International acclaim for the novels of P.D. Martin

THE MURDERERS' CLUB

"Martin provides solid entertainment
as she takes a high-concept premise and runs with it.
The narrative is fast-moving, the protagonists likable,
the police detail and dialogue believable and
the serial killers just as evil as they need to be."
—*Publishers Weekly*

"Just as gripping and original as the first…
The Murderers' Club is certainly a riveting read."
—*Herald Sun*

BODY COUNT

"A taut and terrific debut novel… Martin is a real find.
Can't wait to read her next."
—*Women's Weekly*

"A great, gripping read."
—*Woman's Day*

"P.D. Martin…ticks all the right boxes."
—*Sydney Morning Herald*

"Martin's debut is truly superb, combining enough
procedural details to satisfy CSI junkies with humor,
emotion and a generous number of chills."
—*Romantic Times BOOKreviews* [4 ½ stars]

Also by P.D. MARTIN

THE MURDERERS' CLUB
BODY COUNT

P.D. MARTIN

FAN MAIL

MIRA®

MIRA

Recycling programs
for this product may
not exist in your area.

ISBN-13: 978-0-7783-2613-7

FAN MAIL

www.MIRABooks.com

Printed in U.S.A.

ACKNOWLEDGMENTS

First I'd like to thank the fabulous crew at MIRA Books in the U.S. and Canada (especially Linda McFall, Adam Wilson, the design team and the sales team) and my agent, Elaine Koster.

A huge thank-you goes to retired U.S. cop Jim Tuttle for answering my never-ending questions. Jim's knowledge has been instrumental in completing this book, and all deviations from the reality of policing are my mistakes or things I didn't check with him or artistic license! I'm so glad he lives in Melbourne, Australia, now!

Also for their professional expertise, I'd like to thank Paul Spenceley for all his ideas and help making the IT side of *Fan Mail* realistic and interesting; and for their insights into profiling, ex-FBI profiler Candice deLong and Victoria Police profiler Deb Bennet.

I'd also like to thank Marty and Sharna Alderette for help with some L.A. facts, Aaron Snowberger for my Web site design (www.pdmartin.com.au), Sisters in Crime for their support, Nicole Hayes and Merran Holman for their feedback, and Gil Broadway for the Kung Fu training.

Finally, I'd like to thank my family and friends for their support, and thanks to all my readers and Sophie fans.

Prologue

Three months ago

The voice is deep and smooth. "Agent Sophie Anderson?"

"Yes." I stop typing and give the person on the other end of the phone my full attention.

"It's Justin Reid."

The last time I saw Reid was about a month ago, after I'd arrested Heath Jordan, his R&D manager and long-time friend. Jordan, using the online ID of AmericanPsycho, had brought together three other killers and formed an online club called the Murderers' Club. Collectively, the group had killed seventeen people—including twelve workmen who'd built the bunker where the victims were held. That's some toll. But even so, Reid couldn't accept Jordan's involvement; at least he couldn't back then.

"How can I help you, Mr. Reid?"

"Actually, I'd like to help you."

I pause, letting him continue, but when he doesn't I prompt him. "How so?"

"I think you might be right about Heath, Agent Anderson."

It's not exactly a revelation to me, but I can imagine what Reid must be going through and I try to be sympathetic. "The computer evidence is overwhelming, plus we've got positive visual IDs for the kidnapping charges." I'm referring to the victims who escaped from the bunker and later identified Heath Jordan as their abductor.

"Yes." His voice is sad, like even though he believes me, he still hasn't come to terms with it. But murder is hard for most people to understand, especially multiple murders. "I'd like to help," he says.

"I'd like to help you find this NeverCaught."

NeverCaught was one of the four members of the Murderers' Club, the only one who got away. He remains nameless and faceless—all we've got is his online pseudonym. We still haven't been able to trace him, and the fact that he slipped through our fingers chills me, especially when I know what he's capable of doing to young women. He may have already killed again or be selecting a target right now. A cold shudder travels through me as I visualize some of the crime-scene photos of NeverCaught's handiwork—women stabbed to death in a frenzied attack and then wrapped in plastic and dumped. I want Never-Caught real bad, but it's Bureau business, not Reid's.

"Special Agent Gerard is working on that," I say. Gerard, a senior consultant in the Bureau's Cyber Crime Division, has also admitted to me that tracking down NeverCaught will be a long haul.

"Yes, and I'm sure he's more than capable, but we've got a new specialized search engine in testing that I think will help you and Agent Gerard. We're still ironing out all the bugs, but I'd happily turn the code over to the FBI to help you catch this killer." He sighs. "Maybe it will make up for what Heath did."

My anger is immediate. "Nothing can make up for what Heath Jordan did, Mr. Reid. For the lives he took."

"Of course…" Reid's on the back foot. "I…I didn't mean it like that."

I cool down a little. I know I'm being harsh on Reid—he's an innocent bystander, caught up in this through his employee's actions, and now I'm giving him a hard time. "Sorry, Mr. Reid. I know you're just trying to help."

"Yes." His voice softens. "And please, you really must call me Justin." The hint of flirtation that characterized our previous conversations returns.

"Okay, Justin," I say, but I make sure my voice is neutral, with no hint of anything other than the professional. "I'm not sure how this new search engine of yours would help us."

"Well, it analyzes Internet-browsing habits to build a user profile." He pauses. "I'm not sure if you have any information about your killer's online behavior, but if you did, this could then be matched against an existing user, and their IP address."

While I have a pretty good grasp of computer basics, it's time to hand Reid over to someone who can really speak his language. So far it sounds promising. I know IP stands for Internet Protocol, and an IP address is a unique identifier electronic devices use to communicate on a computer network, including the World Wide Web. An IP address is pretty damn specific and should give us a name.

"Agent Gerard would be the best person for you to talk to. Can you hold the line while I put you through?"

"Sure thing, Sophie. I'll speak to you later." Again the flirtatious voice, this time coupled with the uninvited use of my first name. Reid's a powerful man, used to getting his way, used to women falling for him. I want to pull him up, but then think the better of it—I don't want to be antagonistic toward a man who may help us catch Never-Caught. I hit the transfer button and dial Gerard's extension.

"Hi, Anderson," he says warmly as soon as he picks up the phone. "What's up?"

"I've got a call I'd like to put through to you, Gerard. It's Justin Reid from San Francisco. He says he's got some new search engine that he thinks will help us find Never-Caught. He's talking about browsing habits and matching a profile against an IP."

"Really?" The interest in Gerard's voice is obvious. I'm not the only person haunted by the one that got away.

"Will it help us?" I ask.

"Yeah. Especially if he's thrown money and resources at the code."

"Which I'm sure Reid has," I say. Reid may only be in his thirties, but he owns SysTech, the world's biggest computer security company, which is worth billions.

"Exactly." Gerard pauses. "We've got search engines that routinely go through ISP logs and flag any IP addresses that are accessing our target child-pornography sites, but if this search routine is based on browsing habits, that's a little different." Gerard pauses. "I've been working on the case on and off, actually. And not just NeverCaught."

"Really? Why?" As far as I knew, everything had been handed over to the lawyers.

"There are a few anomalies on Jordan's computer, and I want to make sure the computer evidence is watertight by the time we get to trial. I don't want some computer-whiz witness for the defense outsmarting me on the stand."

"Fair enough," I say, but given Gerard's skills, not to mention his IQ, I think he's being a little paranoid.

He sighs. "It's not my priority at the moment, though."

"I understand." Gerard's usual focus is predators who stalk children online.

"Anyway, put him through. If he can make my job easier or faster I'm not going to say no."

"Okay. Call me back as soon as you're done."

"Will do."

I hit the transfer button again, connecting Justin Reid with Agent Daniel Gerard.

With each minute my excitement builds. I want Never-Caught. The fact that one of the murderous group got away keeps me awake at night—literally.

I find myself pacing when the phone rings five minutes later. Gerard's name is on the display. "Well?" I say.

"He might have something, Anderson. He's putting it onto a secure server for me now and I'm going to download it. If it does what he says, we could have NeverCaught's real name by the end of the day."

"Holy shit," I say, unable to contain my excitement. "How?" I pause. "In terms that I can understand."

The line's silent for a while, presumably while Gerard mentally translates into layperson's terms.

"Well, we know that while NeverCaught was logged on to the Club's shared laptop, he accessed other Web sites."

"Uh-huh." All members had a special Club laptop, but there was also a communal laptop kept at the house where they took the victims. We never found NeverCaught's Club laptop, but we know he logged on to the Club's communal laptop a couple of times.

"Well, we can plug the Web sites accessed under the user ID NeverCaught into Reid's search engine. The software will then compare that user profile with Internet Service Provider records. And because Reid's company has got marketing agreements with all the major ISPs, we'll have instant access to a comprehensive data set without having to contact the ISPs ourselves and get permission or warrants for this stage of the process. The program will simply spit out any matching IP addresses, which we can then trace back to an individual through the ISP."

"Okay, I get it."

"It's pretty impressive stuff. You should see the heuristic search algorithm, it's really advanced, and…" Gerard trails off, realizing he's getting too technical.

"Whatever gets your motor running, Gerard." I stifle a laugh.

"Sorry, but it's good code. And that, coupled with Reid's access to the ISP databases… I'll let you know the minute I have something." Gerard hangs up, probably as keen to get this moving as I am.

The thought of going back to the offender psychological profile I was working on and ignoring what could be happening down the corridor is unbearable, so instead I bring up the profile of NeverCaught. An offender profile is usually quite detailed, covering everything from age to occupation to the kind of car an offender drives. We use a four-step process—analyzing the profiling inputs, which include the crime scene, the victimology, the forensic information, the preliminary police report and the crime-scene photos; reviewing decision models, which include the type and style of murder, the primary intent of the murder, the time taken by the offender and information about the location; an assessment of the crime; and then drafting the profile itself. It's not an exact science, but it is something that has been highly refined by the Bureau since the seventies, when a team of agents started looking at commonalities between perps and crime scenes. Never-Caught's profile is based more on the murders we were able to link him to in the past, rather than his activities in the Murderers' Club. Using signature elements plugged into VICAP, a national database of violent crimes, we were able to tie him to seven unsolved murders from 2002 to 2007. I'm confident the profile is accurate, especially given I had so many murders to draw on. Generally, the more crime scenes and victims, the better the profile will be—heartbreaking, but true.

Sex:	Male
Age:	Chronological: 20-25 Emotional age: 16-20
Race:	Caucasian—but hunts across non-Caucasian races and is attracted to difference.

Type of offender:	Organized—well-planned murders, transports victims before and after death, intelligent. Knife attacks are frenzied, but still organized (similar knife wounds from victim to victim and clean crime scenes forensically). Frenzy is indicator of youth, and the need to bolster his ego.
Occupation/ employment:	White-collar but likes his victims to be lower than him in socio-economic status and intelligence. Office worker in middle management—has some power but not enough to satisfy him.
Marital status:	Single but sexually active with casual partners. Sexual partners more likely to be his equals (college-educated).
Dependents:	No dependents—stereotypical bachelor.

Childhood:	Quite a privileged upbringing—knife wounds and the savagery of the rapes indicate a spoiled brat who's used to getting his own way.
Personality:	Charming, but also very manipulative of others. Can be impulsive if things aren't going his way. Needs to exert power through rape and murder because he cannot exert this violent power on his peers. Hides his own sense of inadequacy by acting like an egotistical playboy. Channels these feelings of inadequacy into murder.
Disabilities:	None.
Interaction with victims:	Keeps his victims for a day or two (based on forensics). Long enough for multiple rapes and for him to feel in control. Stalks his victims and knows their routines. Nabs them at night, when they are in vulnerable positions (e.g., the barmaid disappeared on the walk home from work—something she did every night). Spends time with them postmortem—elaborate positioning of the body.

Remorse:	The plastic wrapping indicates some feelings of remorse because he's symbolically covering the victims. Yet the fact that the plastic is clear shows that he's not overwhelmed by shame. Positioning a body facedown is normally done by a killer who doesn't want the victim "looking" at him or "judging" him, but in this case the facedown position is more about the sexual pose. He poses the victims in what he feels are provocative stances, with their legs slightly parted.
Home life:	Lives alone in a modern apartment or town house—classic bachelor pad. Would spend a lot of his wealth on his home, which would have the latest gadgets and be decorated in a modern yet stark style.
Car:	He transports the victims, so he must own a van or SUV. More likely an upmarket SUV to tie in to his "wealthy bachelor" look. Also possible he has two cars— one for show, and one for dealing with his victims.

Intelligence:	High IQ
Education level:	College-educated (although he probably spent more time partying at college than studying). Takes education for granted because his family is wealthy.
Outward appearance:	Highly educated and well-groomed—all the girls seemed to go willingly with him so he must look trustworthy in some way (although women are more likely to trust a man in a business suit with a nice car than a man covered in tattoos on a motorbike). Well-dressed at all times—designer suits or more casual wear.
Criminal background:	Probably no criminal record but it's possible he was charged with something at college such as drug possession or DUI (wealthy boy away from parents).

Modus operandi (MO):	Stalks the victims, getting to know their routines. Lures the victims into his car but then takes them to a remote location (not his house). Ties them up and repeatedly rapes them before stabbing them to death. Transports victims to wooded location for dumping (not much blood at dump sites, so he transports them postmortem).
Signature:	Frenzied knife attack. Posing of body postmortem, with plastic.
Post-offensive behavior:	May revisit the dump site and look at his victims—clear plastic facilitates this.
Media tactics:	This killer will follow the media very closely and will want to see his actions in the paper. He uses the media reports to fuel his ego (and cover up his underlying sense of inadequacy). This could be dangerous—if he gets lots of media coverage, this will excite him and may propel him into action in terms of taking his next victim.

Reading the profile brings back images of the seven women in North and South Dakota—one had over a hundred individual knife wounds, mostly centered around her breasts and abdomen. The killer, NeverCaught, wrapped his victims in plastic and dumped them in the woods in posed positions. They were placed on their stomachs with their arms reaching above their heads and their legs parted. The women were all young with dark, exotic complexions. I remember the cases, the girls, easily. His first victim, as far as we know, was a nineteen-year-old Italian girl. But soon he struck again, and again, and again. These women are the reason I lie awake at night, thinking about NeverCaught.

Please let Reid be right. I pace in my office a bit before remembering Detective Darren Carter. The Murderers' Club is his case, after all. I punch the familiar number into my phone. Darren and I started out as colleagues, but we quickly became friends.

"Homicide, Carter." His voice is hurried.

"Hi, Darren. It's Sophie."

"Hey." His tone changes instantly. "What's up?" Darren's using the expression as a greeting, but in this case there really is something up.

I launch straight into it. "We might have something on NeverCaught."

"Really? What?"

I relay Reid's phone call and update Darren on our current status.

He lets out a whistle. "It'd be nice to nail him." The words may be casual, but I know Darren's never casual about an investigation. Just like with me, NeverCaught will be on his mind most of the time. Darren and I have more in common than I care to think about.

"How's everything else going?" he asks.

"Good...good. You?" Normally I could happily chat to Darren for hours, but not today, not now.

"All's well here. Guess you need to get back to it, huh?" He senses my hesitation.

"Yeah. I'm going to talk to Gerard. But I'll call you as soon as we have something."

"Look forward to it."

I'm standing up before I've even hung up, ready to head down to the Cyber Crime Division.

Gerard shakes his head when he sees me. "I'm not surprised."

"I couldn't go back to my other case. How's it going?"

"It looks good. This search routine is amazing...." His voice and face are animated, excited.

"Amazing how?"

"The algorithm...it's really smart...creative...and clean."

At this point I'd normally have another dig at Gerard's excitement over computer code, but I can't bring myself to be flippant when I'm still visualizing the women's dumped bodies. "So, will it help you find NeverCaught?"

Gerard looks up at me and cocks his head to one side. "You've been looking at the files." He's serious now too. "Reviewing the profile and remembering the photos." He winced. "I just have to plug in all the Web sites he visited when he was logged on as NeverCaught on the communal laptop and see what hits we get back."

"What sort of sites?"

"We've got an online game called Kill Kill, a custom-made-knife retailer, CNN and the *New York Times*."

"And that will help us find NeverCaught?"

He nods. "We'll search the ISP's records through

SysTech's live links with them and see if there's a user out there who visits all those sites on a regular basis. I'd expect to get way too many hits if we only had CNN and the *New York Times,* but when we're cross-referencing that with the more obscure sites of the online game and the knife retailer, we might get lucky."

I motion toward Gerard's screen. "I guess Reid did throw some money at this."

"Yup." Gerard nods. "But don't give him a knight-hood…he's using this code for marketing and growing the SysTech empire. He didn't do it for us." Gerard stops working and turns to me. "Now, shh." He puts his index finger across his lips. "Or I'll make you wait at your desk." The gesture manages to lighten my mood a little.

Less than five minutes later, Gerard turns to me and circles his index finger in a theatrical motion before hitting the enter key one more time. *"Voilà."*

I lean forward, but can't see anything that makes sense on the screen. "And?"

"We wait." He stands up. "Coffee?"

"How can you be so calm? How long do we have to wait?"

He smiles at me. "Sometimes you have to wait, Anderson. You know that."

I manage a smile at his dig. Everyone I work with knows patience isn't my strong suit.

"It could be up to an hour. It's a big database of users." He starts walking. "Maybe you don't need the caffeine, but I do."

I follow him, but it's to keep myself busy rather than to get a coffee—caffeine is the last thing I need at the moment.

Back at his desk, Gerard plants his rear end on the seat and shoves his coffee cup to one side. "I'm going to work on something else while the search program runs in the background."

I nod.

"You sure you want to stick around?"

"Uh-huh." I probably should go back to my desk and do some work, but I'm too agitated to think about any other case. Sitting here watching the gibberish on Gerard's screen is better than sitting at my desk.

I lean back, willing myself not to ask questions. I don't want to break Gerard's concentration. But half an hour later I'm more than restless. As much as I want to make something happen, it is pointless waiting here. "I'll be at my desk. Call me—"

"The minute I know something."

I don't get much work done in the next fifteen minutes, but at least I'm out of Gerard's way. When the phone rings, I snatch it up quickly.

"Well?" I ask.

"We've got a few matches. The best one is a ninety-two percent match on an IP address of 64.12.96.54."

"What's his name? Where is he?"

"One thing at a time, Anderson. The IP belongs to an AOL user, but if we want a name we'll need a court order. We did the hard bit without warrants, but there's no way AOL will give us specific user info without one."

"Unless it's a life-threatening situation," I say, knowing that in those circumstances we could follow up with the paperwork later. But while it's true that NeverCaught could be targeting someone right now, locating him comes under the scope of a historical investigation, so we'd better play it safe and get the court order first. "I'll draft the request now, and make sure it's fast-tracked."

"Okay, I'll ring AOL and line us up a good contact."

Two hours later, Gerard and I are faxing the court order to AOL from my office. Gerard must have done a good job convincing his contact of the urgency of our request, because it's only a few minutes later that Gerard's cell phone is ringing.

He scribbles something down and hangs up. "The IP is registered to an A. Picking from Seattle."

"Seattle?" I raise my eyebrows. "But his previous killings are in North and South Dakota."

"Hey, I'm just the messenger, remember?"

I laugh. "Fair enough. What else you got?"

Gerard waves a Post-it note. "His address."

I stand up. "Let's go."

"Do you want to see what he looks like first?" He motions to my computer. "May I?"

I stop in my tracks. "Sure." I push the keyboard closer to him and move my chair in the opposite direction to give him more room.

He minimizes Word. "Let's see what we've got on him." Within a few keystrokes the interface for the Washington State Department of Licensing is on my computer. Gerard types *A* as the first initial, then *Picking* as the last name and then types in the address.

We get full details of twenty-five-year-old Andrew Picking, including his social security number. Another few keystrokes and Gerard's in the IRS database, typing in the number. On his last tax return, Picking listed his occupation as "manager" and his industry as "telecommunications." He fits. I'd profiled NeverCaught as twenty to twenty-five years old, white collar and in middle management.

"He matches the age and the occupation." I cross my arms and grin. "Let's go catch NeverCaught."

Twenty-four hours later, Darren and I are in Seattle, having confirmed Andrew Picking as a very real suspect. He matches the profile in just about every way, and the office he works for has an operation in Bismarck, near the murders in North and South Dakota. After discreetly speaking to his employer, we've put him in Bismarck at the time of all seven murders in North and South Dakota between 2002 and 2007. From there, we focused on the most recent South Dakota murder, locating Picking's rental car for that trip. Forensics found traces of human blood in the trunk. The DNA's still being processed, but it was enough to get us a search warrant for Picking's Seattle home and an arrest warrant. With these important documents in hand, it's time to get our man. Our team is made up of local police, SWAT and FBI.

Picking will no doubt have a weapon. Knives do it for him when he's with his female victims, but he's the type to have several guns in the house, for his "enjoyment" and to make him feel more powerful. At the moment we have the element of surprise, and we need to make the most of that. Picking's probably feeling pretty safe because it's been a month since everything went down, but a man like that is always prepared. I profiled Picking as a spoiled brat who's used to getting his own way, so I don't believe he's the type to negotiate. We need to take the offensive.

The SWAT leader positions his people: four sharpshooters on neighboring roofs, and two team members for each of the four escape routes we identified—the back door, two side windows and one back window. It's probably overkill for one suspect and no hostage, but you can never be too careful in this business. And for all we know, he could have his next victim in there.

I refasten one of the straps on my bulletproof vest, pulling it tighter across my chest.

I take a deep breath. The mixture of excitement, anticipation and fear builds as I run through the many possible scenarios. We know he's home, know that we're not barging into an empty house, but other than that anything is possible. Even though Picking's normal hunting ground is Dakota, he could have a victim with him right now—he didn't kill his victims in the woods, he killed them beforehand. We could take him quietly, or maybe the execution of our warrants will turn into a shoot-out. I take another deep breath and push my fears aside. If I did busts like this regularly, the job might just turn me into an adrenaline junkie.

Darren gives me a smile and a discreet wink.

"Thirty seconds," the SWAT leader says into the comms link. "Everyone in position?"

The units all respond in the affirmative.

"Shooters, can you see anything?"

"Negative, blinds are drawn."

I'd prefer it if our sharpshooters had a target in their sights, but I also want Picking taken alive. I'd rather make him face the families of his victims and see him suffer in prison than go down clean and quick with a slug in his chest. Is that vengeance or justice? Sometimes the line is blurry.

The SWAT leader counts down the final ten seconds

into his mouthpiece, and then gives the order to go. We move single file up the stairs to the front door. One of the SWAT guys tries the door handle very, very slowly, checking to see if the door's unlocked. It's not, so they get ready to break the door down. With his hand up and visible, the SWAT leader counts to three, his lips mouthing the numbers in unison with his hand gestures. On what would have been the fourth count, he points toward the door with his full hand and mouths, "Go." The door only takes two hits before the lock gives. The team files in, SWAT leading the way to secure the house. I'm the fifth person in the living room, with Darren directly behind me, and there's already yelling, but thankfully no shots.

We've caught Picking off guard, lying on the couch watching TV in only his jeans. He looks at us, his eyes wild with anger, and I eyeball the gun on the table, only a few inches away from his left hand. I wonder if he's been carrying that everywhere with him since the rest of his Club members were arrested last month.

"You're right-handed, Andrew." I keep my stance open and solid, ready to take the shot. "You'll never make it."

He could reach for the gun with his left hand, but he'd never get a shot off before we fired. And if he had to reach across himself with his right hand…

"You're screwed, whichever way you look at it," I say, hoping my thought processes are in sync with his. What else could he be thinking, faced with so many guns trained on him?

"What the fuck's going on?" He screams it so violently that his body bucks.

I keep my gun pointed at him, while one of the SWAT

guys moves toward the coffee table and takes the gun, all the while keeping his eyes on the target.

"It's loaded," he says, taking the magazine out of the gun.

I scan the area, making sure there are no other weapons in sight.

"Hands on your head, slow," says the SWAT leader.

Andrew Picking, aka NeverCaught, moves his hands up slowly, but his body is still tense. He should be frightened, but I know from getting inside his head and profiling him that it's anger taking hold of his muscles.

His hands reach his head. "What's all this about?" His voice is calm now.

I move forward, ignoring his question. "Interlace your fingers and then sit up, real slow."

His dark brown eyes look almost black in the dimly lit room and he focuses all that anger on me. I'm ignoring him, and to someone like Picking, that's plain unacceptable.

"Well?" he demands, but he has followed my orders and is now sitting on the couch.

Knowing Picking's got six guns trained on him, I put my gun back in its holster and take out handcuffs. "Stand up, hands behind your back."

He hesitates. "Answer my fucking question."

My natural reaction is to laugh at his petulance, but I know that would push him over the edge. "Sure," I say. "Once I cuff you."

"You're smart, I'll give you that," he says. "You're right to be wary of me." He turns around, giving me his back.

What an arrogant SOB. He's turning this situation into an ego boost. I can imagine what's going through his head, what stories he would tell: "They needed SWAT, cops and FBI to take me down…."

Once he's cuffed, he yells, "Tell me!"

"Murder, Andrew. You're the last one, NeverCaught." I use his online pseudonym. "DialM's dead and Black-Widow and AmericanPsycho are in jail." I pause. "But I guess you knew that."

One

Present day

I lie on top of my bed fully clothed, and breathe deeply. I'm hopeful rather than optimistic, hopeful that something I see may help save her.

"Her" is a Montana girl called Tabitha, the only file in my Inbox and the last case I'll be profiling in my current job at the FBI's Behavioral Analysis Unit in Quantico. Tabitha disappeared on her way home from school in Helena and it's the second disappearance in the area, with the first happening six months ago. The case details swirl in my mind—the locations; the crime-scene photos; the police reports; and the photos of both girls, happy and smiling for their school portraits.

I take another deep breath and let it out slowly. Like the first girl, Tabitha's eleven years old, an age that many predators like because girls are on the brink of adolescence, showing the first signs of physical development. I shudder at the thought of what *he,* whoever he is, would be doing to her now—if she's even still alive. They never found the first girl.

I clear my mind of its daily noise, hoping something will come to me. The past four months I've been in training. Just like I exercise my muscles, I've learned to exercise whatever part of my brain it is that lets me tune in to other people's lives—and deaths. The images come to me in either dreams, or as waking visions. But they're not just images—they're all the emotions of the situation too. Sometimes the vision or dream is played out like a movie and I'm watching the events unfold, but often I'm in the killer's or the victim's shoes. I've come a long way since I realized I had this gift, accepting and learning to control it more. But ultimately, inducing visions is still a bit of a crapshoot. And if I do see something, it may be unrelated, or just a replay of what we know…but sometimes it gives us something meaningful.

The discovery of my ability has been a rocky road. I had my first premonition at eight, but was so distressed by it that my subconscious repressed the memory, and my gift. It wasn't until nearly a year ago that my latent abilities resurfaced with the D.C. Slasher case when a serial killer got close. But after the case my sixth sense dived underground again until I was out in the field, watching a body being uncovered. The vic was on his back, his arms tucked underneath him, and a bright red love heart had been drawn on his chest with body paint. But suddenly I wasn't looking at a dead body, I was having sex with the victim and he was very much alive. For a few seconds, I was the killer. Over the next few weeks the visions kept coming—they were back with a vengeance. With the help of Darren, whose aunt had been a professional psychic, I realized that being at the scene, instead of viewing crime-scene photos months or years later like I normally do, gave me a connection to the case. And even though I have some control over my gift now, my "remote" episodes still don't seem to be as strong or detailed as when I'm at a crime scene in the field.

Finally, the dizziness that usually accompanies my visions engulfs me. I see flashes from the Montana case, flashes of things that aren't in any police report or crime-scene photo. At first the images are of Tabitha's life—she's blowing out candles at a birthday party, she's playing at school, she's giving her mom and dad a kiss good-night—but then the visions become more sinister. A car with tinted windows. The passenger window glides down. Tabitha moves closer to the car. Then she's in a dark room. I don't know if the scene's from the past or present—I can never tell. She may be cowering in the room now, or she may already be dead.

I concentrate on the dark room, zeroing in on what I know will be important details. A single window is boarded up, I think from the outside. I can make out the silhouettes of a bed and a toilet, but there's nothing else to help me in the room. No wallpaper or anything else on the walls, no other furniture…nothing. So I shift my attention to the house. What's it like? Where is it? I'm rewarded with a flash of the house's exterior. This image only pops into my head for a second. When nothing else follows, I break my concentration on getting a vision and think back to the scene. Using my memory, I re-create the image, getting a fix on things. A small log cabin, surrounded by woods. Out front is a dark gray car. I can't make out the license plate.

I jot it all down in a notebook beside my bed before returning to my relaxation techniques.

Another ten minutes go by, but nothing else comes. I open my eyes and sit on the edge of the bed, still a little dizzy and now also feeling drained. I would have liked to have gotten more, but then again I'd always like more. If I'd been at the place where Tabitha went missing, maybe the vision would have been more vivid, more accurate or more detailed. Then we'd have a better chance of finding Tabitha, of saving her. And that's why I had to ask for the transfer. I need to be in the field again, where I can do the most good with this gift of mine.

I look around my half-packed bedroom. Another week and I'll be in Los Angeles, working out of the Bureau's L.A. Field Office. It took a couple of months for the right position to come up, but the L.A. profiling job was a perfect fit. And the West Coast means warmer weather and living slightly closer to my family in Australia.

Maybe in a few years I won't need to be out in the field anymore, maybe by then I will have learned enough about my abilities to get the same vivid sensations simply by looking at photos. Then I might come back and work for the Behavioral Analysis Unit again. I'd like that.

I arrive at the Quantico offices at 8:00 a.m. and fire up my computer. It whirs to life as I make my way to our small kitchenette…and coffee. I end up with the dregs from the bottom of the pot, and set another jug in motion. Back at my desk I find my replacement, Bessie Jackson, sitting in my spot.

Bessie is a five-five African-American dynamo with pure muscle packed tightly around her short frame. She's about my age, midthirties, and has been working in the Bureau as a field agent for nearly ten years. Making this team has probably been her dream for most of that time. The Bureau has profilers stationed at our busier field offices, but most profilers start off in the Behavioral Analysis Unit. If you want to be a profiler, you need to focus on getting a job on this team. Everyone wants into this unit, despite the macabre nature of most of our cases. The Behavioral Analysis Unit tends to get the worst of the worst, almost exclusively violent serial offenders. Occasionally we may get called in to profile a series of armed robberies or a kidnapping, but most of our work is of a much more gruesome nature.

"Sorry." Bessie stands up. "I just had to make a call."

I smile. "That's okay." I'd hoped the Bureau would find a replacement for me quickly, to give me time to hand over my cases properly, but sharing a desk is going beyond the call of duty. At least they managed to get a laptop for Bessie. Otherwise the situation over the past week would have been unbearable.

Bessie returns to the desk behind mine, which was cleared of junk especially for her. After today, the desk situation won't be an issue. Today I wrap up the Montana profile and officially finish all my desk work. Then tomorrow I've been assigned to entertain Loretta Black. Great. Babysitting a famous crime novelist isn't exactly my ideal way to spend my last day at the FBI Academy.

Coffee in hand, I go back to my profile. In this case, the only crime scene we have is where we found Tabitha's school bag, where we assume she was abducted. The street was between her school and her home, a journey she often made by herself.

I move on to the victimology to get an insight into the

victim. By getting to know the victim, we can understand the perpetrator. Based on information we have about Tabitha, I don't believe she would have gotten into that car without good reason. She was a smart girl who tended to be shy rather than outgoing. From my vision, I know she approached the car willingly, but the evidence of her school bag at the scene indicates that some force was involved—why else would she leave her bag? Tabitha was very close to her family and I can imagine the perpetrator using this to his advantage, perhaps telling her that one of her parents was ill. The family did have a safety-word system in place, but something made Tabitha move closer to the car, even though the man couldn't have known the family's special code word. Maybe Tabitha knew him, maybe not. Once she was close enough, he was able to grab her. As a child, she's a high-risk victim…trusting and innocent. But most importantly, how can an eleven-year-old girl physically fight off a grown man? It sickens me to think about guys like this perp. I focus on the profile, trying not to get caught up in how I *feel* about the crime and about the little girl.

Next I would normally look at forensics, but in the case of Tabitha we don't have anything—no body, no fibers, no blood, no DNA—so I move on to the police report. There were no witnesses to Tabitha's abduction, at least none that the police could find, and the police have included a basic sketch of the area and some general neighborhood information. I absorb it all, getting a feel for the location.

The final profiling input is the photos, which in some ways are the single most important factor. Like the saying goes, a picture tells a thousand words. Generally, each crime scene will have many photos. A complex murder case could have hundreds. But in this case, with no body, the photos I have only help to paint a picture of the neighborhood, helping me understand how it was possible for the perp not only to fit in, but to take Tabitha unnoticed.

Tabitha is only half the picture, and before I can think about drafting the offender profile, I need to get to know the first victim, Sue-Anne. Again, I go over the victimology, the police report, the case photos and the forensics—or lack of it. Like Tabitha, Sue-Anne was eleven years old and grabbed on the way home from school. The only differences between the cases are that Sue-Anne had stayed back for an after-school practice, and there's nothing to pinpoint the exact abduction site. She was last seen by a school friend just after 5:00 p.m. out the front of the school. She never made it home, and was abducted somewhere during the two-mile walk, again with no witnesses. As far as the police were able to establish, the girls didn't know each other or have any other connection with one another. They lived ten miles apart and attended different schools. But certainly, looking at their photos, we have a victim type: long blond hair, slim but athletic builds and girls who, unlike their peers, actually seemed to dress their age.

For both girls I'm already assuming the worst—kidnap, rape then murder. It's got all the hallmarks of a sexual predator targeting young girls. And statistics tell us that during a stranger-child abduction, most of the victims are killed within an hour or two. Still, there's hope yet, at least for Tabitha. Our guy's different—he keeps them for longer than that. Why else would he take them to the cabin I saw in my vision? But how long does he keep them for? While I can't answer that question, I know one thing for sure—

he's going to keep going until we stop him. And if he escalates, which he might, the time between abductions will increase—not a comforting thought for Montana families.

The last thing I need to consider before drafting the actual profile is the interaction between the girls and their abductor. This is always an extremely important factor when assessing a crime and drafting a profile. Both girls were smart enough, and sensible enough, *not* to get into a stranger's car. So what went wrong? Or did they know their abductor? Two possibilities emerge. One, a killer who's composed and convincing, so much so that he's able to persuade the girls that he's been sent by their families. In this case, part of his stalking process would include gathering enough information about the families that he could carry it off. He'd have to mention both parents by their first names, maybe pretend he worked with one of them, or drop another relative's name or some other pertinent information. The second possibility is that the girls knew the killer, perhaps only in passing. Maybe they met him at a barbecue or through friends. But even so, our perp followed the girls' routines carefully. They weren't victims of opportunity, these were planned abductions, carefully tied in to the times the girls would be walking home from school. And once the girls were in the car, he could drop the ruse, if there was one, or even simply knock them unconscious and push them onto the car floor, out of sight of any nosy motorists. The abductions were fast and well-planned, especially given there were no witnesses.

With all my background work finished, I'm ready to paint a picture of the Montana perp. The standard profiling process can take anything from hours to days, depending on the complexity of the case, the number of victims and offenders, etc. I've allocated one more day to Tabitha and Sue-Anne—today.

My profile covers the standard areas—sex, age, race, type of offender (organized or disorganized), occupation, marital status, dependents, personality, interaction with victims, home life, car, post-offense behavior, intelligence, education level, outward appearance, criminal background and any signature elements of the crime. In this profile, I'm able to add in the cabin from my vision this morning, rationalizing it by saying I believe he keeps his victims for some time and so he must have somewhere quiet and isolated to take them. The fact that he plucked the girls so boldly from the streets indicates he knows the area well, so his primary residence or workplace will be close to the abduction sites, within ten kilometers, and the cabin wouldn't be more than an hour's drive away—he needs to see his victims regularly. I look up a state map of Montana and notice the number of national forests around Helena. The cabin is probably near one of these, but the local cops will know the area and can identify suspect sites.

Before I finalize the profile I jump online and surf a few car Web sites until I find the car from my vision—a Lincoln Zephyr. In the profile, I write it as *Upmarket sedan (but not European), such as Lincoln Zephyr, Ford Crown or Buick Lucerne.* We normally include the type of car—sedan, pickup, sports car—so it's not unusual to be so specific in a profile. The Montana perp likes his girls "fresh" and "simple" and I believe these tastes would run to his car too—he'd see a European sedan, pickup or sports car as too flashy, just like a young girl wearing clothes and makeup to look like something she's not. The Ford Crown and Buick Lucerne are similar to the Lincoln Zephyr; this is my "padding" around the real car. No one in the FBI knows about my visions and I intend to keep it that way.

It's 6:00 p.m. by the time I finish the profile and e-mail it to the task-force head in Helena. I'm happy with the profile, but experience tells me this case won't be resolved anytime soon. The perp's been careful so far, and that's what he'll keep doing. I'm helpless to do anything more about it. I lean back in my chair and flip the manila folder over. The red cardboard cover floats down slowly, hiding the smiling face of Tabitha, the first photo in the file. Bile rises in my stomach as I see a flash of Tabitha, her body too still for anything but death.

Two

The next day when I arrive at headquarters, Bessie is at my desk again, but this time she's there for good. With all my cases officially handed over, I'm relegated to the laptop and the cramped spare desk—with no phone. But I won't be at a desk today anyway.

I hang my jacket on the back of my chair and Bessie smiles at me apologetically. Loretta Black is due to arrive at 9:00 a.m., which gives me half an hour to check my e-mails and get enough coffee into my system to make the day bearable—and today that could be a tall order.

At ten minutes to nine my boss, Andy Rivers, calls me into his office.

"How's it going, Anderson?"

"Under control. Finished off that Montana profile yesterday and everything else is handed over to your new gal."

He nods and grunts his affirmation and then pauses before going on. "I guess it's no use then, trying to convince you to stay on my team."

I smile at the use of "my"—it was a strategically planted word to make me feel disloyal. "Come on, you know it's not personal, Rivers."

Now he smiles. "I've tried everything else to convince you to stay—that was my trump card."

We both know human behavior all too well.

"We'll miss you, Anderson." He stares out his window for a second before looking back at me. "I'll miss you."

"Me too, boss." If Rivers only knew how much I'm going to miss it, all of it—him, the job, the unit, the Academy, even Quantico and all the buzz cuts. Working in the FBI's Behavioral Analysis Unit has meant everything to me and I've never felt so professionally fulfilled as I do here. But I'm not doing this for *me*. If I was driven only by what I wanted, I'd stay here indefinitely. But I've always felt such a strong loyalty to victims and potential victims that I have to go where I'll do the most good. And at the moment, that's in the field. But I can't tell Rivers any of this. Instead, I have to play it cool. "Who knows, maybe I'll be back one day."

He stares at his desk and fiddles with the small, gold-rimmed glasses in his hands. "I'm sorry…sorry about what happened." His eyes only meet mine on the last word.

I force a small smile. "I know. So am I." Rivers is referring to the D.C. Slasher case twelve months ago—the killer got close, real close, and it was nearly my undoing. Nearly. But I've moved on now, although I'm still not entirely comfortable about being intimate with a man. "That's not why I'm going. You know that, right?"

"Right," he says, but without conviction.

His intercom buzzes. "Yes, Janet?"

"Loretta Black just passed through the security checkpoint."

The checkpoint is at the outer rim of the base, and the FBI's buildings are in the grounds' belly, so I've still got ten to fifteen minutes up my sleeve.

"Thanks." Rivers releases the intercom button. He looks at me. "You're on."

"Joy oh joy. After this final torture, maybe I won't come back."

Rivers smiles. "It's not that bad. All you have to do is answer Black's questions."

I resist complaining about the fact that I've had to work sixty-five hours a week for the last four weeks to clear my cases and fit Black in. She must know someone pretty high up to be getting this sort of treatment.

"You read any of her books, sir?"

"No. But my sister's a big fan."

"Really?" Maybe Rivers is the source of the preferential treatment. "Well, I hope you get a few autographed copies out of this."

Rivers smiles. "Hell, I better. My sister's been at me for months, since I first told her about Black's request."

I nod. "Guess I should read one of her books, huh?"

I turn to leave and Rivers yells after me, "And don't be late for your send-off!"

At the elevator doors I envision what Black is like. She's probably lovely…entertaining, interesting, inquisitive. I sigh and think of my half-packed apartment. Man, so much to do and so little time. Five days to finish packing, get over to L.A. and settle in before I start work. Maybe Rivers is right—this isn't such a bad way to spend my last day. At least I'm not madly trying to close off files and hand over last-minute cases. And maybe Black will be charming enough to keep my mind off the packing. It's a big move. A scary move. Especially when I am happy here.

The elevator doors open and I'm greeted by a tall woman, around six foot, who's immaculately groomed and appears to be in her early fifties. Her jet-black hair is swept up into a bun, and several loose strands of hair fall on her face to ensure the bun looks casual and stylish rather than severe. Her makeup is spare and tasteful and she wears trendy square-framed glasses. Next to her is a shorter, younger blonde, who, by the look of her notebook and pen at the ready, must be Black's assistant. Damn, two of them—I forgot about that. I stifle a large yawn. I need another cup of coffee already.

I hold my hand out to Black. "Hi, Ms. Black, I'm Special Agent Sophie Anderson."

She gives me one firm pump and looks over my shoulder, like I'm the appetizer and she's waiting for the main course to be served up.

"I'm a profiler on Andy Rivers's team. I'll be showing you around and answering your questions."

"Fine," she says briskly.

The assistant holds out her hand. "Deborah Holt. Wonderful to meet you, Agent Anderson." Her handshake is firm but friendlier, more prolonged, and I sense genuine admiration in her voice.

Black takes control again. "Is Andy Rivers here?"

Rivers really is torturing me. "He's in. I'll introduce you later."

Her lips tighten. She's acting as though she was expecting a personal tour from the head of the unit. Get real.

Besides, she would have been told I'd be showing her around.

I lead the way to a small meeting room I've booked for the day, even though we'll probably only need it for a few hours this afternoon. I sit down and Black and Holt follow suit, Black still pursing her lips and Holt still smiling.

I give Holt a quick smile before turning my attention back to Black. "I've reviewed the request you sent through to our Future Publicity Department. I thought we'd start by having a look around the Academy, giving you an idea of where we work and how we work. Then we'll come back here and I'll move on to your specific questions about profiling and the unit."

"Fine."

"Thank you, Agent Anderson." Once again, the assistant's personality has to make up for Black's.

"You can call me Sophie." I smile at Holt with some sympathy. I bet Black goes through assistants.

"Thank you, Sophie," Holt says, again with a warm smile. "It's so exciting to be here and meeting a profiler."

"Debbie." Black's voice is a warning.

"Sorry." Holt hangs her head, like she's done something wrong.

I look at the pair questioningly.

There's silence for a few seconds before Black rolls her eyes. "Debbie is writing a little book of her own and it involves profiling, I believe." She pauses. "But we're not here for that. We're here for my research. For my next book."

I stand up, ready to start the tour. While many of the facilities are located in this central complex, the Academy has a substantial three hundred and eighty-five acres, and I decide to start with the outdoor stuff—it's a nice day out and I need some fresh air. I lead the way back to the elevator and Black trails after me, with Holt hot on her heels. The ride down in the elevator is silent. My natural instinct is to talk, to smooth things over. But I resist this instinct for no other reason than my initial dislike of Black. Petty, but hey, it is my last day and it's not like Black's a life-and-death case.

Black breaks the silence once we're in the parking lot. "How long have you been working here, Sophie?" She nudges Holt, who responds instantly by bringing her pad up to her chest, her pen hovering above it. No doubt she's practiced in walking and writing at the same time. *Bet she's not wearing high heels.* Rather than looking down to check my assumption, I visualize Holt's shoes from the initial once-over I gave her—black flats. It's the details that matter in law enforcement, especially profiling, and I've trained my mind and memory.

I force myself back to the conversation. "Eighteen months. But I was a police officer for six years in Melbourne, Australia, before coming over here."

"I see. And what sort of cases have you worked on recently?"

I wonder if this is my job interview—am I worthy of her attention? I rattle off the rough details of some of the cases, but make sure not to include any specifics, like names or locations. I include the Montana kidnappings but refer to it simply as a child-abduction case, and explain why we feel the perp kills the girls, even though no bodies or other similar physical evidence such as blood has been found. Black probably knows the dismal statistics for survival rates of child abductees.

She nods. "I see." I notice with interest that she has a level of practiced detachment similar to law-enforcement professionals—in some ways she deals with perps as much as we do…it's just that her bogeymen are make-believe. What a luxury.

She continues. "I did Google you, Agent Anderson. You've made some press in your day, albeit a short day so far."

"True." I'm noncommittal at first, then say, "But the media are intrigued by profiling, you know how it is." Once I've unlocked the car, Black slides in the front next to me, and Holt climbs into the back, hitting her head as she gets in because she's still busy writing.

"Oops, sorry," Holt apologizes.

Black doesn't let Holt's potential pain or the change of location break her rhythm. "You've worked several high-profile cases. The D.C. Slasher, the kidnapping of Senator Robert Keen's daughter, the Wisconsin murders. And they're only the ones in the press."

I shrug. "Guess so."

When Black buckles her seat belt I notice there's even a sense of detachment in the way she moves. It's almost robotic.

"And your name came up associated with that bizarre case in Arizona four months back," she says. "Nasty business, that one."

"Yes." I manage a smile to myself before flicking the ignition of the car. Despite the gruesome nature of the case, we got them all in the end, including NeverCaught.

Case closed. The DNA in Picking's rental car came back as a match for his last victim in Dakota. But better still, like many serial killers Picking took trophies from his victims, and these items will ensure a conviction for the seven murder cases in North and South Dakota. In addition, a search of a storage facility in his name also gave us his Club laptop, and enough evidence to prosecute him for his involvement in the Murderers' Club. I do love it when we get the bad guys.

"There was an interesting signature in Arizona, I believe." Black's oblivious to my sense of triumph.

I concentrate on what she's saying, the signature…the detail she's talking about has been made public, so I feel no hesitation in discussing it. "Yes. A love heart was painted onto the victims' chests with body paint."

She nods. "I like it. I've used something similar in my latest book."

I try to ignore Black's "I like it" comment—the victims sure as hell didn't like it. Black's looking at it not as a crime but as a story. Again, I don't have that luxury.

A look in the rear-vision mirror tells me Holt's buckled in too—can't be breaking the law in my car. "What's the book about?" I ask Black.

"A serial killer who targets women he meets at speed-dating evenings." The succinct sentence has a practiced ring to it, but I guess lots of people have asked about the book.

"Realistic," I say. And for the first time, I don't have to force my interest. Perps are hunters who need an area where they can select and stalk their prey. For some it's their local video store, for others it's the random selection of someone walking down the street. Speed-dating events would have lots of single women, many of whom probably live alone. One date with Black's fictional character…

"I thought so." Black crosses her arms and nods.

"So what's the signature?" I ask.

"The women are strangled with torn-off panty hose, which are then pulled over their heads. On top of the panty hose is a kiss mark, drawn on with lipstick."

"It's a great book," Holt says from the backseat.

Black acknowledges the compliment with a slight nod. "I know it's not exactly like the Arizona case." Black's voice is authoritative. "But the signature indicates the same romantic overtone."

I let myself imagine it was a real case, a real signature. "True. And the stocking also has the sexual element." Women's panty hose do it for many men.

"I've used a highly sexualized pose too. My killer pulls his victim's knees upwards but with the soles of her feet together, exposing her, and also cuts off her breasts."

Most sexual homicides demonstrate the killer's need to leave the body in a highly sexualized pose, with the woman's legs open to expose her genitalia. Sometimes there's sexual mutilation, sometimes not. It's all about a man's desire to degrade his victim and punish her sexuality as much as possible. I'm about to comment on this as I turn the car's steering wheel to guide us toward the parking lot's exit, when a slight dizziness hits me. Shit. Not now, I can't have a vision now. I fight it off, like I used to when I was running away from my gift, and it only takes a couple of seconds for the sensation to subside. I come back to the conversation—Black's book, the signature. A flash of Black's fictional signature element passes across my imagination. "It's good," I say, acknowledging the plausibility of Black's idea.

"Thanks." Black smiles genuinely for the first time, but it's gone in an instant. "Do you read crime fiction, Agent Anderson?"

"I get enough crime at the office," I say. "I do like reading, but fantasy's my favorite genre." I don't add how much I enjoy letting myself get into a fantasy world, rather than a killer's world. I'll take wizards, dragons and magical worlds over rape and murder any day.

Black seems disappointed I'm not a potential fan.

We pull out of the parking lot and after a few beats of silence, I say, "What's your next book about? The one that's brought you to the Academy?"

"I'm starting a new character. It's very exciting. A woman this time, Angie Base. She's a criminal psychologist who lectures at New York University and consults for the police. I hope she'll be as popular as Benson, and I'm thinking of moving her to the FBI in a few books' time." She pauses for a breath. "Debbie suggested I should find out how a Behavioral Analysis Unit works firsthand."

"Well then, you've definitely come to the right place."

I head for the outdoor running track and start my tourist-guide duties with pride, if not gusto. In some ways it's fitting that I get to show off the FBI's setup on my last day. Who knows when I'll be back again? And I really have loved every minute of my time here.

After the running track, we come to the defensive-driving track before moving on to Hogan's Alley—the Bureau's famous simulated town. I stop the car and from our vantage point it's possible to look down into the fake ten-acre town, which includes a post office, a bank, a hotel, a laundromat, a barbershop, a pool hall and suburban homes.

Once we're out of the car, I start the spiel. "Hogan's Alley is used to train new recruits and is also used by many other agencies for training exercises. You'll often find the Drug Enforcement Agency, police officers from all around the States and even international law-enforcement professionals down there. In fact, that was my introduction to the FBI."

"You came over from Australia officially?"

"Yes. The Victoria Police sent me on the International Training Program. I met Rivers, and we got talking after one of the profiling sessions. When I mentioned my dad was American I had a job offer."

"The Bureau's citizenship criteria," Black says.

"Uh-huh." To apply for the Bureau you have to be an American citizen. I hold dual citizenship, thanks to an Australian mother and American father.

Black nods. "I see."

I move back to Hogan's Alley and the tour. "The town can be set up to simulate any criminal activity, like a bank robbery, a kidnapping, a murder, a terrorist attack, etcetera."

"It certainly looks impressive in real life." She turns to her assistant. "Debbie, you getting this?"

Holt nods and writes furiously, switching from looking at Hogan's Alley to her pad, where she must be taking notes on layout and other items Black might need for her research.

Black peers over her glasses at the town. "Let's go down and have a better look." She starts to walk down the embankment.

I grab her arm. "I'm afraid we can't go down there. A training exercise is scheduled for later this morning and it's off-limits." I point to the activity in one corner of the fake town. "They're setting up."

Her lips purse slightly again, like a petulant child who hasn't been given the sweet they're demanding. I wonder if a tantrum's brewing.

We wait in silence for Holt, whose pen is still dancing across the page of her notebook. When she's finished, I take the two of them back to the main complex. We spend the next couple of hours wandering around the dormitories, dining room, library, auditorium, chapel, gym and finally around the offices. While the Academy is primarily a training ground, it also houses several centralized departments that operate from Quantico rather than the D.C. head office. The National Center for the Analysis of Violent Crimes, which my unit sits under, is one of these departments. I finish up there and take Black and Holt to the three divisions—the Child Abduction Serial Murder Investigative Resources Center, the Violent Criminal Apprehension Program and my unit, the Behavioral Analysis Unit. After I've explained each area and shown Holt and Black some of what the center does, I finish up outside Rivers's office. Once Janet announces us, we crowd into the office.

Rivers extends his hand. "Ms. Black, lovely to meet you."

"Thank you, Special Agent Rivers. And you."

Black doesn't make a move to introduce Holt so I do it for her.

After he's shaken Holt's hand, Rivers turns back to Black. "My sister's a big fan."

"Yes, we have…" Black turns to Holt and is about to snap her fingers when she thinks the better of it—perhaps only because she's in company.

Holt fishes out seven books. "This is the George Benson series, to date, including the new one." She passes the books to Rivers. "They're made out to your sister, sir," she adds.

"Thank you. That's very kind of you…and efficient."

Holt gives him a small nod and a slightly embarrassed smile.

Next Holt pulls out another book from her bag of tricks and passes it to me. "This is a copy of the new one for you too." She smiles.

I take the book. "Thanks…congratulations," I offer, studying the striking, glossy book cover. A woman lies dead on white tiles, and a large lipstick mark is embossed across one quarter of the cover. On the bottom *Loretta Black* is written in big black letters and the title, *Ladykiller*, is in red at the top. Not surprisingly, given that the killer poses the victims with their legs open, the cover image only shows the top half of the girl's body. The breasts are attached but blood trickles from a cut on one of them.

"So, how are you finding the tour so far?" Rivers asks Black.

"Very informative." Black says it without appreciation or passion. I make an inward *humph* sound—it's a damn good tour, if I do say so myself.

"Anderson is one of our best. It's a pity we're losing her."

Black turns to me. "You're leaving?"

"This is my last day. I'm transferring to the L.A. Field Office."

"Oh," she says with no emotion.

"Really?" Holt adds her voice to the mix, and I can tell from her face that she's thinking. Then she says, "You should come to the launch party."

"Um…" I have no desire to go to Black's party.

"When do you fly?" Holt asks.

I pause, wishing I knew when the party was so I could name a date after that. "Friday night." I give her the truth.

"No good." She seems genuinely disappointed. "The launch is tomorrow night."

The buzz of the intercom interrupts us and Janet's voice comes over the speaker. "The sandwiches are in the project room, Sophie."

"Thanks," I say. I would ask Rivers to join us, but I don't want to impose. Then again, it would be a fitting punishment for dumping Black on me—I bet he knew she was a pain in the ass. "Why don't you join us for lunch, sir?"

Black jumps in quickly. "That would be lovely."

She thinks Rivers can give her more information than I can. He's got more experience, yes, but anyone in the unit will be able to answer her questions about the Academy and profiling.

Rivers looks at the papers on his desk but only hesitates for a second. "That'd be great. But there's probably not enough food." He looks at me with a slight pleading look in his eyes.

No way is he getting out of this. "Of course there's enough food. Janet will have organized enough for an army, she always does." I give him a smug smile and he forces a smile in response.

I'm leading the way to the project room when a wave of nausea envelops me. I make it to the door and steady myself against it, trying to be as discreet as possible but also ready for whatever I'm about to see and feel…and ready for the dizziness.

A woman's running through woods. Someone's chasing her.

Three

I jump at the sound of my ringing phone before hunting around for it in the rubble that is my bedroom—now half unpacked on the other side of the country. My new apartment is on Veteran Avenue in Westwood. The rent's costing me a fortune, but the place has got everything I need, including a small swimming pool for the hot summer months and a fitness center that I can use whenever it suits me. The apartment complex itself is only six stories high, with approximately thirty apartments arranged in a square shape around the pool and landscaped gardens. The ground-floor apartments have small, enclosed patios, and the higher apartments have balconies that stretch across the living rooms and usually a bedroom. I'm in a one-bedroom place on the second floor, set in the front of the complex. It's very different to the high-rise apartment building in Alexandria where I lived while working in Quantico.

My front door opens directly onto the living room and a small kitchen that's tucked away in the left corner. The hardwood floors of the living room lead to glass doors and my balcony, with two doors off the small living space opening to a carpeted bedroom and a compact bathroom.

I find the phone and pick it up. "Hello?"

"Hi, honey. How are you settling in?"

"Hi, Dad. Good. You're my first phone call."

He laughs. "Your mom's been making me call every hour, just to see if the phone was on yet."

"That'd be right." I sit down on my bed.

"Are you sure about this move? I don't know about L.A."

Dad grew up in Providence and he's always been very pro East Coast.

"It'll be great, Dad. And maybe I'll run into some movie stars. Get some autographs for you."

"Mmm." He sounds neither hopeful nor impressed.

A loud click on the line tells me that Mum's picked up the other phone. "Finally, darling. I thought they'd never connect that phone of yours."

I shake my head. "Mum, they said Saturday morning. It's 11:00 a.m. here."

"I know, I know. But…" She trails off, presumably realizing that there's no logical way to finish her sentence.

"And you could have called me on my mobile."

"We wanted to speak to you in your new home." She quickly moves on to her next topic. "Are you unpacked yet?"

"Almost." It's an exaggeration more than a lie. The removalists put all the furniture in place, leaving me with only the unpacking. I started with the kitchen, essential bed things and the bathroom, and now I'm making my way through all my clothes and other bedroom items before tackling the living room. My bedroom furniture has a definite Japanese theme, with a dark-wood slatted bed, two matching bedside tables, a long, skinny tallboy and a three-panel Japanese screen. A small Buddha sits below my bedroom window, and I've placed indoor plants on either side of the balcony doors. Gradually the bland shell of my white-walled, cream-carpeted apartment is looking cozier and more like mine.

"I wish we were there to help," Mum says. "Or that you had someone." Her voice is melodramatic. "Someone special."

I roll my eyes, but I guess it's fair enough. I'm a thirty-five-year-old single woman and her only hope of grand-children—of course she wants me to settle down. "I'm fine on my own, Mum. Honest."

"L.A.'s a dangerous place." Her voice is still full of drama. "I don't like the idea of you being there at all."

"Come on, Mum, you didn't like me moving to D.C. either."

She's silent for a while. "No."

We all know the real thing she's unhappy about—my job. My dad's not exactly over the moon about my chosen career either, but at least he doesn't go on and on about it.

"Mum, L.A.'s going to be great for me. Warmer weather and, don't forget, I'm closer to Melbourne now. It's only fifteen hours away." Fifteen hours is small fry for Australians. Heading north from Melbourne it takes over five hours to clear Australia's coastline. "And we can meet in Hawaii for your holidays this year."

My cell phone rings and I'm almost as surprised to hear it buzzing as I was to hear my new landline ringing. I move to the kitchen bench, where I left my cell. I look at the number coming up, but don't recognize it. Curiosity gets the better of me. "Hold on a sec," I say to Mum and Dad.

I answer my cell and hear the sobs before the person on the other end manages to speak.

"Hello?" I say. I repeat my name. "Sophie Anderson."

"Agent Anderson, it's Debbie Holt." More sobs. "Loretta Black's assistant."

"Yes?"

"It's…it's about Loretta."

"Yes?" I repeat, trying to coax her out of the panic. "What is it, Debbie?"

"She's dead. Loretta's dead."

"Dead?" I repeat loudly, then realize Mum and Dad can probably hear me. Damn.

More sobs from Holt on the other end of the phone. "Loretta's husband found her this morning. She was…she was strangled. But…"

"Yes?" I want to tell Holt to hold on while I deal with my parents, but I can tell she's teetering on the edge, about to break down completely. There's something she needs to get out, now.

"She…she had the stocking, the lipstick and…and her legs were spread, and her breasts were—" Holt's voice cracks and she doesn't finish the sentence. "It's just like her book."

This *is* bizarre news. I automatically visualize the front cover of *Ladykiller,* the face and upper body of the dead redhead lying glassy-eyed on a stark white bathroom floor. Even through the stocking that covers her face you can make out the open eyes, the slightly startled look. "Sorry, Debbie. But I need you to hold on for a sec. Okay?"

"Sure." Holt's voice is more even now that she's managed to verbalize the distressing news.

I move back to the landline. "Mum, Dad, I've got to call you back."

"Who's dead?" Mum yells.

"It's a case, Mum. No one you know."

"Oh, darling." Mum's voice is disapproving, but there's also a hint of hysteria to it and that's something I can't deal with now.

"I'm sorry, Mum, I've got to go. I'll call you back. Love you."

It's Dad who answers. "We love you too. Be safe, sweetie."

"Always, Dad, always." I hang up and move back to Holt. "Sorry, Debbie, I was on the phone to my parents."

"In Australia?"

"Yes."

"I'm sorry. I shouldn't have bothered you. I just—"

"It's fine, Debbie. Where are you? You have called the police, haven't you?"

"Oh yes, we called the police straightaway. I'm at Loretta's house in Beverly Hills." The tears start again.

"Who's we, Debbie?"

"Scott, Loretta's husband, and me."

I process the information. He'll be the prime suspect, even more so if he found the body. "Just tell me everything that happened."

Through Holt's tears I manage to pick up the basic facts. Black and Holt arrived back in L.A. on Thursday morning, ready for the launch. Black's husband had to fly out to an important meeting in Chicago on the Friday morning and returned to L.A. Saturday morning—this morning. He claims to have spoken to Black on the phone at 10:00 p.m. last night, but then when he rang this morning from the airport there was no answer at home or on her cell. He caught a taxi home and found his wife dead in the bathroom, with a stocking over her face and a kiss-shaped mark drawn on her cheek with lipstick.

Holt sobs some more on the phone and I'm at a loss— what do I do? I can't exactly jump in a cab, race to the crime scene and work my way into the investigation— that's not the way things are done. It would be the equivalent of slashing my wrists, professionally. And it's not a federal case…murder in Beverly Hills is the jurisdiction of the Beverly Hills Police Department.

"I'm not sure what I can do to help," I say.

She takes a few seconds to respond. "When I organized that tour for Loretta and I, we were told you were the best. I know Loretta's family would want the best to investigate. Loretta would want you involved too. She spoke very highly of you."

I stop myself from spluttering with surprise at this last comment. If Black felt that way she sure didn't show it. "The problem is, Debbie, it's not my jurisdiction. I haven't even started at the L.A. Field Office yet, and the Beverly Hills police are more than qualified to handle a murder case. If they want FBI help they'll contact the field office." Beverly Hills PD would probably ask for assistance from the sheriff's department first, anyway.

"Then they could assign anyone. Loretta would want *you*." Holt's adamant, and I can almost imagine her pursing her lips and digging her heels in, just like her boss…ex-boss.

"I'm sorry, Debbie. Sorry to hear about Loretta and sorry I can't be of more help. Let's wait and see how things pan out in the next forty-eight hours."

She starts sobbing again and I feel guilty, not to mention professionally curious.

"Tell you what, why don't you explain to the lead detective that you were at the Academy earlier this week and that you'd like him or her to give me a call."

She sniffles. "Okay." More sniffles. "I'll do it now."

"The police are still there?"

"Yes. They're all over the place. I haven't even seen Scott since they arrived, but I think they're still questioning him."

No surprise there—it's standard practice to separate witnesses at the scene and I'd still be questioning Scott too, because the old adage "the husband did it" often turns out to be true.

"Thank you, Sophie. And I'm sorry I interrupted your phone call with your folks."

"That's fine. Call me if you need anything else."

We say a brief goodbye and I disconnect. I probably won't be hearing from Beverly Hills' finest, at least not today. They'll have plenty of leads to follow without wanting to pull an FBI profiler into the mix at this early stage. I think back to Black's visit and, with a sickening sense of dread, I remember the dizziness in the parking lot. I'd fought off a vision when I was with Black—was it of her? Her death? It *was* while we were talking about her killer's signature. Maybe if I'd let the vision come, Black would be alive now. Images of Black posed like the front cover of her book flash across my field of vision. Dammit! A minute ago I felt empathy for Holt and was intrigued, but now guilt is riding me hard.

I pace up and down for a bit before I suddenly remember my parents. I wouldn't want to make my mother any more hysterical by not calling back. I make the call, but only spend ten minutes on the phone before cutting the conversation short with the excuse of unpacking. I know they worry about me, especially after what happened to my brother, but sometimes I just wish they'd accept that I love my job and am not going to change it for anyone, not even them.

Half an hour later I've made some progress on my apartment, managing to unpack my wardrobe, but I haven't been able to keep my mind off Black. Eventually I succumb and hunt out her book. Flicking through it, I find the section on the first murder scene and read from the start of the chapter.

The media throng surged forward, spitting out the man with the badge, Detective George Benson. But he wasn't released without a fight from the many journalists, hungry for the story, willing to do just about anything to find out if the body in the motel room was the fourth victim of the city's serial killer. The killer had been labeled the Terminator for his violent killings, or maybe it was just a name some smart-ass journalist came up with—it was usually the media rather than the public who dubbed serial killers.

Benson ignored the frantic and aggressive questioning, pulling long and hard on his cigarette and making sure anyone and everyone close enough got a dose of his secondhand smoke. *That'll teach the fuckers,* he thought as he watched the closest journalists back away from his cancer stick. Benson's rationale was that he was more likely to die from a bullet than lung cancer, so he'd prefer to indulge his bad habit—each cigarette could be his last. He burrowed his cigarette butt in the sandbox outside the motel-room door. He still remembered the days when you could smoke inside, smoke anywhere you darn well liked…those were the days.

"You the first responder, boy?" he asked the officer on the door who, while he did look young, could hardly be called a boy rather than a man.

"Yes, sir." He answered with respect and fear. He'd heard about Benson. Cranky old bastard, they all said, but a damn good detective. Rumor had it that he used to have a wife and daughter, used to be a nice guy. Until a car accident took them away and changed him forever.

"Anyone else been on the scene since you arrived?"

"No, sir."

Benson smiled, enjoying the show of respect. "You touch anything, boy?"

"No, sir!"

"Good…good—" he gave the officer a slap on the shoulder and glanced at his name badge "—Officer Graves."

The uniform offered Benson a schoolgirl smile and they stood there grinning at each other for a couple of seconds before Benson put his hands in his pockets.

"Guess I better go in."

"Yes, sir." He nodded. "Holler if you need anything."

Like a coffee? But Benson only thought it. He

wasn't that much of a bastard…not today, at least. Besides, he needed someone standing guard at the motel room. He moved closer, toward the open door.

"Was it open when you found it?" Benson yelled back to Officer Graves.

"Yes, sir. Cleaner opened the door, saw her and ran, leaving the door open. Then the manager on duty came and saw her but said he was real careful not to touch anything, including the door. He's a *CSI* fan."

Benson tried to smile but it came out more like a grimace. "Isn't everybody? He's probably already decided whodunit."

The officer laughed briefly before making eye contact with the manager, who was well within ear-shot. The manager's eyes burned with humiliation and the officer's face fell before he gave himself over to the standard blank stare. Who knows when or where they learn it, but every cop can do it.

Benson slipped into the motel room, sucking in his paunch so as not to touch the door or the door frame as he squeezed through the open door. No contact was quite a feat, given the size of his beer gut. Benson's attitude was, If you can't smoke and drink beer and bourbon, life just ain't worth living.

A chair sat in the middle of the room, with rope partially draped around it, falling down one side and coiling at the chair's legs. The rest of the room looked normal. Benson noticed a woman's round handbag on top of the TV. It was molded rather than softened leather, and it sat up perkily. Benson smiled, drawing an analogy between the handbag and a good pair of tits. But the smile faded when he remembered how long it had been since he'd seen a good pair of tits...unless you counted dead bodies...which he didn't. Particularly not the ones in this case.

He moved into the bathroom. The tall, curvaceous redhead lay still on the white tiles. Her lily-white skin was covered in light freckles from top to bottom, and the positioning of the girl made sure everyone knew right off that the girl was a true redhead. Her feet were pulled up in a froglike pose, and her exposed genitals were directly in line with the bathroom door, so her full frontal slapped you in the face—hard.

Benson's eyes moved up her body. A circular cut extended around each breast, but Benson couldn't tell if the killer had detached the breasts or simply cut around them. Only a closer examination would reveal if the underlying breast tissue was cut through. Stretched thinly over the woman's face and head was a light-colored stocking, just like the first three girls. *Fuck, how did that female cop describe it? That's right, sheer.* It was sheer all right. Despite the panty hose, her facial features were easily distinguished. Her mouth was large and pouty, her jaw squarish and her cheekbones high. Her blue-green eyes were open but lifeless, now a window to nothingness, rather than to her soul. Drawn on her cheek in bright red lipstick was a pair of lips. Unfortunately for Benson, it wasn't a real lip print—some labs were printing lips and ears, not just fingers. Benson noticed that there weren't any toiletries in the bathroom, none of the usual crap that a woman had to travel with, and there was no suitcase, no clothes. The redhead was checking in for a fuck…but who was she fucking?

Despite the fact that the redhead's murder is the fourth, it's the first one in the book, the place where the reader comes into the crime investigation. I can only assume there are more murders after this one, or perhaps flashbacks to the first three girls. This particular victim is also obviously the one on which the front cover was based. Even though I haven't seen Black's body, the similarities are disturbing. Is the crime scene *exactly* the same? If not, how does it differ? For a start, the fictional murder took place in a motel room, and Black's was in her home. I think about Black's detective, Benson—I hope the lead detective on Black's case isn't like him. Benson's just the sort of cop I'd hate to work with—a self-destructive misogynist. And unfortunately, those characteristics aren't unique in this job.

I can't do anything useful from here for Black, so I force myself back to the unpacking. The thought of boxes everywhere for days or weeks is good motivation. I like my house neat and tidy, in stark contrast to my work desk, which is usually covered in a thick layer of papers and at least one or two old coffee cups.

I'm working on a box of clothes for my chest of drawers when my cell phone rings. The caller ID says Private Number and curiosity gets the better of me again.

"Sophie Anderson."

"Hi, Agent Anderson. It's Detective Dave Sorrell here from Beverly Hills Homicide."

"Detective." I keep the surprise and excitement out of

my voice. I want in on the investigation and I want to see the crime scene firsthand, and fresh.

"Sorry to bother you on a Saturday, Anderson, but Debbie Holt was persuasive, to say the least."

"So she's been bugging you to call me—" I look at my watch "—for the last hour."

"Uh-huh." Sorrell's tone of voice says it all.

I respond to his tone by playing it cool. "Well, I told Ms. Holt I'd do everything that I can to help, but I don't know if I can shed much light on the case."

"No offense, but my thoughts exactly."

"None taken." I pause. "Although the signature elements are interesting…and certainly something that holds a professional interest for me." Truth be told, it's exactly the sort of case that most cops would at least consider calling in a profiler for, though perhaps not this early on.

"Holt says you're the new profiler at the Bureau's field office here."

"That's right. I start on Monday."

"Should I call you back then?"

"No, that's fine," I say.

"So, the signature." Sorrell accepts my interest and moves back to the case.

"It's intriguing. Especially given the book's only just been released, so, realistically, how many people could have read it and then had time to plan and reenact the murder?"

"That's what I thought, until Holt set me straight. Holt reckons a new release of Black's would normally sell a few hundred thousand in the first week, plus preorders. Its official release date was Wednesday, three days ago. I'm trying to get the book pulled off the shelves so we can at least limit the number of people who know about the book's plot and crime scenes."

"I bet the publisher will love you for that," I say, though it's unlikely Sorrell will get anywhere with his request. For a start, to pull a book nationwide would take a federal directive, which means FBI, and that's unlikely when the book itself isn't breaking any laws. Movies have been pulled by the FBI before—one case that comes to mind is Traci Lords. She made dozens of adult movies when she was sixteen, using a fake birth certificate and driver's license as proof of age. The feds found out her real age and pulled and destroyed every one of the videos she made before she turned eighteen. But showing a minor in sexual acts is a criminal offense and writing a crime-fiction book isn't. Besides, Black's basic plotline would already have made its way onto the Web and into newspaper reviews. Can't pull all that too.

"Everyone will want that book if they find out Black's murder replicates the story line," Sorrell says. "And once that happens, it'll be much harder to track down who had the book *before* her murder and who bought it after."

I don't want to put a damper on Sorrell's plans and tell him he hasn't got a hope in hell, so I change the topic. "Do you think it's worth me coming down to the crime scene?" I keep my voice cool and only slightly interested.

"Maybe."

Silence. I ride out the silence, not wanting to push...not yet at least.

About fifteen seconds pass before I hear an intake of breath on the other end of the phone. "I probably would have got a profiler on this eventually. What the heck. You may as well see the crime scene at its freshest."

I smile. He's right about that...especially if I want to

increase my chances of using my visions to find Black's killer. I didn't like Black, but I sure as hell didn't want her dead.

Dear Ms. Black,

I read the latest George Benson novel with both fascination and repulsion. While the killer was fantastic and inventive, I think you've taken it too far. All you authors these days are committing horrible crimes against our society. What if someone read your work and was inspired to act? To kill?

Think about our youth. Your stories give them a terrible, terrible role model to follow, maybe terrible, terrible ideas. Do you want to be responsible for some poor woman's murder?

You seem to be able to capture the heart and soul of a killer. Do you know what it's like to feel a person's life literally in your hands? To have the power to drain their blood, ounce by ounce? And the way your victims' legs are spread is such an exciting and suggestive concept for a man. Do you know how strong that imagery can be for us? How powerful the desire to see a woman laid out like that is? Your words could make someone act.

You must stop writing this filth. It can only bring you pain, believe you me.
Yours sincerely,
A fan

Four

There's more than the usual crime-scene circus outside Black's house. The road, sidewalk and nearby driveways are littered with cars and media vans. There's always press, but not like this, and there must be over a hundred people congregating around the house's gated entrance. It's not just interested bystanders or neighbors, as with most crime scenes; these people are fans, mourning the loss of one of their favorite authors. The news sure has traveled fast…but then again, this is L.A. and Black's famous. What did I expect?

I drive slowly toward the gate, the mass of my car forcing the crowd to part. For much of the slow crawl to the entrance, I'm completely surrounded by people—some blocking my path in front, people on the sides ogling inside my car, and a sizable crowd surging forward behind me, trying to use the momentum of my car to get closer to the Black residence. I'm not claustrophobic, but I'm no lover of crowds either, and being boxed in by a group this size makes me anxious. The unease manifests itself physically—my heart pounds and my body temperature sky-rockets. Darren, the only person who knows about my gift, says part of the reason I hate crowds is my sixth sense. He reckons I pick up on people's emotions, like one big buzz of conflicting thoughts and energy.

I finally make it to the gate, which has four uniformed officers guarding it, spaced evenly across a temporary barricade. At the gate, I also notice a small camera—part of Black's security system. So how did her killer get in? Once I've shown my ID to the nearest cop, he removes the temporary barricade and lets me pass, while the other three uniforms hold the mob at bay. I breathe a sigh of relief—I'm clear of the crowd. The driveway snakes up to a home that can only be described as a mansion. Guess I'm in the wrong business. Out of the car, I try to smooth the creases out of my pants—a futile gesture. None of my suits have traveled well, and spending ten minutes ironing once Sorrell had opened up his crime scene to me didn't seem appropriate. Besides, I hate ironing. My body heat will eventually steam the creases out. I straighten up with a deep breath. I'm not looking forward to this. All I can think about is Black, alive and being a pain in the ass. So now I've got the double-guilts. Guilty about the premonition I shoved deep down into wherever they come from, and guilty about thinking ill of the dead. I bite my lip, willing the emotions away.

At the threshold of the front door I take out my ID again. "I'm here to see Detective Sorrell."

The officer's eyes move from the ID to me before he's satisfied. Nice to see he's thorough.

"Sorrell's on the second floor, third door on your right."

"Thank you, officer." I force a small, polite smile and

take a deep breath, aware that a vision of Black's murder could come to me at any time. Seeing someone's death is never pleasant, but I force myself into the house. A quick sweep of the entranceway shows me at least four motion detectors guarding the room. So did the killer get past them somehow or did Black have them switched off?

The crime scene is still busy, and as I walk up the stairs I pass two people dusting the walls for prints. What a nightmare—so much wall and surface space and they'll all be covered in prints. But the killer was here, and if he didn't use gloves, he probably left a print somewhere.

I know the room the officer was talking about not from his directions but because two uniforms are spilling out of the door, giving that room more attention. They look up as I approach and I get my ID ready again. I focus on the cop nearest me, a man in his early twenties.

"I'm here to see Detective Sorrell," I say. I hold up my ID. "I'm FBI."

The officer nods and jerks his thumb over his shoulder. "He's the tall guy."

Not exactly the most helpful description. I resist the urge to say, "Gee, thanks," in the most sarcastic voice I can muster.

I dodge the uniforms until I'm in the center of the room, and then I realize that the young cop's description was perfect. One man is towering above all the other people. He must be about six foot six. I can't help myself—I smile.

Just at that moment, Sorrell turns around, facing me full-on. His eyes narrow. "You Anderson?"

I rearrange my face, wiping away the amused smile and replacing it with a courteous, professional one. "Yes. Special Agent Sophie Anderson." I move forward and hold out my hand.

He gives it two short, yet forceful pumps, but his eyes remain suspicious and he gives me a rapid once-over. His eyes don't change. I guess most people don't walk into a crime scene with an ear-to-ear grin. I'm not winning any points for first impressions. I could let it ride, but I feel the need to explain.

"The officer said look for the tall guy. I didn't think he was being very helpful until I saw you."

My explanation falls over like a bad joke and Sorrell's silent.

I nod, uncomfortable, and take a deep breath in. "So, where's the body?"

Sorrell's eyes soften slightly. Maybe he likes a woman who gets straight down to business.

"Bathroom's through here." Sorrell moves toward the right and an open door.

I do a fast visual sweep of the room, taking in the decor and people—any and every detail can be important. It's a huge room, perhaps originally the master bedroom, but it looks like Black turned it into her writing room. Running partway down the left wall is a small bar, and the rest of the wall is taken up by a built-in bookshelf that's overflowing with books. The far wall is fitted with a floor-to-ceiling window that runs the width of the room, broken only by a few supports and French doors that lead to a small balcony. Against this window wall is a large desk with a computer, printer and fax machine, and to the right of the balcony is a treadmill. The window looks out onto extensive landscaped gardens and, of course, a pool. A couch, two armchairs and a coffee table also fit easily in the room, and I notice that the matching wooden chair for the desk sits about two meters to the left of the desk, facing out as though whoever was sitting in it was looking at the view. But it doesn't seem like the most comfortable chair in which to relax and take in the scenery. To my right, an arched entrance gives me a sneak preview of another, smaller room, and I'm guessing the bathroom's off that. A photographer takes shots of Black's writing space, while three forensic techs are still dusting for prints. Another technician is crawling on the floor, examining the carpet closely—obviously looking for hairs or any foreign fibers. He'll also vacuum the room with a clean bag and someone at the lab will search the bag's contents for fibers or any other trace evidence. Given the time, not to mention the amount of print dust around this room, it looks like the crime-scene techs are almost finished.

I follow Sorrell into the adjoining room.

To the left, Holt sits on a four-poster bed with her legs dangling over the edge. The four-poster is made of a dark wood, with cream curtains drawn around each corner. The bedroom's also got its share of investigators, with two men dusting for prints and one cop standing in the corner, taking everything in.

Holt looks up as I enter the room and slides off the high bed.

"Thank you for coming, Sophie." She holds out her hand to me and I take it with both hands, giving her a comforting handshake.

"That's fine, Debbie. But don't thank me, thank Detective Sorrell—it's his case." I say this for both Holt's and Sorrell's benefit. I want Holt to realize that I'm not the only one doing her a favor, and I want Sorrell to know that I appreciate him inviting the FBI onto his turf, especially this early in a case.

"Thank you, Detective Sorrell." Holt nods at him, although I don't see a lot of friendliness in her eyes. Has Sorrell rubbed her the wrong way? As one of those closest to Black, Holt may be treated as a suspect until ruled out. The husband will be Sorrell's first line of questioning, but maybe he's given Holt a taste of what's to come and she doesn't appreciate it.

"Where's the husband?" I ask Sorrell quietly.

"Another room." He motions with his head toward the main door, presumably in the general direction of this other room. Sorrell would have separated Holt and Scott as soon as he arrived, wanting to minimize any time they had to confer…especially if it turns out the husband and Holt are having an affair.

Holt turns red eyes to me again. "You'll have a look around?"

"That's what I'm here for," I say. Holt's presuming that someone she knows, and trusts, will be more inclined to examine the scene thoroughly than strangers like Sorrell and his team. But it's not necessarily a good assumption— in fact, a stranger is more likely to be objective, and anyone who takes pride in their work will be thorough.

"I'll help Sorrell and his team in any way I can," I add. "And I'll certainly begin work on a profile." I look at Sorrell. "If that's okay with you."

He shrugs, like he doesn't care either way, but says, "Fine by me," with more warmth than the body language and words alone indicate.

I'm not sure what to make of Sorrell. I'm FBI, which in his books could be a strike against me. A lot of cops are territorial, especially when it comes to "the feds." I guess Sorrell hasn't exactly warmed to me. Not yet, at least. I have to earn his respect. Fair enough. Another week and I may think he's the dumbest homicide cop in the world; it cuts both ways.

I go for the straight-down-to-business approach, which seemed to work last time. "So she's in there." I look toward the bathroom, hesitant. What will happen when I'm confronted with the body? I'm used to seeing dead bodies; I can handle that. But when I see Black, I could be invaded by her final thoughts, feelings, fear and pain. Or maybe I'll tune in to the killer's mind.

"We only got someone from the coroner's office a half hour ago."

I nod. Guess there were more deaths for a Saturday morning than they were expecting and Black had to wait her turn. She wouldn't have liked that…if she were alive.

"Let's go." I take a pair of latex gloves out of my handbag and slip them on. The fingerprint guys will have enough prints to sift through without adding mine to the mix—not that I'd ever touch anything at a crime scene anyway. There are only two places for your hands at a fresh crime scene—in your pockets or covered with a pair of latex gloves.

Sorrell leads the way, and Holt hesitates, uncertain.

I pick up on her movement. "You should stay out here, Debbie."

It's a massive bathroom, perhaps even more luxurious than the rest of the area. Large white tiles line the floor and walls, and the centerpiece is an enormous spa bath. Next to that is a shower and on the far wall is a TV—I guess if you can't watch TV in the bath you're just not living. The setup reminds me of Black's wealth. She is…was…a multimillionaire, and Sorrell's going to love that for motive. Hell, I would. Except for the murder scene…it doesn't look like money. It's sexual and ritualistic, not practical. Lying on the floor next to the spa bath is Black. She's naked, eyes wide open. She's on her back, with her left arm raised slightly and her head turned in the same direction. It looks like her breasts have been cut from her body, but then placed back in position. The relative lack of blood tells us it was a postmortem mutilation. It's just like the body in her book. The only things that differ from the fictional scene are Black's hair color and a message written in lipstick on the mirror, which says, *Your turn.* But is the *your* referring to Black or to us, the investigators? If it refers to Black, the only thing that comes to mind is her turn to die. But if the *your* is directed at us, then perhaps the killer's playing a game of cat and mouse—he's had his turn, killing Black, and now it's our turn. Our turn to try to find the bastard.

I concentrate on the mirror and take in another deep breath, aware of all the people who will witness my response to a vision. But I've already blocked one vision that was probably about Black's murder; I can't do it again. I'm ready for anything I might see, but I also stay focused on the crime scene.

"That isn't in the book, is it?" I ask Sorrell, pointing at the basin mirror. It wasn't in the section I read.

"Apparently not," he says. "But I haven't read it yet."

I nod and take in the rest of the room. It's covered in fingerprint dust too, but there's only one other person in here—the forensic pathologist from the coroner's office. Obviously the techs did this room first before moving on to the bedroom and living area of this section of the house, and Sorrell's had to wait for someone from the coroner's office to arrive before he can move the body. Poor Holt, sitting here for hours, only meters away from the body.

"You've got lots of men on this," I say, commenting on the number of uniforms and lab technicians.

"The more the merrier."

I wait for the smile but it doesn't come.

"Besides, may as well make use of my search warrant."

"You got one for the whole place?"

"Uh-huh."

With defense attorneys challenging the admission of so much evidence these days, we have to be extra careful that everything's done by the book. Even though this is a crime scene, it's still private property, and a search warrant covers everybody's ass. Point to Sorrell for ensuring it's sewn up from the outset.

"Highly sexualized pose," I say, moving closer. It's not a revelation, more a running dialogue.

The forensic pathologist looks up. "Yes."

"I'm Special Agent Sophie Anderson from the L.A. Field Office." It's not entirely true, not yet, but who's going to argue about thirty-six hours?

"Lloyd Grove, coroner's office." An unspoken acknowledgment ensures we don't shake hands—his are busy.

I crouch down next to Grove and Sorrell follows suit. Even this close to her body, nothing's coming to me. No dizziness, no nausea and no vision. Being in the field, at crime scenes, was supposed to bring more visions, not fewer.

"What have you got, Grove?" Sorrell asks.

"When I get her back to the office I'll know more, but looks to me like she died sitting, not lying."

I nod, knowing that he would have made that discovery from lividity—the way the blood settles after death.

"Did you notice the chair in the other room?" I ask Sorrell.

"Yeah. It's out of place. Not behind the desk. The crime-scene techs did find something on it. Possibly rope fibers. That ties in with her—" Sorrell points to Black's body "—and apparently with the book too."

"She was tied up before death," Grove explains, pointing to marks around Black's wrists—rope marks.

"Probably tied to that chair, but the killer took the rope with him," Sorrell says.

I study the rope marks. "Time of death?"

"Rectal temperature and rigor indicate roughly twelve hours," he says.

Sorrell nods. "Looks like she died between ten last night and nine this morning."

I look at him, waiting for more information.

"The husband called at ten and I've verified that on Black's cell phone. They spoke for twelve minutes and ten seconds. He called again from the airport at nine this morning—the missed call came up on Black's cell. We'll need to check that the phone hasn't been tampered with, but it certainly looks like a solid time frame."

It's just like Holt told me on the phone. "What else have you found?" I look at Grove expectantly, even though I know he'll wait until he gets Black on the table before he says much. Forensic pathologists don't like to disclose solid details until they're in their rooms doing the official autopsy. Jumping to conclusions too early can be dangerous.

"Asphyxiation seems likely, given her eyes." He points to some small burst blood vessels in Black's open eyes. "The breasts have been almost completely detached from the torso, but the killer didn't do a great job of it. We're *not* looking for someone skilled with a scalpel or knife, that's for sure."

I study the hands more closely, noticing the jagged lines.

"Not much else at this stage," Grove says.

I shift my focus back to Sorrell. "Anything on point of entry?" I ask him. Finding out how the killer got in will be one of the first areas of his investigation. Did he break in? If not, perhaps he was let in by Black, which means she probably knew him or had some other reason to let her killer inside her home. And either way, was the killer caught on the security system?

"He came in from the back. One of the glass doors that leads to the pool was broken."

"Was the alarm system armed?"

"No. But the husband says they usually only put it on when they go out."

I'd have thought Black would have been more security conscious, given the type of research she was exposed to. Once you know what…or who…is out there, the world becomes a much scarier place.

"What about the camera on the gate? Did that catch anything?" I ask.

"The camera's activated by movement, rather than being on 24/7, and any video images are stored on a hard drive for seven days. A preliminary check of the hard drive indicates the last activation was six o'clock last night, when Black came back from a walk. But our tech guys will confirm that."

I nod and look down at Black's body again. "You notice the tiles?"

"Sure," he says. "Just like the book's cover. The killer probably knew this house, this room."

Sorrell would already have assumed Black knew her killer—most homicide victims do know their assailants—but it's good to get evidence to support that theory. And certainly the killer seemed to know he wouldn't have to contend with an alarm system.

I can think of one other possible explanation for the tiles so I voice it. "Or the killer may have checked this detail beforehand—" I point to the body on the tiles "—indicating a high level of organization and planning."

I stand up and look down at Black. She doesn't look tough and cold anymore—no victim ever does. I shake my head, getting more and more frustrated by the minute. While my visions are still unreliable, I would have thought they'd be unavoidable in a crime scene this fresh.

I loiter in the bathroom for another minute, staring at Black's body, but nothing happens, so I move back into the adjoining room.

"Sophie?"

I look up at Holt's reddened face.

"Yes?"

"There are a couple of things you should know about." Her voice is raspy.

I glance back at Sorrell, who's still bent over the corpse. "You mentioned them to Detective Sorrell?"

"Yes." Holt talks fast. "The first one is a strange letter that Loretta got recently. It was…creepy. Kinda threatening."

"Give it to Sorrell and I'll get a copy." I play it by the book—I'm merely a visitor in Sorrell's crime scene.

"And there's something else…."

"Yes?"

"Loretta was sued recently. A journalist here in L.A. accused her of stealing his idea. He lost the case, but it got real nasty."

"Violent?"

Holt shakes her head, but slowly. "Not exactly." She gulps. "But he threatened to kill her."

I nod and put my hand on her arm. "We'll look into it." I give her a reassuring smile. "Do you have any idea what *Your turn* means?"

Holt shakes her head. "No."

"It doesn't have anything to do with *Ladykiller?*"

"Loretta didn't have anything like that in any of her books."

"Okay." I make my way back into the bathroom. "Sorrell?"

He turns to me. "Uh-huh?"

"Holt just told me about the letter and the journalist who sued Black."

He straightens up. "Yeah, I'm on it." He says it with authority.

"Mind if I talk to the husband now?"

"I'll take you to him." Sorrell takes us out of the writing wing of the house and leads the way down a long hall.

The door is slightly ajar, but Sorrell gives it two short raps before opening it fully. The room is obviously the main bedroom—big and tastefully decorated. Large bay windows look out onto a small balcony, and a man sits in an armchair to the left of the window. As we enter, his gaze moves from the window to us. Standing in the room is a uniformed officer, who was probably assigned by Sorrell to record everything the husband says and does.

"Agent Anderson, this is Scott Werner, Loretta Black's husband." Sorrell introduces us.

Werner is built like his late wife—tall and slim. His face is boyishly handsome and complemented by a round jaw and salt-and-pepper hair. He stands up and stares for a little while before moving forward to shake my hand. His eyes are swollen and his brow furrowed.

"I'm sorry for your loss, Mr. Werner," I say as I release his hand.

"Thank you, Agent Anderson. And thanks for coming. We appreciate it."

"I told Mr. Werner that Debbie Holt asked you to come down," Sorrell explains.

Werner's brown eyes shift to Sorrell and harden slightly. "I want to see my wife." He sinks back into the chair, his head in his hands.

"It won't be much longer now, Mr. Werner."

He looks up and shakes his head. "This is an outrage." He stands up again. "And what about Loretta's father? Has he arrived yet?"

"Yes, Mr. Black is here. He's downstairs in the living room. I'll finalize your official statements shortly and then bring everyone together."

Werner seems to be oscillating between grief and anger.

"First, if you could just answer a few questions for Agent Anderson."

Werner turns impatient eyes to me. "How many more questions do I have to answer?"

"I'm sorry, Mr. Werner, please bear with us. We're just trying to find your wife's killer."

He sighs. "Go on."

"Debbie mentioned a strange letter. Do you know anything about that?"

"Not really." He crosses his arms. "Loretta got negative mail from time to time, and it honestly didn't seem to bother her that much. She rarely spoke to me about it."

"Why did you say 'not really'?"

"Debbie did mention a letter a couple of weeks back."

"And?"

"Do we really have to do this now? My wife's dead. Can't you give me time to grieve?"

I apologize again, but press him. "Debbie said the letter was from someone who thought crime fiction was damaging our society. It became a dinner-conversation topic," he says.

I nod. "And what about your wife's lawsuit?"

Werner's jaw muscles tense. "Randy Sade. You think he did this?" At first Werner seems shocked by the prospect, but then his face changes. "That bastard did threaten her." Werner is lost in thought, but I bring him back.

"What's your relationship with Debbie Holt?" I say it abruptly, hoping to catch him off guard.

He rolls his eyes and looks at Sorrell. "You lot all think alike, don't you?" He turns back to me and says in a stern voice, "Debbie was my wife's assistant. We see a lot of each other, and we get along. But that's it."

Werner seems to be telling the truth, but it can be dangerous to take someone's words at face value, especially when that someone could be your prime suspect.

"What about the phrase *Your turn*. Does that mean anything to you?"

"No. I…I didn't know what it meant when I saw it, and I don't understand it now. It wasn't in her book and it doesn't sound familiar."

I move on to the security system, wanting to see Werner's face for myself when I ask the questions. "You know the alarm system wasn't armed, Mr. Werner?"

"Yes. Detective Sorrell mentioned it. And like I explained to him, that was normal. My wife and I only ever put it on if we were both going out."

"So she felt safe here?"

"Of course she felt safe in her own home."

I don't say anything, but I'm surprised Black didn't know better. While most people *think* their own home is safe, stats show us that it's a false sense of security. Witness the many people murdered or assaulted in their homes each year. But perhaps in Black's case her comfort level was because she knew the full picture, knew that the number of murders in people's homes is related to the fact that most people know their killers. Black's sense of safety may have been about the level of trust she had for those around her, including her husband. But was that trust misplaced?

I look around my apartment, triumphant. I know it's only a one-bedroom place, but I still feel like I've accomplished something by unpacking within twenty-four hours. Especially given I was called out to a crime scene yesterday. The last item that needs a new spot is the metal box that holds my brother's file. For the moment, it's sitting on my bed until I can figure out what to do with it. My brother, John, was abducted and murdered when I was eight years old, and that's the first time I remember dreaming about something that came to pass—my first premonition. The dreams started about a week before John disappeared. They were vague at first—a young boy running and someone chasing him. But on the sixth night that I woke up from that same nightmare, John was gone, abducted from his bedroom. And as I stood in the doorway of my brother's room looking at his empty bed, I was hit by an onslaught of images and emotions from the killer's perspective. I was looking down at John, and when my hand reached out to touch him, it was a man's hand. John was crying, and I felt pleasure in his pain. My hands encircled John's neck and squeezed, harder and harder. John was gasping for air, but I had a tight grip on him. John went limp and my pleasure and adrenaline peaked with his death.

All those years ago, I collapsed on the floor as soon as the vision had finished. When I came to, nobody would believe that John was in danger. I was an eight-year-old child, distressed by her brother's departure. The police wrote him off as a runaway, but just over a year after his disappearance his body was discovered.

The case is still unsolved, even though there were two similar murders before my brother and one after. Every year I look at the case files, hoping time will give me fresh eyes, but so far it's been useless. When my gift resurfaced again four months ago, I thought perhaps it would be the key to solving his death. I started trying to induce a new premonition about him, but all I got was the same vision, over and over again—me strangling John. I gave up a month ago, too traumatized to relive his murder anymore.

I'm still sitting on the bed and staring at the box when my cell phone rings. I jump and look at my bedside clock—I've been mesmerized by the metal container for twenty minutes, yet it seemed like a minute or two. I answer the phone.

"Anderson, it's Sorrell."

"Uh-huh." I pick up the box absentmindedly and put it on the shelf in my closet, below my suitcases.

"I'm following the money." Sorrell pauses. "Black's worth some serious dough."

I resist the urge to say, *What gave it away—the house, the pool, the huge garden?* Instead, I say, "Do you know how much?"

"Not exactly, but we're talking millions, and lots of them."

"So who stands to benefit the most?"

"The husband, of course." He sighs heavily down the phone, like he's bored by having to retell me the key facts. "They were married before she hit the big time, so no prenup. The family's agreed to give us access to the legal documents, and I've got a phone call scheduled with Black's lawyer for tomorrow, first thing."

"Great," I say, eager to get things moving.

"Black's also got a brother, sister and father who'll presumably be very rich," he says.

"What about the husband's alibi? How's that looking?" I ask.

"Pretty tight. It's possible he chartered a plane to L.A. and back again before catching his commercial flight, so we're looking into that. It's also possible he paid someone to kill his wife and gave them instructions on how to pose her."

I mull it over. Sorrell's following the money, but I'm not so sure. "The murder was kinda ritualistic for a money-motivated kill, don't you think?"

"People will do anything for money," he responds half jokingly and half judgmentally. "Maybe it was personal and someone wanted to 'shove her words down her throat,' literally."

Sorrell's idea is interesting, symbolically—she was made to eat her words by being killed just like the women she wrote about. So what if it is personal? Who would be angry with Black? Maybe Scott Werner couldn't handle his wife's success. Maybe that anger built up. Or maybe Black has got some serious sibling rivalry going with a brother or sister who felt overshadowed by her success. Until we find out more about her family, this is all just blind speculation. But you've got to start somewhere. Set up a few possibilities and knock 'em down or build them up, depending on where the evidence takes you. And we've still got the letter and the journalist too.

"Anything from the lab or the forensic pathologist?" I know it's probably too early, but you never know your luck.

"The autopsy's scheduled for tomorrow morning and the evidence is still in the queue at the lab. We've also taken Black's fan mail, including that suspicious letter Holt mentioned, and Black's computer for analysis." Sorrell pauses. "Well, that's it, Anderson. Speak to you tomorrow."

"Okay…" I manage to say before the phone goes dead. Just when I thought we were playing nice.

I lie back on my bed and pick up *Ladykiller*.

Benson poured maple syrup on his bacon, eggs and waffles and dug in. His side order of fries arrived and he used them as a chaser for the rest of his breakfast.

Forensic pathologist Dan Keller shook his head. "I know exactly what your arteries would look like on my table."

"Whatever, Doc," Benson replied, his mouth full of food. "Just finish telling me about the girl. Or maybe I'll take back my offer to buy you breakfast, if you can call that mush breakfast." Benson shoved his fork toward the pathologist's oatmeal.

Keller's face reddened a little, but he managed to regain his cool. Even though he knew it was no good fighting with Benson, he found it hard not to worry about him. Maybe one day he'd see sense. Maybe today?

"I'll miss you when your heart or lungs or both give out, Benson."

Benson pulled a face. "Yeah, you and the rest of Boston."

"Guess I'll be your pallbearer." Keller's face dropped, realizing the mistake too late. "I'm sorry…I wasn't thinking." Keller had stood next to Benson as they carried Benson's wife's coffin. The five years had passed quickly for Keller, but it had been a lifetime for Benson.

Benson shoveled another overloaded mouthful in and ignored the comment. "Back to the girl. You were saying you found something different with this one."

"She was pregnant. About six weeks along."

Benson paused, his fork an inch away from his mouth. "Well, what do ya know. You getting me some DNA or what?"

"It's at the lab. Give it a week."

"A fucking week. Can't you work any faster?"

Keller took a sip of his coffee. "No." He was used to Benson's prodding and he had learned a long time ago it wasn't worth raising *his* blood pressure over. "You'll have the results as soon as possible. Got any suspects to compare the DNA to?"

Benson's eyes narrowed. "You know I don't, Doc. Told you all of ten minutes ago I ain't got shit."

Keller shrugged. "Maybe the daddy-to-be has a record."

Five

The thought of being late for my first day at my new job makes me anxious enough to ensure a lousy night's sleep. At 6:00 a.m. I wake up for about the tenth time, but this time I'm covered in a thick film of sweat. I prop myself up on my elbows and lean my head back. "You gotta be kidding me," I mutter, recalling my dream. Black was tied to a chair, gagged and a figure was pacing in front of her. My dream is consistent with the evidence. In fact, if I didn't regularly have dreams and visions that came true, I'd assume it was just my imagination taking over from the case—the ligature marks, placement of the chair and plot of the book tell us she was tied up, so I dreamed about it. But it's not that simple. Not with me.

Again, a sense of overwhelming anxiety fills me—why didn't I let myself see that vision in the parking lot that day? It was a logical decision—I was driving, plus I was with two strangers.

I think back to the dream. Black was gagged and her

hands seemed to be tied behind her back, yet oddly enough she didn't seem scared. I visualize her face. It was almost devoid of emotion, certainly there was no fear in her eyes. There can only be two reasons for that—she was acting, presumably trying to out-psych the perp, or she genuinely didn't realize her life was in danger. Maybe it was someone she knew? Maybe someone she thought would never harm her, like her husband? He could even have presented it to her as a sex game.

I decide to get up rather than toss and turn for another forty-five minutes. I crawl out of bed and put on a pot of coffee before even thinking about any of my usual morning rituals. I feel as if I've hardly had any sleep, which means this latest dream wasn't my only disturbing nightmare—but for better or worse I can't remember any of the others.

I gulp down some warm water and lemon juice (hopefully that will counteract the imminent coffee abuse) and then do my twenty-minute Pilates DVD workout followed by fifty push-ups. I throw myself into the exercise and try not to think about Black or what I should do about the dream. I fail miserably, and by the time I'm eating breakfast I'm visualizing the crime scene and going over everything in my head. The autopsy report should come through today.

I tear myself away from Black long enough to think about what to wear. I choose my favorite suit for my first official day and go with pants rather than the skirt. Now that I'm in the field again, I'll probably always wear pants—it's much easier to move around crime scenes. You never know when you'll have to climb a fence or do something else that's not skirt-friendly, and flashing my underwear at my work colleagues isn't on my top-ten to-do list. I even give the suit a quick iron, although some of the creases have dropped out since I hung it up on Saturday afternoon.

I allow plenty of time to get to the L.A. Field Office at 11,000 Wilshire Boulevard, including factoring in time for the infamous L.A. traffic and for the possibility of a wrong turn—or several—even though my apartment is close to the office. I'd prefer to walk, but I really need my car for mobility once my day starts.

I drum my fingers on the steering wheel, nervous about my first day. What if my boss is a prick? What if no one likes me? What if I hate the job? What if I don't cut it? I shake my head of the negativity and think of the positive… I'll be in the field, making better use of my psychic abilities, which should translate into more criminals behind bars, faster. And the warmer weather is an added bonus, which shouldn't be underestimated for a southern-hemisphere girl.

But inevitably my mind drifts back to Black. I picture her hair plastered to her face by the panty hose, her dark green eyes devoid of life, her legs shoved up and open and her body mutilated. I wonder what her last few minutes were like. Did she know she would die? She wrote about murder, delving into the minds of the perpetrators and victims—and now she was one. Dammit.

I crawl forward another meter or two in the traffic and decide to call Rivers. See if he's heard the news. Janet picks up after two rings and puts me straight through.

"Let me guess, you want to come back."

I laugh. "No. Sorry." I move forward another couple of meters. "I was ringing to see if you'd heard about Black."

"Hard to miss, Anderson. Been on the news all weekend."

"Of course." I flash back to the media around her house. "I've been kinda busy. Haven't switched on the TV yet."

"Unpacking, huh? Better you than me."

"Yeah, the unpacking…and something else." I pause. "Debbie Holt rang me on Saturday. Wanted me to investigate the murder."

"What did you say to her?" Rivers's voice is guarded, hesitant.

"That it wasn't my jurisdiction unless the Bureau got a formal invite."

"Good. Glad to hear you can say no sometimes, Anderson."

"Ha, ha. I did end up going down to the crime scene though." I don't give him details, not yet. I love pushing his buttons.

"Anderson!"

"Don't worry, Beverly Hills PD called me."

"Maybe, but did you go through the right channels? Did *they* go through the right channels?"

"Um…I'm not sure." Now my stomach tightens with worry.

"It's not up to you or some homicide cop to decide whether you work a case, it's up to your boss. Your detective should have contacted the FBI directly, and they would have assigned you, if that was appropriate."

I gulp, my fear of my first day suddenly tripling…no, more than tripling, way more.

"Shit," I murmur.

Rivers sighs. "How'd you swing the call anyway?"

"I told Holt that if she really wanted me involved, she should suggest it to the lead detective."

Rivers lets out a little snort. "So, what did you make of the crime scene?"

"It's a classic sexual homicide…except that she was killed just like the victims in her book."

"Replicating a fictional crime scene is a very unusual MO." Rivers's voice is detached, showing his scientific interest. "A twisted fan, maybe. She have any stalkers?"

"Apparently she did get a strange letter a couple of weeks ago. And there's also a journalist who tried to sue her last year in the picture."

"I bet Black's worth a pretty penny. And a prime target for lawsuits."

"Uh-huh," I say.

Silence.

"You going to profile the case?"

"It's as good a first profile as any, I guess." I feign disinterest. No need for Rivers to know this case has got me sucked in already.

"How's your first day treating you?"

"It's only seven-thirty here. I'm still in traffic."

Rivers laughs. "You could have avoided all that if you'd stayed here."

"Sorry, what was that? I was taking my sweater off because it's so warm."

He laughs again. "You're not making me jealous. I'm not a lover of warm weather like you, Anderson. Besides, it's August—it's even warm in Virginia."

"Can't blame a girl for trying." I'm happily distracted by our banter—I don't want to think about being in trouble on my first day.

"I'll step outside and take a breath of fresh air for you, shall I?"

Now I laugh. The Academy is forty-five kilometers away from D.C., and in a rural setting. No smog there. "You got me, sir."

When I arrive at the L.A. Field Office, I'm a little frazzled from my peak-hour experiences, even though it was such a short trip. When I worked at the Academy, I lived halfway between Quantico and Washington, D.C., and I was nearly always traveling against the traffic. It's going to take some time to get used to the crawling pace of peak-hour again. I'm also tense from stressing about being in trouble with my new boss.

My new pass is waiting for me at the security desk, complete with an updated photo. This one isn't much better than the last, but at least I've got a slight smile on my face rather than a wince. It's a head-and-shoulders shot, but it makes my strawberry-blond hair look almost brown, and my relatively slender frame look slightly fuller—at least my face seems rounder. My hair is cut in layers that fall to my shoulders, and streaks of copper and a lighter blond accentuate the textured hairstyle. Today I wear it down, just like in the photo, but I've got an elastic band around my wrist so I can sweep it into a ponytail quickly and easily. Who knows what my first day will hold?

I wait at the tenth-floor reception for Miles Brady, Assistant Director in Charge, FBI Los Angeles. Within a couple of minutes he emerges through a security door to the right of the reception desk, buttoning his jacket. Brady is in his midforties, with blond hair and tanned skin—it is L.A. He's about six foot and I'm betting quite muscly under the suit. His face is angular and clean shaven, and his expression is tense.

"Special Agent Anderson." He puts his hand out and we shake, but he doesn't seem happy to see me.

I manage a small smile. "Nice to meet you, sir."

"You found us okay?" Again his tone is abrupt, like he's forcing himself to be polite.

"Yes, sir."

"You'll get used to the traffic," he says, almost breaking into a half smile…almost.

We start walking. "So I hear you've already officially been at work?" He raises his voice slightly, making it a question.

I clear my throat uneasily, not sure if I'm in trouble or not. "Yes, sir. I hope you don't mind. I met Black and her assistant at the Academy only a couple of days before she was killed. Holt called me and managed to convince Detective Sorrell to contact me directly."

He nods. "I know the story, Anderson. Sorrell filled me in about half an hour ago. Covering his ass like you. He's filling in the paperwork now."

"I'm sorry, sir. I just didn't think to call the office first." Brady wouldn't have been in, but I guess I should have at least tried to contact him or someone at the field office.

He grunts and leads me through the security door. We weave our way through the open-plan floor until we reach his corner office. As we move through the ranks, most people look up briefly—checking out the new girl—but he doesn't stop to introduce me to anyone. He seems really pissed off at me. Way to go, Sophie.

Brady's office is spotless. His in-tray is an orderly stack of files, as is his out-tray. One notepad, with scrawl, and a pen are the only items on his desk that aren't in holders or files or tucked away somewhere else. My desk will look like his for the first hour, if I'm lucky. Two bookshelves are lined with criminal-law and law-enforcement books and journals, including many titles that are on my own bookshelf, and multiple copies of the FBI's monthly bulletin. Brady moves behind his large wooden desk and motions to one of the chairs in front of the desk. I sit and manage a tentative smile. God I hate first days.

"So…" Brady plucks a file from his in-tray and hands it to me. "My assistant, Melissa, prepared this file for you. It's got our org chart, our current case list, that sort of thing."

"Thank you, that's great."

He nods. "Obviously you'll be working on the Black case first." He crosses his arms. "What's done is done." His tone of voice and body language don't back up his words.

"Yes, sir. If that's okay with you." I know I'm kissing butt, but I sure as hell don't want a reputation as someone who doesn't follow procedures.

He looks up but doesn't smile or confirm that it's okay. "Melissa will show you around the office and introduce you to everyone."

He pauses and I fill the silence. "Thank you, sir. I'm really looking forward to being in the field again. And sorry about Black."

He picks up the pen and rubs it between his fingers, but doesn't accept my apology. "Obviously it will take a little while before the cops start asking specifically for their requests, but this field office covers the largest population in the States and, let's face it, L.A. doesn't exactly have the lowest crime rate in this country."

I nod. "Yes, sir. Are there any other cases you'd like me to work on straightaway?" The L.A. Field Office has been without a profiler for three weeks, but I couldn't get away from the Academy any sooner.

"There are a couple. But make Black your priority for now. It's a high-profile murder. But I'd still like you to meet with our four main divisions—Counterterrorism, Criminal, Counterintelligence and Cyber Crime. They'll talk about their requirements going forward. We'll ease you into it. I don't want you quitting on your first day." Although obviously a joke, Brady delivers the line with no hint of sarcasm or frivolity. That could be his manner, or maybe it's because he's annoyed with me.

I try to lighten the mood. "Don't worry, sir, I like the weather too much to leave."

He flashes a white, toothy smile for the first time. "I'll bet." He punches a key on his phone. "Melissa, can you come in here, please?" He looks back up at me. "Melissa will help settle you in."

In what seems like only a couple of seconds, a flaming redhead in her midtwenties is standing beside me shaking my hand. With her heels on she's taller than me, but I'd say shoeless we'd be about the same height—five-eight—but her frame is skinnier than mine. Her long, curly hair is held off her face with two combs, and her thick locks hang down her back to the bottom of her shoulder blades. An intense and vibrant energy is already emanating from her, even though so far all she's done is said "Hi," and assured Brady she'll look after me. Her voice is expressive and loud, and she's obviously the sort of person who's always on the go.

Once out of Brady's office, Melissa maneuvers me into the nearest meeting room and, talking a million miles a minute, takes me through the file. She's both professional and friendly, and as she goes over the org chart she includes personal information about each person, including helpful tips like, "Don't talk to her until she's had at least two cups of coffee." Even this information is delivered to me in a cheerful manner, as a friendly tip rather than a bitchy warning. I like Melissa already.

"Everyone's real friendly in the office, which makes it a great place to work. You'll be working across all four departments, but the last profiler mostly worked with the Criminal and Cyber Crime divisions."

Good—I'm more comfortable with those areas. Even though profiling is already a specialized area of law enforcement, within profiling most of us have areas of expertise too. Counterterrorism is a field I haven't done any work in and I'll certainly be handballing the terrorist profiles to my colleagues at the Academy. My specialty is murder, particularly serial killers. I like working on homicides, because not only can we bring the perp to justice, we can also save potential victims by stopping the perp from killing again. Serial child abductors are also high on my hit list…very high, given my personal experience.

"So, are you ready to meet everyone?" she asks.

I smile. "Ready as I'll ever be."

She leads the way around the floor, introducing me to the staff and pointing each person out in the org chart. It's overwhelming to meet so many people in such a short space of time, but I'm sure no one expects me to remember their names…not yet.

"Now it's time to get you settled at your desk!" Melissa leads me to a small nook in the east corner of the building. "This is the old profiler's desk. You've got a view and all." She points to a window that's only a few steps away from the desk. Excellent…I like staring out a window when I'm profiling. It helps me vague out and move into *their* world.

"I've set you up with everything you should need. Trays, pens, pencils, highlighters, folders—" she points to each item as she reels off the list "—a file stacker for current cases, and I've cleared out this filing cabinet here." She gently kicks the bottom drawer of a three-drawer return. "Everything else I put in this filing cabinet." She points to a large four-drawer filing cabinet that stands against a partition.

"Wow, thanks, Melissa. This is…this is fantastic."

She smiles. "You're welcome, Sophie." She taps the computer screen, moving on quickly. "Now, your username and password shouldn't have changed—you've just been set up as an L.A. Field Office user. But we better make sure. Go for it."

I turn on the computer, and once the log-in screen appears I type in my username and password. The transition is seamless from the FBI Academy's system to the L.A. Field Office, and I now have access to the L.A. drives. "I'm impressed," I say.

"Me too. IT gets it right sometimes." She gives me a wink. "I'll just check your printers." Melissa pulls up a seat next to me and reviews the default printer. "Yup. So, you're set up with everything you should need—Word, Outlook, Windows Explorer, Internet Explorer and you've got the VICAP link on your desktop."

I nod. The Violent Criminal Apprehension Program was created in the early eighties to investigate serial offenses on a nationwide basis, and has two main offerings: the VICAP Web-based software and twenty VICAP consultants based in Quantico. The software system is an online database of violent crimes. Now I'm in the field I'll be using it mostly for searches—a crime comes up with certain patterns in L.A., I search VICAP and see if there have been similar cases logged here or in other states. It's a great system. The only problem is that not all cops use it, so similar murders might not be in the database. It's also my responsibility to make sure any violent cases that come across my desk are logged with VICAP.

"Sophie?" Melissa brings me back from my thoughts.

"Sorry."

Melissa smiles, unfazed, and continues. "I've set you up a folder on our drive, the G drive. You're under *Profiling,* then *Anderson.*"

"Great. Thanks again. You've really looked after me, Melissa."

She smiles and blushes slightly. "You can go through the team-meeting minutes to check out our current cases for each of the four divisions. See where they're at. Your business cards are due from the printer this morning. I'll bring them around as soon as they come in." Melissa stands up. "I think that's it. Anything I've forgotten?"

"Hardly."

"Well, Brady's got a quick lunch meeting organized for you with a few of the key people you'll be dealing with internally, plus me. Nothing fancy—we're just going to the café across the street. See you at twelve-thirty?"

"Great." Maybe this won't be such a bad first day after all. "Oh, there is one other thing," I say.

"Yes?"

"Do you know much about a Detective Sorrell in Beverly Hills Homicide?"

"Sorrell." She sighs. "He's dreamy. You know him?"

Dreamy? I hadn't noticed. "He's working Loretta Black's murder and I was just curious if he uses our services much."

"He called the old profiler in on a few cases."

"Okay, thanks." Good to know Sorrell likes to play with the Bureau, but it makes it even more of a bummer that I made a bad first impression. I'm not doing well so far—first Sorrell, now Brady.

After Melissa's gone I put my handbag under my desk and fish out my phone. I have two missed calls. I take the phone off Silent and check my messages. One from my parents wishing me good luck for my first day, and one from Holt asking me to call her back ASAP.

I study the phone on my desk, wondering what Holt wants. I pick it up and punch in the number she left in the message.

"Hello, Debbie Holt."

"Hi, Debbie, it's Sophie Anderson."

"Sophie, thank you so much for calling me back."

"No worries." I don't think I'll ever get out of the habit of using this Australian expression—it's too ingrained. "How are you holding up?"

"Okay." She pauses.

I let the silence lengthen, allowing her to give me a truthful answer. She obliges.

"I don't know. I'm still in the denial phase."

"Understandable."

"Yeah." Her voice is vague, dreamlike. Another pause before she strings a more complex sentence together. "Have you found anything new?"

"I'm afraid it's early days, Debbie. Although the autopsy report will probably come through today, and that may give us something. And then forensics will drip through in the next few days, maybe even a week."

"I'm glad you're working on this, Sophie. I…I don't like Detective Sorrell. He was…" She searches for the right word, either for herself or the word she thinks is most appropriate to use with me. "Well, to be honest he was rude."

The comment makes me think of Benson, Black's fictional detective. But I don't think Sorrell's that bad, or that jaded. Hopefully he's not a misogynist like Benson either.

"Think about it from his point of view. He's only trying to find Loretta's killer."

"Is he good?"

The truthful answer is, I don't know. How can I when I only met the man two days ago? But you've got to be good to get a homicide gig in any department, and a good bedside manner with the victim's friends and family isn't necessary for being a good cop. Sometimes it can even be detrimental.

I avoid answering Holt's question. "Don't worry, Debbie. We'll work this case hard."

Several seconds pass before she speaks again. "It's just…Detective Sorrell spoke to Scott and me like we were Loretta's enemies."

"You've been involved in Loretta's research, yes?"

"Yup."

"So you know how it goes. Solving a case is as much about elimination of suspects as it is about finding suspects."

"You're right…I know." Another pause. "It's just different when it happens to you. When it's your life. You know what I mean?"

Unfortunately, I know exactly what Holt means. I take my job seriously; I take it personally, but I've also been involved with abduction and murder firsthand…up close and personal. I bite my lip. "I know what you mean, Debbie."

She's silent.

"Were you and Loretta close?" I ask, unable to see how Holt could have liked Black, given how her employer treated her at the Academy.

"Yeah, I guess we were." She pauses. "I know Loretta could come off as rude, but that was just her manner. She didn't mean to be nasty and she could even be kind at times."

I'm not sure if Black's apparent ignorance of her rudeness makes it better or worse.

"Will you keep me in the loop?" Holt asks. "Detective Sorrell's not telling us anything."

"It's only been forty-eight hours, Debbie."

"Exactly. And I know how crucial those first forty-eight hours are."

Holt's right—if they're going to be solved, most homicide cases are solved quickly.

"You know that's got more to do with the type of homicide than anything else," I say, making assumptions about Holt's knowledge based on the research she would have done for Black over the past four years.

"I know." She sighs. "A guy gets shot and soon the cops learn that the victim had a new girlfriend, and that her ex-boyfriend was the jealous type."

I continue with Holt's hypothetical situation. "And witnesses confirm a male was seen leaving the crime scene around the time of the shooting. *Voilà,* case solved." I pause. "Most murders aren't well planned. They're committed by disorganized offenders acting in the heat of the moment. They leave clues, and usually plenty of them. It's only about one out of seventy or eighty homicides that are trickier, more complex. And for the moment, this case, with its elements of ritual and Loretta's standing as a famous crime author, is one of those more difficult cases."

"I know, I know. And I do feel better knowing you're working the case."

"Thanks," I reply politely. "I presume you realize that Loretta's bathroom tiles are the same as the ones in her fictitious motel room?"

"You think it's significant?"

"Could be. Do you know if there was any particular reason that Black chose white tiles for the novel?"

"Lots of writers use their surroundings or places they know when they're writing."

"Really?"

"Oh, yeah. Loretta told me once that Benson's apartment is furnished just like one of her first boyfriends' places." She pauses. "Loretta probably would have also used white tiles because the victim had red hair. It was symbolic of blood on white...contrast."

"It certainly was striking on the cover," I comment.

"Exactly." She takes a breath. "Anything on that strange letter?" Her voice trembles. "I've been thinking about the letter and the writing in the bathroom."

"Go on."

"Well, I thought maybe it meant her turn to die. Loretta's turn to die."

I leave this hypothesis alone for the moment— I want to think about it some more before I respond to Holt, even though it's one of the two options I came up with too, and the most obvious interpretation.

"It's still too early for anything on the letter I'm afraid, Debbie."

"What about the journalist, Randy Sade?"

"We're looking into him." To be honest, I don't know exactly what Sorrell's doing on either count. But there's a lot of evidence and witnesses to process in this type of case. I move the conversation away from specifics about our status and back to the letters. "Did Black get many hostile or negative letters?"

"Hardly any. Her fans loved her work, loved her characters."

"Well, one fan didn't."

Six

I'm barely off the phone with Holt when another incoming call buzzes. The display shows a private number.

"FBI…L.A." I only just remember to say L.A. rather than Behavioral Analysis Unit. "Agent Anderson speaking."

"Good. Thought you might be on Krump's old number. It's Sorrell."

"Good morning, Detective."

"Ah, yes…morning." He seems thrown by having to wind back to the pleasantries. "What you doing?" he asks.

"Um…settling in."

"Do you want to come and speak to Randy Sade with me?"

Maybe Sorrell's ears were burning when I was on the phone with Holt. "Sure," I reply, downplaying the fact that I'm thrilled to get the invite.

"I'll pick you up out front in ten."

The line goes dead. I look at the receiver and shake my head.

Ten minutes later I'm standing out the front of our building. I've been waiting for less than two minutes when a horn honks, and I make out Sorrell behind the wheel of a dark blue Ford Lancer. He double parks and I climb into the passenger side.

"Hi," I say, buckling my seat belt. I'm pretty sure I make a better visual impression than Saturday. At least today I've got my best suit on, no creases, and I'm not grinning weirdly at a murder scene. Always a plus.

"Hey." Sorrell pulls into the traffic. "Sade lives in Venice."

I actually considered Venice when I was looking for a place to live myself. It's close to the beach and close to work, but in the end I opted for Westwood, which is also nice and close to the field office.

Sorrell takes La Cienega south.

"Where's the autopsy at?" I ask.

"The ME's finished, but I haven't got the report yet. Should be through in the next couple of hours. Cause of death was strangulation, and the ligature marks on the neck are consistent with panty hose. Time of death has been fixed at the early hours of the morning, we're thinking between midnight and 4:00 a.m. Grove also found a beige fiber in Black's hair."

"A fiber. Great. They know what it is yet?"

"No, it's with the lab." Sorrell fishes through his briefcase on the seat between us, alternating his gaze between the road and the briefcase. "Autopsy also indicated no sexual assault."

"Really?" This strikes me as odd, not only because it's a departure from the book, but also because it's inconsistent with the sexual nature of the crime scene, specifically Black's posed body and the sexual mutilation.

"I know," Sorrell says. "Not in line with the crime scene. Unless it was the husband."

"Thought you said his alibi was tight."

"It is. We checked the airports for charter flights and he's clear on that one. But the possibility of a contract killer is growing on me. Werner can't stomach the thought of someone violating his wife, so he orders the posing but not the sexual assault."

"That's definitely plausible." In most people's minds sexual violence is very different from "straight" violence and while Werner may have been prepared for someone to kill his wife, rape would probably be a different kettle of fish altogether. "But what about the mutilation? Could he order that to be inflicted on his wife?"

Sorrell shrugs. "It was postmortem."

"Maybe the killer can't perform." Often when there's no evidence of sexual intercourse at an obviously sexual crime, it reflects the perp's inability to get, or maintain, an erection.

"Yup. That's the other possibility." Sorrell finds the folder he's been looking for in his briefcase and hands it to me. "This is everything we've got on Black so far."

"Excellent. Thanks." I flick through the file's contents, including the overwhelming number of photos.

"The body was moved postmortem," Sorrell says, confirming another element the forensic pathologist mentioned on scene.

"She die on that chair?" I ask, even though I know from my vision that the answer is yes.

"Looks like it, but we still don't have forensic confirmation. But she did die sitting, not lying down." Again he confirms one of the forensic pathologist's on-scene conclusions.

"Just like the book." I shake my head.

"Yeah. In the book the perp meets the woman at a motel, overpowers her and then ties her to a chair. Next comes verbal abuse, and lots of it, before he strangles her, rapes her postmortem, moves her and finishes with the posing elements and the mutilation."

"Nice." I try not to linger on the many photos of Black, dead. Instead, I move to the security system. "How about the security system?"

"Computer forensics are looking at that now to see if it's been tampered with. We should hear back this morning."

"I've been thinking about the writing. *Your turn* could be an obsessed fan or Sade. Assuming the killer was referring to Black."

Sorrell nods. "Her turn to die like her fictional victims or her turn to pay for what she did to Sade."

"Exactly." I stare out the window. "The *Your* could also be referring to us. Our turn."

"But if he does mean our turn, we're doing what he'd expect…investigating the case and looking for him."

Sorrell's come to the same conclusion as me—if the killer's message was for us, it's not going to change the way we work the case.

Sorrell takes a right at Venice Boulevard. "Is this hard for you? Given that you met her?"

I'm surprised by Sorrell's comment, surprised by his perceptiveness. Or maybe I'm letting my guard down.

"A little," I admit. "But I only met her once."

Sorrell nods, but doesn't say anything else, so I move the subject back to the case. "When do you expect forensics?"

He shrugs. "They should confirm the rope today, but we're looking at a couple days, maybe more for all of the forensics. Although the publicity might push it through faster."

"The crowd at her house on Saturday was unbelievable."

"Black's sold millions of books and she's got lots of fans."

I start chewing on my bottom lip. "Have you started on them yet? The fans?"

He sighs. "I spoke to Holt about it. Black averaged fifty letters a month and a couple hundred e-mails."

I wince. "Oh, that sounds like fun."

"I'll say," Sorrell replies, with a roll of his eyes. "Then there's that strange letter, from 'A fan.'" He marks air quotes as he says it.

"An obsessed fan is a definite contender. Whether it's the fan who wrote that letter or not."

Sorrell grimaces. "That's a big lead to chase down… and God knows how much fan mail will pour in over the next week or two." He sighs. "Still, it's doable…if we've got the manpower."

The success of an investigation can hinge on many things, and unfortunately resources is one of them.

About two kilometers after we cross the I-405, Sorrell takes a left off Venice Boulevard and then another series of turns until we pull up on a residential street.

"Which one is it?" I ask.

Sorrell points across the road. "One hundred and twelve."

The place looks like a two-story house that was built in the sixties and then subdivided into four apartments.

"He's number two," Sorrell adds.

As we cross the street, a faint, cool breeze hits me, diluting the heat of the summer sun.

"Do you think he'll be home?" I look at my watch—11:00 a.m.

"I called the *Los Angeles Times* and he's off today, so hopefully he's in."

"How'd you go with the will?" I ask as we climb the steep set of brick-and-concrete stairs.

"The house and Black's other possessions, which include two cars, a yacht and a home in the south of France, go to Werner. He also gets forty-five percent of copyright income, unless he remarries. Fifty per cent of copyright is split equally between the father, brother, sister, niece and nephew, and Holt gets five percent."

"Holt? Really?"

"You spent quite a few hours with them at the Academy. I take it they didn't seem especially close to you?"

"In my opinion, Black didn't treat her very well. Although Holt did say they were friends."

"Well, I guess the proof's in the pudding…or in this case, the will."

Sorrell's right. They must have been close for Holt to get a mention in the will.

"What would copyright be worth?"

Sorrell shrugs and rings the doorbell. "Lawyer said it's hard to say, but there'll probably be an initial surge in sales, particularly of *Ladykiller,* and then things will level off. But if she sells three million copies of *Ladykiller* in hardback, that's over six million dollars, minus her million-dollar advance."

"Whoa."

"Yup." Sorrell rings the doorbell again, this time holding it down so it rings several times.

Finally the door opens, revealing Randy Sade in nothing

but his boxers. Sade's in his late thirties or early forties, although it's hard to pick which because his skinny frame makes me think thirties but the wrinkled skin suggests forties. He's around six foot with messy blond hair and blue eyes, which are barely half-open.

"What is it?" His voice is hoarse and gruff.

Sorrell takes out his badge. "Detective Sorrell, and this is Special Agent Anderson from the FBI. We're investigating Loretta Black's murder."

He shakes his head. "She just won't leave me alone."

Sorrell and I share a glance. Not exactly the response a badge usually gets.

"Would you like to elaborate on that statement?" Sorrell asks.

Sade sighs heavily. "Whatever. Guess you ought to come in." He wanders back into his apartment and we follow, closing the door after us.

He flops onto the couch and props his feet on a small coffee table. Sorrell and I remain standing, unable to find a piece of couch that isn't already occupied by a dirty plate or magazine.

"Can you believe it—after everything that I went through with Black, my editor made me stay up around the clock all weekend covering the murder? Said I had insight into the story because of my history with her." He leans his head all the way back on his sofa and rubs his eyes.

I wonder if Sade's always like this or if it's sleep deprivation making him so blasé with law enforcement. Judging from the state of his apartment, this could be his usual demeanor.

"Man, I need a coffee. You guys?" He stands up, but it seems to take a lot of effort.

I shake my head. "I'm good," I say, thinking about where he'll find a clean coffee cup…and what his definition of clean will be.

"I'll have one."

I'm not sure if Sorrell doesn't care about hygiene or if he's simply playing polite with Sade.

The apartment is small, so the kitchen is only a few steps away from the living room. "So, what do you want to know?" Sade calls as he rinses a coffeemaker and two cups in the sink. I bet the water's not even hot.

"When did you find out Loretta Black was dead?" I ask.

"Saturday morning, when my editor called to tell me."

I lean on the doorway. "What time was that?"

He fishes out a paper filter and fills it with coffee. "About ten-thirty or eleven, I think."

The press did find out quickly.

Sorrell takes over. "You asleep when you got the call?"

"Sure. I tend to work late, finalizing stories for the next day's edition, so I'm rarely up before eleven." He puts his hands on his bony hips and stares at the coffeemaker. I know from experience giving it dagger eyes is not going to make the coffee flow any quicker.

"Damn, I wish this thing was faster." He looks up and manages a smile before he comes back into the living room and sinks into the couch again.

"So, tell us about this lawsuit and Loretta Black." Sorrell moves a couple of magazines and a dirty dish onto the coffee table and sits down in the cleared section of the sofa.

He shrugs. "She stole my idea. End of story." Sade's either no longer angry about it, or his response is practiced. It's hard to tell which.

"Go on."

He sighs heavily, as though he's told this tale a hundred times. "About four years ago I interviewed Black for a profile piece in the newspaper. The first Benson book was going to be on the big screen, so that was the focus. I'd heard she could be a bit of a bitch, so I decided to interview her over lunch. Thought maybe a few glasses of wine would loosen her up a bit."

"And did they?" I ask.

He shrugs. "Don't think so. She was still pretty aloof during the interview, although because I was doing a piece about her she was trying to be nice…sort of." He shakes his head. "The wine loosened me up though, and I told her about an idea I had for a serial killer who hunted for his prey while driving a taxi."

"Cruising," I say, remembering one of Black's books with a taxi on the front cover.

He snaps his fingers at me. "Exactly." But instead of continuing, Sade stands up and goes to pour the coffees. He's silent that whole time, and Sorrell and I both ride it out.

After Sade's taken a few sips of his coffee he continues. "I even had the conversation on tape. I always record my interviews."

"So how'd it get thrown out of court?" I ask.

Sade's fists clench, showing the first signs of anger. "She had a better lawyer than me. The judge ruled that the taxi environment was too small a part of *Cruising* for it to be crucial to the plot and characters, and that Black hadn't infringed any copyright laws." He shakes his head. "But the taxi angle was the whole premise." He grits his teeth. "She even laughed at me in court." The gritted teeth turn into a smile. "But she isn't laughing now, is she?"

"No, she's not, Mr. Sade," I say. "She's dead."

Sorrell comes in straightaway. "Where were you Friday night?"

Sade doesn't seem surprised or perturbed by our question. I guess he expected it, given the history between him and Black. "I was at the office until eight and then I came home, smoked a joint and watched TV." He smiles, enjoying flaunting the illegal joint-smoking. He takes several gulps of his coffee. "Believe you me, I didn't know Black was going to get herself murdered and that I'd need an alibi."

I watch for Sorrell's reaction, but he keeps his face blank and focused on Sade. "So, no one saw you that night? No one can verify that you were here?"

Sade shrugs. "I ordered a pizza, which arrived about ten. Maybe the delivery guy remembers me or maybe my order's on a computer somewhere." Again, he's very casual for someone being questioned by police and FBI.

We take down the details of Sade's local pizza place before Sorrell stands up, draining his coffee. "Thanks, Mr. Sade. We'll be in touch if we need anything else."

As we're at the door and leaving, Sorrell turns back. "One other thing, Mr. Sade."

"What?" Sade's acting as if we're trying his patience.

"We've had reports that you threatened Black. That true?"

Sade hesitates, looking a little concerned for the first time. "Yeah, it's true." He clears his throat. "After the judge ruled in her favor I confronted her outside the court. I called her a few names and then…" He clears his throat again. "Told her I'd kill her. But it was just an expression, man. It wasn't a real threat."

Sorrell gives him a nod. "Thanks for your time."

Once we're in the car, Sorrell says, "So what do you think?"

"Revenge as a motive fits with the message on the bathroom mirror and with the mutilations although perhaps not the sexual nature of the disfigurement." I pause. "Maybe Randy figured she screwed him and it was time to turn the tables, and the book provided his MO."

Sorrell sighs. "You think he's got it in him?"

It's a good question—a question homicide cops ask themselves all the time. In this case, it's hard to know after only a ten-minute interview. I shrug. "Everyone has their breaking point, and he'd probably see it as poetic justice…he uses her words against her by replicating her fictional murder. Especially given his claim of plagiarism."

Sorrell pauses. "Revenge fits with some elements of the crime scene." He shakes his head. "But then we've also got the money…."

"Sade doesn't gain from the will." I finish Sorrell's point. "You wanna go talk to Scott Werner again?" I ask. "He's the number-one beneficiary."

"I'd definitely like another crack at Werner. But let's wait until we've got more info. Maybe forensics or the autopsy will give us something we can use when we talk to him again. I've been dodging his calls all morning, hoping to have something before I talk to him again."

I nod. It's not surprising that Werner's chasing Sorrell— it's normal to get lots of calls from the family.

"You think Sade would pose her like that?" Sorrell asks.

Again, it's hard to know one way or another for sure with only a brief insight into Sade's personality. "Given there wasn't rape, the sexual pose might be more about replicating the book than the killer's need to make the scene sexual. It's almost staged."

Staging refers to a perp's attempts to disguise the scene, to make it look different to what it really is. For example, a perp might stage a robbery after an assault, to make it look like the victim was simply in the wrong place at the wrong time. The hope is that the police will look for a burglar and not a rapist.

On the way back to the field office, we make a quick detour to visit Sade's pizzeria. Sure enough, a computer ordering system confirms that Sade ordered a large pepperoni pizza at 9:45 p.m. on Friday night and that it was delivered around 10:10 p.m.

Out on the street, Sorrell leans on the car. "That still gives Sade plenty of time to eat his pizza and get his ass to Beverly Hills. Time of death is between midnight and 4:00 a.m."

By 11:45 a.m. I'm back in the office in one of our meeting rooms, studying the Black photos. Moving my gaze from one to another, I also sip the cup of hot coffee I've been craving since I smelled the brew at Sade's place.

I slow my breathing and close my eyes, letting the photos of Black and her house swirl around in my conscious mind. Snippets flash in front of my eyes, fast, as I recall some of the images. I take a deep breath and push the images away, forcing my mind from Loretta Black to blank. This technique is something that Darren helped me with during our Arizona case. It was how his aunt tuned in to a person before she opened herself to any sort of psychic episode, and it seems to work for me. I repeat the process—thinking about Black and then clearing my mind—until I get something.

The room is dark, but the faint glow of a half-moon and lights from the neighboring building give outlines to the room and people. A woman lies on the carpet, still. Her eyes are open, the moonlight reflecting off them—she's dead. A shadowy silhouette leans over her body and takes hold of her two hands. The killer drags her across the room, out of the moonlight and shimmer from the other buildings, and into more darkness.

A flash of light shows black on white.

It was Loretta Black all right. The last bright light showed such contrast that the shapes were initially hard to make out, but visualizing the image tells me exactly what it was—the white was the tiles and the black was Loretta's jet-black hair. The contrast reminds me of *Ladykiller*'s cover, but instead of red on white, it's black on white. But the vision didn't really tell me much, beyond the fact that she was moved postmortem, which we knew from the forensic pathologist anyway. Although I can sometimes control *when* I get the visions, I can't control what I see—and how helpful or otherwise the images are.

A knock at the door breaks my concentration. "Come in."

The door opens a crack and Melissa's head pops around the corner. "Oh, here you are."

I give her a small smile, unsure why she's looking for me.

She laughs. "You're one of those."

"What?" I say, confused.

"Absorbed in your own world. It's twelve-thirty. Lunchtime."

"Twelve-thirty?" I glance at my watch, needing verification. It doesn't seem like forty-five minutes has gone by since Sorrell dropped me off.

"We'll wait for you at the elevators," Melissa says before disappearing.

I leave the project room as it is, with the crime-scene photos strategically placed on the table, and quickly gather my stuff for my lunch meeting. Time to find out more about the field office. On the way to the elevator, my cell phone vibrates, still in silent mode from when I'd been trying to induce the vision.

"Anderson," I say into the mouthpiece.

"Anderson, it's Sorrell. I just heard from computer forensics."

"Yes?"

"The security system hasn't been tampered with, so the last activity at the gate was at six last night. The killer must have gotten into the property some other way."

"Which means he knew about the camera at the main entrance."

"Yup. Knew personally or was told about it." Sorrell's hinting at Werner again, and the possibility that he hired someone to kill his wife.

Just as Melissa told me, the café is low-key, and has a menu consisting of sandwiches made to order, a small selection of hot meals and some premade salads. I grab a Diet Pepsi from the fridge and order a smoked-salmon bagel. The others' orders range from a healthy chicken salad to a carb-loaded lasagna and chips.

Around the table sit Brady; George Rosen, the head of the Criminal Division; Ed Garcia, the head of the Cyber Crime Division; Sandy Peters, the head of Counterintelligence; Brad Jones, the head of Counterterrorism; and Melissa. While Melissa, Peters and I wait for sandwiches, the others dig in to their ready-made meals.

"So, how's your first day treating you?" asks Rosen, popping the lid on his iced tea.

"Good. Busy."

"I hear you're working the Black case." Jones loads his fork with a mouthful of lasagna. "Tough first case."

"Hopefully it won't end up being too bad," I say.

They all laugh, a little too heartily for my liking.

"What's the joke?"

Melissa gives the others a scowl. "Don't listen to them. It's only because it's a high-profile case, and the media will be all over our asses…well, more specifically, your ass."

I smile, relieved there's nothing more to it than that. "I'm good at keeping a low profile. Wait and see." Two resourceful journalists have already left messages on my voice mail. Who knows how they found out I was working the case. Maybe they took my picture at Black's house on Saturday and hounded their contacts until they got an ID on me. Or perhaps they've got a buddy who works for the Bureau or the Beverly Hills Police Department. "So, do you guys have any cases you'd like me to work? After Black?" I make eye contact with the four heads, waiting for a response.

"There are always cases," replies Peters, the only female head. "It's just a matter of where your attention is best focused." She glances at Brady, the one who calls the shots. Although I'm not as high up on the food chain as the division heads, just as they do I report directly to Brady. He'll be managing my cases, largely based on what the four divisions have on their books and who needs profiling expertise the most.

"I'll be honest, Sandy. I haven't done any work in counterterrorism before."

She smiles. "I'm sure you'll pick it up fast."

"I've got contacts at the Academy who specialize in that area, so I'll call on their expertise if need be."

"Anderson's specialty is homicide, particularly serial homicide," Brady explains. "So that'll be you, Rosen."

George Rosen nods. "You're on my radar." He gives me a kind smile. "But I'll let you settle in first. Let you get past the Black phenomenon."

"Gee, thanks."

"It *is* your first day." There is just a hint of sarcasm in Rosen's voice.

Peters's chicken sandwich and two smoked-salmon bagels arrive at the table, one for me and one for Melissa.

"A lot of our work is organized crime and drugs. I do have a rather unusual homicide that's come in. But it can wait a bit."

Terrorism, organized crime and drugs—L.A.'s certainly a whole different ball game to the Behavioral Analysis Unit. I hope I've made the right decision, hope that being in the field is as necessary as I think it is. My strikeout at Black's yesterday is making me question the theory that being in the field will help with the frequency and accuracy of my visions, help me to solve cases and save lives. It sure as hell hasn't helped Black yet.

Seven

Back at my desk, I check my messages—two. The first one's from Scott Werner, asking if we've got any new information, and the second is from Sorrell, asking me to call him. I guess Werner decided to try me when he couldn't get ahold of Sorrell. But like Sorrell, I decide to avoid Werner for the moment.

I punch in Sorrell's direct line and he picks up after one ring.

"Beverly Hills Homicide, Sorrell." His voice is gruff and sounds a little deeper than a couple of hours ago.

"Hi, Sorrell. It's Anderson. Got your message."

"Good. First off I've got some forensics in. The particles found on Black's chair are definitely tiny strands from a rope. They've matched it, but it's a common brand, so we'll have to wait until we have a suspect."

I don't bother voicing my understanding. Hopefully we'll find the same brand of rope at a suspect's house, and it will form part of our evidence.

Sorrell continues, "We've also got a match on the lipstick. It's Estée Lauder, Summer Blossom."

It's amazing what they can do in the lab these days. In this case, the sample of lipstick would have been run through a gas chromatography procedure to identify all the different chemical compounds and their levels. This would then have been compared to the lab's database. But again, until we've got a suspect and a search warrant for their house, the brand of lipstick doesn't help us much, particularly when it's such a popular brand, like Estée Lauder.

"I've also sent you the autopsy report. You checked your e-mails?"

"Just got back to my desk," I say, clicking on my e-mail icon. I scan my Inbox. "Yup, I got it. Was there anything extra in the report? Anything unusual we didn't cover this morning?"

"No. Only a minimal amount of alcohol in her system and trace amounts of a painkiller."

"So she wasn't pregnant or anything?" I hadn't thought to ask Sorrell this question this morning, but presumably he would have mentioned it.

"Pregnant?" He seems stunned. "Oh, the book. She's a bit old for that, Anderson."

"A sixty-year-old gave birth a few years back, Sorrell. It's amazing what modern medicine can do, particularly if you've got money."

"She definitely wasn't pregnant." He still seems a little disturbed by the prospect, although I'm not sure why. Black looked younger than she was, so I didn't think my question was that left field.

"You got enough to profile the killer?"

"Not quite." I've got most of my profiling inputs except

for a detailed victimology. It would be arrogant and sloppy of me to assume that just because I spent a day with Black at the Academy I have an insight into her personality. We all have faces, masks we wear for different situations, and maybe I only saw one of those masks. And the fact that Holt actually liked Black is proof—I doubt anyone could like the woman I saw. "I'll need to talk to some of Black's friends and family to expand the victim profile. That, in conjunction with Black's autopsy report and everything else we've got, should be enough."

"Time frame?"

If this were my first conversation with Sorrell I might be offended by his gruff demand, but less than one official day on the job and I already know personal relationships aren't his strong suit. Hell, that was probably polite for him.

"Depends who I call and who I go and see in person." It's always better interviewing someone in person. That way you can observe their body language as well as analyze their responses and tone of voice. But it also takes a lot more time. It could take me all afternoon to talk to one or two people if they're across town.

"Who do you want to speak to?" Sorrell asks.

I go through the list of the contacts from the police report that I'd like to follow up on one way or another. "Black's father, sister, brother, Scott Werner and Black's agent and editor. Of course, it's kinda hard when so many of them could also be suspects."

"Let's kill two birds with one stone. I'll take the suspect questions, you can take the victim-profile questions."

"Sounds reasonable." I pause. "But I do need to speak to the husband and I know you wanted to wait with him."

"That's okay. I don't think I can dodge him any longer anyway. When I spoke to Werner yesterday, he mentioned they were finalizing the funeral arrangements today. We might be able to catch the family together."

"Sounds good to me."

"Leave it with me and I'll call you back." Sorrell hangs up.

While I'm waiting for Sorrell, I decide to call Black's agent. Given that she's based in New York, I'll be sticking to an over-the-phone interview with her, at least for the time being.

I punch in the number and the phone is immediately picked up by the receptionist. After I identify myself, I'm put through to Black's agent, Linda Farrow.

"Agent Anderson, is it?"

"Yes, that's right. I'm investigating Loretta Black's murder."

"I still can't believe she's really gone. And murdered? It just doesn't make sense."

"Murder never does." I pause. "I'm sorry to have to call you under these circumstances, Ms. Farrow."

"How can I help?"

"I'd like to ask you a few questions about Loretta."

"Yes?"

"The more we know about her as a person, the more we can deduce about the killer, so I need you to be as honest as possible. That's crucial."

"Sure. If it will help."

"It will." I start with the first question on my list. "How long have you known Loretta?"

"Um…ten years. I've been her agent since 1997. She sent me her first crime novel and I agreed to represent her."

"Is that your specialty? Crime?"

"I represent lots of different authors, but I guess crime is one of my main areas of focus."

I type her response, my touch-typing only just keeping up with her. "How would you describe your relationship with Black?"

There's a pause on the other end of the line before she speaks. "Loretta could be warm and kind, but she could also be difficult." Farrow's choosing her words carefully.

"Yes, I understand that." I don't bother telling Farrow that I met Black, that I know what a pain in the ass she could be.

"We had a good professional relationship, but she was demanding. She didn't make my job, or the publisher's, easy."

"How so?"

"Loretta was first and foremost a businesswoman and she always wanted to know what was going on. She insisted on daily updates, on everything from sales here in the U.S. to sales around the world."

Farrow's being honest all right. "So you won't miss her." I know the question is cold; it's meant to be. I want to gauge her reaction.

"That's unfair, Agent Anderson. Yes, Loretta wasn't always the easiest person to deal with but I'll still miss her. And I owe a lot to her and I'll never forget that."

"Go on."

"Do you know much about this business, Agent?"

"No, I don't." I admit my ignorance openly.

"One client as successful as Loretta *makes* an agent. Loretta and I started out together. I'd only had my own agency for a year when Loretta contacted me and, to be honest, we weren't doing so hot. Loretta had tried some of the bigger-name agents but with no luck. We both offered each other something. I believed in her, something all authors need after countless rejections, and she repaid me by sticking with me over the years, after she'd become a bestseller."

"I see." I pause. "So how will her death affect your business?"

She laughs, not a kind laugh but a disgusted laugh. But my responsibility is to Black, the victim, not Farrow.

"My business will suffer, Agent Anderson. That is what you wanted to hear, isn't it?"

I ignore the dig. "But surely sales will go through the roof now that Black's dead. Won't you get a cut of that?"

"Yes, sales will probably spike. And yes, I get a cut of that." Her voice is defensive, tight. "But Loretta's earning potential is based on her bringing out new books. A book a year, in fact. That's where my future revenue would have been coming from." She pauses. "I won't lie. I can't say I've lost a good friend, but I've lost a woman I have a huge amount of respect for and I've lost my biggest client."

"So you won't benefit from her death."

She laughs, this time a hearty laugh. "Certainly not, Agent. Quite the opposite."

I go to the next logical question. "Who will benefit?"

She thinks about this for some time before she answers. "Her family, I guess. I imagine her husband stands to gain a substantial amount."

I don't bother telling her she's right. "Do you know him very well?"

"Not well, no. But Scott was involved in the business side of Loretta's work on and off over the years. For a while I even thought she'd dump me for him."

"Does that happen?"

"With Black's name and reputation, my job wasn't about the contacts or getting her read by the big publishing houses. It was about contract negotiation and keeping Loretta happy. Scott could have done that, I guess, but I think he wanted his independence from the Black empire. My personal opinion…it was a good decision. I wouldn't wish managing Loretta professionally and living with her on my worst enemy."

Makes sense. Why put more pressure on a marriage? "Did Loretta have any enemies?"

Farrow releases a small snort-laugh. "A few publicists, that's for sure."

"Go on."

"Each time Loretta released a new book, she'd go on tour. Loretta was always high maintenance, but when she was on tour she was the bitch from hell. And I really don't understand why. It's not like public speaking bothered her. She had no problems talking to the media or fans, but the support staff around her were treated like shit. She didn't like the hotel, it was our fault. She didn't like a restaurant, again, our fault. You'd get her a coffee and if it was too strong or too hot or not hot enough, she'd shove it back at you, demanding you fix it."

This is how Black treated Holt at the Academy. Obviously she treated lots of people like dirt, so maybe she was nasty to the wrong person.

"How much of a grudge do you think these publicists might hold?" I ask.

"Not enough for murder. That is what you're asking me, isn't it?"

"Yeah."

"Loretta's got a reputation in the industry for her demanding nature. No one would have thought less of her publicists for getting into a disagreement with her. They were all personally upset and perhaps a little angry, but I can't imagine it would lead to violence, of any description."

Some people's idea of "enough" motivation for murder is pretty scary, but I don't bother pointing this out. Instead, I take down the names of the publicists on Loretta's hit list, including two she personally got fired.

"So they're all women?" I ask as I look at my list of names.

"Yes."

Loretta Black certainly worked in a female-oriented world, and she wasn't popular. Could one of these women have been motivated enough to kill her? Anything's possible, but the crime scene screams male killer. Especially with the sexual mutilation.

I move it along to one of our stronger leads. "What about fans?"

"Loretta's fan mail was handled by Debbie. Occasionally I'd get something and forward it on, and the publishers got a lot. But her Web site had an e-mail address and a post-office box, so I believe most of her fan mail was via e-mail or the box."

That ties in with the information Holt gave us.

I ask Farrow some questions about the specific financial arrangements of the Black book empire, then hang up.

Sorrell still hasn't called back, so I follow up the Farrow interview by contacting Black's editor, but the editor doesn't add anything new to my perception of Black. Both women knew the tougher side of Black, but I wonder if her family has a different picture.

I'm about to ring the two publicists that Black got fired when Sorrell calls.

"The family's at the father's house. They're expecting us."

"Great," I say.

"May as well go in one car again. I'll pick you up out front in ten." The line goes dead.

I manage to get in touch with one of the publicists before heading downstairs, but again, the phone call doesn't tell me much. She isn't a fan, that's for sure, but she's moved on, just like Farrow assumed.

Eight

Sorrell and I pull up outside the Black patriarch's Pasadena home. The houses on the street are mostly older, but all large and distinctive. The home in question is one of the smaller ones on the block, more modest than its neighbors. But even so, either Black's father has his own money, or Black set Daddy up. Sorrell pulls into the driveway and presses the call button on the driver's side of the large gates.

"Yes?" a female voice answers.

Sorrell identifies himself and the iron gates open. The house is set back about a hundred meters from the front gate and wall, and the gardens are expertly landscaped and maintained. We stop in front of the redbrick house, where an older man waits for us on the doorstep.

He greets us politely, but his voice is flat and grief-stricken, and he looks like he needs sleep. George Black is spry for his seventy-odd years, and walks us quickly into a large front room where he introduces us to the rest of the family—Sandra Black, Loretta's younger sister; Mike

Black, the older brother; Mike's wife, Tracy; and their two adult children, Georgia and Harry. Both kids look to be in their early twenties. Also in the room is Scott Werner.

The family resemblance between Loretta and her sister, Sandra, is striking. Though Sandra is at least ten years younger, she has the same raven hair, green eyes, rosebud lips and sculpted face. There'd be no mistaking the family connection, and framed photos of a woman who could only be their mother make it clear the girls take after her. Mike Black, on the other hand, looks like his father. His features are much broader, his face rounder than his sisters' and his eyes are blue.

Werner's sitting in an armchair, as is Sandra Black, while Mike and his wife and two children take up a large, three-and-a-half-seater couch. Their faces all show grief in its many guises. The women's eyes are red, their faces slack, while the men's expressions suggest tension and underlying pain—except for Harry, whose eyes also show the telltale signs of recent tears.

I shake Werner's hand. "Sorry I didn't get a chance to call you back, Mr. Werner."

He nods but is obviously annoyed with me. He's the husband…of course he's hounding us.

Tracy Black offers us a drink, and both Sorrell and I take her up on the offer of coffee.

While she's out of the room, Sorrell updates the family on the investigation, briefly covering the autopsy results and letting the family know that we're pursuing several leads and waiting for forensics. Next he explains that he's called me in to profile Black's killer and that I need to get a better idea of Loretta personally before I can start that process. All the family members seem on edge in one way or another. They're all grieving, yes, but most smart people would realize they'd also be suspects when this much money is at stake.

I have two questions I'd like to ask them collectively before I start interviewing the family members one by one. "As you know, the front cover of Loretta's latest book featured a woman on white tiles. Just like the tiles in the bathroom where Loretta was found."

They all nod their understanding.

"So who's seen that bathroom?"

George Black answers, "Well, obviously we've all been to her house, Agent Anderson. Then I imagine her work people—like Debbie and her agent?" He looks at Werner for confirmation.

Werner nods his head. "That's right."

"Anyone else?" I ask.

"Our friends, of course. And she was interviewed by *60 Minutes* a couple of years ago," Werner says. "They did the whole piece in that area of the house."

I shoot Sorrell a look. *60 Minutes* has got a big audience—that's a lot of people who might have known that killing Loretta in her home and leaving her in the bathroom would replicate the front cover of her book.

"Do you have a copy of that interview, Mr. Werner?"

"Back at the house. I'll get it couriered to you today."

I thank Werner and give him one of my cards. "I understand you had the reading of the will this morning," I say, moving on to the second topic I want to address while the family's together.

"Yes, that's right." Werner seems tense. Perhaps he's worried we'll go for him, the primary beneficiary. Mind you, some husbands would be pissed off with only forty-five percent of copyright, despite getting all the possessions.

"Did you know about the structure of the will before?" I ask, looking at them all and waiting to see who responds.

"I did." Werner answers first.

"And what about everyone else?"

Only George Black confirms that he also had prior knowledge of the will's contents.

"And how did you feel about it?" I ask Werner.

He shrugs. "It was Loretta's decision, but I thought it was very fair."

"And the rest of you?"

But all's quiet in the Black family. Maybe they think it was fair and equitable or maybe they're keeping their mouths shut for other reasons. Still, with the sort of money copyright's worth, I wouldn't be complaining.

"So you knew Debbie Holt was entitled to five percent of the copyright?" I address Werner and George Black, but watch the entire family's reactions to see if anyone is pissed off that an employee got a cut, albeit small.

They both nod, and Werner adds, "In many ways, Debbie was more than an assistant to my wife. Loretta relied on her for administration and research, yes, but she also used her as a sounding board during the creative process and valued her input. Loretta added Debbie to the will a couple of years ago in recognition of that."

"Did Holt know she was in the will?" Sorrell asks.

"No. Not that I'm aware of."

For the individual interviews, I set up base in the large study, calling in each family member one at a time while Sorrell sits with the rest of the clan, also asking them questions. I start with George Black. The study walls are lined with bookshelves, and an old-fashioned globe sits in the middle of the room, next to a large wooden desk. The room's classical look matches my initial impression of George Black as an old-fashioned gentleman.

"Again, Mr. Black, sorry for your loss."

He nods, but launches straight into father mode. "So what are you doing to find my daughter's killer? And why are you insisting on interviewing us separately? It's a disgrace to treat my family like this."

I find it interesting that Black waited until we were alone to question my motives, but he's probably simply being protective of his family. Even though Sorrell updated the family only minutes ago, I understand Black's grief and frustration—and his need for answers. "I'll start with your first question, Mr. Black. Detective Sorrell and I are investigating numerous leads. My area of expertise is profiling—analyzing what sort of person your daughter's killer is. Once we have a profile, we can use that in addition to forensics and other leads to track down the perpetrator."

"Do you have any suspects yet?"

"It's very early in the investigation, sir."

"In other words, no." He pauses. "So are we suspects?" He doesn't seem shocked by the possibility. "I can tell you now, Agent Anderson, no one in my family killed Loretta."

I give him small nods and a smile. "Thank you, Mr. Black, but we must investigate all leads. I'm sure that's what you'd want."

"What I want is for you to focus on the real leads, and not waste your time with us." He crosses his arms. "And I don't like you coming in here and making judgments about my family."

"We're not making any judgments, sir." I try to reassure him.

"So why am I in here by myself?"

"Before I can profile the killer, I need to have a thorough understanding of Loretta. And, to be frank, sir, people, especially family, will often be more open if their brother or sister or father isn't sitting next to them."

He's silent for a little bit, then gruffly says, "Go on."

"What can you tell me about Loretta?"

George Black doesn't hold back in his glowing description of his daughter. He focuses on her talent, ambition and drive to succeed. He certainly paints the picture of someone who was unforgiving in pursuit of her goal, but he describes it positively, as ambition and drive. He also talks about his daughter's generosity—buying him this house, sending her niece and nephew to the best schools and college.

"And what about your other daughter?"

"What about her?"

"Was she on the receiving end of Loretta's generosity too?"

"Of course. Sandra lives in a beautiful little town house in Hermosa Beach. Courtesy of Loretta."

All of the people in the family are indebted to Black in one way or another. Did she withdraw support from one of them? Is that the motive?

"Did you notice any changes in Loretta's behavior in the past few weeks leading up to her death?"

George Black mulls this over for a minute or so. "No, can't say I did. She was the same old Loretta as far as I could tell. And I saw her every week. She always came to visit me on a Saturday afternoon."

"No fights or disagreements with her brother or sister?"

"No." The annoyance returns.

"So, is there anyone you can think of who might want to harm Loretta?"

The question calms him down and he gives it his full attention before responding. "No. She was…she was everything. A wonderful daughter to me and sister to Sandra and Mike, a wonderful wife to Scott and a talented and successful writer. My baby girl had it all. No one disliked her."

His vision is rose-colored, like most parents'.

"I gather Randy Sade disliked your daughter."

"He was trying to get a free ride from Loretta. Honestly, as if my daughter needed any help with her writing!"

I ask the rest of the family the same questions, but they don't give me any additional information on Black. They all comment on her generosity and her ambitious nature, and both Mike and Sandra acknowledge that their sister could be a little abrupt at times. But no one can give me any names of possible suspects or someone who held a grudge against Black—except Randy Sade. The whole family knew that the lawsuit got ugly.

"Well?" Sorrell says as soon as we get in the car.

"They were very careful with their words," I say. "Very cautious."

"You mean they didn't say anything negative about Loretta," he says. "They were like that with me too."

"The brother and sister did acknowledge that she could rub people the wrong way, but I think they were all holding back, realizing that they may be suspects."

"And I played nice too." Sorrell gives me a little grin. "Didn't give them reason to get nervous."

"But were you hard on Scott Werner at first?" I remember Werner's reaction to Sorrell.

"Sure. He was the husband, first on the scene…."

"So maybe he told the others and put them all on guard."

"Possible. What did you make of the sister?"

"There was a bit of tension there. She seemed intimidated by Loretta's success."

"That's what I got too. I definitely sensed more sibling rivalry from little sis than big brother."

"Yes," I say. "She even admitted to me that it was hard living in her sister's shadow."

Back at the office I continue working on Loretta's victimology, calling the other publicist before I write it up. My interviews tell me that Loretta Black had two distinct sides, arrogant and aloof or warm and tender, but the latter only seemed to come to the surface around those she was closest to, like her family and Holt.

I'm putting the final touches on Black's victimology when my phone rings. The screen displays *Melissa*.

I pick up. "Hi, Melissa."

"Hi," she says, almost squealing with excitement. "Guess what?"

"What?" I say warily.

"You've got a delivery."

"A delivery? What do you mean?"

"There's a bunch of flowers here for you."

"Really?" I can't hide my shock. Who'd be sending me flowers?

"Come on, I'll see you in a sec."

On the walk to Melissa's desk I'm thinking through the possibilities. Okay, there's Mum and Dad. They could have sent me a good-luck bunch of flowers, but it's not really their style and they would have sent them to me at home, not work. They know I'd kill them for embarrassing me at the office. Then there's Detective Darren Carter, but again, I wouldn't have thought flowers delivered to my workplace would be his style. He knows the kind of grief I'll cop from my male colleagues. Plus, although he's interested, he hasn't pushed me at all. He realizes I need some time out on the love-life scene and that I'm still uneasy about being with any man after what happened with the D.C. Slasher. Then there's my ex-boyfriend here in the States, but we've barely been in contact over the past few months so I can't imagine he's suddenly decided to send me flowers. Let's face it, I'm stumped.

As soon as I come around the corner, I see the flowers propped on Melissa's desk. Looking at the roses, I can't help myself—I smile. I haven't been sent flowers very often, and certainly not recently, and it's hard not to be flattered as well as embarrassed.

"Someone likes you." Melissa beams. "A dozen red roses." She pauses only for a second. "Who are they from?"

"That's the million dollar question," I say. "I've got no idea."

"Well, go on, open the card." She points at the small envelope pinned to the front of the bunch. Melissa's already hyper enough without the added excitement of flowers.

I undo the small pin that fastens the envelope to the paper, and open the card. *Welcome to the West Coast, Agent Anderson. Perhaps we can meet for dinner one night? Justin Reid.*

"Well?" Melissa prompts.

"They're from Justin Reid," I say.

"Oh my God!" Melissa, like many people, knows exactly who Justin Reid is. "How do you know him?"

"I met him on a case I worked a few months ago."

"Wow." Melissa gives a little sigh.

As well as being the owner of SysTech, Justin Reid's also handsome, single and charming, which is probably why he gets a lot of press and constantly appears in the social pages.

"You don't seem too happy. Why aren't you happy?" Melissa's eyes narrow, unable to comprehend why any woman wouldn't be thrilled to receive flowers from Reid.

It's a compliment that Reid sent me flowers, but I don't know him well enough to be truly interested in him. He's an attractive and charismatic man, not to mention successful, but it wouldn't be appropriate for me to date him, even if I wanted to. "I arrested one of his employees," I explain to Melissa. "At some stage there'll be a trial, and I'll need to give evidence and so will Reid. It's a conflict of interest."

"You gotta be kidding me! Justin Reid has sent you flowers and you're going to ignore them? You *have* to go out with him!"

I laugh. Maybe Melissa's right. Would it be that bad to see a witness? I shake my head at my momentary lapse of professionalism—the answer is yes. "It's not a good idea."

Melissa hands me the flowers. "Well, you can set me up with him. I'm single."

I laugh again and take the flowers from her. After a few steps, I hesitate. How did Reid find out I'd moved to the L.A. office?

"What's up?" Melissa asks.

Looking over my shoulder, I say, "I didn't tell Reid I was moving to L.A."

She shrugs. "A man like that has got some serious contacts."

I nod slowly. "I guess so." I take the flowers back to my desk and manage to find a vase in the kitchen. I pop the flowers on top of the filing cabinet and can't help but smile. They are beautiful.

Sitting back at my desk, I look through the victimology again and continue to work on it. An hour later I save the document and close Word, reverting to my desktop. I stare at the VICAP icon in the top-left corner. What if we're going about this the wrong way? The fact that Black's murder reenacts her book's story line makes the death more unusual, and the ritual elements could point toward a serial killer. In that case, VICAP might have something for us. I could try the signature—the strangulation, stocking, lipstick, mutilation and posing—but given it's an exact replica of her book, I doubt I'll get any hits. The writing on the mirror is more likely to reap rewards, because that is part of our *killer*'s signature. I double-click on the VICAP icon and search for both the stocking and the lipstick marks, even though I'm confident there'll be no murders matching these elements, unless Black actually based her book on a real killer. I don't bother with the sexual posing or mutilation, because it's so common in sexual homicides that it would bring back way too many matches.

While VICAP does spit out a few homicides with some similar elements, I quickly rule them out due to date, state or modus operandi. Next I do a search on the writing, typing in *Your turn.* To my surprise, I get one hit, from four months ago in San Francisco. And not only were the magic words at the crime scene, the victim was an author. Coincidence? I doubt it. I click on the link to view the whole file. Her name was Lorie Rickardian.

I pick up the phone straightaway and punch in Sorrell's number.

"You won't believe this," I say as soon as he answers. "Another crime author was murdered. In April."

"What?" His shock is obvious. He was too focused on the money to think about a serial killer. "Who?"

"Lorie Rickardian."

"Never heard of her. And I don't remember hearing about an author being killed either. How'd you find this out?"

"VICAP. *Your turn* was written at the crime scene."

"Damn," he says. "Was it written with lipstick? Estée Lauder, perhaps?"

"I don't know. I've just found the VICAP entry. Hold on a sec." I click back on the full VICAP file and start reading through the details. "She was forty-one, an English teacher and author. File says she only had one book out, so low profile, I guess. There are photos…." I click on one of the image links.

Lorie Rickardian was a woman who looked all of her forty-one years. She had gray-streaked brown hair, which she wore shortish—not long enough to tie back, but long enough that the top layers fell onto her face, framing her features. Her face was full from extra weight, and her brown eyes and thin lips seemed to be overwhelmed by her tanned and wrinkled skin. In the photo she's wearing a conservative brown jumper with a butterfly design on the front. Middle-American frumpy.

"She look like Black?" Sorrell's searching for other similarities between the victims. It may be a leap to expect something else, especially when we've already got the statistical anomaly of two crime novelists winding up dead.

"No, nothing like Black. She's kinda frumpy, not glamorous at all." I think about Black's muscled but slender frame; Rickardian's almost the opposite. "Yup, here it is. The message was written with lipstick, but not Estée Lauder. It was Revlon's Plum Dynasty."

"It's still lipstick. Anything else?" He asks the question but doesn't give me time to answer. "Screw that. I'm coming over. I want to talk to you about this thing anyways."

"Okay, I'll…"

"See you in fifteen."

I'm left with a dial tone. Maybe Sorrell *should* work on his bedside manner.

Fifteen minutes later I get a call from the security desk informing me that Sorrell's here to see me. Sorrell's got his badge, and probably even knows the security people, but protocol's protocol. I pick him up by the elevators and lead the way to the meeting room I've booked, which contains the fledgling Rickardian file I've pulled together since our phone call. We sit down at the table and I flip the folder open. On top sits the first, slightly pixelated color printout of the scanned photos of Lorie Rickardian. The VICAP software includes the capability to upload as many digital images as the law-enforcement officer lodging the crime sees fit—from the normal pic of the person to all the crime-scene photos. In this instance, we've got a photo of Lorie Rickardian alive, and five of her dead. We've also got four photos of the inside of her house and one of her street. It's not like having the full case file, but it's enough to give you an instant sense of the crime scene and how the person lived and died.

I spread the photos of Rickardian out on the desk between us. We both focus on the photo of her bedroom, and the message on her dressing-room table's mirror.

"Shit," Sorrell says, verbalizing the obvious connection.

"Yup. They're definitely linked." I bite my lip, only too aware of what it means. Two murders, both targeting crime-fiction authors, both with the words *Your turn* written at the crime scene. "We've got a serial killer."

Sorrell sighs before eventually agreeing with me. "Yeah." He shakes his head. "Shit. I hate those bastards."

"Not particularly high on my Christmas list either."

Sorrell seems taken aback by the joke, but it does have the desired effect and he smiles. Then he's back to business. "Kinda eliminates Sade, Werner and Black's family too." Sorrell says it, but without conviction. Serial killers don't murder for revenge or money, they do it for pleasure.

"Yeah," I say. "But we should still track down each lead, even though we have to look at them in a different light now." I'm telling Sorrell something he already knows. "And it makes that letter all the more important. A fan fits for both murders."

"True. How does the murder compare to her book?"

"Not sure yet. I found the book on Amazon, and the cover blurb says it's about a murdered teacher. Rickardian *was* a teacher but according to the VICAP file she was killed during a B and E that went wrong."

Sorrell nods. "Cause of death?"

"The blurb mentioned hanging, but Rickardian died of blunt-force trauma to the head. Four hits."

"What did the police say?" He shuffles paper until he finds the police report, but I give him a verbal summary anyway.

"The break-and-enter was the kitchen window downstairs, which was jimmied open. They figured he broke in after Rickardian had gone to bed. Not much forensics, although they did find a carpet fiber near the bed. Unfortunately they never had any suspects or samples to match it against."

"What color was the fiber?"

"Navy."

Sorrell moves it along. "Did San Francisco Homicide make anything of the book?"

"It's not mentioned in the police report."

"How about the writing?"

"The report just says they couldn't link the message to anyone or anything."

I look at the photos of Rickardian's bedroom. There are some signs of a struggle, including clothes strewn across the floor, but other than that the room is pristine. In fact, from the few crime-scene photos we have, the house is extremely neat. Unless the killer happened to catch her on cleaning day, Lorie Rickardian took a great deal of pride in her home.

Rickardian lies facedown, and the forensic pathologist said she was hit from behind with something heavy, maybe even the crowbar that the killer used to break in. Next to Rickardian's right hand lie a broken china dish and some broken glass. They look like they were knocked down by Rickardian as she fell forward.

"She went down hard," I say. "The autopsy report indicated a broken cheekbone, and the pathologist felt it was from the impact of the fall rather than an injury directly inflicted by her attacker." I slide the autopsy report across the table, closer to Sorrell.

"Mmm," he says, picking up the report and scanning it. I know he'll read every detail many times, but for the moment he's happy for me to take him through it. "Anything else of note in here?" he asks.

"No. Tox screen was negative, even for alcohol. No skin under the fingernails, or other defensive wounds, except for this." I point to a close-up of one of the autopsy photos, one that's been taken with a UV light source. In the picture, you can just make out a bruise that forms an almost perfect ring around Rickardian's wrist, where someone had grabbed her tight. The forensic pathologist always examines a body under a UV light source because it reveals bruises invisible to the naked eye. Either they're old and faded, or they're recent and haven't had time to show on the skin's surface before death. Alternative light sources can also show hair, pollen, saliva and semen. In this case, the UV light shows much darker patches where someone's thumb and forefinger held Rickardian.

Sorrell picks up the image and examines it closely. "She either tried to break free of his grip, or he held her so tight she bruised. But it all must have happened quickly, because there aren't any other defensive wounds."

"It may not have taken much to subdue her, given the victim profile," I say. "You can read it later, but she was definitely a more passive type. Not a fighter."

"He may have promised her he wouldn't hurt her if she didn't struggle. She probably just thought he was going to rob her. In that case it would make sense not to fight."

I nod. "But then he killed her. The first strike would have been enough to ensure she couldn't put up much of a fight even if she tried. After that…" I leave the sentence unfinished and move on. "No other injuries—just the minor bruising on her right wrist, the cracked cheekbone and the four head wounds."

Sorrell shuffles through the papers on the desk again. "Who found the body?" He finds the police report but waits for my answer rather than flipping the document open.

"Her sister. Rickardian didn't show up for work on 21 April, and the school's principal rang the sister, because it had never happened before. When the police interviewed the principal, she said Rickardian always arrived early and hardly ever took a sick day, even after the first book was launched, so she was worried enough to call the sister after Rickardian was a no-show for the first class. Little sis had a spare key and that's what she found." I point to the photo of Rickardian, dead on the floor.

"I see the coroner's office fixed the time of death as between 11:00 p.m. and 2:00 a.m.," Sorrell says.

"Yeah. And that's consistent with her clothing." Rickardian was in her nightdress.

Sorrell leans back. "Guess we better get a copy of her book and read it through properly."

"I called a few of the bookstores in the area after I spoke to you, but no luck. So I've ordered two copies online. We should get them tomorrow."

Sorrell cocks his head slightly and then nods. I'm definitely making progress since that bad first impression.

"Great," he says. Then, with a sigh, "More reading."

I laugh.

"Have you read *Ladykiller* yet?" he asks.

"Almost finished. You?"

"I finished the darn thing last night."

"And?"

"It's darn close. Except for the writing and the sexual assault."

"From what I've read it certainly seemed like a replica. I hope to finish the book off tonight."

He nods. "Anything else interesting in Rickardian's case?"

"They found a partial footprint near the kitchen window. The tread was smeared, but forensics said it looked like some sort of work boot, size ten to eleven. They couldn't be more precise with the shoe size because the print had been smudged over." I place the final photo on the table.

A knock at the door interrupts us.

"Come in," I say.

Melissa enters the room, a small rectangular parcel in hand. "This just came for you, Sophie. I thought it might be important." She passes it to me.

The parcel is the shape of a DVD case, and the sender sticker says *Scott Werner.* "The *60 Minutes* interview," I say. "Thanks, Melissa."

She gives a smile and nod before disappearing, but the smile's directed more at Sorrell than me.

I place the DVD in the DVD player in the far corner of the meeting room, turn on the TV and press Play. The interview's a fifteen-minute segment, which aims to give viewers an insight into Black's writing process. The writing-retreat part of her large home does feature heavily in the interview, and many shots include the bathroom, white tiles and all, in the background.

A few minutes in, I say, "The white tiles are a dead end. They were probably never going to lead us to anything significant, but sometimes it's small details that can give you the break in a case, so it pays to follow them through."

Sorrell nods his head. "Anyone who saw this would know they could lay the body out just like the cover of *Ladykiller.*"

"Uh-huh," I say.

Sorrell looks at his watch. "Let's see if I can't rustle up some extra officers on this. See where we're at tomorrow morning."

"I'll talk to Brady too. Find out what he wants to do."

"Had you started on the profile?"

"No, but this changes everything. I finished my victimology on Loretta Black, but now I'll need to look more closely at Rickardian before I even consider drafting the offender profile." The profiling inputs just effectively doubled, and to ignore Rickardian's murder would be like leaving out half of the ingredients in a cake.

Sorrell nods.

"I'd like to see if the vics have other things in common, besides their occupations," I say. "I'm also interested in examining the two crime scenes a little closer. I know the MOs aren't the same, because they follow different fictional books, but I will be looking for any similarities."

"Okay. I'll feed through forensics as soon as I have it."

"Thanks." I stretch my arms back, trying to correct my posture. "I'm going to San Francisco to check out Rickardian's place and her contacts firsthand, but I'll have my BlackBerry with me so just call or e-mail me."

"Will do." Sorrell stands up and is disappearing out the door before I can even say goodbye. Again the conversation is cut short abruptly. I guess I'll get used to Sorrell eventually.

Before I start planning my to-do list, I give Holt a quick call in response to a couple of messages she's left for me today. The fact that I met her before Black's murder makes it harder for me to ignore her calls.

The phone rings several times before she answers. "Hi, it's Debbie." Her voice is ragged.

"Debbie, it's Sophie Anderson."

"I was hoping it was you. Any news?"

"Not really. Did you know the autopsy was completed this morning?"

"Yes, Scott told me."

"Okay, well we're also following up some trace evidence."

"Did you speak to Randy Sade?"

"Yes, we did."

"And?"

"It's too early to make any firm conclusions." I decide to withhold the new link, the link to Rickardian. For the moment I'd rather this latest twist remain quiet. "I'll be drafting a profile of the killer in the next day or two and we're getting more resources on board."

She's silent at first, then: "And the letter?"

"It's with forensics."

Holt lets out a long breath. "Thanks, Sophie. I knew we could count on you."

Nine

Today is a running day in my exercise schedule, and while the last thing I feel like doing is getting my ass to my apartment's gym, I force myself. I pull on the shorts, sports bra and singlet top I set out last night in anticipation of my morning lethargy, and then hunt around for my shoes and socks. Picking up my MP3 player and a bottle of filtered water, I make my way to the ground-floor gym. It's busy, and I take the last of only three treadmills. Lots of gym junkies in L.A., I guess. I walk for five minutes to warm up, before hitting my usual ten-miles-per-hour pace. I keep thinking about the case, going over it step by step as I push my legs hard to keep up with the treadmill. It's the only danger with morning jogging—for the first ten minutes I always feel close to a stumble. Then I push past that, and the rhythm and music win the battle. Soon I'm taken over by the steady thudding of my shoes and the bass that's pumping in my ears. Fifty minutes later, having completed my sit-ups and cool down, I head back to my apartment.

The earliest flight I could get to San Francisco was 8:30 a.m., and when my alarm went off this morning I was glad of the extra time. It took me ages to get to sleep last night, probably because I'm still getting used to being in a new place. Different sounds, different shapes, different smells… I guess it'll take a couple of weeks until it feels like home.

Once I'm on the plane I fish out Black's book. I'm almost finished and the flight should see me through the final pages.

"So, you met her speed dating. How'd it go?" Benson took out a cigarette. "Mind if I smoke?" he asked, already lighting up.

"Sure, why not?" David Brown was clearly annoyed, but he answered Benson's question. "I was attracted to Lara as soon as I saw her. She is…was…a beautiful woman."

"You always go for redheads?"

"I'm attracted to a person, Detective, not the color of her hair."

Benson blew out a thick trail of smoke. "Yeah, right." He held his cigarette out, examining it. "Got an ashtray?"

David Brown sighed heavily and stood up. A minute or so later he returned to his living room carrying a small bowl. "This is all I got."

"Great." The bowl arrived just in time to catch Benson's first cylinder of ash. He liked to pull hard on his cigarettes, and it didn't take him long to get through one…or a pack for that matter.

"So, you were saying that you're attracted to the woman, not the color of her hair."

David Brown smiled. "That's right, yes."

Benson took a drag. "So, you fuck her or what?"

Brown winced, like he had been slapped in the face.

"Come on, David, it's just us guys sitting in your living room." Benson sucked on his cigarette like a hungry newborn on its mother's breast. "I bet she was good, huh?"

Finally Brown smiled.

Benson threw himself back in the chair. "Knew it. You dog."

Brown's smile grew wider.

Benson stared out the window. "She had great tits, that one."

"Yeah, man, she did." Brown's eyes clouded over a little as he relived it.

Benson leaned forward. "Of course, I didn't get to hold 'em, like you would have."

"They felt good. Just right." Brown held his hands up in a cupping motion. "A nice big handful."

Benson nodded, but not enthusiastically anymore. He took a drag of his cigarette and the smoke oozed out with his words. "Course, I only saw them when she was dead. And they were cut up real bad too."

Brown was silent and no longer smiling.

"You know she was pregnant, David?"

Brown's jaw dropped open, but then he regained his composure. "So? Nothing to do with me."

"She was pregnant with your child, David."

Brown started shaking his head, over and over again. "Bullshit!"

"You were *so* happy to supply us with a DNA sample too, so confident we had nothing on you."

Brown's eyes darted around the place. "So we had sex. Doesn't mean I killed her." He shook his head. "She said she was on the pill. Not to worry about it."

Benson shrugged. "You used a condom with her later. The last time. You weren't leaving your semen in her when you were about to kill her. You're too smart for that."

"I didn't kill anyone." Brown stood up. "I think you should leave now."

Benson stood up too, but reached into his inside pocket. "I don't have to leave, David, I've got a search warrant for your house and a van full of technicians out front." Benson let a chunk of ash fall on David Brown's pristine carpet. "We're going to nail your ass."

Brown's breathing got heavier and faster, and Benson knew it was just a matter of time before he popped. Benson mentally crossed his fingers, hoping Brown would do something to warrant him emptying his .38 into the suspect.

But it wasn't Benson's day.

Two days later

"What you find?" Benson stood outside the county's lab building, waiting. Next to him was a pile of over forty cigarette butts. "Tell me we've got enough to nail this bastard, even without a confession."

Jimmy smiled. "We got enough. The ends of the rope from the latest crime scene match the rope we found at the house."

Benson nodded, going over the evidence they'd collected and thinking about it from a jury's point of view. They had the rope, and they also found condoms that matched part of a wrapper that was recovered from the first girl's murder. They'd linked Brown to all the girls—he'd met them through the speed-dating nights and had had at least one date with most of them. Then there was Lara, the redhead, and her unborn fetus. He'd had more than one date with her before he killed her.

Benson stubbed out his cigarette. Signed, sealed and delivered. He took the back of Jimmy's neck and cradled him closer. "You're the best, Jimmy."

Jimmy smiled…he'd waited for Benson to praise him for a long time. "Thanks, Benson. Thanks."

I put the book down. In terms of our case, I didn't really get much more from reading the whole book than I did from reading the specific crime-scene sections. The similarities between Black's book and her death are limited to the MO and the killer's signature. There's no baby, no redhead and no speed-dating. Still, I guess it's possible we'll find stockings and the matching lipstick at our suspect's house. I think about the killer's motivation in replicating the authors' plots. Assuming *Your turn* does mean the authors' turn to die like their characters, then the killer could be punishing the authors, presumably for their dark imaginations; but the MO replication could also appeal to the killer's sense of creativity, his sense of humor. This is going to be a hard one to profile.

I catch a cab from the airport to the San Francisco FBI Field Office, and when I arrive I'm greeted by Special Agent Dusk, an FBI agent I worked with in bringing down the Murderers' Club. I called him after I'd booked my flights and we decided it made sense for him to act as my liaison in San Fran. He knows the two detectives who worked Rickardian's case, and he knows me.

Dusk's fairly short at about five-six, and his thin frame makes him seem even smaller. Even with only one-inch heels I feel like I tower over him. His ash-blond hair has some natural red undertones, and his beard is speckled with blond, red and a touch of gray.

"I like the beard," I say as we shake hands.

"Thanks." He runs his hand over his chin. "And welcome back to San Francisco."

We start walking toward his desk and a few strides in he says, "So, Rickardian."

"Yes. Any luck getting her file?"

"I've organized to meet the detectives, Perez and O'Shaughnessy, at Rickardian's house in one hour. They said they'd bring the full case file." Dusk doesn't sound enthusiastic.

"What are they like?"

He pauses only for a second. "O'Shaughnessy's a pain in the ass. He's arrogant and he doesn't have any time for me because I was never a cop. Maybe he'll give you the time of day."

"I may have been a cop before the Bureau, but I'm also a woman."

Dusk laughs. "You've profiled him well already."

"Sounds like it'll be a fun afternoon."

"Mmm…" Dusk pauses. "The only reason they even lodge their files in VICAP is because their captain insists." He sighs. "Are you getting lots of press on Black?"

"Oh, yeah. I've got heaps of voice mails from journalists. All of which I'm ignoring." The first two had soon been joined by many more.

He laughs before moving back to the case. "The writing on Rickardian's mirror wasn't released, so we're definitely talking serial."

"Yeah, we are." I pause. "We're keeping the writing quiet for Black's death too."

It's standard practice to release some information to the victim's relatives and the press, but withhold other information, especially on a high-profile case like Black's. For a start it helps us weed out the crank callers ringing up to confess to the crime. The officer taking the call simply asks the caller if he left anything at the scene. The caller will usually make something up, but unless he's the killer he's going to strike out. It also stops potential copycat killers fooling us into believing a scene is related, and when we do have a suspect it can help us during the interview process. If he lets something slip and claims to have read it in the newspaper when it wasn't public knowledge, then we have him. In both Black's and Rickardian's cases, the family knows about the writing, but that couldn't be helped.

"Rickardian's death is real close to her book too."

"Really? It didn't sound like it from the cover blurb. Have you read it?"

He gives me a sheepish smile. "I'm actually a bit of a crime-fiction fan. When I found out a local author had released a new book, I picked it up."

At his desk, Dusk motions to a chair opposite him.

"Is it any good?" I ask, sitting down.

"Excellent. I was looking forward to her second."

"The back cover said something about a teacher who was found hung?"

"Yeah, that's right. It starts with her death and works back. Eventually the lead detective discovers that the teacher suspected one of her students of a break-and-enter that ended in murder. But the student's part of a new, violent gang and they ordered him to silence her—permanently." He pauses. "It's not reflected on the cover, but the book's actually more about gangs than the teacher's murder, plus it's got lots of twists and turns along the way."

"But it does have the B and E murder. How could the cops miss that?"

"It was such a small part in the story line, so they chalked it up as a coincidence. And they did question her students."

"Big coincidence."

He shrugs. "You and I are looking at it in a new light, thinking about Black. But from their point of view four months ago? Rickardian lived in a rough neighborhood that was usually subject to lots of B and Es. Apparently Rickardian kept a thousand dollars in her bedside drawer, which was missing. The cops figured it was a drug-related robbery gone wrong."

I try to see it from their eyes. "Talks like a duck, walks like a duck, it is a duck?"

"That's what they figured."

I open my briefcase, still not one hundred percent convinced the detectives were thorough enough. "So, how do you want to do this?"

"We've only got about fifteen minutes before we need to hit the road. I'd like to spend that time on Black's case file so I'm not flying blind. Sound okay?"

"Sure." I fish the folder out and briefly take Dusk through some of the photos, the police reports and the autopsy report, before completing the story with my victim profile.

"She's a very different kettle of fish to Rickardian," Dusk says once I'm finished. He glances at his watch and I instinctively check the time myself, and notice it's been nearly twenty minutes since I started taking Dusk through the case.

"Besides their occupations, I haven't found anything else in common between the victims." Serial killers have patterns and their victims usually have something in common. It may be something obvious—they could look alike, or all work as prostitutes in a specific area—but sometimes that similarity can be harder to find. And it's the victim commonality that can help you find the killer, so it's extremely important to carefully compare victims. Often a relatively obvious link can be hard to find—for example they may have all frequented the same café as the killer, but when you're retracing a victim's steps their favorite cafés aren't usually the first thing mentioned. In our case, the occupation is a mighty big link. The population of crime-fiction authors is very small compared to other occupations, plus the replication of the fictional crime scenes is ritualistic, again, usually an indicator of a serial perpetrator. It also tells us that the murders did have something to do with the women's writing. But why these two crime-fiction authors? What have they got in common?

"Time to go," Dusk says.

Within five minutes we're on the road. The drive to Rickardian's compact house in Excelsior, a suburb of San Francisco, is spent discussing Rickardian's case. By the time we get there, Dusk and I have caught each other up on the elements of both murders.

Rickardian's street is suburban poor. Parked out in front of her home are two cars, an older white Volvo station wagon and a late-model Ford Fusion. Two plainclothes cops lean on either side of the Ford; one's on the phone and the other's staring at the house. We pull up behind them and they both look at us, initially without moving. Dusk and I are out of the car before the one looking at the house, who I'm guessing is Perez from his olive skin, approaches us. As he pushes himself off the car door, I can see he's holding a file in his hand. At least we're heading in the right direction. O'Shaughnessy keeps his eyes on us, but continues his conversation.

Perez holds out his right hand. "Perez."

I shake his hand while Dusk introduces us properly.

Perez motions with his head over his shoulder. "O'Shaughnessy won't be long." He thrusts his left hand forward. "And here's a copy of the file."

"Thanks." I give him a smile before opening the folder and having a quick flick through. I look up when I hear the driver door of the white Volvo opening. The family resemblance makes it immediately obvious that the Volvo driver is Emily Rickardian, the victim's sister. I close the manila folder, not wanting to cause her any unnecessary distress.

Perez clears his throat and leans in to us. "She's not one of our biggest fans."

I nod, now understanding why the three hadn't been waiting together. I wouldn't have expected them to be waiting for us inside—it may have been four months ago, but I'm sure Emily Rickardian wouldn't be keen to be in the house where her sister was murdered—but I would have assumed they'd be waiting together on the front lawn. Things must be pretty bad for Emily Rickardian to stay in her car until we arrived. And she obviously doesn't want us inside the house unless she's present.

A Realtor sign that sticks out of the front lawn leans to one side. The sign's tilt and its slightly weathered look tell me it's been there a while. Again, not surprising that Emily Rickardian has put her sister's house up for sale and that there hasn't been a rush of potential buyers. No one wants to live in a house where someone got murdered. It creeps the average Joe out. And we're not talking San Francisco's most exclusive suburb either. The crime rate here is high enough, without adding a known murder to your house's history.

Emily Rickardian is petite, and her clothes look as though they belong to a little girl—jeans and a bright pink jumper with a blue teddy bear embroidered on it. She walks past Perez, making a beeline for Dusk and me.

"Are you from the FBI?" Her voice is soft, tentative.

I let Dusk answer. "Yes, ma'am. I'm Special Agent Dusk from the San Francisco Field Office and this is Special Agent Anderson from the L.A. Field Office."

Rickardian shakes both our hands and is friendly in every way. Either she's on her best behavior or O'Shaughnessy and Perez deserve the cold shoulder.

"I'm glad you're looking at Lorie's murder again." Her voice is appreciative but I also catch the small look she gives the detectives. Perez is right; she's not a fan.

Perez manages a sheepish look, which I think is guilt, and O'Shaughnessy takes Rickardian's contact with us as a cue to finish his conversation.

He snaps the phone shut and strides over to us. "O'Shaughnessy." He holds his hand out to me and I take it, introducing myself.

"Nice to meet you," he says. "We always like having the Bureau on board."

I sense a hint of sarcasm in his voice, but I leave the bait dangling. I don't think I'm going to like O'Shaughnessy one little bit. Perez still has the slightly sheepish look on his face and I'm already making assumptions about the partners. O'Shaughnessy's the dominant one, and while Perez may not like his partner's attitude, I don't envisage him speaking up too often.

I smile. "Shall we go inside?"

A hint of fear flashes across Emily Rickardian's eyes.

"How long has the house been on the market?" I ask her.

"Two months." She seems happy to be distracted and I start us walking toward the front door while she continues. "The first couple of months I couldn't do anything, couldn't bear to sell it. This was my sister's home for over ten years."

"She lived alone, right?"

Emily Rickardian slides the key in the door and turns it. She takes a deep breath before pushing the door open. "Yes, that's right. We're both spinsters. Never married, no children." She manages a small smile that's innocuous in every way—I can't tell if she's happy to be single or longing for a family. Interesting.

"But you didn't live together?"

"Not since we were kids, no." She steps inside hesitantly and we all follow. "Lorie was a neat freak and me…well, she'd call me a slob. We loved each other dearly, and I used to spend a couple of hours over here most days, but we couldn't live together."

"Where do you live, Ms. Rickardian?"

"A five-minute drive around the corner." She pauses. "In the daylight I used to walk here, but I drive everywhere now, since…"

She doesn't need to complete the sentence for me.

The house is a little larger than it looked in the photos, and now a fine layer of dust coats the interior surfaces.

Emily Rickardian notices it too. "Lorie would kill me if she saw the place now. She always kept it just so."

"Yes, I noticed that from the photos."

Rickardian winces. "Photos of my Lorie?"

I look her straight in the eyes. "Yes. The crime-scene photos."

She nods—small, fast movements. She found the body, so she knows exactly what it looked like.

"I…I couldn't believe she was really dead." She closes her eyes.

"I know." I touch her shoulder briefly.

O'Shaughnessy pushes past us. "So, the killer entered from the kitchen window over here." He strides down the hallway and I give Emily Rickardian a quick smile before tailing O'Shaughnessy. He's standing by the window impatiently when I arrive in the kitchen all of a few seconds after him. He starts as soon as my foot crosses the threshold. "The window was jimmied open by a crowbar by the looks of it."

I nod, picturing the photo that was taken outside the window, where tool marks had scratched the window frame.

"Then he made his way into the living room." O'Shaughnessy leads and we follow him. "Then up the stairs." O'Shaughnessy pauses to eyeball us all before moving upstairs. The others follow, but I take my time in the living room. I've only seen one photo of this space and, like the house, it's a little bigger than it looked in the photo. An older-style television sits in the corner, with a couple of armchairs and one couch placed around it. I can tell by looking at the furniture which chair was Lorie Rickardian's, because one armchair is well worn while the others look almost new, except for the dated floral design. Lorie didn't entertain much in this room. Another armchair faces out of a bay window, and this one looks even more worn than the one near the TV. Obviously Lorie spent more time gazing out her front window than watching the box.

Except for two ornamental units and a couple of framed paintings, the walls are lined with books. I look through the collection.

Emily comes back down the stairs. "Lorie loved to read."

I smile. "In that chair?" I look toward the bay window.

"Yes. It catches the late-afternoon sun and she just adored it. She spent hours there."

I nod and go back to the bookshelf. I recognize many of the names as crime-fiction authors, including what looks like Black's complete collection. "She liked reading crime, as well as writing it?"

"That's what inspired her to write. She loved reading the stuff so much, she decided to write her own. Funny, she was such a quiet, reserved person and everyone found it hard to believe she could write such—" she searches for the word "—nasty stuff."

"How did it do, her first book?"

Emily shrugs. "Just okay. But Lorie didn't mind. She was quite happy to write in her spare time. She wasn't looking for a quick buck."

"We better go up," I say, looking at the stairs.

Emily nods, but I can tell she doesn't really want to think about her sister's death. I move first, but stop in my tracks when I suddenly feel giddy. I take ahold of the stairs' railing.

A dark silhouette stands over me. I gasp, but a gloved hand reaches over my mouth and then I'm pulled out of bed within a couple of seconds. I stand with someone holding on to my wrist tightly.

My breathing is raspy and shallow with fear. I'm standing in front of the dresser, and I turn. The shape is still only a silhouette, but I can make out dark eyes under a balaclava. I'm shocked when I feel the dull pain of something hitting my head. I fall forward, reaching my hands out uselessly on the way down. I knock a couple of things off the dressing table and fall. I push my hands out in front of me, trying to crawl away, but then I feel another dull thud, followed by blackness. Hands reach up my legs, pushing my nightdress up.

I'm running through woods and someone's behind me.

I open my eyes, staring at Emily Rickardian's face, which is now very close to mine.

"Are you okay?" she asks.

I close my eyes and nod, still coming back to reality. "I'm fine. Just a dizzy spell." I start up the stairs.

"Are you sure you're okay?" She doesn't make a move.

"Yes, thanks, fine." I make sure my voice is authoritative and calm.

I replay the vision, looking for anything new, anything that can add to what we know. The point that sticks out is the nightdress—all the photos show it down, covering her ankles, but in my vision the killer pushed it up, exposing Rickardian's underwear.

And then there was the last part, being chased in some woods. That's the second time I've seen that image in the context of this case. And it seems more than a little familiar. I try to think where I may have seen or read about a woman running through a forest. I go over all my cases from the Behavioral Analysis Unit, but come up with nothing. Then it hits me. It's something I saw over a year ago, during a vision when I was working on the D.C. Slasher case. But a case involving a woman in the woods never came across my desk.

When we reach Lorie Rickardian's room, Emily hangs back, obviously unwilling to set foot inside the room in which her sister's life was taken. O'Shaughnessy gives me an impatient glare but then continues his monologue, like he never stopped. "Lorie Rickardian was probably asleep—" he points to the bed "—and woke up when the perp went for her cash." O'Shaughnessy taps the bedside table where Rickardian's thousand dollars was kept. "He pulled her out of bed and forced her over to the dressing table." He crosses the room and stands next to the dressing table. "He probably wanted her to get jewelry or other valuables for him. But she struggled, and he hit her over the head with the crowbar." O'Shaughnessy makes a small swiping movement. "She grabbed at the dressing table on her way down, knocking over a small glass vase and an ornamental frog." O'Shaughnessy points to the spot where Rickardian's body lay. "The killer hit her three more times before running." O'Shaughnessy looks up to the bedroom door, indicating the killer's escape route, before crossing his arms and looking at me...waiting.

I smile. "Or..." I look around the room. "Our perp arrives with one thing on his mind and one thing only— murder. He breaks in through the kitchen window and comes straight up here. He then drags Lorie Rickardian out of bed."

"Are you saying..." Emily comes closer, one leg actually in the bedroom "...are you saying that she knew her attacker?"

"Not necessarily, although it is possible."

Emily's face crumples with concentration. "Lorie would have screamed if it was a stranger. No one reported a scream." Now she turns to O'Shaughnessy, her look an accusation all by itself.

He shakes his head. "We've been over this, Ms. Rickardian. She was startled out of her sleep. Maybe she screamed and wasn't heard or maybe she was too shocked to scream. It happens." O'Shaughnessy looks at me with unpleasant eyes.

"He's right. Often people are so shocked during a confrontation that they don't think to scream, or their voices literally close up. Like the saying goes, paralyzed by fear." I pause. "It's also possible he cupped his hand over her mouth," I say, adding in one element from my vision. "Let's take the scream out of the equation for the moment. So, Lorie is out of bed, and maybe the attacker promises she'll be all right if she keeps her mouth shut." I look at Emily. "Another reason why there could have been no scream."

She nods reluctantly.

"But he doesn't keep his promise. The attack catches her by surprise and she goes down, without any chance of fighting. The writing on the mirror makes it personal, not just a robbery gone wrong." I look at O'Shaughnessy again, wondering how hard he's going to cling to his original findings. Most people don't like to be wrong, and I don't suppose O'Shaughnessy is any different.

He is quick to come up with a hypothesis in response to my blank stare. "The writing could refer to a student's vendetta. Maybe she was mean to some kid and he decided it was Rickardian's turn to be on the receiving end."

That would make the case even closer to Rickardian's book, but according to the police report, O'Shaughnessy and Perez investigated the students extensively at the time of the murder.

"Lorie was loved and respected by her students!" Emily looks as if she can think of nothing better than slapping O'Shaughnessy across the face. Perhaps he deserves it.

But she controls her anger. She turns to Dusk and me. "I'll be waiting outside." She gives O'Shaughnessy a scathing look before moving quickly down the stairs.

I glance at O'Shaughnessy and shake my head.

"What?" he says.

Perez strokes his chin. "Told you Emily Rickardian wasn't a fan."

I move back to the case. "The police report indicated that none of the students stuck out as a genuine person of interest."

"Look, lady…"

Here we go. I'm no longer "Agent," just plain "lady." Let's face it, for guys like O'Shaughnessy I've got three strikes against me—I'm FBI, I'm a woman doing what he thinks is a man's job and I'm a profiler, which many old-school cops think of as subjective mumbo jumbo. And to top it all off, I'm not even bloody American!

"We're kinda busy up here, you know. And not every murder can be solved." He takes a breath, about to keep going, but I cut in.

"I know." I try to break his train of thought, at least momentarily, and with some supportive words. It has the desired effect and he seems a little bewildered that I'm agreeing with him.

"He exited from the back door?" I ask.

O'Shaughnessy nods slowly and seems happy enough to go back to the evidence. "Yes, the back door was open when Emily arrived but there were no prints so he must have worn gloves."

I stand with my hands on my hips, going over things, visualizing the crime and the crime-scene photos. The others are courteously silent.

"Who was the first responder?"

"One of our uniforms," O'Shaughnessy says. "Why?"

"The scene definitely wasn't tampered with?"

"No!" His outrage is obvious. "You think I'd leave something like that out of the report?"

"Just covering all bases." I pause. That only leaves one person. "This was a planned murder," I say, making sure there's no hint of accusation in my voice. "If there were any doubts before now, with Black's murder and the same message at the crime scene…" I let the sentence hang.

O'Shaughnessy comes up with a compromise. "Maybe Rickardian was his first kill, and it was accidental or personal with her, and then he decided he liked it." It's an unlikely hypothesis, but it is possible that the perp killed Rickardian for personal reasons and is now targeting victims like her—authors—to relive that initial thrill.

I give him a nod. "Could be," I say, even though the evidence points to a high degree of planning in both murders, and to a serial killer.

I lead the way downstairs and out. Emily's waiting at her car for us. O'Shaughnessy and Perez loiter on the front lawn, and I go over to Emily, who's leaning on her car, deep in thought.

"Thanks for letting us back into your sister's house, Emily," I say.

She looks up. "Not at all. It's good to see you're looking into my sister's death and taking it a little more seriously now." She leans in, conspiratorially. "I never thought Detectives Perez and O'Shaughnessy showed my sister the respect she deserved." She pauses. "I'd like to ask you something, Agent, if I may."

"I'll answer if I can." I'm careful not to commit myself to something I may not be able to deliver on.

"I can't help but notice the renewed interest in my sister's case is straight after Loretta Black's murder."

"Yes, it is." I keep my voice neutral, still unsure of how much I want to tell Emily.

"That's not a coincidence, is it?" She holds my gaze and I'm reminded of her cool announcement that the sisters were spinsters. Again, her voice is devoid of any emotion, leaving me nothing to interpret. For whatever reason, she's used to hiding or controlling her emotions. Or maybe that's just me in overanalysis mode. One of the hazards of life as a profiler—you tend to profile everyone.

"I'm afraid I can't discuss Loretta Black's case at this

time." I know my answer sounds like it's been fed to me by a lawyer, but policy is policy. It's a standard response— one that probably was originally written by a lawyer.

"Agent Dusk said you were from the L.A. Field Office. Are you working on Black's murder too?"

"Again, I'm afraid I can't talk about that. I'm sorry. All I can tell you is we're reopening your sister's case. Hopefully this time we'll catch her killer."

The last sentence has the desired effect and it brings a smile to her face. "Thank you, Agent Anderson." She gives me a knowing nod, pretty much telling me that she can see the link between Black and her sister, but I keep my face blank.

Not many people know about the link—not yet. There'd really be panic in the book world if they knew Black was the second author murdered, not the first. It's lucky for us that Rickardian's not very well known, but sooner or later a journalist or someone else is going to remember the robbery gone wrong and put two and two together, questioning Rickardian's death. I'd like to delay that moment for as long as possible.

"It's imperative you keep any theories you have to yourself, Emily. You understand that, don't you?"

"Yes, Agent, I do." She gives me an officious nod.

"It could harm the case if details are leaked or discussed with *anyone*."

She nods and smiles again.

Satisfied, I move on to the fan mail. "Emily, did Lorie get any fan mail?"

"Yes, she did." Emily Rickardian smiles, a wide, telling grin. "I've never seen her so happy as when she got those letters."

"Did she get very many?"

She shrugs. "Only about twenty, I think."

"Are they inside?"

"No, I've got them. I wanted them close to me, you know?"

"Those letters could really help this investigation."

"You think…you think one of her fans did this?" Emily visibly tenses with the thought.

"We need to look into every possibility. Were there any unkind letters?"

"No," she says. "Everyone who knew Lorie loved her and everyone who read her book loved it."

Emily is in proud-sister mode, but her "no" was a little too emphatic for my liking. She also broke eye contact for a split second, a telltale sign of a lie. This is one of the advantages of talking to people in person. Over the phone, the "no" may have fooled me, but not in person.

"If Lorie received a letter that was anything but flattering, it's really important you tell me. Even if it seems inconsequential." I rest my hand lightly on Emily's upper arm. "You understand that, don't you, Emily?"

She slowly nods, and hangs her head. "There were two letters that upset her."

"Have you got those?"

"Yes. I wanted Lorie to throw them out or burn them, but she wouldn't. I collected them from her house with the others and haven't got around to doing anything with them yet."

"Did the police ask for them?"

"No. They didn't."

I hide my disappointment. It should have been an area they covered.

"What about e-mails?"

"No. Lorie didn't have a Web site or anything like that set up, so it was just the letters."

Sorting through Lorie Rickardian's fan mail will be a lot easier than Black's.

There's one more thing I need to ask. "Emily, did your sister know a journalist called Randy Sade?"

Emily stares into the distance for a couple of seconds before shaking her head. "Doesn't sound familiar." She pauses. "Not that I know of."

It's still possible Sade did, in fact, come across Rickardian in his work. And maybe O'Shaughnessy *is* onto something about Rickardian being a test run. Maybe Sade wanted to practice before he went for Black.

"We're finished with the house if you want to lock up," I say. "I'm going to talk to the detectives for a few minutes."

The tiniest smile lights up her face, and I wonder if she thinks O'Shaughnessy and Perez are going to get in trouble for their sloppy investigative work. But alienating them like that is the last thing I want to do. I need them on my side. Besides, I'm sure they don't care what some Fed thinks of them.

I continue, "And then I'd like to come over and get those letters."

"Sure thing, Agent Anderson."

"But don't touch them until I get there. They could be evidence."

"Okay."

She gives me directions to her house before moving to her car.

"One more thing, Emily."

"Yes?" she says, turning back to me.

"Did you touch your sister when you found her? Touch anything in that room at all?"

"No." She drops eye contact for a millisecond.

I move closer to her, giving us even more privacy. There's no way the guys can hear us. "Emily, if you've misled us in any way, now is the time to set things straight."

"I don't know what you're talking about." She seems to be regaining her resolve.

"Emily, I know you don't like Detectives O'Shaughnessy and Perez, but this is your sister's murder. Your sister's *killer* we're talking about."

She holds on to her car-door handle and puts her head down. "I pulled her nightdress down. It was…no one should have seen her like that. I couldn't stand the thought of her exposed, and once I met O'Shaughnessy and Perez…well, they were so rude. So smug. They don't care about Lorie." She bites her lip. "I'm sorry." She looks at the two detectives. "Are you going to tell them?"

"Yes. I have to."

She nods, but seems embarrassed. "It's just…once I hadn't told them, I didn't feel like I could go back on that, not hours later. And then hours turned to days, and days to weeks. It was too late."

I nod my understanding once more, even though I'm frustrated by Emily Rickardian's actions. I can see *why* she did it, I just don't think she realizes the implications. A lifted nightdress makes it much more obviously a sexual homicide and much less like a B and E gone wrong. It wasn't just O'Shaughnessy and Perez who fouled up this case—Emily Rickardian did her fair share too.

After Emily Rickardian drives off, we all hover around

the detectives' Ford and I fill them in on my discovery. They're pissed off, not surprisingly.

"Jesus," O'Shaughnessy says. "How could she keep that from us? All this time?"

I don't respond.

He sighs. "In light of this and Black's murder, it seems like we're looking for a serial killer."

I feel like jumping up and down and shouting "Hallelujah!" But if it wasn't for Emily Rickardian's revelation, chances are O'Shaughnessy would still be plugging away at the B and E gone wrong.

"We're looking into fans for Black's case, so we'll do the same for Rickardian. I'm going to get the letters from Emily now."

"Rickardian had fan mail?" O'Shaughnessy seems taken aback.

"Yes." I try to keep my voice neutral; there's no reason to point the finger now.

O'Shaughnessy shrugs. "Emily didn't tell us about that either."

I swallow my words. *Because you didn't ask.*

"Do you mind if I take them back to the L.A. lab? It'll be much easier if we analyze the letters alongside Black's mail."

There's silence. Officially Rickardian is their case, their forensics. But I'm hoping they'll see reason.

O'Shaughnessy gives me a grumpy affirmation, but I don't care how much of a bad mood he's in, because I got what I needed—the letters with me. We part company with the detectives, and once we arrive at Emily Rickardian's house, Dusk and I put on gloves. No one mentions the nightdress, but she can barely look us in the eye—guilt.

Emily takes us into a spare room and points at a small, expandable folder. "They're in there, under *l* for *letters.*"

I remove the loose pages carefully.

"We also had some of the early ones framed," Rickardian says, disappearing into another room. She returns a couple of minutes later with four frames. I scan those ones and then go on to the file, reading each letter briefly.

Then I see it, a letter signed "A fan."

Ten

"Here you go." Dusk stops at a spare cubicle a few across from him. "You can plug in to the network there if you need to." He points to the network cable.

"I'll just use my hard drive," I say, but then immediately get nervous about not having a backup copy. "Actually I might plug in."

I start connecting the leads.

"So, what are your thoughts?"

That's the big question. "If it was Black's case alone," I say, "I'd hypothesize sexual homicide, possibly by someone she knew. Revenge would be a strong contender for motive, and the money would bother me enough to keep on the family too." I plug in the laptop's power cord and switch it on. "But with Rickardian's case in the mix, we're talking sexual homicide with escalation—from exposing Rickardian's clothed lower body slightly to the highly sexualized pose of the naked Black and the sexual mutilation. And I believe the sexual escalation will continue, probably with sexual assault at the next murder, if our guy's physically capable of it."

"You think he might not be?" There's no hint of surprise in Dusk's voice. Anyone who's worked a few sexual homicides knows that it's a pattern with some offenders.

"It's a possibility. Black's body was left with her genitalia exposed, but no obvious interference. And that deviates from her book."

We're silent for a while, both thinking while we watch my computer boot.

"The fact that our killer is targeting crime-fiction authors is significant," I say. "It's too specific to not mean something. So I think the doer sees himself meting out justice."

"Go on."

"You know how some people think pornography incites rape and so they exact revenge on pornographers?"

"Yup." Dusk leans on the cubicle partition.

"Well, what if someone thinks crime fiction encourages violence and murder, so they silence one of the country's most prominent authors, in Black?"

"Interesting." He pauses. "But why Rickardian? She's not in the same league as Black in terms of fame."

Dusk's right. The choice of Rickardian, such an obscure author, doesn't jell. "Maybe Rickardian was a practice run." I voice one of the possibilities we've come back to a couple of times—even O'Shaughnessy put it forward earlier today. "Then he moved onward and upward to Black, the big fish." My computer screen comes to life. "Or maybe he realized Rickardian wasn't a big enough statement."

"Because she didn't get much press."

"Exactly. Which means *he* didn't get enough press. If we are talking about someone who's punishing the authors, he's similar to a religious zealot or anyone else championing a cause with no regard for human life."

"A vigilante." Dusk slips his hands into his pockets. "So he'll strike again?"

"Most definitely. Probably in three to four months' time if we use the gap between Rickardian and Black as a guide." For most serial killers, the compulsion to kill is satiated with murder itself, and they can maintain this sense of satisfaction by reliving the murder. That's why so many serial killers take trophies, things that will remind them of the kill. Once the memory doesn't fulfill them anymore, the cooling-off period is over and they start looking for their next target. While the gap between victims can change, many killers sit on a cycle with roughly the same interval between victims—assuming nothing happens to propel them into action, and murder, sooner.

Dusk nods. "You think this letter is related?" He points to Rickardian's letter from "A fan," which is now in a plastic sheath.

"It's a link between Black and Rickardian. Both letters are judgmental in nature and dwell on the sexual violence of the authors' books. For the moment, I'm going to use the letters in my profile." An offender profile is a living, breathing document that may need to be changed when new evidence comes to light, but unless we can discount the letters, they're our strongest lead, so I'll use them to get a better understanding of the writer.

Dusk nods and looks at my screen. "There's one other possibility, Anderson."

"Yes?"

"What if you're looking for a struggling author? Someone who's jealous of their success?"

I think about Dusk's suggestion. Black would epitomize the successful author, but Rickardian? "Rickardian doesn't fit. If you're jealous of success, why kill such a fledgling author?"

"Back to the practice-run theory." Dusk grins.

I smile back. "You've got me there." I lean back and think on it. "It's a competitive world, right?"

"Yes, extremely. It's darn hard to get published. Only a small percentage of authors make it. And of those who get published, fewer again are truly successful like Black."

"It was certainly lucrative for Black."

"Sure, but you need to have a bestseller…or ten." He smiles again and pushes himself off the cubicle partition. "Well, guess I'll leave you to it."

"Thanks," I say, still deep in thought. "I'll let you know when I'm heading off." I guess we do need to take a closer look at Black's competition. But if the killer is an unpublished author, how will we track them down? It might be something to talk to Black's and Rickardian's publishers about.

I've got three hours before I have to leave for my flight back to L.A. and I hope to get most of the profile down on paper by then. While I can finish it off tonight, I'm planning to go to a kung-fu class at 7:00 p.m. and I don't want to miss it—I've been studying kung fu for seven years and I'm keen to continue in L.A. So the more I get done now, the better.

I've read the letter several times since Emily Rickardian handed it to me, including once over the phone to Sorrell. The links between the two cases continue to grow and I doubt we'll be able to keep them quiet much longer.

I read the letter one more time.

Dear Ms. Rickardian,

I'm sure it must be hard to launch a career as a novelist, and congratulations on releasing a book. However I don't think you've chosen a good genre. Your characters and prose are excellent, and worthy of a much more refined genre than crime. Especially with the humor you bring to your work, I can see you writing something else. Why crime? Don't you think there's enough evil in this world without adding to it? And how would you feel if someone you loved became a victim of such a horrible killer? It's a terrible thing you do, Ms. Rickardian, terrible. You should think about the victims more. How would you feel being a victim of a violent or sexually violent crime? Yours sincerely,
A fan

It's milder than the letter to Black, less threatening. But I'd expect that, given Rickardian was his first. His rage grows all the time and he thinks killing and enacting his form of justice will release the anger and make him feel better. Interesting also that he calls himself a fan, yet most of the letter is far from complimentary. A clear picture of the killer is beginning to form, so I open my standard Word template.

Sex:	Male
Age:	Chronological: 35-50 Emotional age: 30-40
Race:	Caucasian.

Type of offender:	Organized: • Well-planned murders. • Not much forensic evidence left at the crime scenes (had the presence of mind to deal with the footprint at Rickardian's house by smudging it). • Highly ritualistic and sexualized postmortem posing (Black). • Restraints used for Black but not for Rickardian (although she was physically restrained by her wrist). Conflicting behavior in terms of high-risk or low-risk offender: • Rickardian's murder was low-risk offender behavior. She lived alone and he entered late at night in a suburb known for its high crime rate. He had privacy and time, if he needed it. • Black's murder was high risk—the murder took place in her house with a full security system. However, the alarm wasn't armed and the size of the grounds also ensured that once he was inside, he'd go unnoticed.

Occupation/ employment:	Blue collar. Could be involved in some sort of security work—feels like he "polices" something and now "policing" authors. Other possibility is a rival author— perhaps published but more likely unpublished.
Marital status:	Recently separated—something sparked him into action four months ago, and relationship breakup is most likely. A job loss is also the possible trigger.
Dependents:	He either has children himself or has children he's close to (e.g., nieces and nephews). It's his sense of protecting these children from the dangers of the world that's making him take action against crime-fiction authors.

Childhood:	Something happened in his early years that led to an overdeveloped sense of justice. That was kept in check for many years and probably only released through his job (security, shop manager or similar), until a trauma roughly four months ago left him needing more control over his life and with a sense of needing to take action. That was soon channeled into crime-fiction author Lorie Rickardian.
Personality:	Loner. Competent socially, but prefers one-on-one situations to groups.
Disabilities:	None.

Interaction with victims:	Rickardian: He chose a low-profile author in Rickardian, possibly because he wanted to "practice" or because he wanted to silence her early in her career, before she could write more books he'd see as "damaging" society. Killing her at such close range was personal, although he struck her from behind and didn't have to see her face. Black: He wanted Black to pay for her words, pay for her career as a crime author. Although he was really only following a script, set up by Black herself, he did take control of the situation and openly confronted her while she was tied to that chair. He used this time, before the murder, to punish Black further, quite possibly through verbal abuse, much like the killer did in Black's book.

Remorse:	Rickardian: Felt some remorse for her—hit her over the head, but from behind, because he couldn't face her while he killed her. She then landed facedown, which was less confrontational for him. Black: No remorse. Murder, post-mortem posing and mutilation are evidence of this, especially given she was lying faceup with her eyes open. While this replicated her book, if the perpetrator felt remorse he would have felt compelled to close her eyes or cover her in some way, deviating from the "script."
Home life:	Lives alone, in a simple manner—basic apartment or small house.
Car:	Older sedan—sensible car. Our guy's not about flashiness, rather he sees himself as sensible, and he believes in an ordered and logical society. Most probably American model.

Intelligence:	High IQ, but not as high as many organized serial killers. He's copying someone else's ideas rather than creating the MOs and signatures himself.
Education level:	Definitely high-school educated and could be partially college educated.
Outward appearance:	Blends into his surroundings—again, he likes things plain and simple. During the murders he's playing the part of vigilante/redeemer, but would dress in clothes that wouldn't bring attention.
Criminal background:	No criminal record. He's been sent over the edge recently and is killing for punishment/fanaticism.
Modus operandi (MO):	Chooses his victim and then uses their book and the MOs they create as his script. However, he didn't rape Black, like in her book. This probably indicates an inability to perform sexually, or is a factor in escalation (nightdress raised for Rickardian, Black's genitalia exposed and her breasts mutilated, and his next victim may be sexually assaulted pre- or postmortem).

Signature:	His signature is the presence of something from the victims' fictional worlds at the real crime scene. His personal touch, the writing, is also a signature element, as it's something he can't leave the crime scene without doing.
Post-offensive behavior:	Rickardian: Some staging elements to make it look like a robbery (taking the cash), plus he cleaned up any potential forensic evidence (footprint near kitchen window). Black: Detailed posing, as per Black's fictional book *Ladykiller*. The mutilation was also carried out postmortem. He wanted to deface her sexually, but didn't feel the need to torture her while she was alive.
Media tactics:	Fine line… Media coverage will draw attention to the killer's cause (punishment of the authors), which is something he wants. However, too much media or not enough may incite him to kill again, or sooner. Link with Rickardian should be hidden from media for the time being until we see what leads turn up.

Eleven

The kung-fu class has about twenty advanced students, including four women, which is quite a high ratio in martial arts. I watch as they finish their warm-up with a hundred crunches and eighty push-ups. This school is close to my new apartment, and it's tiger and crane kung fu, the same style I used to study in Melbourne—perfect. Plus the instructor, Sifu Lee, comes highly recommended. While the Bureau does train us in hand-to-hand combat and self-defense, I took it upon myself years ago to start kung fu. I'd been part of the Victoria Police for a few years, and was keen to move up the ranks and start working some more challenging cases. But I felt like I needed an edge, particularly given that any potential confrontation I'd have on the street was more likely to be with a man, someone who would be physically stronger than me. I haven't really had to use my kung-fu training on the job yet, but I love the classes and find it reassuring to know the moves are there if I need them. It's also great exercise and a good way to release the day's tension—and you need an outlet in this job.

After the warm-up, Lee moves the class on to forms,

which are sequences of movements drawing on different stances, blocks, punches, kicks and so on in a simulated fight sequence. The forms can be done at a variety of speeds, including incredibly slowly, so the movements resemble Tai Chi more than kung fu. I love doing the forms this slowly, as they become meditative and I can forget about the horrors of murder and rape.

Next, the class moves on to punching drills for fifteen minutes, before splitting up into groups based on their levels. The rest of the class is spent on punches and strikes within the person's level before Sifu Lee brings the group together again for a five-minute cooldown. After the class I talk to Lee and arrange to join the club, starting with my first class tomorrow night.

It's nearly 10:00 p.m. by the time I get home, and I'm starving. I had a quick snack on the plane, knowing I wouldn't get time to have dinner before watching the class, but it's not enough to tide me over, and with my stomach making enough noise to wake the dead, I've got no chance of sleeping. I resist the urge to order a pizza and go for the healthy alternative instead—one poached egg on rye toast. It only takes me a few minutes to bring a small saucepan of water to the boil and, once I've added a little vinegar, I crack in the egg and count to one hundred before fishing it out and placing it on the toast. I dig in and give myself a metaphoric high five for the show of willpower. Once I'm finished eating, I fire up my laptop to make the final touches on the profile.

When I arrive at work the next morning, there's a parcel on my desk—two copies of Rickardian's book, which arrived yesterday while I was in San Fran. I undo the packaging, but decide to get the profile off to Sorrell, Dusk, O'Shaughnessy and Perez before I start flicking through the book. The profile isn't as concrete as I'd like, but with the differences between Rickardian and Black in MO and victim interaction, I've had to be necessarily brief in some areas. I've also drawn on the two letters and their judgmental tones to draft the profile, so if our fan isn't the killer, the profile will need some major revisions. I explain all this in the e-mail and I've barely hit Send before the phone's ringing.

"Good, you're in." It's Sorrell.

"Good morning, Detective," I say. "I've just sent you the profile."

"Uh-huh." He seems totally disinterested. "Have you seen the paper this morning?"

"Paper?" I say hesitantly, already guessing what this morning's edition must cover. "Did they lead with it?"

"No, but it is front page, just below the headline about that train crash in New York."

"Damn." I sigh. "I'll go rustle up a copy. Tell me there was no mention of the message at the crime scenes."

"No, we've still got that. The headline is Black The Second Author To Die, and the article talks about the two authors and their murders."

"It was only a matter of time before someone linked the crimes. As long as we've got the killer's message up our sleeves the rest doesn't matter. I'll call you back about the article soon."

"Hold on…guess who wrote it." Sorrell's voice is more theatrical than normal, and that can mean only one thing….

"Randy Sade."

"Yup." He pauses. "I've got more. Good news this time. We got forensics back on the fiber the pathologist found in Black's hair. It's thirty percent wool and seventy percent polyester, in line with a sweater."

I imagine the killer standing over Black, strangling her, his jumper close to her hair. "I wonder if Sade owns a beige sweater."

"We don't have enough for a search warrant. Not yet," Sorrell says. "You're still on for Black's funeral?"

"Funeral?" Then I remember—a 4:00 p.m. service and 6:00 p.m. for drinks and food. "Damn, I forgot all about it."

It's common practice during a homicide investigation for the cops and other investigators to attend the funeral. It's amazing how often a killer visits his victims' graves or attends their funerals, sinking into the background. We'll have a crime-scene photographer or two on hand to photograph all the mourners, but sometimes being there in person can tip you off to the person who's crying too much or not enough. Guilt takes many forms.

"See you there at four?" Sorrell asks.

My only real commitment is my first kung-fu class tonight, which I can reschedule. But the thought of a funeral makes me balk—I'm scared of what I might see if I'm that close to Black's body again. "Yeah, I'll be there." I force the fear out of my voice and quickly change the subject. "What's the latest with the fan mail?"

"The last six months of letters are all with the crime lab. They're scanning copies and sending them through to us today, before they start examining them. Black's computer is with forensics too."

"Great. I've got Rickardian's fan letters on me. I'll get them couriered to the lab so they can add them to their evidence."

"We could hook up at the lab this morning. Then you

could personally deliver the Rickardian letters and we can see how they're going with Black's stuff."

"Sounds good. The sooner I can review those letters the better. And I've got your copy of Rickardian's book too."

"How's an hour?"

"Done."

He pauses. "We'll definitely be assembling a task force soon."

"So your boss is in favor?"

"Yup, he's on board. What about Brady?"

"I spoke to him briefly about it yesterday on the phone and he asked me to put together an e-mail about the cases and my recommendations for the task force. I did that from San Francisco late yesterday afternoon."

"He wants the paper trail."

"I guess."

"Brady likes his procedures."

I smile. "That wouldn't surprise me, going by his desk."

Sorrell laughs, a deep chuckle, and it startles me. "He's a neat freak," he says, and then his laughter stops as abruptly as it started. "Don't suppose the profile fits Sade, Werner or anyone else in the Black family?"

"Not really, no. But for the moment I've drafted the profile using the letters as part of the evidence, and if they turn out to be unrelated, I'll need to revise it."

"So we should still keep our minds open?"

"Always."

This time Sorrell actually says goodbye before hanging up. I must be making progress with the man.

It only takes me five minutes to locate a copy of this morning's edition of the *Los Angeles Times* in our office. I read through the article on my way to Brady's office, managing to miss most obstacles as I read and walk. When I was a kid I once walked into a tree when I was reading and, until the X-rays came back, the doctor suspected I'd broken my jaw. Guess it pays to watch where you're going.

"You saw it?"

I look up to see Melissa, a cup of coffee in hand, sliding in behind her desk.

"Yeah. Sorrell just told me." I flip to page twenty, where the article continues. "Is Brady in?" I try to keep the nervousness out of my voice. I'm not sure if Melissa knows about my procedural stuff-up with the Black case, and regardless I'm still uneasy about Brady. I hate it that we got off on the wrong foot.

"Sure is." She sits down, and her hand hovers over the phone. "You want to see him?"

"Give me a few seconds. I just want to finish this." I linger in the hallway and finish reading. I'm relieved to find there's nothing that will harm our investigation. Although it will mean the number of calls we get about the case will go through the roof.

"Okay," I say, looking up at Melissa.

She calls Brady using the phone as an intercom and announces that I'm here to see him.

"Send her in." His voice is stern. I take a deep breath and am barely in the door when Brady says, "Well?" He's looking at the paper.

Straight down to business is the best tactic. "It was only a matter of time before the murders were linked. It's all public knowledge, sir."

"And its effect on the case?"

"It won't harm us, sir. But I do think we need to talk to the media formally. Just so we have some control over what information gets to the public."

He gives me a curt nod. "I'll call our media officer, Jan Logan, so she can weigh in on this too."

As a profiler, I deal with how our responses to the media could affect the perpetrator, not how it could affect the FBI's public face. "From my point of view, now that the murders have been linked in the media, the killer will be watching what's reported carefully. Better to drip-feed real information than let the media create a frenzy of misinformation." Although it's probable both will happen.

"Take a seat, Anderson."

I read the article again while Brady gets the FBI's official media line from Logan. I try not to listen to the conversation, but it's hard when I'm in the same room.

He's only on the phone for a couple of minutes before he hangs up. "Okay, let's do this."

I already knew the end result from listening to one side of the conversation, but I nod my agreement anyway. "You'll run it?"

"Joint. It'll be me and Chief Saunders from Beverly Hills PD. Assuming he agrees."

"He will, won't he?"

"Yeah—formality, really. I'm going to try to hook it up for later this morning."

I fold the newspaper. "I might have updated information for you if you can hold off until, say, eleven or twelve. I'm meeting Sorrell at the crime lab in an hour."

"Fine. I'll talk to Chief Saunders and then get Jan and Melissa to set up the media conference. I'll make sure you're notified of the final time." He speaks quickly, but I'm not sure if that's his usual tone or an indication that I'm still not his favorite employee.

"Thank you, sir."

Back at my desk I call Sorrell to tell him about the media conference.

"Now that's good news. And it'll mean more people to

help us out. They may even announce a hotline, and that means they'll have to staff it."

"You can never say no to extra resources," I say. "So Saunders will give the go-ahead."

"Sure. He has to respond after that article. And a joint announcement will be good for public perception."

"Beverly Hills PD and FBI working together, like one big, happy family."

"You said it." He pauses for a second. "Gotta go."

Bang, dial tone.

I shake my head, but despite the bad bedside manner, I can't help but like Sorrell. He's professional and thorough, and obviously very dedicated to his work—all good qualities in my book. And while he's not as easy to work with as some colleagues, things could be worse—he could have O'Shaughnessy's charm…or Benson's.

I'm still holding the phone, thinking of the other call I need to make. Today's shaping up to be a busy one, to say the least, and before Black's funeral I've got to call Detective Darren Carter, the only person in the world who knows about my psychic abilities.

For extra privacy, and because I'm plain running out of time, I call him from my car phone on the way to the lab.

He picks up after one ring. "Detective Carter."

"Hi, Darren. It's Soph."

"Sophie, hi. How are you settling in?" His voice is warm and engaged, as it always is when we talk, reminding me how lucky I am to have him in my life.

"Getting there. The apartment's unpacked but I've been thrown in the deep end at work. I'm on the Black case."

"Ah, yes, the famous crime writer. A nice way to make your mark in a new town," he teases.

"Yeah, I'm thrilled." I force as much sarcasm into my voice as possible.

He chuckles.

"Merge in one hundred feet."

I glance at the navigator system on the dashboard and see that I'm supposed to be merging onto the I-405S. I see the sign and change lanes.

"Where are you off to?" Darren asks.

"Sorry about that. On my way to the crime lab, and I haven't been there before so we'll have to put up with the computerized voice interrupting us every now and again."

"Sure."

I merge onto the freeway and the navigation system tells me to continue for 1.7 miles.

I could chat to Darren the whole way without bringing up the real reason I'm calling him, but I don't. Instead I get straight to the point. "I'm going to Black's funeral this afternoon."

"I see."

Silence.

"And you're worried." Darren's voice is soft and reassuring, as is the fact that he knows exactly what I'm worried about.

"Uh-huh," I say, recalling the case four months ago when a victim's…spirit…came to me in one of my visions. I don't even really believe in ghosts…at least I didn't until a few months ago. I've managed to gain some control over my visions, but if Black's spirit comes to me, I might not be able to control that. I know it, and Darren knows it too. "So, any words of wisdom?"

"Do you *want* to see her?"

"I don't know." Being at Black's funeral will be as inappropriate a setting as they come—I'll be officially on duty and supposed to have my wits about me, plus Sorrell will be there, the press will probably be there and so will a host of strangers. They'll all be potential witnesses to my response, which at the very least will be me looking distracted and at the worst could be me going down for the count. "I'm willing to see anything I can that will help me find Black's killer, but I just don't see me getting any privacy whatsoever. This funeral will be packed."

"You might not have a choice."

"I know." I bite my lip. "Did your aunt ever talk about this?"

Darren's aunt was a professional psychic and helped him out on cases from time to time—until one killer decided to take her out. Maybe that's part of the attraction between Darren and me: we both lost someone we loved at the hands of a killer.

"You're most likely to see Black where she died. After that, usually it's her home, then the funeral."

"Well, I got nothing at the murder scene, which was also her home."

"That's strange." He pauses. "But it doesn't mean it won't happen at the funeral."

"Great." My stomach clenches at the thought of what I might see. "Strategies?"

"Want me to fly up?"

I laugh. "Darren, that's got to be the sweetest offer ever, but I can't get you to hold my hand every time I might see something that scares me."

"I wouldn't mind."

I can imagine his tentative smile on the other end of the phone, and the dimples puckering at his cheeks. I'd love to see him, but it's not practical. He's got his cases, and God knows I'm more than busy with Black's and Rickardian's murders.

"Thanks, Darren, but I need to do this myself."

"The killer might be there." There's a hint of concern in his voice, but he's smart enough to know how I'd respond if he became too protective.

"Maybe Loretta Black will point him out to me." Even though Darren can't see my smile, he'll know from my tone of voice that I'm not serious.

"Sounds like you've got it all worked out."

I laugh. "That's me." But I know it doesn't work like that. Often all I get is vague flashes or symbols, and it's like putting together a jigsaw puzzle. With one missing person case I profiled a month ago, the only new thing I got from my gift was an image of a dog. It didn't mean anything to me at the time and there was no mention of the victim having a dog, nor was there anything at the crime scene to indicate a dog was present. It certainly wasn't something I could work into my profile. Then, three weeks after I completed the profile, they found the missing person, dead, and the body was in a stream behind an English-style pub called The Old Dog. Unless I'd been walking past the damn pub, *that* interpretation would never have occurred to me.

"Merge in one hundred feet." Again, I glance down at the on-screen map to check the upcoming turnoff, this time onto the I-10E, heading west toward downtown L.A.

"Are you sure, Sophie? I can probably get a flight out and make it in time."

"Thanks, but no."

He doesn't respond straightaway, perhaps wondering how many times he should offer. Finally he says, "Tell me how it goes?"

"Of course."

"And don't be a stranger. We're much closer now than when you were in Quantico." He pauses. "Maybe I can come up for a visit?"

The last part of Darren's sentence is cut off by the navigation system telling me to continue on this road for eight miles.

"Sorry, I did hear that. And it'd be really nice to see you, Darren."

"We've got Heath Jordan's pretrial conference on Monday. Want to come down this weekend and hang around for that?"

"I'll probably still be working Black's murder," I say. "How's everything going with Jordan anyway?"

"You know. The usual."

It's been four months since we arrested Heath Jordan, the president of the Murderers' Club, for murder, kidnapping, conspiracy to murder, conspiracy to kidnap and unlawful imprisonment, plus a whole host of other charges relating to his use of the Internet to facilitate his crimes. Both California and Arizona had wanted to prosecute, but in the end Arizona won that battle—after all, that's where the bodies were found. I flew back to Tucson for the preliminary hearing soon after Jordan was charged, and the judge found probable cause and held Jordan over for trial. And the beauty of conspiracy charges is that all of the defendants are judged for the sins of one, so Jordan and Picking—NeverCaught—will stand trial together for their roles in the Murderers' Club. Their lawyers have petitioned for separate trials, but without any success so far. The only surviving member of the Club who won't be sitting as a defendant with Jordan and Picking is Brooke Woods, aka BlackWidow. The Arizona D.A. cut a deal that will keep her in prison and away from the lethal injection. She's still been charged with the same crimes, but the death penalty is off the table and she's been promised a separate trial. She's even managed to escape the death penalty for all the murders she committed before she became part of the online scheme. She got a good deal, all right, but at the time we didn't have Picking and we needed testimony from someone in that club.

"Will Jordan try to cut a deal?" I ask, knowing that often the pretrial conference is all about negotiation.

"Probably. But he won't get it."

"Good."

I hear a woman's voice in the background, and recognize it as Stone's, Darren's partner.

"Hold on, Soph." It's a minute or so before he comes back on to the phone line. "Sorry, Stone's been looking for me. I've gotta go. Let's talk in a couple of days in case you can come down to Arizona."

"Will do. And thanks for the words of wisdom."

"I don't know about wisdom, but I'm here if you need anything."

"Thanks, Darren. You're a great friend." But as soon as I say it I regret it, knowing that Darren wants to be much more than friends.

Twelve

Just as I pull up at the Scientific Services Bureau on West Beverly Boulevard, my cell rings. It's been a busy morning.

"Special Agent Anderson."

"You didn't call." The voice is male and is playacting at being offended.

"Sorry?"

"Dinner."

My mind makes the mental leaps, trying to work out who could be calling me about dinner. Then I realize who this is. "Oh, hello, Mr. Reid." I'd normally tell Reid I was busy, but that would be pretty rude after the guy sent me flowers. Not to mention that he gave me the lead that busted NeverCaught.

"Please, call me Justin."

"Okay, Justin," I say, but don't invite him to call me Sophie. "Thanks for the flowers."

"You liked them?"

"Of course, they're beautiful."

"But you didn't call for dinner."

"No." I sigh. "But you are in San Francisco and I'm in L.A."

"You know I could be there in an hour." He manages to deliver the claim without any hint of arrogance. Via his chopper or personal jet, he could be here pretty damn fast. "I've been waiting for your call," he says.

I laugh. "Somehow I can't imagine you waiting by the phone."

"Okay, I've been hoping." His voice is thick with flirtation.

"I'm actually running late for an appointment, Justin." I glance at my watch. Five past nine.

"Of course. I'll let you go. But I will call you back." Again, the flirtation.

"Okay. I'll speak to you then," I respond politely. "Goodbye." I hang up my phone and sigh. Sounds like he's going to be persistent.

When I finally get inside, Sorrell's waiting for me in the reception area.

"Sorry I'm late."

He shrugs. "Only a few minutes. Renee Watts oversees the document-examination area and she's on her way down now."

I nod and hover near the reception desk with him. Watts is obviously our centralized contact for all the document work, and she'll liaise with the actual lab techs. A couple of minutes go by before a woman in her late twenties to early thirties comes out of the elevator. She's a couple of inches shorter than me, and carries an extra twenty or so pounds, mostly around her middle and face. Tight blond curls are held back by a red silk scarf, which matches her red pants. A loose cream shirt falls just low enough to cover most of her hips and butt.

"Hi, Renee." Sorrell shakes her hand. "This is Special Agent Sophie Anderson. She's the new profiler for the Bureau here."

Renee Watts holds out her hand and we give each other a smile and a firm handshake. On the way up in the elevator, she comments on the accent, and I do my best to dispel a long-standing myth when she asks me if I had a pet kangaroo. There were lots of kangaroos in Shepparton, where I grew up, but I focus on my later childhood in Melbourne, which was kangaroo-free. And I don't tell her about the kangaroo found in Melbourne several years ago. It was spotted by office lunchgoers in Flagstaff Gardens, right in the heart of the city center. Who knows how it got there.

On the third floor, Watts leads us into a meeting room and gets down to business. "We only just got started on this."

"Yes, of course," I say, acknowledging that although it's been a few days since Black's murder, the document and computer evidence wasn't officially gathered until Monday, and one full day, Tuesday, in a lab as busy as L.A.'s, is nothing.

I fish the sealed evidence bag out of my briefcase and hand it over to Watts. "These are the letters Lorie Rickardian, the San Francisco victim, received before her death. I'd like them reviewed as part of Black's case." Although the chain of custody is a more unusual one—from Emily Rickardian in San Francisco to me to the L.A. crime lab—it remains unbroken because I've sealed the evidence and kept it on my person.

Watts takes the evidence bag from me. "Did you get a chance to fill out the log form?"

"Oh yes, sorry." I take that out of my bag and pass it to Watts. She reads over the details before taking a sticky layer off the back of the form and adhering the documentation to the evidence bag. She carefully places it to one side.

"Okay." She smiles. "So I've got a PDF file of the compiled letters, ready to e-mail to you guys if you still want it."

"Thanks, Watts," Sorrell says. "It'd still be good to have that, even though we'll look through some of the originals this morning."

"I'll send it as soon as we're done here." She opens an extremely large two-ring binder with dividers and flicks it open to the first section. "So, using the scanned letters, we've done a search on the suspect words *murder, love, stocking, panty hose, love heart, strangulation* and *kill,* but we got a lot of hits on these, given the content of Black's books. We also searched for swearwords and all the different expressions for female genitalia. One hundred and eighty-eight out of the three hundred and twenty letters contained one or more of the words. These are copies of the letters that came up with matches." She hands us a wad from the top. "They're ordered in terms of the most hits."

Each letter has been reproduced on standard printer paper, and the suspect words are highlighted in red. I flick through the top few pages, but nothing immediately catches my eye. Most of the references seem to be to the plot of *Lovers' Lane,* Black's book before *Ladykiller.* Makes sense that the last six months of letters would be focused on her second-last book. I'll add the letters to my reading pile, along with Rickardian's book.

I hand the letters back to Watts, who puts them back in place. "Court's team is starting a fingerprint analysis on the letters today."

Once every single fingerprint has been lifted from the letters and then scanned into the computer, they'll be run against AFIS, the Automated Fingerprint Identification System. But a match will only happen if the person who sent the letter has been arrested before, or belongs to one of the many government agencies that take compulsory fingerprints of their employees. Given that I don't think the killer has a criminal record, unless we're lucky enough that he works for the United States Postal Service or was in the armed forces, or something similar, we won't get a match. But the prints will act as an important cross-reference point once we've got a suspect in custody—then they could be damning evidence.

"Only latents, I take it?" A latent fingerprint is transferred onto a surface because of the oils and salts in our skin. They are generally invisible to the eye, but can be seen when an object or surface is dusted. The other two types of fingerprints are patent prints, which are clearly visible because they've been made in a substance like blood or ink, and impressed prints, which occur when a fingerprint is indented into a malleable surface like gum or wax. It's possible, although highly unlikely, that a patent print or at least a partial patent print may be on one of the letters if ink leaked or spilled. An impressed print would only be present if the writer used a wax seal. But in our case, Holt didn't keep any of the envelopes, so we've got nothing like that. The lack of envelopes also means we can't test them for DNA, which would normally be present if the sender licked the envelope to seal it.

"They looked at all the documents quickly—no patents," replies Watts.

I nod. "Do you know how long the fingerprints will take?"

"They have to fume each letter, so I guess it will be a few days, but you'll have to check with Court to verify that."

The most common method for lifting latent prints on paper is fuming using superglue, a cyanoacrylate. The letter is suspended in an airtight container, and once the superglue reaches its boiling point of just over 120°F, chemicals in the fumes attach to the print, building up a white substance. The paper can then be dusted with black or colored powders, photographed and digitized for database comparison in AFIS. It is a lengthy, multistage process and each letter could contain many prints, including the writer's, Holt's and Black's.

"What about the e-mails?" Sorrell asks.

"You'll have to check with the computer guys about any leads, but they did give us printouts." Watts opens the other binder she carries. "These are printouts of all the e-mails over the past six months. Five hundred and forty-five in total. Again, they've been compiled and sorted by occurrence of key words, and then alphabetically by the sender's e-mail address. I believe our computer guys are checking out all the addresses and flagging any unusual ones plus all public accounts like Yahoo and Hotmail."

Our killer is an organized offender, so he should be smart enough not to use a personal e-mail, which means if he did e-mail Black it would have been through a public e-mail service. But it's the letters I'd like to see, because the originals might tell us something. For example, if colored or patterned paper was used, that might be the killer's way of drawing attention to himself and trying to make his letter stand out. I'm also going to be very interested in any critical or abusive letters, besides the one from our fan. We need to look at all the letters to make sure we don't develop tunnel vision in the case. Any negative letters could be the first time our vigilante spoke out, before he decided to take action. Holt also mentioned that "A fan" was a repeat letter writer, so I'll certainly be looking for any previous letters from him and looking for any changes in the tone. In fact, I'll need to ask Holt about letters pre-dating the six-month mark. Ideally we'd submit all letters from the last twelve months, or longer, to the lab, but the resources just aren't there, not when Black got so much fan mail. It'll be hard enough getting through what we've got so far.

"It'd be good to have a look at some of the original letters now, Watts. If that's okay with you?" I say.

"Sure." She stands up. "Prints are probably working on them as we speak." Watts leads us through several security doors until we reach a glassed area with four separate labs. The glass gives the impression of a more spacious working environment, something I'm sure the technicians appreciate. Watts takes us into one of these mini-offices, where two lab techs are at work on the Black letters. One of the lab techs is a woman, and one a man. The fuming process is underway, with one letter held firmly inside the chamber. While the woman stands over the slightly smoky chamber, the man is dusting another letter with black particles. They both pause momentarily as we enter.

"Court, McAvey, you know Detective Sorrell, and this is Special Agent Anderson from the Bureau. They're working on the Black case."

Court, the woman and head of the department, stands

up from the chamber and shakes our hands. "Yes, I saw your names on the request."

McAvey looks up and gives us a nod, but decides not to interrupt the delicate brushing process. "Sorry, I'll just finish up this one." He continues lightly brushing the letter with the black dust before taking close-up photographs. "About ten prints on this one," he says.

"All different?" Sorrell can't keep the shock out of his voice.

McAvey shrugs his shoulders. "Don't know yet." He smiles. "I'll take a closer look at them on the computer. We've recovered prints from at least two different individuals off your first five letters so far, though."

"And how many letters?" Sorrell's pointing out the math rather than asking for a reminder of how many letters there are. He knows that detail. Over three hundred letters will give us at least six hundred prints. Presumably one on each letter will be Holt's, but even with that duplication, you're still talking well over three hundred prints. Pre-computers, analyzing that many prints for one case just wouldn't have been possible. Thank God for the computer age.

McAvey moves over and shakes our hands while Court turns back to the fuming process and adjusts a knob.

"How long do you think it will be?" I ask, looking at the setup.

"It'll be another day or two lifting the prints manually, but we'll run them against AFIS as we go and feed you any matches as they come through."

Computers make the search process fast. A print can be run against the complete AFIS database in minutes. It's the human component of actually getting the print in the first place and then digitizing it that takes the time.

"We'd like to have a look at some of the letters while we're here," I say.

"Sure." McAvey goes over to one of the desks and pulls out two sets of gloves, then gathers a thick folder full of evidence bags in his other hand. "We've only processed a few so far, so this is most of them."

I take the folder and one set of gloves, and McAvey holds the other set out to Sorrell.

"There's a room through here you can use," McAvey says, already starting to lead the way.

But Sorrell lingers. "Anything on the prints at the murder scene?" he asks Court.

"Yeah, I finished them off about ten minutes ago." Court types the case's ID number into her computer. "Here it is." She clicks on something on the computer screen. "There were a total of eleven different prints on scene, and one unaccounted."

Under Sorrell's guidance, the police would have collected prints from Werner, Holt, all the household staff and anyone else at the murder scene. These prints, in addition to fingerprints from Black herself, would have been passed on to the lab and compared against those found at the crime scene. The fact that they found one unaccounted print could mean it was left by the killer, or it could simply mean there's one person who was in the house legitimately but wasn't on our list.

"And there was no match in AFIS."

"So we might have the killer's fingerprint," I say with a smile.

"Yup. We'll need to rule out a few more people first, like the family." Sorrell looks at Court. "Thanks." He starts moving again.

The room McAvey leads us to is small, only large

enough for a meeting of two or three, but it serves our purpose.

"I'll take some of the letters so we can keep processing them on our end," McAvey says, holding out his hand.

I pass him a small wad of plastic-sheathed letters before he leaves. With our hands gloved, Sorrell and I start cautiously examining the letters. Given that each letter has been carefully placed in a clear plastic covering sheet, the gloves really only serve as a backup for cross-contamination.

The letters come in all shapes and sizes. Some are on writing paper, some simply on lined notepad paper, and others have been typed and printed out on standard printer paper. And they also vary from only being a few lines, to one letter that's eight pages long and goes into detailed analysis of Black's books. Most of the letters are what I'd expect of fan mail—simply congratulating Black on a particular book or all of her books. But a few letters stray from that theme. Out of our batch of one hundred and ninety-eight, there are only five that can be described as hate mail, but they seem to be randomly targeting someone in the spotlight. Still, I put these five documents aside for priority forensics, and will also get the four that are handwritten analyzed by a writing expert.

"This is the one Holt was worried about," says Sorrell, holding up the original, which is typed on cream printer paper. He reads it out: "'I read the latest George Benson novel with both fascination and repulsion. While the killer was fantastic and inventive, I think you've taken it too far. All you authors these days are committing horrible crimes against our society. What if someone read your work and was "inspired" to act? To kill? Think about our youth. Your stories give them a terrible, terrible role model to follow, maybe terrible, terrible ideas. Do you want to be responsible for some poor woman's murder? You seem to be able to capture the heart and soul of a killer. Do you know what it's like to feel a person's life literally in your hands? To have the power to drain their blood, ounce by ounce? And the way your victims' legs are spread is such an exciting and suggestive concept for a man. Do you know how strong that imagery can be for us? How powerful the desire to see a woman laid out like that is? Your words could make someone act. You must stop writing this filth. It can only bring you pain, believe you me. Yours sincerely, A fan.'"

"I wonder if he's talking about *Ladykiller*," I say.

Sorrell shrugs. "No date on the letter, but he does talk about the spread legs."

"True. Holt told me the letter was recent, but she didn't mention if it was in the last few days or weeks." I pause. "Werner said they'd discussed it a couple of *weeks* ago over dinner."

"So maybe the killer had an early copy of the book."

Most organized killers plan their murders for weeks, if not months, rather than days. "Maybe we should be looking at anyone who had early copies."

Sorrell nods. "Like people at the publishing house, the media, that sort of thing."

"I wonder if Sade got a copy." Something about Sade makes me suspicious, even though he doesn't fit the profile.

"That would be interesting."

"Yup. Who knows how many people had access to the manuscript or finished book before its official release date? Let's call the publishers now. Especially given it may affect how we look at these letters."

Sorrell nods. "We may as well confirm the letter's timing with Holt first. The date the letter arrived needs to be as accurate as possible."

I give Holt a call. "Debbie, it's Sophie. Just a quick one."

"Yes?"

"We're looking into that letter some more, and it would really help us if we knew exactly when you received it."

"I think it was a couple of weeks ago."

"Can you be more specific?"

"Hold on a sec, I'll just check my diary."

Less than a minute passes before she comes back on the phone. "Okay, it was two weeks ago today. We talked about the letter at dinner that night, and I just double-checked the dinner reservation in my diary."

I nod…Werner's dinner conversation.

"Thanks, Debbie. I'll speak to you later." Holt says goodbye and we hang up.

"Well?" Sorrell says.

"She got it ten days before Black's murder. So who had the book a week and a half before its official release date?"

Sorrell takes his gloves off and fishes his notebook out of his inside pocket. He flips back a few pages. "Laura Cue, acquiring editor," he says, tapping his finger on his notebook.

"Dusk and I were talking about the possibility of the killer being a rival author, maybe even an unpublished one."

"Yes?"

"While we've got Cue on the phone, I'll ask her about the process for unsuccessful manuscripts."

Sorrell leans to one side to access his pants pocket and, phone in hand, stands up before dialing the number. Once he's got Laura Cue on the other end, he puts his phone on speaker and holds it out between us. With his height, he has to hunch right over, so I stand up, allowing him to straighten out almost fully. He'll thank me when he's seventy.

"I've got Special Agent Anderson from the FBI with me too."

"Hi, Laura," I say, having already spoken to Laura once when I was completing the victim profile of Black.

"Hi." Her voice is crackly, and no doubt the poor reception is because we're in the middle of an office building. "What can I do for you?"

Sorrell takes the lead.

"We're trying to find out the exact date *Ladykiller* would have been available in bookstores or online, and who might have had a copy before the launch date."

"We aim to fill all orders with both online suppliers and bookstores about two to three weeks before the official pub date. In the case of bookstores, it allows them to unpack the boxes and arrange their shelves at their own pace. They're not supposed to put it out before the official release date, but some do."

"How far before?"

"Couple of days, maybe a week or more—unless you're talking Harry Potter, which is much more carefully monitored than most books."

It's cutting it fine, but it does give our fan enough time to read the book, write the letter and then commit the murder.

Cue continues, "Then you've got your preorders. Some booksellers will fill preorders as soon as the stock arrives, others will wait until the official release date."

"Like how far before?"

"Again, they're not supposed to ship before the release date, but I have heard of readers getting their books a couple of weeks before, especially if they preorder online."

I roll my eyes. What a logistical nightmare to track. "Obviously you've got records of who stocked *Ladykiller*."

She gives kind of a snort, in between a laugh and a groan. "Sure, we've got the records, but you're talking…" She pauses. "Hold on, I'll just look it up." About a minute goes by, and during that time we can hear Cue tapping on her keyboard. "Okay, our sales reps had orders for three million copies of *Ladykiller*. And that's for August alone."

I hold back a groan. "To how many stores or online retailers?"

Again, more tapping before she says, "One thousand, two hundred and sixty-six."

"Oh, man." Sorrell shakes his head.

"Any way of telling how many sold up to last Saturday, when Black was killed?"

"There's BookScan, but it only gives you about sixty percent of the total because it doesn't include every bookstore. The BookScan figure as of Saturday was—" more tapping "—six hundred and fifty-four thousand, four hundred and fifty-two copies. Other than that you'd have to check with each individual store."

It's so depressing I almost want to laugh. Instead I move us on to the next question. "And we assume the press get advance copies?"

"Yes, that's right. We send out over one hundred copies to newspapers, magazines, radio stations and other reviewers."

"When would those have gone out?" I ask.

"Months ago. We have to give them time to read it and write their review before our release date. And in the case of magazines, they're usually closing off copy two or more months before their on-sale date."

Sorrell and I exchange a frustrated look, but he writes it all down.

"Was Randy Sade of the *Los Angeles Times* on that list?" he asks.

"I'm not sure. Maybe. I'd have to check with publicity."

"We'll need to see that list. Can you e-mail it to me?" Sorrell gives Cue his e-mail address.

"And who else would have read *Ladykiller* before it was released?" I ask.

"Well…there's a few of us here, obviously. Me, a freelance copy editor we use, my boss and a freelance proofreader. The desktop publishers don't actually read the work, but the designers would have known the basic plot for some time, given the cover's usually done about six months before release. Who else?" she asks herself that, and then pauses, thinking. "Her publicist, our marketing director and then, of course, her agent, her husband, Holt and anyone else Loretta may have passed it on to, like family, friends or her sources."

"That's it?" Sorrell's voice edges on sarcasm, and I guess it's his attempt at it.

When both Sorrell and Cue are silent for a few seconds, I broach the subject of unpublished authors.

"Laura, we're also looking at the possibility of an unpublished author targeting Loretta and Lorie Rickardian. How many books do you get sent for consideration?"

She whistles. "Lots. Although our policy is only agented authors, so that cuts it down some."

"What sort of numbers are we talking?"

"Several hundred a month."

I give Sorrell an exasperated look. "Were there any that stood out in terms of being particularly disturbing? That seem to have been written by someone who was extremely angry?"

"No. That sort of stuff wouldn't get past an agent."

"What about strange responses to rejections? Authors who took it personally?"

She's silent, thinking. "Not exactly. But since you mentioned Randy Sade, his agent did send in his manuscript a while back."

"He's written a book?" I ask. Sade mentioned the idea of a serial-killer taxi driver, but he didn't say he'd actually written that book, or any other.

"Yes."

"Is it the idea he was suing Black over? The taxi driver?"

"No. It's about an investigative journalist who gets drawn into organized crime in L.A."

"Any good?" Sorrell asks.

"Yeah. We were close to publishing it, but I knew about Loretta's history with Sade. The court case was still happening so I decided to speak to her about it. She made it clear that if we signed Sade, we'd lose her. The choice was easy."

"A debut author or a known bestseller." I verbalize the obvious. "How did he respond to the rejection?"

"Not well. He rang me once a week for a couple of months, leaving messages demanding to know if it was because of Black. It was difficult."

"Fair enough." I move back to other prospective

authors. "Did any other rejected authors threaten you, or send you strange letters?"

"No. Nothing like that. Like I said, we deal mostly with the agents and once we say no, that's it."

We finish up with Cue and call Rickardian's publisher, but it's the same story—lots of rejections but no over-the-top reactions.

"Sade's life sure is mixed up with Black's," Sorrell says.

"Uh-huh," I say.

"No wonder he was pissed with her...I'd be pissed."

"But would you kill her? And Rickardian?" I ask.

"I wouldn't. But would Sade?"

I try to picture Sade as our killer again, and while there is something about Sade that bothers me, I'm still not convinced he's our perp. "Let's keep him on our list, along with our fan." I tap the letters in front of me. "And anyone else we might find in here."

We force ourselves back to the letters, sifting through them again, this time separating ones dated within three weeks of the book's official publication date to identify people who might have read preordered copies of *Lady-killer*. That gives us fifteen letters plus the five nasty ones for the lab techs to put at the top of their list. For the moment, we leave any undated letters in the middle of the pile.

We're still reading when my cell phone rings.

"Agent Anderson."

"Hi, Sophie. It's Melissa. The media conference is set for eleven-thirty, and Chief Saunders will be there." She says it all in one long stream, not giving me time to respond to her initial "Hi."

"Great. Thanks, Melissa."

"See you back here before eleven-thirty?"

"Tell Brady we'll be there." I hang up.

Sorrell looks questioningly at me.

"The press conference is set for eleven-thirty at the FBI field office."

Sorrell nods, but his face crumples ever so slightly at the mention of the location.

"Rickardian," is all I say in explanation.

If it was just Black's murder we were dealing with, it would have been held at Beverly Hills PD, but with Rickardian and San Francisco in the picture, the killer has crossed state lines, which makes it the Bureau's baby.

Sorrell nods again before checking his watch. "We don't have much time if we want to brief Saunders and Brady before they front up to the media."

"No." I knew today was going to be hell. Just one of those days when you're constantly fighting the clock. We've managed to chew up an hour on the letters, and we still need to touch base on other elements of Black's crime scene.

"Should we check in with DNA?" I say. "We can look at the letters later, in the PDF Watts sent through."

"DNA is Sam Gold's area. I'll give him a call."

Sorrell's on the phone for less than a minute. He shakes his head. "Not yet. Maybe tomorrow but more likely Friday."

DNA is always a tricky one, because you have to be smart enough or lucky enough to collect it from the right place. Forensics couldn't swab Black's entire house, hoping to pick up samples. And even if they did, the lab could never process that much material—no lab's got those sorts of resources. So they had to pick the most likely places to swab, in the hope that something would show up. The guidelines from the National Institute of Justice suggest swabbing fingernails, tissues, cigarette butts, straws, glasses, phones, bed linen, eyeglasses, used condoms and any items like rope used as ligatures. In the case of Black, the stocking was swabbed extensively, in the hope that some of the perpetrator's skin cells would have been sloughed off during the strangulation process. The chair was also swabbed, especially around the areas where rope particles were found, and swabs were taken from underneath Black's fingernails, from a tissue and a cotton bud found in the bathroom bin and from the phone in Black's writing room. The toilet was also examined under an alternative light source, and traces of urine were visible at the base of the toilet, so this area was swabbed, in case the killer was the one who missed the bowl. Some perpetrators get nervous enough or excited enough when they're committing a crime to feel compelled to relieve themselves. In our case, if the killer followed Black's fictional scenario, he may have spent a while with her, making a toilet stop mandatory, irrespective of nerves.

Next we check in with the computer techs, but, as with the fingerprints and DNA, they're still sorting through the influx of evidence from Black's case.

On the walk to the parking lot, I broach the topic of the profile.

"So, have you read the profile?" I can only assume that Sorrell read it this morning, even though he still hasn't commented on it. I'm not looking for a pat on the back, but some feedback would be nice.

"Uh-huh."

I give him room to expand, but once again he's not forth-coming. I can't tell if it's because he disagrees with it or if it's more of his bad bedside manner. "And?" I finally prompt.

He nods. "A vigilante." Again, he leaves the conversation hanging.

"Yeah. I think Rickardian and Black were punished. Black's murder was elaborate, but that was more about her book and the killer's desire to…" I search for the right words "…punish her with her own words, rather than the killer's own personal fantasies coming into play."

"How would that tie in with Sade?"

I screw my face up. I hate this part. Normally we profile blind—it's better for us if we don't know any of the sus-pects so that their personalities don't taint our interpreta-tion of the crime scene and other profiling inputs. I gain a lot by being active in the investigation, but I do lose some of my ability to profile objectively. "He did want to punish Black, yes. But I'm not so sure about Rickardian. I think our fan is a more likely contender. It adds up better."

Sorrell nods, taking it in. "So would you rule Sade out?"

I bite my lip, thinking. He does match some parts of the profile—age, race, lives alone and, as I've just discovered, he's a budding author. And even his job as a journalist could be seen as "policing" in some ways, because his normal beat is crime. "Has Sade been married before?"

Sorrell shakes his head.

"I doubt he's our man, but I think we should keep an eye on him. It's not impossible."

"Writing that story is certainly a way to involve himself in the investigation."

I nod. Serial killers often need to contact the police or insert themselves into the investigation in some way—it helps them relive the murders, the excitement. "Let's call him," I say. "See what he says about this morning's story."

"It'll be quieter from my car." Sorrell leads the way through the lot and we both clamber into his car. On speakerphone, he dials the number.

"Hello?" The echo in Sade's voice and the background music make me think Sade's driving.

"Mr. Sade, it's Detective Sorrell and Agent Anderson."

He sighs. "Hi. I bet I know what this is about."

"Really?" Sorrell leaves his response open.

"My article."

"How did you find out about Lorie Rickardian's murder, Mr. Sade?"

"A guy I went to college with is the crime reporter for the *San Francisco Chronicle*. He's in Hawaii on his honeymoon and saw the news about Black for the first time yesterday. He gave me the heads-up."

"Why you? Why not his paper?"

"He knew that Black and I had a history so he decided to give me the jump on it. That's what friends are for, right?"

"Yeah." I pause. "You don't mind if we verify that, do you?"

"Knock yourselves out." There's a hint of amusement in Sade's voice. "He's staying at the Hilton in Honolulu. Stephen Wright. But remember, the guy is on his honeymoon."

"We'll keep it in mind," Sorrell says.

"Yeah, I bet you will." Sade's voice is sarcastic. "Well, if that's all, guess I'll see you guys in half an hour."

"At the press conference?" I ask.

"That's the one."

We say goodbye and hang up.

"What do you think?" Sorrell asks me.

"He's one cool customer, that's for sure."

"Yup." Sorrell stares out the windshield. "He's certainly not acting like he's got something to hide."

Thirteen

The media conference has been set up in a large training room in the foyer of our building, and the invitation has gained the interest of print, radio and TV. Randy Sade sits front and center and gives both Sorrell and me a quick nod and a small smile. Cheeky bastard. Sorrell called Hawaii from his car, and Sade's story about his reporter friend checked out. Maybe Sade can afford to be cheeky.

The conference is scheduled to last for thirty minutes, but after only five minutes I'm getting antsy. My mind ticks over the rest of the day—or at least all the things I should be doing. We've got Black's funeral service and wake, that's a given, but I'd also like to at least start on Rickardian's book and preferably get a sizable chunk of it read, and I'd like to review the letters in more detail and look through the e-mails. Plus, I want to call Holt to organize a visual review of the fan mail going back further than six months. I wonder how far back her record-keeping goes. I catch myself chewing on my bottom lip—great, that'll probably end up as backdrop in some paper somewhere. It's almost as bad as being caught biting my fingernails. It's not good for one of the lead investigators on a case to look overtly stressed.

"How d'you think it went?" Sorrell asks as we file out of the room with Brady, Saunders and the others.

I shrug. "Fine, I guess. It's all standard stuff."

He nods. "You've been involved in high-profile cases before?"

"Yeah, I have. What about you?"

He smiles and holds his hands out, open and wide. "I work Homicide in Beverly Hills…."

"Point taken."

I look at my watch, worried about time. "I want to talk to Holt before the funeral this afternoon. Want to come?"

Before Sorrell can answer, Melissa powers toward us, her face missing its usual happy and relaxed expression. "Sophie, the Blacks are here."

"What?" Brady says from behind us.

"They came in the middle of the press conference and wanted to barge in, but I managed to convince them to wait in a private room."

"Good job, Melissa," I say, looking back at the room and all the journalists packing up. It would have turned into a real circus if the Blacks had crashed the conference.

"You got this one, Anderson?" Brady asks, with Saunders hovering behind him.

"Sure, sir." I turn to Melissa. "What room are they in?"

"The boardroom on our floor."

Sorrell and I hotfoot it to the boardroom.

We've barely got the door open when Werner shouts, "When were you going to tell us about this other author?"

Sorrell and I both move into the room and close the door.

Werner is standing, pacing, and George Black is also on his feet. They've brought Sandra, Mike and Tracy along with them too.

Sorrell leans against the wall. "I'm sorry, Mr. Werner, but there are some things in a case we can't disclose."

It's true, we couldn't disclose it yesterday, but we should have called the family first thing this morning, in the hope that we'd get to them *before* they read the paper.

"So you knew about this other author?" It's George Black who takes over. Like his son-in-law, his voice is full of anger. "How long have you known?"

I take this one. "Not long, Mr. Black. We discovered the possible link late on Monday and I flew up to San Francisco yesterday to confirm it."

"And we had to read about it in the paper?" Werner moves in closer to Sorrell and me, and it certainly has the effect he's after—I feel boxed in. The room's big, but the family is down our end, crowding us.

"I'm sorry about that," I say. "We've been working on leads all morning, but you're right, we should have called you." Honesty is often the best policy. And when you're wrong, admit it.

"What leads?" Sandra Black's voice is tentative, hurt.

"We've been looking at your sister's fan mail." I give her a sympathetic smile.

"Oh. The letters."

"Yes."

"Have you found anything?" she asks.

"It's early days yet."

"How long will it take?" Werner asks, his voice a sharp contrast to the whisper of Sandra Black.

"There are a lot of letters," Sorrell says. "We're working

through them all for fingerprints and other trace evidence, but it's a big job."

There's silence from the family, perhaps accepting that we are working on the case. I hit them with confirmation of our commitment. "We're assembling a task force to work both cases to find Loretta's killer. It was just announced in the press conference."

George Black nods, and then adds, "Good. Because you better find the bastard who did this to my daughter."

Silence for a few beats before Sorrell takes his chances. "While we've got you here, it'd be good if I could ask you a few more questions," he says. "It'll help us with the case."

George Black sits down and Werner follows his lead. Both men give their nod of approval, and both are now calmer.

Maybe they'll let their guards down now that they know we're investigating a serial killer and not pursuing a money-motivated kill. This time we question them as a group.

"I just…I just don't understand it." George Black shakes his head, the transition from anger to despair complete. "Why would anyone do this to Loretta? And to that other author?"

"That's what we're working on, Mr. Black." I address them all. "Do you know if Loretta ever met Lorie Rickardian. Did she ever mention her?"

They all shake their heads. "I've never even heard of her," Werner says.

"I have," Sandra Black offers. "She was very good."

"Not as good as my Loretta." George Black's voice is full of pride.

Sandra fidgets, and George Black notices it, giving his daughter a disapproving look.

Sorrell picks up on it too. "Ms. Black, if there's something you know, something you think might be important, you should tell us. No matter what it is."

George Black rolls his eyes. "I'm afraid it's nothing like that, Detective. Sandra is jealous of Loretta."

"She was no Agatha Christie, you know, Daddy."

The gloves are off now.

"You of all people should know what an achievement it was for Loretta to get published, let alone become the success that she did."

Sandra bites her lip and seems close to tears.

"Why you of all people?" I ask her softly.

"I've written two books, but haven't been able to get them published…yet."

Little sis is jealous. There was a hint of it at my first meeting with Sandra Black, but nothing like this. She really was on good behavior on Monday. Or maybe it's just that Daddy wasn't in the same room, pushing her. Sandra Black's status as a fledgling novelist only has a bearing on the case if Dusk is right and the killer's a rival author. But the pose and mutilation are sexual, and it's hard to imagine a woman doing that, especially to her sister.

"What about you, Mr. Black?" I ask, addressing Mike. "Ever hear Loretta mention Lorie Rickardian?"

"No. But she didn't really talk about other authors—not to me at least."

"We spoke about it," says Werner. "She often liked to talk to me about the 'competition,' but the name Lorie Rickardian doesn't ring a bell. It couldn't have been someone she felt threatened or impressed by in any way. But you should ask Debbie about it—part of Debbie's job was to keep up to date with what was on the market."

I nod. "What about your children?" I ask Mike Black. "Would they know?"

"I doubt it. Although Georgia did write some sort of paper on crime fiction, and I know she consulted Loretta."

"Are they back at the house?" Sorrell asks.

"Yes. We didn't want to involve them in this." He gestures with his hand—"this" obviously means the possibility of a hostile confrontation with Sorrell and me.

"They'll be at the funeral this afternoon?" I ask.

"Yes."

"We can talk to them there," Sorrell says to me. "Or I'll give them a call before we go."

"So…so, you really think the killer could be there this afternoon?" Tracy Black's voice is full of fear.

"Don't worry, Tracy, the kids will be safe." Werner turns to us. "It's invitation only and I've organized for security, given Loretta's fame."

Mike puts his hand on Tracy's knee. "They'll be fine. And they'll be back at college in a couple of days."

Yes, back to their expensive colleges, courtesy of Loretta.

"How did you feel about Loretta paying for the kids' college?" Sorrell asks, obviously following the same train of thought as me.

Mike shoots Tracy a look before studying his feet. "We were very grateful."

With two looks, Mike's told us that he felt shame about his sister helping him out financially, but that his wife was part of his decision to accept the money. It's amazing how people lay their lives out on the line with a few well-timed looks or fidgets.

"Yes," Tracy says. "They've had the best education that money can buy."

It's obvious from looking at Tracy Black that wealth is important to her. Just like the first time we met, she's wearing designer clothes and expensive jewelry. Clearly Loretta's money wasn't just spent on the kids' education.

"If you've finished, Detective, Agent, we'd like to get back to the house." George Black stands up. "We've still got preparations to make for this afternoon."

"Actually, there is one more thing. Have any of you been to Loretta's house recently?"

"Loretta usually came to visit me," says George Black.

"And we haven't been there for a while," Mike Black says. "This is our first visit to L.A. in about six months."

I nod—Mike and Tracy live in New York.

Sorrell looks at Sandra.

"I'm not sure when I was there last." She looks at Werner questioningly.

"Probably your birthday."

Sandra Black nods. "Yes. That was in March."

Sorrell scribbles it down. "We have found one fingerprint at Loretta's home that's unaccounted for. We'd like to take all your prints for reference purposes—hopefully we've got the killer's print and not one of yours."

"Don't you need a warrant for that?"

"Sandra, don't be ridiculous." George Black gives his daughter a scathing look. "If they've got the killer's fingerprint, we need to know."

Sandra's right—we need a court order to compel them to provide their fingerprints, but in cases like this, you assume the family's going to be helpful.

Sorrell looks at his watch. "Excuse us for a moment." He takes us both away from the action. "We've only got four hours before we have to be at Watson Brothers and

Sisters, funeral directors to the stars." He says the last part with more humor than I'd expect from him.

"Like that, is it?"

"Well, not really the stars…just the rich, which in L.A. is usually the same thing."

"We need to talk to Holt about the fan mail," I say.

"Yeah, but we've also got to brief a couple of uniforms that Saunders has given me, and print the family."

We both pause—there's no reason why we can't split up. In fact, we're both more used to working alone.

"I'll take Holt," I say. "But call me if you hear from Watts or find out anything useful."

"Like an ID on that print from the house?" he teases.

I smile. "Yeah, like an ID on an unaccounted print." God, I'd kick his ass if he didn't call me about that.

"I'll get the family's prints before they leave. Given AFIS didn't find a match on the print at Black's house it'll be useful to eliminate the family members as the source." He takes a breath. "Then I'll brief the uniforms. See you at four." He pauses. "And I'll organize two photographers from the lab for the funeral too."

"Great."

He holds his hand up in a wave before turning on his heel and going back into the boardroom. Wow, I am making progress. I even get a wave.

Back at my desk, I ring Holt.

"Have you got news?" Her voice is eager and I feel horrible letting her down.

"No, sorry. More questions, I'm afraid."

"Oh." She pauses, making me feel worse, before saying, "Okay, shoot."

"We're following the fan mail angle pretty closely."

"I knew it had something to do with those letters!"

"Have you kept all her letters?"

"I started as Loretta's assistant four years ago, and I've got all the letters since then."

"At Loretta's house?"

"No, here at my apartment. I used to work from home quite a bit, and all my files are here."

"Okay. I'd like to come over now, if that's okay."

"Um, sure. I guess. But I've got Loretta's funeral…" She stops midsentence but eventually pulls herself together. "The funeral's this afternoon and I want to be there."

"Don't worry, I'm going too, so I'll be out of your hair before then."

"Oh?" She seems taken aback at first, but then adds, "I'd forgotten that's what you guys do for murder cases."

"Yes." I pause. We'd told the family of our intention to attend the funeral, but not Holt. "So I'll leave for your place now?"

"Sure. I'll see you soon."

But before I jump into the car, I wait for the printer to spit out all five hundred-odd pages of the PDF Watts's team created, and grab several evidence bags in case any of the letters at Holt's house are noteworthy enough to get the Questioned Documents team involved. The last thing I do before leaving is jump online and go to Google. I type in "Lorie Rickardian" + "Loretta Black" to see if I can find a link between the victims online. I get only twenty-nine results, and quickly click on each link. They're mostly review sites and online bookstores, including a few eBay results, but the authors are mentioned separately. Certainly there's nothing like joint appearances or an article that featured both authors. It was worth a shot.

* * *

Holt lives in a small but modern two-bedroom place in Los Feliz. The two-story apartments are laid out in a U-shape, with a swimming pool in the middle. It could almost be the set for the nineties show *Melrose Place.* Holt's second-floor apartment is decorated in a modern yet homey style, with off-white carpets, dark wood furniture and a few splashes of dark purple and burgundy to add contrast. A fresh-looking vase of tulips in the center of a low coffee table also adds warmth. She leads me into the second bedroom, which she's got set up as an office.

"This is everything," she says, plucking four files from a wooden, filing cabinet. "I've got one folder for each year, but this year's is pretty small—" she holds up one labeled 2007 "—given your lab's got most of the letters."

I take the 2007 folder and open it on her desk. "May I?"

"Sure." She pushes a couple of books to one side, making more room for me, and sits the other three folders on top of her stack of books.

Sitting down with a fresh pair of latex gloves on, I flip through the letters. Again, some are dated, some not. Some have names and return addresses, some just names, and a few are simply signed. The 2007 folder only has what looks like about thirty letters in it.

Starting at the top of the pile, I read each of the letters quickly, turning them over facedown onto the other side of the open folder when I'm done.

"Do you want a coffee?" Holt asks, only a couple of letters into the process.

Caffeine…definitely time for another hit. "That would be fantastic, Debbie," I say, with the fervor of someone being offered their first bite of food in days.

She smiles at my obvious desperation. "I'll be right back."

When I'm about twenty letters into the 2006 file, Holt returns with a mug of steaming coffee in hand.

"Thanks, Debbie." I put the mug on the desk, far enough away that I'm not at risk of knocking it over as I flip through the letters.

Despite the volume, the work is fast-going, with most of the letters only being a paragraph or so long. About halfway into the 2006 stack, I come to another letter from "A fan." Like the letter we already have, it's printed, but unlike our current sample, it's also dated—12 July, 2006. Unfortunately the writer hasn't put down a name and address.

Dear Ms. Black,

Congratulations on your new book. I did enjoy Lovers' Lane *thoroughly, but probably not as much as some of your previous books. The level of graphic violence in your books seems to be increasing, and I simply don't think that's necessary. Is this your decision? Do you feel that it's needed in order to keep your fan base? Believe you me, this is one fan who sees so much violence on TV, both real and fictional, that it concerns me. Our children and society in general are becoming desensitized to violence, and upping the ante in fiction is not helping.*

Again, congratulations, but perhaps you will consider this bit of feedback for your next Benson novel.
Yours,
A fan

I take a sip of my coffee. There are similar characteristics to the letter we already have, with the writer's disapproval of the violence in Black's books. However, this letter is calmer, almost academic. I think it's raising a point rather than suggesting the need to take action. Perhaps he was disappointed that Black didn't heed his advice.

Holt left me to it after she brought me in my coffee, but now I have questions for her. "Debbie?"

She answers, "Yes?" before appearing in the doorway.

"Was *Ladykiller* more violent than *Lovers' Lane?*"

"Um…" She stares vacantly at her bookshelf. "I guess. Maybe. Certainly Loretta's descriptions of some of the kills became longer and more vivid." Holt pauses. "And Benson became more hardened over the series too."

"Have you read Rickardian's book?"

"Yes." She pauses. "I can't believe…I can't believe Loretta is this psycho's second victim." Her face wrinkles, threatening to be invaded by a flood of tears, but I need answers and don't have time to comfort Holt.

"When did you read Rickardian's book?" I ask, bringing her back to the question.

She regains her concentration. "As soon as it was released. Loretta liked me to read as much crime fiction as possible. You know, to make sure a new book she was working on wasn't too similar to someone else's, and to keep an eye on the market in general. I think she also liked to be aware of what her competition was doing. Loretta was a very talented writer, but she was also a businesswoman and *very* competitive. I used to read pretty much every new release and give Loretta a summary of the plot and a critique."

I nod, having heard about Loretta Black's business sensibilities before. "Did they ever meet?"

"No. Certainly not since I've been working for Loretta."

"Not at a writers' festival or something?"

Holt shakes her head. "Sorry."

That backs up my Google search, but it is disappointing. I move back to the letters.

"Do you want more coffee?"

"Sure." I pass Holt my nearly empty cup.

It's two hours and several more cups of coffee before I finally find myself reading the last letter from the oldest pile, the 2003 letters. It's been a tedious afternoon, but very fruitful—especially given I found a handwritten letter from "A fan." In total I've picked out eight letters for further review: three from the mysterious "A fan," including the important handwritten one, four hate mails and one letter that suggests the writer may have been stalking Black.

Black was a prominent person in some circles, so I'd expect she'd get threatening letters, just like celebrities do, and while these usually turn out to be harmless, in some cases they can lead to stalking and more aggressive behavior down the track. Maybe in Loretta Black's case they led to murder. If we were investigating Black's murder in isolation, we'd put a lot of investigative power into the hate mail, but as always with serial killers, it boils down to finding the link between the victims…and that's the letters from "A fan."

Fourteen

I sit in my car out in front of the Watson Brothers and Sisters funeral parlor. After dropping the letters from Holt's files off at the Scientific Services Bureau and waiting for high-quality prints of them, my time is running low, to say the least. Soon I need to be actively surveilling the area, but what little time I do have needs to be spent on Rickardian's book. I flick through the first few pages of copyright information, acknowledgments and dedications, to the prologue. I skim a few paragraphs then read more closely.

The scream echoed in the empty auditorium. Mandy pulled herself away from Tom.

"Katie!" she yelled, already on the run, assuming Jake was getting too friendly and forcing her friend into something she didn't want to do.

Mandy vaulted the stage stairs with Tom hot on her heels. She fumbled through the curtain. Her jaw dropped—it was not what she was expecting to see.

Jake and Katie were locked in an embrace, but Jake was comforting a distressed Katie. And next to them was the source of Katie's hysteria.

Hanging from the school's twenty-foot stage rig was their geography teacher, Jan Somers. She was naked, except for a straitjacket, and the angle of her neck coupled with bulging eyes left nothing to the imagination.

Half an hour later, forensic pathologist Sarina Robertson was on the scene, helping the detectives and uniforms lower the body. Once she was close enough to the victim for her initial visual inspection, she knew the death was not the bizarre suicide it first appeared. Somers had been hit on the head, and was at least unconscious if not already dead when she went off the stage rig and broke her neck as the rope pulled tight and jerked her body in the opposite direction to gravity. Sarina would have to confirm cause of death back at the morgue, but one thing was certain: Jan Somers didn't jump.

A tap at my car window gives me a fright.

Sorrell, actually managing a grin, is staring at me. "Good?"

I open the car window. "Only just started. You're here early." A glance at the dashboard confirms that it's 3:25 p.m.

"I wanted to see if anyone was hanging around." He shrugs. "Besides you."

I motion with my head to the passenger seat and he walks around the car and hops in.

"So, how'd you go with Holt?"

"Good. I found some letters to add to our pile, including three more from "A fan" and one that looks to be his first. It's handwritten and on proper writing paper."

"Really?" Sorrell takes his eyes off the funeral entrance and shoots them my way, clearly as happy as me with this latest find.

I look at my watch. "I've got copies with me. We got time?" But I know the answer. If the service is at 4:00 p.m., people will arrive before, probably mostly coming around 3:45 p.m. That doesn't give us much time to get inside and process any early attendees.

Sorrell also checks the time. "No. We need to get going. I've got the list of everyone the family invited." Sorrell takes a piece of folded paper out of his inside pocket. He looks back at the entrance. "Mind if I put one of the photographers in here? You've got a better view of the front than me." Sorrell points out his car, which is on the other side of the street and a little farther away from the funeral home. "The other photographer can stick with us for the time being."

"Sure," I say. "Did you get a chance to talk to the niece and nephew?"

He nods. "On the phone a couple of hours ago. The nephew Harry didn't know anything, but her niece Georgia said Loretta did suggest she read and profile particular authors for her paper, but Lorie Rickardian wasn't one of them."

"Holt says Rickardian and Black never met." I sigh. "I'd feel a whole lot better about this case if we could link Rickardian and Black together somehow, in addition to that letter."

"You and me both."

"I did a Google search on their names together, but nothing out of the ordinary came up."

Sorrell gets out of the car and leans in before he closes the door. "Let's talk about those letters tonight, after this is over." He jerks his head in the direction of Watson Brothers and Sisters. "See you inside in five?"

"Yeah." I smile, but it's forced, because I'm suddenly reminded that soon I'll be in the same room as Loretta Black's body.

When a lanky kid with a camera around his neck and a camera bag over his shoulder comes running up the street toward me a couple of minutes later, I'm still chewing on my bottom lip. He stops and checks the number plate before looking at me hesitantly. I give him a smile and roll down my window, letting the L.A. heat surge into the car.

"You Agent Anderson?" he asks at my window.

"Yup." I get out of the car and throw on my suit jacket. It's more professional, but also more appropriate for a funeral. It's too hot for it, but it'll be air-conditioned inside. "The keys are in the ignition," I say.

Buttoning up my suit jacket, I cross the road. The funeral home's already put up a small sign that reads Loretta Black, Main Parlor, with an arrow. I follow the arrow, but the door is locked.

"We'll be opening up in another five or ten minutes."

I turn around to the source of the voice, an older man with snow-white hair and a cleft chin. "Hi, I'm Special Agent Sophie Anderson." I show him my ID.

"Jake Watson."

"Ah, one of the Watsons." I smile and he returns the gesture.

"Precisely." He fishes some keys out of his pocket and

unlocks the main parlor. "The family arrived a couple of minutes ago. We have a small room set aside for them." He holds the door open for me. "Did you want to join them?"

"Thank you, no. I'll wait in here." I hesitate as I enter, my eyes drawn to the open coffin at the other end of the room.

"Is there anything we can do to help?"

I pull my eyes away from the mahogany casket. "No. That's fine."

He gives me a quick nod and leaves me to it. I glance nervously around the room and walk slowly toward the coffin, inexplicably drawn to see her body one more time. As I get closer, my heart pounds faster. Feeling someone's gaze on me, I turn around expecting to see Sorrell, Jake Watson or someone. But I'm still alone. I keep walking, and as I get nearer, I see part of the coffin's interior, which is white. Within another step her face comes into view and I'm relieved to see that she looks more peaceful than the last time I saw her. Her eyes are closed and a layer of makeup makes her look happier somehow. The last feature that comes into view is her hair, which has been left down to fan out across the plump white coffin lining. The effect certainly is striking…as it was in her bathroom.

I close my eyes and let out the breath I've been holding. Silly to get all worked up over nothing. I open my eyes, but I'm not the only one. As my eyes open, so do Black's. I instinctively grab for the side of the coffin to steady myself, but also take a step back, wanting to get away from her. My stomach swirls with butterflies and my head starts to spin. I realize I've also closed my eyes, so I steel myself for what I might see before opening them once more. Black's looking at me, her face very much alive, but then within less than a second her corpse is lifeless once more. I look around again, but I'm still alone. I let go of the coffin and, once again, breathe a sigh of relief.

I feel a hand on my shoulder and spin around, expecting to see Sorrell. But it's not.

Black stands in front of me with the sheer stocking pulled over her face. Her eyes are wild, shocked and frightened, but her lips are set in determination. She starts shaking her head. Her lips move, but there's no sound. I take a step toward her and she raises her hand, palm facing toward me. She wants me to stop and I do so, midstep. Then she points behind me, but when I turn all I see is her coffin.

I turn back but Black's gone.

I stumble toward the nearest seat, only just managing to control my descent. I focus on slowing my heart rate, which is pumping as hard as if I've just run a marathon.

A few minutes pass before I feel a hand on my shoulder. I jump, and my whole body tenses as dread envelops me. But I want to know, I want to help her, so I turn around slowly, ready to see her dead again.

But this time it's Sorrell. "Sophie?"

I'm startled by his voice, and realize that everything has been silent, perfectly silent, since Watson left the room. But now I can hear the faint hint of street noise, voices in the distance and the soothing music being played in the main parlor.

"Are you okay?" Sorrell's voice is full of genuine concern. God knows how many times he said my name. Well, a lot, if he resorted to using my first name.

"Yeah, I'm fine. Sorry. Didn't get much sleep last night."

He looks at me strangely and takes a breath in, presumably about to quiz me some more, but I'm saved by the sudden appearance of Jake Watson at the door.

"The first guests, Agent, Detective." He nods at both of us in turn and then moves to the side, allowing a smartly dressed middle-aged couple to enter the room. They look sad, but not grief-stricken, so I peg them as distant friends or relatives, maybe professional acquaintances. Sorrell ticks them off his list and we station ourselves at the door, alongside the private security Werner hired. Scott Werner and George Black are the official welcoming committee, and we're...well, as far as the guests are concerned, we're probably pains in the ass, but I doubt Loretta Black or Lorie Rickardian would see it that way. Sorrell phones the photographers and gets them to reposition themselves so one's directly out front to take pictures of the guests as they arrive and one's inside to photograph everyone once they're seated. Now that people have started to arrive officially, the photographers don't need to be discreet.

The guests turn up in a constant stream and I get to put a face to the name for both Black's editor, Laura Cue, and her agent, Linda Farrow. But not surprisingly, the two publicists I spoke to aren't on the invitation list—Black did fire them, after all.

When Sorrell's cell rings at 3:50 p.m., the family glares at him. He bows his head in apology, and mouths "Lab" to me before picking up the call.

While I'm dying to hear what the lab has to say, I keep my mind on the job at hand and continue marking people off while Sorrell takes the call. He sidles up to me a few minutes later.

"It was McAvey," Sorrell says. "They've come up with their first AFIS match from the letters."

"And?"

"His name's Robert Wendell, arrested for auto theft in 2002. I'm getting Edwards in my department to find out more about Wendell now."

Just before four, the peaceful tone of the preceremony activities is interrupted once again, but this time much more dramatically than by a ringing phone.

"Get out of here, you bastard!" Scott Werner lunges forward toward a man. I move closer, to intervene, and my line of sight is now cleared so I can see the source of Werner's distress—Sade.

"What the hell are you doing here, you sick bastard?" Now Werner's got his hands on both of Sade's shoulders and is a threatening force.

Sorrell and I grab Werner at the same time. "Scott!" I say.

He turns hurt, tear-filled eyes my way. "He killed her. I know he killed her."

"We've got it under control, Scott." Sorrell loosens his grip on Werner's shoulder. "Leave it to us, okay?"

Werner looks at Sorrell, then at me, then at Sade. "Get out of here. You're not invited and you're not welcome." He spits the comment through gritted teeth.

Sade gives a small smile. "You gonna make me?"

I take my hands off Werner and push Sade away from him.

Sade is startled enough that he stumbles backward a few steps. "Hey, take it easy." He holds his hands up. "FBI brutality."

I roll my eyes. "Give it a rest, Sade." I lower my voice.

"Have some sympathy…the man's wife is dead and he's barely holding it together."

Sade looks over my shoulder then back at me.

"Why are you here anyway?" I can't keep the incredulity out of my voice.

"Come to pay my respects. To say goodbye." He smiles. "And good riddance."

A hurried look around tells me we're out of earshot. If I'd been Werner or anyone close to Black, I'd have decked Sade for that comment.

I shake my head. "Just go, Sade. Okay?"

He shrugs. "Fine, have it your way." His hands sink into his pockets and he moves away.

"Hey, Sade," Sorrell says after Sade's only taken a few steps.

"Yeah?"

"Why didn't you tell us you'd written a book?"

"None of your business."

Sorrell moves closer. "Black shafted you twice, didn't she?"

"Like I said, good riddance." He pauses. "But I didn't kill her." He looks Sorrell and me up and down. "That it?"

Sorrell gives him the cop cliché. "For the moment."

He shakes his head and keeps moving.

The rest of the guests arrive without incident and by 4:00 p.m. there are over one hundred people squeezed into the exclusive funeral home's chapel. Most of the attendees are impeccably and somewhat extravagantly dressed, making Sorrell and me look a little out of place and the two crime-scene photographers look downright shabby.

At a couple minutes past four, the officiant introduces herself and welcomes everyone to "this somber event, the service for such a bright star tragically taken away from this world, her fans and from you, her friends and family." Sorrell and I loiter up the back in case anyone sneaks in or lingers at the doorway. We need to account for everyone. The officiant speaks for about ten minutes before calling Werner up for the eulogy. Werner gives a touching speech, filled with just the right amount of love, admiration and genuine emotional distress. He then calls up Black's father, who walks slowly to the podium, eyes down. Werner welcomes him and then returns to the family front lines, taking hold of Sandra Black's hand on his return. It's hard to see who's comforting whom and I can't help but think about Sandra's jealousy. Crocodile tears?

"What do you think?" Sorrell asks me.

I shrug. "Nice eulogy."

"You think he's clear?"

I look at him, puzzled. Of course I think he's clear. Werner doesn't fit the profile, certainly not in terms of his possible motivation, and he's got an alibi. He's not our guy and Sorrell's only dwelling on him because he's hard-pressed to give him up when there's so much money at stake. Yes, that would be simple: husband gains millions if wife dies, so he kills her. But things don't always fit together like a nice, neat jigsaw puzzle and this case could end up being a one-thousand piecer, with five hundred pieces dedicated to a blue sky.

I hesitate. Could Sorrell's instincts be better than mine? I've seen tunnel vision cloud many an investigation—could I be guilty of that? But I still return to the facts—serial killer. Unless…

The father's address is long, recounting some of Loretta Black's childhood moments and the many highlights from her illustrious career. He goes on to talk about what she would never achieve and how her mark will be forever left on the book world. He has everyone's complete attention, but his delivery isn't as smooth as Werner's.

I glance around the room again, watching the heads of the mourners. "I'm going up front," I say to Sorrell. I use an outside aisle, trying to be as discreet as possible. Out of respect for the mourners, I also don't move up level with the podium, but stop at the first pew. From here, I angle my body slightly so I'm turned between the podium and the congregation. This way I get an excellent view of everyone's faces without becoming too conspicuous. Every minute or so I flick my eyes into one section of the crowd, reading their faces. But all I see is grief, in its varying degrees. Some people are crying, some look stoically up at the podium, some fixate on their hands in their laps and others lean on loved ones. It's the same story across the congregation and nothing strikes me as out of place, except, of course, Sorrell, me and the two photographers.

Black's father finishes and the officiant takes over again. I stay standing but move back slightly as she leads us in a hymn. I notice a man in the middle of one of the pews making his way to the inside aisle and I manage to catch Sorrell's attention. As the man leaves, Sorrell follows, stopping him at the entranceway. Sorrell and the man talk for a few seconds before Sorrell leads him out the door.

I make my way back and join Sorrell and the mystery man in the foyer.

Sorrell looks up as I enter. "Peter Blake was just telling me he's an author with the same publishing house as

Black." Sorrell looks down his invite list. "Yup, here it is, Peter Blake." Sorrell studies the man intently. "You got some ID on you?"

Blake shakes his head in annoyance, but fishes his wallet out of his inside jacket pocket. He shows us his California driver's license.

I'm reminded immediately of Dusk's notion of a rival author. If it's not Sade, maybe Blake's got a few screws loose. Could he be a killer?

Sorrell hands back the license. "So why are you leaving early, Peter?"

"Prior engagement."

"Must be something important to ditch a funeral," Sorrell says.

"It is. I'm working to a deadline for my next book. But I had to pay my respects."

"Did you know Lorie Rickardian?" Sorrell asks.

"God, no." It has suddenly dawned on Blake that we're asking questions that could implicate him in murder and he's instantly nervous. "I never met Lorie Rickardian. Never even heard of her."

"But she was an author."

"So? I don't know every author's name, you know." He looks around nervously. "Look, I really have to go. I'm already late with this book. Just a few more chapters and I should be done. Here's my card. Call me if you've got any more questions."

"Before you go, Mr. Blake, I do have one more question for you." I talk fast, not wanting to give Blake time to think or make something up. "What were you doing last Friday night, between 11:00 p.m. and 4:00 a.m. Saturday morning?"

Does Blake have an alibi for Black's murder?

"Um…I went to a Dodgers game and out for drinks afterwards. I got home around midnight."

"Who'd you go to the game with?" I ask.

"Couple of other guys."

Sorrell prompts Blake for the names and writes them down. "And which bar?"

"Tearaway in West Hollywood."

"Do you live alone, Mr. Blake?" I ask.

"Yes."

"So no one can verify your whereabouts after midnight?" Sorrell scribbles as he talks.

Blake scrunches his face. "I guess not. But I was home, in bed."

"I bet." Sorrell doesn't sound convinced, but it could be part of a scare tactic with Blake, rather than his actual feelings.

We let Peter Blake rush off to his waiting computer and those last few chapters.

"I'll check his alibi out tomorrow," Sorrell says. "But no one can alibi him for Black's time of death."

"No, not when he was home alone between midnight and four." I bite my lip. "And if the killer isn't a fan, a rival author's a good fit."

"So that gives us Blake as well as Sade now."

"Uh-huh."

No one else makes a move until the procession starts. We let the immediate family exit but then place ourselves directly after them so we can get out first and watch the others spilling down the steps. The photographers are with us, taking more snaps, but I'm confident we've already captured everyone by now.

As she files out of the funeral home, Laura Cue approaches us. "Did I see Peter Blake in there?"

"Yes," I say. "That's correct."

She licks her lips and seems puzzled.

"Something wrong?" Sorrell asks.

"I'm just surprised he was here. Surprised he got an invite, actually."

"Why?"

"Bad blood."

"Go on."

"They used to be friends. Good friends, I believe. But then Loretta hit the big time and Peter…well he didn't. He hasn't been able to let go of the differences in their career directions."

"What do you mean?" I focus on Cue, but also keep an eye on all the guests flowing down the stairs behind her.

"Peter was always complaining about the preferential treatment Loretta received. Said her covers were better than his, that she had more publicity and marketing for her books. That we weren't doing enough for him, enough to promote his name and books."

"Any truth to those claims?"

She looks at me like I've asked a stupid question. "Loretta is…was…our biggest author. Of course we put money and resources into her books. But we could afford a bigger marketing spend on them, because of the revenue she brought in."

"Sounds like a catch twenty-two," Sorrell pipes up. "You need to be a bestseller to get the publicity, but you need the publicity to be a bestseller?"

Cue gives him a patronizing smile. "Not exactly, Detective. Everyone in our business knows that word of mouth is the strongest factor in a book's success."

"But how do you start that word of mouth?" I ask.

She shrugs. "It's a bit of everything, Agent Anderson. And if there was a magical formula all our authors would be bestsellers." She smiles. "His last name makes it even harder for Peter."

"How so?"

"It's very similar to Loretta's…Black and Blake. They're often near each other on the shelves, and his name and books are obscured by hers." She pauses. "I've got to find some of my other authors. I'll be around if you need to talk to me some more."

"Thanks for letting us know about Blake."

She gives us a nod before disappearing into the crowd.

"Let's see how Blake got the invite," I say, looking for Holt or Werner. I spot them together, with the Black family, and it looks like they're moving toward the cars. But they both look distraught.

Sorrell picks up on it too. "It can wait until later tonight."

From the funeral home, a small procession of cars moves on to the cemetery for a private ceremony, which only lasts twenty minutes. From there the family, Sorrell and I meet up with the rest of the mourners at 6:00 p.m. at Le Grand Crux, an exclusive and pricey French wine bar and restaurant. The wake is an extravagant affair, and by the time the last mourners, some of whom have become revelers, leave, it's 9:00 p.m. Once most of the guests are gone, we take the opportunity to talk to the family.

"I'm sorry to ask you this, but we do have a question for you." I stand in front of the family, addressing no one in particular.

"Yes?" Werner answers.

"Who invited Peter Blake? He's one of the authors from Loretta's publishing house."

"Debbie gave me a list of who I should invite from the book world," Werner answers. "I presumed my wife knew Peter Blake, that they were friends."

Sorrell and I both retreat, trying to be as respectful as possible. I look around for Holt, and spot her coming out of the ladies' room. "Holt," I say, and Sorrell follows my gaze. As we move toward her she smiles, and I can tell from the slight laziness of her eyes and her overtly relaxed walk that she's had a few drinks—more than a few.

"Detective Sorrell, Sophie, hi." Her voice is warm, even when she says Sorrell's name.

"Sorry to bother you, Debbie," I say. "But there's one person on the invitation list we'd like to ask you about."

"Shoot!"

"Peter Blake."

"Ah, Peter. You know then?"

"Know what?" Sorrell doesn't hide the interest in his voice.

"Oops." Holt giggles and brings her hand up to her mouth. "Me and my big mouth."

Half of me thinks maybe we should wait until tomorrow to talk to Holt, but the other half wants to take advantage of the fact that the alcohol may give her loose lips. "Debbie, this is a murder investigation. You need to tell us anything and everything you know."

"Sorry. You're right." She tries to pull herself together. She leans in closer to us and tries for a more serious tone. "Well. It's about Peter…and Loretta."

"Yes?" I prompt.

"I don't like to gossip, but I think they may have been having an affair."

"What?" Sorrell's interest is really piqued now.

"At Left Coast Crime in 2004, the three of us were up drinking in Loretta's room on the final night. I left at 2:00 a.m., but Peter was still there."

While it's interesting, and potentially incriminating, it doesn't mean anything happened between the pair once Holt left the room.

"That's all?" I say.

She shakes her head. "When I asked Loretta about it the next morning, she seemed upset. Like she was guilty. She explicitly asked me *not* to tell Scott that she was drinking with Peter." She gives us a wink. "Sounded like things hotted up after I left."

"You said you thought maybe they were having an affair, not a one-off indiscretion."

"You're right. I guess maybe 'affair' wasn't quite the right word." Holt sways a little. "That's the only time I suspect."

"Did she get phone calls or anything from Blake?"

Debbie shrugs. "When I first started working for Loretta I believe they were in contact on and off. But not in the past couple of years."

I nod. "Debbie, how are you getting home?"

She puts her hand on my shoulder and leans on it. "Don't worry, I'm not driving."

"Good." I pause. "Do you want me to call you a cab?"

"Already done. I'm going outside now."

"Want me to wait outside with you?" I ask, just a little anxious about letting Holt stand alone in her current state.

"That's okay. Sandra's going to wait with me." She swings her handbag over her shoulder. "Good night, then?"

"Thanks, Debbie. That's it for now."

She starts walking but then turns back, gently taking hold of my arm. "Sophie, you will be discreet about this, won't you? It'd kill Scott."

"Sure." At this juncture in the investigation there's no point telling Scott Werner that his wife might have cheated on him.

Once Holt's out of earshot, Sorrell says, "So maybe Mr. Blake was holding out on us."

We start walking toward the exit. "Maybe." A glance at my watch tells me it's 9:15 p.m. "I think we can wait until tomorrow to find out if the rumor mill's been working overtime or if Black and Blake had something more than friendship going."

"Yup, tomorrow," Sorrell says as we emerge onto the street just in time to see Sandra Black closing the cab door for Holt.

She turns around and spots us. "Good night, Detective, Agent." She looks exhausted.

We say good-night to her before she goes back inside, and we continue walking.

"Man, I'm beat," Sorrell says on the way to his car, which is parked closer to the restaurant than mine. "I could use a drink too."

"It's been a marathon of a day all right." I roll my shoulders a few times, trying to release some of the day's tension. "Do you still want to look at the letters?" I ask, praying he'll say no. I know it's early, but all I can think of is bed…and getting these shoes off. I've been on my feet for most of the past five hours.

He blows out a breath through pursed lips. "How about two for one? Letters and a knock-off drink?"

"I'll come for one drink." I really don't feel like a drink, but I want to be sociable with Sorrell. Chances are I'll work with him again, possibly often, depending on what cases come his way, and so I'd like to put a bit of effort into getting to know the guy. "Do you know a place around here?" I ask, given my knowledge of L.A. bars is zilch.

"Yeah, there's a bar you'll like a few miles away. All the women seem to go for it. Great cocktails." He smiles, a look I can't interpret. I'm not sure if he's making fun of me or my gender or just making an observation.

"I'll follow you," I say.

Sorrell gets in his car and waits for me to swing around before driving off.

Fifteen

I use the time in the car to return some phone calls. First on my list is Darren, who left a message a couple of hours ago to see how it went at the funeral.

"Hey, Sophie," he says as soon as he picks up. "Well? You okay?"

"Yeah, I'm okay. Thanks."

"What happened?"

"I saw Black."

Silence for a beat, then: "And?"

"She only appeared to me for a few seconds and it didn't mean much."

"What did she say?"

"Nothing. Everything was silent, and I mean everything. I couldn't even hear background noise while she was there or for a while after."

"Black was responsible for that."

"Really?" I'm shocked, partly because she was trying to talk to me.

"Not on purpose," Darren explains. "She's…" He

pauses. "I know what you're like but this is serious stuff. No laughing, okay?"

I laugh.

"Hey, I said no laughing."

"Okay, I promise to behave."

"Right." Darren's all business. "She's not fully accustomed to her current…status…and she doesn't have control over how she appears to you."

"At first she had a stocking pulled over her face, like the way I saw her at the crime scene. Did that mean anything?"

He pauses. "Probably not. If Black's struggling to come to terms with her own death…well, she may not even realize that she's dead."

"I see." I can understand her lack of control—after all, I didn't have much control over my gift a few months ago, and even now I'm by no means a master. I feel more like a toddler, taking tentative steps.

"So, what did she do?" Darren asks.

"She touched my shoulder and—"

"You felt her?" Darren's surprised.

"Yeah," I say hesitantly, unsure of the significance.

"Did it feel like a normal touch?"

I think back to that moment near her coffin. I thought it was Sorrell at first, so it must have felt real. But there was a coldness to it. A shiver runs through me, just thinking about it. "It felt real, but cold."

"Okay."

Silence.

"What does it mean?"

"It means either she's strong or you're strong. And given she wasn't able to give you sound, it's the latter. My aunt said it took her years to reach that level."

"Oh…." I don't know what else to say.

Up ahead of me Sorrell makes a left, and I'm so involved in the conversation with Darren that I only just manage to indicate and swing the car around in time.

"Go on, what happened next?" he asks.

"She started talking, but I couldn't hear anything. I moved closer to her and she put her hand up, stopping me, and then pointed behind me."

"And what was behind you?"

"Just her coffin. Was she asking if she was dead?" I shrug instinctively, even though Darren can't see me. "Pointing out to me that she was dead?"

"Um…"

"You're clueless too." I laugh.

"Pretty much, yeah." He sighs. "Either of those is possible. But if we assume she's still disoriented, she was probably just pointing to her coffin out of confusion—you know, 'Why am I lying there in a coffin?' Maybe you should go back to her grave or her house, see if she comes to you again."

"Maybe," I say, without conviction. I won't be doing it now, that's for sure—there's no way I'm trying to see a ghost at night. It's illogical, I know, but there's a part of me that's always been a little afraid of the dark. I think it stems back to my brother's disappearance, because he was taken at night.

Darren lets it slide. "How's the case going? Any leads?"

"We've got a few possibilities we're chasing down."

In front of me Sorrell takes a right, and again I only just pick it up in time.

"I better go, Darren. I'm supposed to be following the lead detective on this case and I keep almost missing the turns."

"Sure."

I say goodbye and hang up, giving Sorrell my full attention. It's only a couple of minutes later that he slows down and points toward a car space next to him. He drives on, letting me take the spot. I park but wait in the car, not knowing where we're going. Ten minutes later I'm starting to get worried, when Sorrell comes around a corner, half jogging toward me.

"Sorry," he says once he's within a few steps of me. "Couldn't get a space for a few blocks." Perspiration beads on his forehead threaten to turn into drips, before he keeps them at bay with a back-handed wipe. "It's this way."

I follow him back the way he came and down the first street. Even though it's late, heat still radiates off the sidewalk and road, hitting us as we walk. I presume it's L.A.'s famous smog that's trapping the heat and ensuring the day's stickiness remains well into the night. Within half a block I feel the first small dribble of sweat trickle down between my breasts, and small beads are forming on my upper lip.

"I had a message from Edwards at the station. Remember the prints on that fan mail, Robert Wendell?"

"Yeah."

"He's twenty-nine years old, lives in Vegas and works as a waiter at one of the casinos."

"It's kind of young in terms of the profile," I say. Then again, Sade's not that much older.

"Yes. But I'll still give him a call tomorrow, confirm he sent a letter to Black and see if he's got an alibi for last Friday night."

I nod.

It's only half a block before we move into the artificial

coolness of an air-conditioned bar. The bar's decorated in a modern, chic style, with white walls and stainless-steel trimmings, complemented by cream leather seats and brown tables. The bar has two main sections, a front section that has low tables and comfy couches, and a back section with high stools and small bar tables. The menu board lists at least thirty cocktails.

When I notice movement in one of the comfy areas, I nod to Sorrell.

"Great." He seems as relieved as I am by the prospect of sitting down. "What do you want to drink?" he asks.

"Gin and tonic." It's perfect weather for a cool G and T, with ice and a slice of lime. No cocktail for me. While I stake out the seats, ready to move in, Sorrell gets the drinks. It takes him about five minutes to get served, and by the time he gets back I've settled into the cream sofa and am imagining falling asleep in its soft folds.

Sorrell's juggling a bottle of beer and my drink in a highball in one hand, and a small bowl of Japanese rice crackers in the other hand. Probably came with the drinks, because it's not something I'd imagine Sorrell ordering. Despite managing to grab a few items of finger food at Black's wake, I still feel unfed, so I nibble eagerly on the snacks in between sips of my G and T.

"You been to L.A. before you moved here?" Sorrell asks.

I'm a little thrown, and relieved, by the more personal question. Like all professions, it's the people you work with as much as what you're actually doing that can make you happy in your job. Besides, socializing is important for building professional relationships. "Twice," I reply. "I came here for a couple of days with my parents when I was about twelve, and then stayed a week with an ex-boy-friend. We were on our way to Europe to do the backpacking thing."

He smiles. "I think that's more popular in Australia than here."

I nod. Many Australians head to Europe for a few months of backpacking, or make the most of the U.K. working-holiday visa to see that part of the world. I love living in both Australia and America, but I wouldn't mind being able to pop to Paris for the weekend—something you can easily do from England. Still, you can't have everything, and I prefer the day-to-day lifestyle in the U.S. and Oz.

"Have you always lived here?" I ask, suddenly aware that my ear isn't good enough to pick up regional differences in the U.S. accent and that Sorrell might not be an L.A. native.

"Yeah. But I took a year off before I joined the force and did a road trip with a couple of buddies. So I got to see a few other cities then." He smiles as he talks about it.

"Good memories, huh?"

He laughs. "Yeah."

I don't want the details of what three or four guys got up to on the road, so I drop it—I've seen enough movies to fill in the blanks.

Sorrell takes a gulp of beer and moves us on to the case. "So, why Black and Rickardian? How did he choose them?"

I mull the question over. "There has to be another link between Rickardian and Black, we just haven't found it yet."

"Yeah." He's silent, sipping his beer in contemplative thought. After a few minutes he says, "There's their location. Both West Coast authors, living in close proximity."

"At the very least it's for convenience." I sit back and have another sip of my drink. I'm feeling much cooler now and the G and T is going down well, so well I'm beginning to think Sorrell's idea of a knock-off drink was a great one, despite our current roadblock on the case. "But it's still not the *reason* he chose Rickardian and Black."

"No." Sorrell finishes a small handful of Japanese crackers. "So, the letters."

I take the papers out of my bag and show him copies of the fan mail I collected from Holt's home office. I decide to take Sorrell through the letters chronologically, starting with the first letter from "A fan."

"Okay, so this is the first letter Holt's got a record of from 'A fan,' the handwritten one. And it's very complimentary." I pass the photocopy to Sorrell and let him read it through himself.

> *Dear Ms. Black,*
> *A friend recently recommended your books, and so I dutifully started with your first one,* The Time Has Come, *and have read all five of your books. You're certainly a wonderful crime author, and have even converted me to this genre. I generally prefer reading literary fiction and some humor, such as the Bill Bryson books, but after starting your Benson series and earlier novels, I'm going to add crime to my reading list. Although I'd love it if you concentrated on the characters more.*
> *Yours sincerely,*
> *A new fan*

"It's signed from 'A new fan,' but I'm sure it's our guy. In the letter to Rickardian he complimented her on the characters, and in this one that's the area he's singled out that he wants Black to concentrate on.

"What do you think the signature says?" Sorrell brings the photocopy closer to him, examining the squiggle at the bottom, underneath *A new fan*.

With the paper close enough to me that I could lick it, I examine the signature. "This letter could be a *J*. Hopefully someone from Questioned Documents will be able to help us with that." Questioned Documents will look at it in the context of the rest of the letter and under a magnifying glass to hopefully give us something more. "I've requested prints, paper analysis, ink analysis and handwriting analysis on this one."

Sorrell takes another swig of beer. "Let's see what we get."

Putting the letter back with the stack, I pull out the two hate mails from 2004. One is typed and the other has been constructed with cut-out letters.

"This one's clearly a crank, from someone with a poor education," I say, referring to the letter made up of different magazine and newspaper cuttings. *You riting sucks. I waisted $8 on you're stupid book.*

"I don't think it's anything to worry about, but I've submitted it for fingerprints anyway. We'll see how our other forensics pan out before doing anything more with this one."

Sorrell hands it back to me and moves on to the typed letter.

"This one's a little more interesting, and it's quite personal," I say.

Dear Ms. Black,
   I have read all your books and have been sorely disappointed each time. I don't know why your books

are so popular. Your writing is clunky and unpolished at best, and your characters lack any depth. I find your writing average in every way and can't figure out why your books continue to make bestseller lists. I have to agree with the Chicago Tribune, and say your work is "mediocre" and "lacking in any depth or well-crafted twists." I hope for your sake and mine that your writing improves, because it certainly needs to. You don't deserve your success.

The letter is unsigned, undated and has no other identifying information on it.

Sorrell looks up. "The last remark's pretty cutting."

"I think it's only someone being critical rather than a threat, but I've submitted it for analysis nevertheless."

He takes a swig of beer. "Do you know a killer is less likely to get caught through forensics in L.A. county than other jurisdictions? They do a bang-up job at the lab but they just don't have enough personnel to handle the caseload."

"I didn't know that particular fact, but it doesn't surprise me." In 2006 L.A. county had four hundred and two murders. The stats indicate that over eighty percent of murders in the county are related to organized crime, but it's still a very high figure, one that keeps everyone—local police forces, the sheriff's department and FBI—busy. It's one of the pieces of research I did before accepting the job here…I don't mind being busy. The more of *them* I can get off the street the better.

We sit in a slightly depressed silence before Sorrell offers me another drink. I get the round, opting for a water.

"So, 2005?" Sorrell says as I sit down.

I shuffle the 2005 letters to the top of the pile. "One from 'A fan' and one that's a little unusual, indicating someone who knows Black or was stalking her."

"Really?" Sorrell raises an eyebrow at the possibility of a stalker. Most serial killers stalk their victims at length before the actual kill. And when you're dealing with celebrities or other high-profile targets, a stalker can get violent and become a murderer.

Despite his interest in the stalker, I pass the letter from "A fan" to Sorrell first.

Dear Ms. Black,
   Again, well done. I really enjoyed the latest Benson novel, although I'm starting to get a little tired of his profanity. Sometimes it makes me question if he really is one of the good guys. Perhaps it's time to tone it down rather than up? And how about giving Benson a serious love interest? Believe you me, even a man like him needs a woman's touch in his life! In fact, maybe it would mellow him. And he needs to move on at some stage. I'm still looking forward to the next installment.
Yours sincerely,
A fan

"This is where he starts to show his first sign of judgment on Black's books and the Benson character," I say. "The judgment element is important, because ultimately that's what I think he sees himself as doing with Black and Rickardian—judging them and then meting out their punishments."

"And the stalker?" Sorrell prompts.

I pass him that letter.

Dear Loretta Black,

You really are doing well, aren't you? Eight best-sellers to your name, a new home, new car and new jewelry. But do you think you've earned your suc-cess? I don't. People like you need to be taken down a peg or two. You write a book in less than a year and get millions for it. That's ridiculous, when you're not even a particularly good writer. Watch your back, bitch.

"Holt said this one really unnerved Black. She did buy a new house, new car and new jewelry within a month or two of one another, and this came soon after her spending spree."

"So someone was watching her." Sorrell puts the letter on top of the pile.

"Exactly. Holt suggested she go to the police, but Black wanted to wait and see if she got another one like it."

"She didn't, I take it?"

"Not one that included personal information like that, no. In 2006 she got one more from 'A fan' and two more letters that seem more like random hate mail."

"Let's have a look at them."

I fish out the final two letters, the 2006 suspect batch, handing Sorrell the one from "A fan" first.

Sorrell's eyes move down the page, and when he gets to the bottom line, I speak. "Notice the mention of our children and society. 'Our children and society in general are becoming desensitized to violence and upping the ante in fiction is probably not helping,'" I quote from the letter. "This is when he starts to feel the need to act, to change or protect society and to protect children."

Sorrell picks out the three letters we have from our fan. "You can definitely see the progression."

"Oh, yeah. They're a classic example of escalation, moving from congratulatory to urging her to cut back on the violence…to quite threatening."

"That's the biggest jump."

I nod. "Yes, the letter that came soon before Black's murder."

"What do you make of the change from handwriting to a computer printout?" Sorrell asks.

Only the first letter is handwritten, and on writing paper. "It could be as simple as the guy buying a printer around that time. But it's also a way to distance himself from Black, to become more anonymous. When he went from handwriting to a printer, he also chose not to sign the note—no sense of personalization. From a profiling perspective, a psychological perspective, it could also be a form of punishment—Black's become too violent and she's no longer worthy of his signature."

"But he still signed it 'A fan' when clearly he wasn't a fan anymore."

"To identify himself only. He wanted her to know that his opinion of her had dropped significantly. I think—" I'm interrupted by my cell phone ringing "—Sorry." I pick it up from the table. "Hello?"

"Can you talk? It sounds noisy."

I recognize the voice—Justin Reid.

"Um…I'm at a bar, but I can talk for a couple of minutes."

"Oh. On a date?"

I'm not obliged to answer his question, but there's no harm in being honest. "No, I'm discussing a case with a colleague."

"Ah, Black? Rickardian?"

"How did you know?"

Reid seems to know my every move—my transfer and now my current case allocation. It's unnerving and I wait impatiently for his response.

"You were on TV."

"What?" I say, horrified.

He laughs. "Don't worry, just in the background of the press conference."

"Oh, that. Okay." Now it makes sense. I stand up and mouth, "Sorry," to Sorrell before walking outside in the hope that the street noise will be quieter than the bar noise.

"I'd forgotten how beautiful you are."

Now it's my turn to laugh. "Very smooth, Justin."

"Can't be too smooth if you're laughing at me." He sounds genuinely upset.

"Sorry." God, I'm not used to dating etiquette. Not that this is a date anyway, but the intent is certainly there on his side.

"I'll live."

And I'm sure he will. Justin Reid hardly needs an ego boost from me.

"So how's the case going? Any luck?"

"You know I can't discuss a case with you."

"Yes, of course." He pauses. "So, tomorrow night. You free?"

"Um…"

"Then it's settled. We'll have dinner in L.A. I know a great Italian restaurant. You'll love it."

I smile. "I'm sure that normally works for you, Justin, but not this time, not with me."

"Why not?"

If he's still at work, I can imagine him reclining in his leather chair behind his desk in Silicon Valley, looking out his window at the spectacular view.

"In case you've forgotten, your employee is sitting in a cell in Arizona, arrested by me."

"How could I forget?" For the first time in the conversation his voice is harsher, no longer playful and seductive.

"I don't mix business with pleasure, Justin."

"Of course you do. Everybody does a little bit." He says it with absolute confidence.

I'm silent, because he's right. I was dating a fellow profiler, I'm still attracted to Darren. It's hard to *never* mix work with pleasure. I mean, everyone socializes at least a little bit at work, right? And for workaholics like me, it's the only way I'm ever going to meet someone.

"I'm sorry, Justin. The flowers are beautiful and I am flattered, but dinner's out."

"Maybe lunch then, something less formal."

I laugh. "Nice try."

"Thank you. So, lunch?"

"Maybe if things were different…" I let the thought trail off, because things aren't different.

"What does it matter how we met?"

He's certainly persistent, and I don't know whether to be annoyed or impressed. "I'm sorry, Justin, but the answer's still no."

"Mmm." He pauses. "I know that tone of voice. It's resolution."

"I'm afraid so. You read people well, no wonder you're a good businessman."

"You're a profiler, you read people too. And maybe you know that I won't give up that easily."

I laugh. "Good night, Mr. Reid."

"Wow, I have taken a step backward. Mr. Reid, huh?" He pauses. "Good night, Sophie." He says the last part softly and then hangs up.

"I take it that wasn't about the case," Sorrell says when I sit back down.

I look at him quizzically.

"You're smiling a little too much for it to be work." His voice has the slightest hint of teasing to it, and I'm embarrassed because I realize I'm not just smiling, I'm grinning. And it's not that I'm even particularly attracted to Reid. As much as I hate to admit it, there is something appealing about being chased by a man.

"No, it wasn't work." I take a sip of my drink and keep my eyes down, hoping to close the conversation.

Sorrell holds up his hands. "Okay, I won't say anything else."

"Thanks." I take the last sip of my mineral water. "So, where were we?"

Sorrell doesn't even have to think. "You were talking about how the fan's opinion of Black has dropped, and you were about to say something else."

I cast my mind back, trying to reignite the train of thought. "Oh, yeah. I was just going to say that I think we need to really push forensics on the letters from this guy."

"Agreed." Sorrell sits back in the comfortable chair and glances at his watch. A clock behind Sorrell tells me it's past 10:00 p.m. Well and truly time to clock off.

"So, the last letter?" Sorrell leans forward again, but it seems to take some effort to pull himself up and out of the clutches of the chair's soft center.

"Another one made with cut-out letters. This one is more threatening, so I've asked forensics to prioritize it too."

I love what you do to the stupid bitches in your books. Women are all whores and need to be put in their place. Sometimes you show them too much sympathy, but at least you always show them cut up or murdered. Keep it up.

"I guess this kinda proves the point Black's fan was trying to make in his letters. This guy—" Sorrell taps the photocopied letter "—obviously got off on Black's books, on her descriptions of women being raped and murdered."

"Yes, but was it enough to make him act? To commit a murder himself?"

Sorrell shrugs. "It made someone act."

Sixteen

Lying in bed, I let the case facts run around in my head. Hopefully two thoughts will bump into each other and I'll recognize their relevance or importance. It actually works surprisingly well. I guess because when you're tired, your conscious mind begins to recede, and the subconscious, which is more likely to notice the little details, comes to the fore. And somewhere in the midst of that shift, the conscious mind can pick up something important from the subconscious and voilà…a revelation. But tonight, it doesn't happen. Instead, my thoughts are so full of what I have to do tomorrow that in the end I get up and grab a piece of paper and pen to write it down.

Once my list is written, I find it easier to relax. Still, it's not quite time to sleep yet. I'd continued Rickardian's book on the couch as soon as I got back, but I want to get some more reading in before the night's out, so I fight tiredness and open up the book at chapter five.

Sarina Robertson's pager beeped, cutting into her sleep like a sharp knife. She blinked her eyes, trying to force them open, but she was never good at waking up in the middle of the night.

"Come on, call in." Her husband's voice was hoarse from lack of sleep, but the nudge came just in time, just as Sarina was in danger of slipping back into her dream world. Kittens...she was dreaming about kittens. She managed to think it was a bizarre thing to dream about before her husband gave the second, deeper nudge.

"Ouch."

"Call in. At least then I can go back to sleep." He rolled over, his back to Sarina.

"Charming," she said, now more awake than asleep. Flicking on the bedside light she checked her pager. Darn, it was Detective Suki Tagara, which could mean only one thing—a homicide. She leaned across her bedside table and groped for the phone in its cradle. She hit speed dial 2, Suki.

"Good morning, Sarina." Suki's voice was light and awake, a sharp contrast to Sarina's.

"Is it? I hadn't noticed."

"You picked the wrong job for someone who likes to sleep."

"Tell me something I don't know."

"Okay. We've got a murder."

"I said tell me something I don't know. You never call me at..." she looked at the bedside clock, squinting to make her eyes focus through the watery, sleep-filled haze "...3:00 a.m. unless someone's dead."

Suki laughed. "Fair enough."

"You need me now?"

"Yes."

Sarina sighed. "Address?" She reached for the pen and paper that she always set up on her bedside table when she was on call for the city's homicide cops. She took the address down. "See you soon." Sarina made sure she hauled herself upright before hanging up the phone. She'd learned from experience that staying horizontal was not a good way for her to get to a crime scene pronto. Like Suki said, not with the way she liked her sleep.

Reading about someone who's half-asleep seems to tip me over the edge, and I put the book down, realizing I've read the last sentence several times. Tomorrow…there's always tomorrow. Turning my light off, I roll over, clutching at the spare pillow that I always tuck under me to support my back.

"Sweet dreams," I say to myself, dropping off practically before the words are out.

I'm tied to a chair and a figure clad in black and wearing a balaclava paces in front of me. The glow of an almost full moon makes the light and shade of the silhouette more pronounced, more ominous. As the figure comes closer, the whites of his eyes seem to shimmer, catching the moon's rays. For the first time, I'm frightened.

Suddenly I'm pacing, shouting at the woman tied to the chair. My fists clench and unclench and I have to hold myself back from hitting her. A buzzing noise rings in my ears.

I wake up, disoriented. I remember the dream, remember the buzzing noise and am surprised to discover it's real…it's my phone. And it's early…6:00 a.m.

"Hello?" I'm not with it enough to manage adding my name onto the greeting.

"Anderson, it's Brady." His voice is even gruffer than usual.

"Oh…hi." God I hope I'm not in trouble again.

"Crime author Katrina Bowles has been reported missing. Last confirmed sighting was midday yesterday in her San Diego apartment."

"What?" I am instantly alert. I was sure our killer wouldn't escalate so quickly…that he wouldn't take another author for at least a few months.

In cases of abduction or kidnapping, the first twenty-four to forty-eight hours after someone's reported missing are crucial, and midday yesterday means the first eighteen hours are already gone. "Who reported her missing?"

"Her live-in girlfriend. She reported it about half an hour ago. Bowles was planning to go to the movies by herself last night, but when the girlfriend got home at five this morning from her night shift, Bowles wasn't there. The detectives in San Diego called it through to FBI, knowing that we're running Black's murder case, and the call got routed through to me." Brady pauses. "What do you think?"

My mind is swirling, and I can't help but feel responsible. Why didn't I get a vision or dream about this woman? Or could she be the one from my dream in the woods? Oh God. I have to find out what Katrina Bowles's book is about. If it's about women who are raped and killed in the woods…

I think back to the question…my thoughts on the situation. "I really didn't think our guy would strike again so soon, sir. Black was murdered only five days ago, and that would make it less than a week between victims." I pause.

"Ultimately the proof is in her book. If it is our killer, it'll be done like Bowles's book."

"I'm at a computer now. Hold on and I'll find out more about her books."

While Brady looks up Bowles, I throw some clothes together for the day, ready to shower.

"You there, Anderson?"

"Yes, sir."

"Okay, she's written two books. The last one was released eight months ago and is called *Missing*. Hold on…."

I hear him clicking in the background, presumably trying to find out more info about the book.

"This is the synopsis—'When a young office worker is missing, believed to have been abducted from her home, P.I. Tracey Hardey is hired by the woman's parents to investigate. The police dismiss the case as a woman escaping an abusive marriage, but P.I. Hardey discovers something much more sinister. When the woman's body turns up, Hardey is thrown into the high-stakes world of corporate espionage.' That's it."

I'm relieved that it doesn't sound like the girl from my vision—no woods, no running naked. But my relief is subdued, to say the least, because Bowles is missing, possibly abducted from her home, just like her character. "It doesn't sound good," I concede.

"We need more information on the book," Brady says.

"If it is our guy and the victim in the novel wasn't killed immediately, we may have some time to find Bowles and save her." My voice rises with hope.

"I'm going to schedule a phone hookup with San Diego and San Fran for eight. That give you enough time to get your ass in here?"

I look at the clock. "Sure. Will you call Sorrell or shall I?"

"I'll call him."

"Okay," I say. "See you soon."

I get into work by 7:00 a.m. and immediately Google Katrina Bowles, and print off a photograph from her publisher's Web site. The head-and-shoulders shot shows an attractive woman in her early forties. She has brown hair in loose waves and strong yet pretty facial features. She seems to be wearing little or no makeup but she doesn't need it—her skin has a naturally healthy glow to it, so much so that I'm guessing she's got southern European or South American blood in her. A tan, real or fake, can never simulate the real deal.

Closing the door of a meeting room, I turn my phone to Silent so I can't be disturbed. I sit down and try to get as comfortable as I can; then, once I've found a moderately relaxing position, I focus on the printout of Bowles. Sometimes just concentrating on a photo will give me flashes of the person, although not necessarily of things relating to the case. With one woman I saw her graduating from college, something she'd done only two weeks before she was attacked by a serial rapist. And with Tabitha I saw her tenth birthday party and flashes of her family life. I prefer these images to the horrific ones of women and children being raped or killed. But unfortunately it's usually the terrifying visions that help the case.

I get nothing from Bowles's photo so I move on to the next stage—relaxation. Putting the photo down on the table in front of me, I roll my shoulders back and start focusing on my breathing, keeping it steady and slow. I try to push all thoughts away, including the sense of guilt I feel over getting the escalation part of the profile wrong. Instead, I concentrate on the rhythmic in and out of my breath. But my mind slips back to the facts. What am I missing? Why did our guy strike again so soon? After a few minutes I manage to clear my mind of the questions. But Bowles, or whoever or whatever gives me these visions, is stubborn and nothing comes to me after nearly fifty minutes of trying. I want to keep going, but I notice the time on the wall clock. I have to get moving.

I bump into Sorrell on the way to the meeting room that's been booked for the conference call.

"Morning," he says with a nod.

"Hi." I look down, embarrassed that my profile was wrong. "I couldn't believe it when Brady called me this morning."

"No, me neither. Let's hope the crime scene in San Diego gives us some evidence."

I nod enthusiastically and we start walking together to the meeting room.

"By the way, Randy Sade didn't personally get a copy of *Ladykiller,* but his paper did. The literary editor there read it straightaway and then passed it on to Sade, so he did have access to an early copy."

"Really?" I say.

"I also contacted Blake's two buddies this morning, and they back up his alibi of the game and then the West Hollywood bar."

"But only until midnight?"

"Exactly."

"You've been busy." I'd like to give Sorrell my update, but I can't tell him I spent the early morning unsuccessfully trying to induce a vision. "And Blake?" I ask.

"I want to talk to him in person. I was thinking we could go to his place this morning, but now…"

"Let's see what happens in here."

Sorrell and I are the last to arrive and we take our seats next to Brady and the head of the Criminal Division, George Rosen. Within less than a minute we've got Dusk, O'Shaughnessy and Perez from L.A. on the line, and Detectives Levy and Sullivan from San Diego Homicide.

After the introductions are complete, Brady starts the meeting. "As I'm sure you all know, Black's death has been linked to that of author Lorie Rickardian, who was killed in San Francisco four months ago."

"So we've got two dead authors and now one missing," says Detective Sullivan, the only other woman on the conference call.

"Yes," I respond. "The replication of the authors' fictional murders makes it clear we're looking at a serial killer."

"So it's likely Bowles has met the same fate here in San Diego." This time it's Levy who speaks.

"We need to find out more about her book." I flick the ring on my little finger. "Has anyone read it?"

"I have."

"Dusk?" With so many male voices on the line, it's hard to distinguish between them. I'm guessing it's Dusk not from the voice but because he told me he was a crime-fiction fan.

"Yeah, it's Dusk."

"How does the book compare?" It's a male voice who asks the question, but I'm not sure whose.

"I've been revisiting the key facts this morning. The victim in Katrina Bowles's book was abducted from her

San Diego apartment. When the body was found a week later, the time of death was estimated at around forty-eight hours after the abduction and the cause of death was a bullet wound to the head, execution style. She'd also been tortured. The only thing they found at the victim's apartment was a tiny chalk *X* on the coffee table. It was made by the killer to represent 'you're out' or 'that's a strike against you.' Did you find anything like that at the scene?"

We wait a couple of seconds before the San Diego detectives reply.

"No, we didn't."

"You may want to go back and look for it. In Bowles's book, the killer put the *X* on the underside of a coffee table and it wasn't found for some time. It was his personal mark, something that his employers wouldn't have wanted him leaving, so he made it extremely discreet."

"I'm looking at a photo of the coffee table now," says Levy, "and there's nothing on the top. Do you want me to call the girlfriend?"

"Do you think she'll be at home?"

"Definitely," Sullivan answers. "She's not coping very well and is convincing herself it's a straight kidnapping. She's hoping for a ransom call."

Brady leans forward. "We'll hold."

It's less than two minutes before we hear a small click on the line as we're taken off hold, and Levy's voice comes through. "It's there."

I shake my head, asking myself the same question again—why the escalation? Has something happened that's fueled the killer's desire to punish another author?

"She's probably still alive, then," Dusk says quietly.

"But if he follows the book we've got just over twenty-four hours left before he kills her."

"Okay, we need to work quickly," Brady says.

"Were the words *Your turn* at Bowles's apartment?" I ask.

"Not that I know of," Sullivan says. "Certainly not anywhere obvious." She's hesitant to rule it out completely, presumably because the *X* was in such an obscure place. But the *X* is Bowles's message, not our guy's, and he likes his personal touch to be obvious.

"We're keeping it quiet, but the words *Your turn* were at both Rickardian's and Black's apartments," I explain for Levy and Sullivan. "That's our guy's signature and his main deviation from the books."

"So why isn't it at Bowles's apartment?" Levy asks. "Or have we missed it?"

"No, you would have seen it. But the apartment's not the primary crime scene this time. The killer *will* leave the message, and thereby his personal mark, but it'll probably be where he dumps the body. Dusk, what happens in her book?"

"The victim was held for two days in a basement. The building was owned by one of her employer's board of directors."

"Our killer will be following that book like a script, keeping to it as closely as possible," I say. "We need to use that to our advantage."

"How?" Sullivan says. "Bowles doesn't work for a company, she's an author."

We're silent for a little while.

I bite my lip, trying to think of a direction to take. "We could try her publisher's board of directors, or the company the girlfriend works for."

A whistle comes down the line. "Could be tricky convincing people to let us in and even trickier getting warrants…the girlfriend works for Wal-Mart."

I can't imagine a judge signing a search warrant for multiple directors based on a hunch. "Could we use the location of the building where the victim was held in the book to narrow things down, Dusk?"

"The building was an old warehouse on the harbor," Dusk replies, "that had been converted into apartments."

"Most of the warehouses on the waterfront are now apartments," Levy says. "We'd be searching a lot of buildings if we can't narrow it down somehow."

Silence.

"Anything else from the book, Dusk?"

"The victim worked for a fictional insurance company, which had real-estate interests on the side. The vic was tortured, and the P.I. on the case figured it was to see how much she knew and if she'd told anyone else."

"What was the name of the company? Maybe the killer will try to find something similar."

"Um…hold on, I will remember it." Dusk pauses for a good ten seconds. "It was Gold…no…Golden Risk Insurance."

"Do you think you can use that?" I ask the San Diego detectives.

There are a few beats of silence before Sullivan answers. "We can look up the companies that have real-estate interests on the harbor and see if anything stands out." Sullivan doesn't sound hopeful and her reluctance is founded. I know it's a long shot but it's better than nothing.

"Anything else, Dusk?" I ask, still not willing to let it go.

"Nothing that I think will help us, Anderson. Sorry."

I nod slowly, and then realize I need to verbalize my response. "Okay, thanks, Dusk."

"So you really think she's alive?" Sullivan asks.

"Yeah. The killer will be torturing her, like in the book." I try not to think too much about what he might be doing to Bowles right now.

Sullivan makes a hissing noise. "What sort of torture, Agent Dusk?"

"In the book the victim was cut up. It started with shallow cuts, then deeper cuts and eventually her fingers were chopped off."

I wince, thinking about what stage the killer might be up to now. Poor Bowles. I've been approaching this case as though we had all the time in the world—well, at least a few months—and now this? I bite my lip.

Sorrell breaks his silence. "We've been looking into a lead over here, letters to both Rickardian and Black that were signed 'A fan.'"

I focus on the leads again, and not Bowles's current predicament. "I think that needs to be our first line of inquiry in San Diego. Have you got her fan mail?"

"No, but we can get it from the girlfriend," Levy answers.

"Anything at Bowles's apartment?"

"The crime scene's still being processed," Sullivan says. "Any other leads in L.A.?"

"Yeah, a few. We've got a fiber from a beige sweater or similar item of clothing, but nothing to match it against. And we've been investigating a journalist who's also a budding novelist here as a person of interest," Sorrell says. "He claims Black stole his idea and he tried to sue her. He was unsuccessful and threatened to kill her."

"But?" It's Sullivan's voice.

"But we can't link him to Rickardian and he doesn't fit some elements of the profile."

"What's his name?" asks Levy.

"Randy Sade."

"Okay, we'll see if we can link him to Bowles, just in case."

"We're also looking at an author called Peter Blake," Sorrell says.

"A rival author," I explain.

"And how does Blake fit?" I think it's Levy who asks the question.

"Apparently Blake was jealous of Black's success. He's with the same publisher and resented the attention she got. And he might have had some kind of relationship with Black a few years ago. We were going to look into that today."

"But no link to Rickardian...again." Dusk's playing devil's advocate with his own theory.

"That's right, Dusk. It's still our stumbling point."

"Alibis?" Brady asks.

"Blake's alibi for the night Black was murdered is only good up to midnight," Sorrell answers.

"With Black's time of death pinpointed as between midnight and four in the morning, we're going to have that problem with most of our suspects," I say. "The single ones at least. And even if someone had their partner lying next to them, it's still possible they could sneak out of the house without the partner waking."

Brady sighs. "True."

"We'll look into an alibi for the night Rickardian was murdered," Sorrell says. "And see if he hopped on a plane to San Diego after the funeral yesterday."

I glance at Sorrell. "He was in a hurry to leave Black's funeral. Maybe it wasn't to finish his book at all."

Brady looks up from his notepad. "Let's keep looking into this Blake character and see what other evidence comes our way. I agree the alibi's going to be tricky in Black's case." He pauses, waiting to see if we've got anything else to add.

"We also came back with an AFIS match on one of the fan-mail letters." Sorrell leans into the speakerphone a little. "We're looking into the guy now. His name's Robert Wendell."

"Okay." Brady looks at me. "What about the media and Bowles, Anderson?"

"I think we should use them. It won't change what he does with Bowles at this stage, but maybe she was spotted by someone when he was transporting her. Given the time constraints, we should hold a press conference as soon as possible."

"We'll get on that straightaway," Sullivan says.

"Levy and Sullivan," Brady says, "okay with you guys if I send Anderson down for a quick look around?"

A few beats of silence before they both agree to an FBI presence.

Sorrell pipes up too. "Mind if I tag along?" He directs the question to me first.

"Not at all," I reply.

It's only a short flight for us, and given we've seen Black's crime scene in person, something at Bowles's house could trigger a breakthrough. We'll be able to make it down there and back in a day, even half a day if need be.

"Detective Sorrell here." He leans in to the speakerphone. "I'll fly down too if that's okay with you guys."

He's asking Sullivan and Levy for their permission. It is their crime scene, after all.

"Okay." Their response is noncommittal.

Sorrell looks at me. "Given this escalation, do you think he could already have selected his next victim, after Bowles, I mean?"

Sorrell's thinking ahead, like me. And if our killer maintains the escalation, the answer is absolutely. "It's something we need to look into."

Brady sighs. "But who's next? How's he choosing his victims?"

"We still haven't been able to come up with anything on that, sir." I pause. "But let's start with a list of female American crime-fiction authors," I say. "At least that will give us a preliminary pool of potential victims."

"Dusk here. I'll look into that one. I could give you quite a few names off the top of my head, but it wouldn't be complete."

"A list would be great," I say.

Sorrell clears his throat. "You could try Black's agent or editor too. They'll probably know, being in the biz and all."

"Will do."

I go back to Brady's question—how he's choosing which authors to target. So far O'Shaughnessy and Perez have been silent, but now it's time to see if they'll play ball.

"O'Shaughnessy and Perez, we need to see if there's some other link between Rickardian, Black and Bowles. I'll work on a list of possible areas, and then can you guys reinterview people there?"

There's a pause and Sorrell shakes his head, frustrated that Perez and O'Shaughnessy aren't more proactive. I'd told Sorrell about my experiences with the pair in San Francisco.

Finally the "boss," O'Shaughnessy, gives us a yes. I want to add, "If it's not too much trouble for you," but I resist the temptation. Instead, I tell them our part of the bargain. "Sorrell and I will do the same with Black and Bowles and then we can compare notes."

"We haven't got much on this end yet," says Sullivan. "But the apartment should be processed soon."

"How did it look?" Sorrell asks.

Sullivan takes the question. "Untouched. But given what we knew about Loretta Black and Lorie Rickardian, we took the report very seriously, so we dusted the apartment for prints. But with no body to autopsy it gives us less evidence."

"Well, if we don't find Bowles in the next twenty-four hours or so, you'll have a body."

The thought that we'll be too late sickens me. I always feel a sense of responsibility to the victims and future victims, but this time I feel like Bowles's abduction and the escalation is something I could have, and should have, predicted in the profile. But even as these thoughts run through my head, my logic rejects them. All indications were that our killer was just getting started and wasn't in a hurry to make his point. Something must have made him bring his next kill forward, but what?

Brady rests his elbows on the table and clasps his hands together. "Okay, let's finish divvying these leads up. So, Dusk is looking into a list of female crime authors, O'Shaughnessy and Perez are going back to Rickardian and Levy and Sullivan will look into harbor apartments and some of the other elements from Bowles's book. We're also looking for something that links all three authors to one another." His eyes move down his notepad. "Anderson and Sorrell will get the first flight to San Diego, and Levy and Sullivan will organize a press conference as soon as possible."

"Do you want us to wait so you can be involved, Anderson?" Sullivan asks.

"No. The sooner the better. Like I said, press won't change our boy's plans, so run it purely as an appeal to the public for information."

"Okay," Sullivan says. "It'll be done by the time you guys arrive."

Brady nods. "Well, that's it for now. Let's get this show on the road." He picks his pad up from the table, ready to bring the meeting to an end. "Unless something urgent comes up beforehand, let's touch base again at twelve-thirty. That okay with everyone?"

We all give positive responses and say our goodbyes, then Brady disconnects.

"Good first week, Anderson?" For the first time he doesn't seem annoyed with me.

I manage a short-lived laugh. "Real good."

"Let me know if you need anything," Brady says, before he heads off, leaving Sorrell and me in the meeting room.

We look at each other silently. I'm feeling guilty about Bowles and I guess Sorrell is too.

"I really didn't think he'd escalate." I shake my head.

"Neither did I." Sorrell places both his hands on the table and gives a deep sigh. "Sometimes they do the unexpected."

Seventeen

We head for the airport and San Diego via Blake's modest apartment in Lennox for a surprise visit. We've only got about fifteen minutes to spare if we're going to make our flight, but that should be enough to press him on his relationship with Black.

I ring the buzzer of apartment 501. After a couple of minutes, I press it again. "Maybe he's in San Diego," I say, thinking of Bowles.

Sorrell raises his eyebrows. "Maybe."

After a few minutes, Sorrell pulls out his cell phone. "Let's see if he's answering his phone."

Sorrell looks up the number in his notebook and punches it in. After a few seconds he shakes his head. "Went to voice mail." He hangs up without leaving a message. "Cell." Again, he punches in some numbers. "It's off."

"So much for him being at home, writing," I say. "We don't have time to track him down, not if we want to make our flight."

Sorrell nods. "Let's go."

An hour later we're about to hop on the plane when our cells ring simultaneously.

"Agent Anderson," I say.

"Anderson, it's Sullivan. We got the fan mail from the girlfriend, but nothing from 'A fan.'"

"Really?"

"Yup."

"Okay…um…we're just boarding, so I've got to go but I'll see you in about an hour."

"We'll be waiting."

I hang up and wait for Sorrell to finish his call. As soon as he's done I fill him in.

"Maybe Bowles threw the letter out," Sorrell suggests. "If it was nasty…."

"It's possible. We can ask the girlfriend, see what she says."

Sorrell nods. "That was Edwards about our AFIS result." He jiggles his phone.

"Yes?" I wait expectantly for Sorrell's news.

"Robert Wendell was working the night shift last Friday in Vegas. He's clear."

I nod. With so much fan mail for Black, it was bound to happen—not all of her fans will be law-abiding citizens, which means their prints are going to be in the AFIS, waiting for McAvey to process the letters and come up with a match.

Within fifteen minutes our plane is taxiing and I'm flicking through the files on my lap, ready to discuss the case with Sorrell.

He glances at the case notes. "Can you give me a few minutes?"

I'm surprised to see Sorrell's head is jammed back hard

into the headrest and his hands are gripping the armrests. Well, what do you know: Sorrell's not a good flyer.

The temptation to tease him is strong, but I resist the urge. "Sure," I say, although he'd probably feel better if he was distracted.

The engines rev.

"So, did you go to San Diego on that road trip of yours?" I ask.

He moves his eyes my way, but not his head. "Yeah."

"What's it like?" Sorrell doesn't answer my question so I think of something else to say. "I've heard it's a nice city."

"It is," Sorrell manages.

"How long did you spend there?"

"Um…" He's torn between concentrating on the takeoff procedure and my question. He answers just as we become airborne. "Two weeks. Summer of '85."

"Nice. Did you have fun?"

"Oh, yeah. Do you like Mexican food?"

"Uh-huh."

"The Mexican in San Diego is even better than L.A."

"Sounds good." I hear the wheels rising, ready to be consumed by the plane's underbelly. "Maybe we'll get a chance to try some."

Silence. Unintentionally, my comment brings us back to reality and the case. We're not flying to San Diego to try Mexican food.

Sorrell looks at the file on my lap and loosens his grip on the armrests. "Let's give it another go."

During an investigation, we'll go through the file and photos over and over again, hoping something will catch our attention or suddenly seem out of place. But in this case, our umpteenth sweep reveals nothing.

I put the file back in my briefcase. "On to the link between the authors."

Sorrell seems much more relaxed now that he's focused on the case and not the flying.

By the time we touch down in San Diego, we've come up with a decent list to investigate—looking for points of intersection between the authors and their killer.

Agent(s)
Publisher(s)
Editor(s)
Publicists(s)
Awards
Other events (e.g., writers' festivals and signings)
University or other writing courses
Writing groups
Online research or book groups
Memberships

If we gather information from each author's friends, family and professional acquaintances, we should be able to come up with a list of their contacts and hopefully find a name in common. Maybe then we'll have some idea who the next target is, or even who the killer is. We'll also find out if Bowles and Rickardian knew Randy Sade or Peter Blake.

Sullivan and Levy are easy to spot, partly because Sullivan's flaming red hair and Levy's darker features are telltale signs of their Irish and Jewish heritages, respectively, and partly because the light catches the police badges they wear on their belts. Sorrell and I make a beeline for the pair and introduce ourselves. Sullivan's a few inches taller than me, and fuller in the figure. Her red hair is cut short, and her blue eyes contrast against milky skin. Levy's got a slim build, is about an inch shorter than his partner at around five-ten and has soft dark brown eyes. His face is made harsher by square-framed glasses and a masculine jaw. With the four of us standing together, Sullivan, Levy and I look like bonsais to Sorrell's six-six frame.

Once the introductions are complete, we make our way to Sullivan and Levy's police-issue Ford, via an airport fax machine that I use to fax my list through to Perez and O'Shaughnessy in San Francisco. With any luck, we'll have all the information for our meeting.

"So how did the press conference go?" I buckle my seat belt.

"Fine. Nothing unusual." Sullivan turns around from the passenger seat. "We'll play the video of it for you when we get to the station."

"Any leads?" Sorrell asks.

Sullivan shakes her head. "Not so far. We've followed up a few elements from the plot of Bowles's book, but nothing."

"Such as?" I ask.

"We looked up the directors of Bowles's publishing house and Wal-Mart to see if any of them have interests in apartment blocks in the harbor, but nothing came up. We also went through the owners of the apartment buildings on the harbor to see if any of them stood out or looked related to Bowles's fictional insurance company, Golden Risk Insurance." She shakes her head. "Nothing."

I nod. It was a stretch, but the lead had to be followed through just in case.

"Forensics has finished in Bowles's home, but no results yet," Sullivan continues.

I mentally go over the leads to decide what we can and should do, and in which order. The first priority has to be Bowles's apartment and the girlfriend. "I'd like to talk to the girlfriend first."

It's not that I don't trust Sullivan and Levy, it's just that…well, okay, I don't trust them, not yet. I barely trust Sorrell and he's proving to be a good cop. O'Shaughnessy and Perez missed the fan mail and alienated Emily Rickardian so much that she withheld vital information. What did Sullivan and Levy miss or do? And on top of this there's also the possibility that I'll get something psychically if I visit Bowles's apartment. That's a pretty good incentive.

"Is the girlfriend around?" I ask.

Sullivan pulls her phone out and flicks through the phone's screen, presumably finding the number. "I guess she'd normally sleep now, being a shift worker, but I doubt she'll be able to sleep at the moment." A few clicks later Sullivan is waiting for Bowles's lover to pick up.

"Hi, Anne, it's Detective Sullivan. Did I wake you?"

I can just make out a muffled response of, "Kinda."

"We've got the officers from L.A. here and they'd like to see you as soon as possible."

This time I can't make out the response.

"Okay. Great. See you soon." Sullivan presses disconnect on her phone. "She's expecting us."

Twenty minutes later we pull up outside a large apartment complex, about fifteen stories high. Painted a pale lemon, it looks as though it was built in the past ten years, with modern, angular lines, blue-gray trim and lots of glass. Sullivan and Levy lead the way, buzzing apartment 425. The security door opens and we make our way to the fourth floor and Bowles's apartment.

Sullivan introduces us. "Anne Cooper, this is Special Agent Anderson from the FBI and Detective Sorrell from Beverly Hills Homicide."

Sorrell and I both shake hands with her. She looks extremely tired, and while her eyes are puffy with heavy, dark circles underneath them, they are clear from the telltale redness of recent crying. Maybe she really was asleep— you can't cry when you're sleeping. Cooper's long brown hair, which falls down her back and around her face, is straggly, like it needs a wash. Her face is gaunt, and even through her baggy pants and loose T-shirt you can tell she's thin—too thin.

"Nice to meet you," she says, but without enthusiasm. She backs up toward the kitchen. "Can I get you a coffee or cold drink?"

I notice the brewer in the kitchen. "A coffee would be great," I say, reassured that I won't be getting instant.

"Coffee sounds good to me too." Sorrell unbuttons his jacket and takes it off. It is rather hot in the apartment.

Not surprisingly, Sullivan and Levy also accept the offer of coffee. I move closer to the kitchen and Cooper, while the others linger in the main living space. As Cooper makes a pot of coffee, I notice her hands are shaking slightly. She's probably hardly eaten or slept.

"How are you coping?" I ask.

She keeps her eyes focused on the coffeepot when she answers. "Okay, I guess. It all still feels surreal."

"That's normal. A normal reaction."

"Normal? I guess so." She seems distant, vague, as well as a little jumpy.

I look at her thin face again and can't help but worry she's not eating. It's funny how people react in one of two ways when it comes to food and stress. Some people eat double what they would normally, and others find it hard to touch food at all. But Anne can't afford to lose any weight. My thoughts instantly flit to how she'll take it when we find Bowles's body, but then I pull myself up…gotta think positive.

"So, you saw Katrina around midday yesterday?"

She nods and smooths her hands down the front of her tracksuit pants. "Yes. That's right."

"Did she seem nervous? Sound strange?"

"No."

"And she hasn't mentioned anything out of the ordinary in the past couple of weeks? No feeling that someone was following her or anything like that?" Given most serial killers and other predators stalk their victims, sometimes the target realizes or senses that she's being followed. Often they rationalize it, but they will occasionally mention it to a loved one.

"No, definitely not. She would have told me too, if she thought that, I mean." She stares at the first drips of coffee as they come through.

I nod. "Detectives Sullivan and Levy mentioned you work the night shift."

"That's right." She momentarily looks past me.

I turn around to see Sullivan and Levy showing Sorrell the coffee table, which would have been thoroughly examined and printed by forensics. Sometimes forensics will take an item back to the lab, and sometimes they can get everything they need from it in situ. In this case they've obviously examined it here.

Cooper continues. "I work nights at Wal-Mart, restocking, 9:00 p.m. to 4:00 a.m."

"Does Katrina make much money as an author?"

Cooper shakes her head. "No, she's just starting out. She only got a small advance for her first two books, and she's almost finished the third one now."

So presumably Cooper supports, or at least partially supports, Bowles. "So you left the apartment around lunchtime?"

"Yes. I was meeting a friend for lunch. Trina…Katrina was supposed to come with us but she said she was on a roll with her book and wanted to keep going. She was planning to write for a few hours and then catch a movie in the late afternoon or evening."

"Did you come back to the apartment before work?"

"Yes. For a couple of hours at about six. She wasn't here. But I figured she was still out."

"And when you got home from work…" I leave the sentence open, ready for her to fill in the blanks.

"That's when I realized something was wrong." She bites a fingernail. "There was no sign of Trina and the bed hadn't been slept in."

"Did you try to call her?"

"Yes, straightaway. And I'd tried before I left for work last night, but it went to voice mail. At the time I assumed she was at the movies, with her cell off." Cooper stares at the coffeemaker, but rubs her hands together. She's strung out all right. She looks up, past me, and I follow her gaze. Sorrell's right behind me.

"The *X* is tiny," he says. "Forensics has taken all their samples but they haven't rubbed it off. You want to look?"

"Sure." I follow him over to the coffee table. To see it

properly, I lie down on my back and slide myself under the table slightly. The *X* has been made in white chalk, in the corner nearest the apartment's front door. It seems a little bit fainter in one small section of the *X*, probably where forensics scraped for a sample.

By the time I've finished examining the coffee table, Cooper is bringing us all mugs of coffee and offering cream and sugar.

We sit down and I open up the questioning again. "So you don't think Katrina received a letter from someone called 'A fan'?"

Cooper shakes her head. "Not that I know of, at least. And I did double-check her files when the detectives called earlier this morning." She looks at Sullivan and Levy as she refers to them. "Is that important? The letter?"

"It's been a common factor with the other authors, but we need you to keep that to yourself, Anne," I say. "It's not something we want to go public with, and if anyone finds out, it could harm our chances of finding Katrina." I want to press my point, but not enough to say the extra part of that sentence out aloud: *alive.*

"I understand." Cooper takes a sip of some fruit juice that she poured for herself. She doesn't need coffee, not like us. Her thoughts can probably keep her awake all by themselves.

"When you came home, did anything look out of place?" Sorrell shifts in his chair and it draws attention to the fact that he's too big for it.

"No." Cooper responds quickly—it's probably a question she's already been asked.

We're silent for a little while before I decide to move things back to the fiction. "What's her new book about?"

Cooper's about to answer when Sorrell's phone rings. He glances at the phone's display. "Excuse me, I've got to take this." Sorrell moves into the hallway, and Cooper's eyes follow him.

"Katrina's book?" I bring her back to the question.

"It's about an organized-crime syndicate. It's very clever." Cooper's more animated, very obviously the proud partner.

"So you've read it?"

"I've read the first two hundred pages. That's where she's up to."

"And you've obviously read the last book she released, *Missing?*" I ask.

She nods. "Oh yes, of course."

"Do you have a spare copy we could borrow?" Reading Bowles's book has to be part of our investigation. Although I'm confident Dusk has a good grasp of the book, reading it myself might give me some helpful information. And I haven't had time since my 6:00 a.m. wake-up call this morning to pick up a copy.

"We do keep a couple of extra copies." Cooper heads into one of the bedrooms, and while she's in there Sorrell moves back into the living room.

"Anything?" I ask.

"One more AFIS match from the letters."

"Great."

"I asked McAvey to ring the name through to Edwards. He can do an initial investigation."

"The lab's getting through them."

"Slowly but surely. McAvey said he's gotten through fifty letters so far, but that he's moving on to another job now."

Cooper emerges with the book in hand.

I flick through it, then say, "Anne, do you mind if I look around? I'm a profiler and it helps me to get a feel for the victim."

She nods slowly. "Okay."

I leave Cooper talking to the others while I head for the two bedrooms. The first room is small, only big enough to be a study or a young child's room. Cooper and Bowles have it set up as a study, and I presume this is where Bowles works. Leafing through some of the papers and mail on her desk, I wait for a vision, but nothing happens so I move into the bedroom. I look around the room briefly before sitting down on the bed. I picture Bowles in my mind and make myself relax. It's difficult, knowing Sorrell and the others are just down the short hallway and could interrupt me at any stage. It's not like I froth at the mouth or anything, but I'm still very self-conscious of what it would be like to be around me when I have a full-on vision. I've already had to explain it away once to Sorrell at Black's funeral and I don't want to have to do it again. I blank my mind, giving myself over to my intuition. But after five minutes I still haven't seen anything, and I know that soon my absence will become noticeable. I return to the others in the living room, frustrated that being in the field isn't reaping the rewards I expected.

"What was Katrina wearing last time you saw her?" I ask, hoping maybe a visual image of Bowles will help me trigger a vision.

"Black shorts and a red T-shirt." Again Cooper responds quickly, making me assume I'm asking her something Sullivan and Levy have already covered.

"Did you check to see if those clothes are here? In case she changed?"

Cooper hesitates. "No. I didn't even think of that." She goes into the bedroom and I can hear drawers being opened and closed.

It's only a few minutes later that she joins us in the living room. "No, she must still be wearing those clothes." Once again, I notice a slight shake in her hands and I feel guilty for pushing her. Her thinness makes her look fragile, and I don't want to do anything that might break her.

I drain the last few sips of my coffee. We're almost done.

"Anne, did Katrina ever meet Lorie Rickardian or Loretta Black?"

Cooper shakes her head. "Not that I know of. I know she's read a lot of Loretta Black's books, but she didn't have any contact with her."

"What about a journalist called Randy Sade?"

She shakes her head.

"Or Peter Blake, the author?"

"I've heard of Blake. I think we've got one of his books around here."

"But has Katrina ever met him?"

"I don't think so, no."

I move us on to other points of intersection, pulling out the list we came up with on the plane. "Who was her agent?"

"Dana Raider in New York."

I write it down. "And her publisher?" I pick up the book, realizing it will be on the book's spine.

"Dorchester," Cooper says, just as I see it on the book. "And her editor?"

"Um…Jane Cliff." She nods. "Yup, that's her name."

I add it to my list. "What about her publicist?"

"Trina didn't have one."

"Okay." I go back to the list. "Did she win any awards or attend any awards?"

Cooper shakes her head. "Not yet. She's really just starting to build her name."

"What about attending writers' festivals or signings or some other events?"

"She did some local signings at a few bookstores in San Diego and some in L.A."

I take the details down from Cooper, so I can cross-reference this information with what we'll get for Black and Rickardian. Maybe L.A. or a bookstore will be a link. "Okay. And did Katrina study writing anywhere?"

"Mostly short courses by correspondence. She didn't study it at college or anything."

I make a note of that too, but don't ask Cooper for the details. I can come back to it if either Black or Rickardian also took some similar courses. "Was she part of a writers' group?"

"Yes. She finds it real useful. There are four people in the group and they meet once a month at a café around the corner."

"Do you know their names?"

"No, not offhand…but I can find them for you."

I nod and wait.

"Now?"

She seems taken aback by the fact that I want this information now. "Anne, I can't emphasize how important time is. The faster you can get us information, the better chance we have of finding Katrina."

She nods her head slowly. "Have you got lots of people working the case?"

Levy steps in. "Don't worry, Ms. Cooper, we're working this hard. That's why we brought in the FBI and De-tective Sorrell here from L.A. We're doing everything we can and we've got people working around the clock on the forensics too."

"So, do you have information about the writers' group?" I ask her softly.

"I'll get it for you now." She stands up and disappears into the study again.

I sigh. "I hope we find her." I say it quietly enough that Cooper won't hear us.

Sorrell nods. "So do I. And then maybe Bowles will be able to lead us to the killer." Sorrell's interested in helping Bowles, but he also wants to close the murder case on his turf—Black.

Cooper reappears, carrying a handwritten note. "I wrote the names down for you."

Taking the list, I press on. "What about memberships? Was she a member of any association or crime-author group?"

"The Thriller Writers' Association."

I write it down and then turn to Sorrell. "Anything else?"

He shakes his head.

I stand up. "Well, we'll get out of your hair now. Thank you." I shake her hand. "You should try to get some sleep."

She makes a small grimace. I guess sleep's the last thing on her mind now.

We all say goodbye, and Sullivan tries to comfort Cooper with a last word. "We've got lots of people on this case, Anne. We'll find her."

But Cooper's past comfort.

Eighteen

At the San Diego Police Station, Levy sticks in the tape of the press conference. Sorrell, Sullivan and I sit around the desk facing the TV, while Levy props himself on the table, one foot touching the ground and one hovering midair.

The video footage starts before the press conference's official opening, and we watch as the last journalists settle in their seats and the camera operators for the TV stations complete their setups. The time stamp shows 8:55 a.m.

"Want me to fast-forward?"

"Nah, that's okay." I study the footage carefully.

On the screen, silence settles across the room as the police chief, Cooper and one other person enter the media conference. Cooper's eyes are red and tear-streaked and she seems more distraught than she did at her apartment. People grieve in different ways—some don't shed a tear for days or weeks, while others can't stop crying. But most people oscillate between moments of emotional distress and catatonia. When we met Cooper at her apartment, she was closer to a catatonic phase.

The other person at the press conference, a woman in her late twenties, speaks first. She's relaxed with the press corps, making it obvious she's the police department's media liaison. She quickly hands over to the chief of police, who announces that San Diego crime author Katrina Bowles is missing. He goes over the facts of the case, including a visual description, when she was last seen and the fact that the police hold grave concerns for her safety, given the murders of Loretta Black last weekend and Lorie Rickardian four months ago. After briefly asking the public for help, he introduces Cooper and hands over to her for the more heartfelt plea.

Cooper is a mess. She holds herself upright on the podium and tears catch in her throat with every word. Her speech pattern is also irregular as she fights off the tears and struggles to make her sentences understandable as she begs anyone with any information whatsoever to come forward.

The press then get their turn to ask questions. The chief fields most of them, leaving Cooper to her grief in the background. It makes a striking picture, one that would certainly encourage most people to act.

Levy stops the video straight after the media officer, the chief and Cooper exit the room. "The TV stations are still running it." He flicks across to the regular TV and moves through the news channels. We catch one station rerunning the story, with a thirty-second snippet from the press conference. It is, of course, the most melodramatic part of Cooper's plea for help to find "my Trina" that's replayed.

Cooper's garbled words are interrupted by a cell phone ringing. Sorrell and Levy both dive for their pockets—obviously they've got the same ring tone.

It's Levy who pulls out the buzzing phone. "Homicide. Levy." He looks up and covers the mouthpiece. "Call center."

I lean forward, trying in vain to hear the other end of the conversation.

Levy pulls out his notepad and starts scribbling in loose, slanted handwriting. "Nope, that doesn't sound right." He's silent again, listening to the caller, and then he writes again. "Okay, we'll look into it just in case." He flips his phone shut.

"What you got?" Sorrell stands up, flexing his tall frame from side to side.

"We've got another possible sighting."

"Really?" I'd like to be eager, but I know most reported sightings turn out to be false. In most cases the witness is simply mistaken.

Levy crosses his arms. "Apparently the caller sounded legit, but the sighting's off base in terms of the book's plot."

"Go on," I prompt.

"It was in Pine Valley." Levy pauses and then looks at me. "That's a small town east of here."

It's nice of Levy to clarify for the Aussie.

"Anyway," he continues, "we're definitely going the harbor-apartment angle, yes?" He looks at me, waiting for confirmation.

"How far east is Pine Valley?" I chew on my bottom lip, knowing this decision could save Bowles…or cost Bowles her life.

"About twenty-five miles."

If the killer follows the plot of Bowles's book like a script, he won't be in Pine Valley. But my instincts are saying to check out the sighting—it's worth a shot.

"Have you got resources to follow it up?"

"I can send a uniform down there. It's not far."

"Great." I pause. "I'm going to look at Bowles's book. See what I can find there."

Levy nods. "Forensics and the call center will phone me if anything else comes through, and I'll let you guys know." He stands up. "But in the meantime, we've got to finish canvassing Bowles's apartment block. What about you, Detective Sorrell? You want to come with us?"

"Maybe. Can you give us a second?"

"Sure." Sullivan and Levy both leave the room.

Sorrell looks at me. "How long do you want to hang around here for?"

I shrug. "Don't know." I think about the question. "Until we find Bowles, I guess."

Sorrell doesn't look happy.

"What's up?" I ask.

"I just don't know what we can do from here. There's virtually nothing at her apartment, and all our real leads are back in L.A...."

"So you think we should head back?"

He shrugs. "It's only a fifty-minute flight if we need to come back here."

"I don't know, Sorrell…what about Bowles?"

"I think we're more likely to find Bowles through the letters and forensics in L.A. We could go to the lab and see if we can't hurry things up a bit, especially now that Bowles is missing."

L.A. county is a large territory to serve and a little pushing never harmed anyone, especially another in-person visit, arguing our case to the lab techs.

"We can expect more results today, yes?" I ask.

"Hopefully from prints, yeah. And DNA will be today or tomorrow."

"What about the first letter from 'A fan'? How many handwriting experts do they have?"

"Daelene Rose is the main person, and she's real good. Plus she's got an offsider…um…can't think of his name. But who knows, they could be in court today."

The forensic expert's job is twofold—to analyze the crime-scene samples and then testify about their findings in court. The more cases in their workload, the more court appearances they have to make, and then the backlog gets worse. If lab techs around the world didn't have to go to court, then the labs could probably keep up with the evidence.

I really want that handwritten letter looked at today and Sorrell's making sense—our presence in the lab may well help to get our items jumped up the queue—but part of me feels like I'd be abandoning Bowles. In San Diego we could help Levy and Sullivan canvass the neighbors in case someone heard or saw something; we could follow up possible sightings that come through the call center, and we could wait for forensics. But Sorrell's right—it's not exactly breakthrough stuff here in San Diego.

"Okay," I say. "Do you want to book the flights while I read?"

"Sure. And I'll call the lab first to make sure Daelene is in and let the others know we're coming."

Sorrell heads out, leaving me in peace in the meeting room. Before I read some of Bowles's book, I need to look at the link between the authors and fill out the information for Black. Some of the details I know myself, but for the rest I ring Black's agent and Holt. It only takes me fifteen minutes to have a complete list for Black.

Agent: Linda Farrow
Publisher: St. Martin's
Editor: Laura Cue
Publicists: Jan Bunt, Heidi Steiner, Vicki Stoker,
Kelly Clarke, Mandy McCleary, Robyn Keen, Kirilee
Swanston
Awards: The CWA Gold Dagger (2000, 2003, 2006),
the CWA Silver Dagger (1998, 2004), Edgar Allan
Poe Award for best novel (2003, 2006)
Other events (e.g., writers' festivals and signings):
ThrillerFest (2000–2006), Vancouver International
Writers' Festival (2003, 2005, 2006), Florida Writ-
ers' Festival (1999, 2002, 2006), Los Angeles Times
Festival of Books (2000, 2005), New Orleans Liter-
ary Festival (2002, 2005), multiple signings
University or other writing courses: None
Writing groups: No
Online research or book groups: Yahoo group, 4MA
Memberships: Thriller Writers' Association and
Mystery Writers of America

For the publicists I've included the full list that I got
from Cue, even going back to Black's first book. And for
the writers' festivals, I only include the North American
ones, even though Black had done several world tours.

I've got twenty minutes before the 12:30 p.m. conference call, so I pull out Bowles's book and flick through it,
finding the part where the bad guy's holding the insurance
worker in the apartment building's basement.

Sarah Brown woke up naked and tied to a chair.
Her legs were spread slightly and tied to each front

leg of the chair, and her arms were tied behind her back. Her shoulders and arms were pulled so far back and down that her spine was heavily arched. She slowly opened her eyes, fearful of what she would see.

Standing in front of her was a large, stocky man, about five-eleven with broad shoulders. His eyes were pale blue and cold, devoid of any emotion except perhaps pleasure. He grinned, revealing a couple of missing teeth from both his top and bottom rows. His head was shaved baby-smooth and he wore one sleeper earring in his left ear. His face was acne-pocked and his nose was already bulbous, despite the fact that he looked about forty. This wasn't the man behind her imprisonment. He was simply the messenger boy, the hired thug.

"Where is he?" she demanded. "Where's Roach?"

"Dunno what you're talking about, lady." He bent down toward Sarah and she was hit by the smell of stale alcohol and tobacco. Her stomach reacted instantly and she almost retched, but she stifled it.

"You know who Roach is. He's the one paying your bills."

He grinned again: tooth…gap…tooth…gap. "I do this for pleasure, not money." He straddled her and rubbed himself against her breasts.

"Get off, you pig!"

"Lady, I'm the one with the knife—" he took a knife out of his back pocket and flicked it open "—and you're the one tied up, so I reckon you should be a bit nicer to Frankie."

The knife scared Sarah, it did, but the effect was

watered down by the guy referring to himself in the third person.

"Okay, Frankie. I'll be nice." She was speaking to the tight denim that stretched across his groin.

"Smart little lady." He stepped back, giving her some space again. He sighed. "I've got plans for you."

"Tell Roach I haven't talked to anyone and I don't intend to. Maybe he and I can come to some agreement."

Frankie glanced upward and Sarah turned her head to follow his gaze. She couldn't be sure, but she bet they were both looking at a camera. The corner was dark, and if it was a camera, it must be a spy-cam.

"You're gonna talk to *me*." The grin was smaller this time, and more unsettling.

For the first time Sarah wondered if maybe this wasn't just scare tactics. What she'd stumbled on was big, but not that big…was it? Or maybe she'd only found the tip of the iceberg.

"Look, you've made your point." She swung around to the camera. "I really don't know much, and I'm not going to go to the cops or anything." It was a lie…she had planned to call the cops or the feds or someone but decided to sleep on it, decided maybe she was indulging a fanciful conspiracy theory. But then she'd woken up to a noise in her apartment, and next thing Frankie was hitting her over the head with her mother's favorite vase, a family heirloom.

She looked up at Frankie. "Did you break that vase?"

He was perplexed by the question, still unsure why the woman in front of him wasn't particularly scared of him. He was used to people just looking at him and being scared.

"Um…yeah. It's broken."

"Shit! Mom's going to kill me."

Frankie shook his head. "Next time your mother sees you, she won't care about no vase." He got up close and personal with her again, this time shoving his face, not his groin, in front of her. "You've got a screw loose, lady. You're in some deep shit. I've been told to do whatever it takes to get you to talk. Whatever it takes." He puts his hand on his groin and re-arranges himself, giving Sarah a visual of what her torture might include.

She was scared again, but unwilling to show it. "What would you want to do that for, Frankie?"

He stood back up and shook his head. "Some women need to have sense slapped into them." He pulled back his hand and hit her hard across the face, almost hard enough to send her back into the land of dreams.

Sarah blinked her eyes rapidly, letting tears run down her face and mingle with the blood trickling from her nose. But Frankie had made his point, and for the first time Sarah believed she was in deep shit. White-collar crime or not, things were getting dirty.

I look up when Sorrell enters the room. "Okay, we're all set for a one forty-five flight back to L.A. And I just heard back from Edwards. This last AFIS match is a dead end too."

"Go on."

"The dates don't match. The guy just got out of prison a month ago. He's covered for Rickardian's murder."

That is a dead end. I look at my watch. "Let's dial in for our meeting before we head to the airport."

Sorrell looks around. "I guess Sullivan and Levy will dial in from their cell phones."

By 12:35 p.m., we're all on the line.

"Did you get the list of potential links between our authors, O'Shaughnessy and Perez?"

O'Shaughnessy answers, "Yeah, got it here. We've got some of the information from Emily Rickardian, but we're also waiting on a call back from the publishers."

"Okay. The only point in common for Black and Bowles that I could find is their membership in the Thriller Writers' Association. Do you know if Rickardian was a member of that one?"

"Yes, she was."

I look at Sorrell, hopeful, but Dusk crushes my hope.

"Anderson, pretty much every crime or thriller writer in the States is a member of that association…sorry."

"So you don't think it's worthwhile pursuing?" I ask.

"Put it this way, I'd make it your last line of inquiry, not your first. In fact, I was going to use their membership list for our main list of American crime authors."

"So you've got a list?" I ask.

"Uh-huh."

"Great. How many names?"

"I went with Wikipedia in the end. They quote two hundred and thirty-five of which one hundred and forty are women."

I whistle and Sorrell makes a face—he's authored out.

"So that's over one hundred potential targets to sift through," I say. Ouch.

"We can't possibly interview one hundred and forty authors or give that many women protection, even short-term." Brady's stating the obvious.

"No. But I'll still take a look at the list. Maybe it will help us find the link somehow. Have you e-mailed it to me yet?"

"Yeah, about thirty seconds ago."

With nothing else to report, our conference call is short.

Once the call's over, I say to Sorrell, "I'm going to get that list of authors off my e-mail. We've got time." In the hallway I find a uniformed officer and he points me in the direction of a computer so I can log in remotely to the FBI's Web e-mail system. Once online I have to jump through a few security checks, but I'm used to that.

Back in the meeting room with Sorrell, I put the three pages on the desk. "So, that's our list of potential victims. If we can find another link between Rickardian, Black and Bowles, we may know who's next." I tap my fingers on the pages, then skim through the alphabetized list, recognizing some names, but not others. Nothing sticks out, but we'll need to find that link before we can predict his next victim. Although...

"You know, it might be worthwhile calling these authors and asking them if they've received a letter signed from 'A fan' in the past six months."

Sorrell whistles. "That'll get them panicking."

"They're probably panicking already. It might put some of them at ease...if they haven't got a letter, they'll feel safer." I gaze out the window, carrying the train of thought through, looking at the pros and cons. "The biggest problem would be releasing the actual existence of any letters. We can't trust over one hundred people to keep their

mouths shut, and we don't want it becoming public knowledge, and 'A fan' realizing we're onto him."

"No, especially not when Bowles's life is in danger."

It's a risk we can't take.

Nineteen

Back in the L.A. lab, our first stop is Questioned Documents and Daelene Rose. Rose is a lanky woman, a feature that's accentuated because she's stooped over a bench. Her black hair is pulled back into a severe bun, but it's probably a functional choice rather than a fashion statement—her hair's pulled back tightly enough to ensure it stays out of her eyes all day. She looks up as we enter and puts on a pair of glasses from her lab coat top pocket. Everything about Daelene Rose, including her pristine work space, tells me she's very particular and very orderly, which are both features I love in any forensic technician.

"Hi, Dave."

"Hey, Daelene. What's up?"

"Same old, same old." She looks around her lab, motioning at the evidence bags.

"Where's your sidekick?" Sorrell asks.

"Vacation." She shakes her head but smiles. "And his name's Jason."

"Jason, that's it." Sorrell looks at me, then back at Rose. "Daelene, this is Special Agent Sophie Anderson, the new profiler with the FBI field office."

"Hi," she says, hand outstretched. "That name sounds familiar."

I shake her hand. "You probably saw my name on a lab request form."

"Yes…" She turns back to her evidence bags and flicks through them. "Here it is." She holds up the clear plastic bag that contains the first letter from our fan.

Sorrell leans on the bench nearest him. "So, how are those cats of yours, Daelene?"

Rose rolls her eyes. "You're as transparent as this bag, Dave," she says. "You want this fast?"

I watch the exchange with interest. I've seen Sorrell be aloof, disinterested and noncommunicative, and I can guess from Holt's reaction he can be heartless and dogged during questioning. And now I've seen him act charming and flirtatious. Will the real Detective Dave Sorrell please stand up? Chameleon or not, I'm beginning to like this guy, and appreciate that he's a damn good detective. When interviewing suspects or witnesses, detectives have to give an Oscar-winning performance every time and Sorrell can clearly deliver the goods.

Sorrell nods his head and becomes more serious. "They're related to Loretta Black's case, but we've got another missing author now too."

"Heard that on the news on my way in." Daelene Rose is also somber.

"And we need to bump the letter over for more tests once you're done," Sorrell adds.

As a document examiner, Rose will do handwriting,

paper and ink analyses and she needs the original for that. But prints need the original too.

Rose looks at the form and reads from it. "Latent prints."

"That's right," I say, given I'm the one who filled out the request yesterday. But I don't think Sorrell needs my input—he's got Rose wrapped up. I'm also reminded of Melissa's description of Sorrell…what did she say? Dreamy. And looking at Rose's face, that's what she sees too. I take another look at Sorrell. I guess he's your classic tall, dark and handsome with that very masculine face—square jaw, defined brow and dark brown eyes. His shoulders are broad and he obviously keeps in shape—at least, I can't see any hint of a potbelly or love handles through his suit. For the first time I'm looking at Sorrell as a man, and not a colleague, and I quickly put the brakes on. I appreciate a good-looking man but, for the moment at least, I've shut down that part of my brain. These days, man equals complication and if I was going to be with anyone it would be Darren. But now I can see why Daelene Rose, despite calling him transparent, is clearly more than willing to get into Sorrell's good books and stay there.

"There are a few more in there too." I make a face of apology.

She flicks through her evidence bags and retrieves the other ones that I submitted yesterday from Holt's files.

"The ones from 'A fan' are our priority at this stage," I say.

"I'll start with the handwritten one. More to do on that one."

"Thanks," I say.

"So, how long you been at the field office?" she asks, making her way back to her workbench.

"Since Monday."

"You are new." Rose pulls on a fresh pair of gloves and puts the document she was examining back into its plastic evidence bag.

"Yup." I find it hard to relax into the small talk when the clock is ticking, but at the same time I don't want to come across as rude.

"I trained at the FBI," she says, putting the document to one side and tossing the gloves.

"Really?" The fact that Daelene Rose trained at the FBI is good news for me, because alumni have automatic and instant access to document databases maintained by the FBI, covering everything from watermark files and printer types to a database of notes handed over to tellers during bank robberies. "When were you there?" I ask.

"Ah…." She does the arithmetic. "Ten years ago." She puts on another fresh set of gloves.

The first change of gloves was because she touched me, shaking my hand, and can't risk contaminating the document she was working on with anything she may have picked up in that brief contact. The second glove change is because she can't risk cross-contamination between her original sample and our letter.

Sitting back on her stool, Rose opens the evidence bag that contains the letter to Black. "Okay, let's see what we've got. I'll check the writing first." Taking her glasses off, she bends her upper body over the letter, stooped once more.

"Right-hander," she says, moving her eyes along a magnified section of the letter.

That decision is always based on the slant of the writing.

Right-handers will slant to the right, left-handers to the left. Even a practiced and fairly straight up-and-down style of writing will slant ever so slightly one way.

"The writing hasn't been disguised," she continues. "All the *Y*'s have a similar size loop." She points to several *Y*'s in the piece. "And again this flatness of the bottom of the *S*'s is throughout the letter."

When someone's trying to disguise their writing, they try to vary some letters and words from their normal style so there'll be inconsistencies within the sample.

Rose continues, "There are also no more lifts than I'd normally expect."

A lift is when someone stops writing for a split second, taking their pen off the paper. Everyone has lifts in their handwriting, but an excessive number can indicate the person is lying, under stress or still hasn't made up their mind about exactly how they're going to phrase the note, so they pause to think. Pauses and the resultant lifts will also come thick and fast if the person is deliberately trying to disguise their handwriting.

Rose scans the document again. "There's a lift on the *a* just before 'a wonderful crime author.'"

"Probably just choosing the adjective," I offer.

Rose nods but keeps her head down. "I'd say so. The other lifts are in places you'd expect them, ends of sentences, at punctuation points and at breaks in the cursive writing." She keeps studying the letter, presumably confirming her initial findings.

Sorrell and I wait in silence for about fifteen minutes before Rose speaks again. "You might want to get a forensic linguist to look at it too."

A forensic linguist will study patterns in speech that

may indicate where a person grew up and their education level, both of which can be very helpful.

"Good idea." It could help us track him down.

"Nothing else, Daelene?" Sorrell's voice is flat, no hint of flirtation.

"Not from the writing, no." She looks thoughtfully at me. "But the paper…" She moves across the bench and turns on a UV light, mounting the paper on top of it. "The paper looks to be about thirty-eight pounds to me. A little thicker than standard writing paper, but…" Again, Rose's head goes down and I resist the urge to crowd her.

Rose is referring to the thickness, expressed as a weight, of the paper. In Australia it's metric and measured in GSM—grams per square meter. Here in the States, standard laser-printer paper would be twenty to twenty-four pounds, and writing paper tends to be a little thicker.

I lean in closer. I don't have the angle she has, but I can still see the faint watermark on the paper. "Do you recognize it?" I ask.

"No." She seems surprised that she doesn't know it instantly. She swivels her stool my way, and I move to one side so she can roll through to a computer that sits on another high bench in the far corner. It seems a little odd to see Daelene scooting along the floor on her chair—somehow too childlike for her personality. But it is efficient, something she'd like.

"I'll just double-check the database."

Again, Sorrell and I wait patiently, watching Rose work. All the things we should, and could, be doing cross my mind, but ultimately these letters are our strongest lead and our presence (or maybe just Sorrell's) is having the desired effect, with our case jumping the queue.

"It's Salurtey." She turns around to us, her face animated. "That's a San Francisco-based niche company. They specialize in high-end writing paper and their distribution network is small. Your letter writer either lives in San Francisco or bought this paper there."

"That's fantastic news," I say. San Francisco also ties in with our assumption that the killer could be based on the West Coast, given the victim locations of San Francisco, L.A. and San Diego.

Rose rolls back to the letter and does yet another change of gloves—potential contamination from the computer. A few minutes later, she says, "I've got something here. A faint impression of writing."

In most cases when someone uses a proper writing pad, they'll write their letter and then tear it off, before moving on to the next letter. That means that our sheet of paper could have faint impressions of any letter that was written directly before the one to Black. And the harder someone presses when they write, the more impressions will be left.

"Man, Sorrell, you owe me." Rose's grin is ear-to-ear and the look in her eyes tells me she wouldn't mind calling in the favor in the form of a date.

Sorrell moves closer to her. "What? What have you got?"

She points to the bottom of the letter. "You can see a very faint impression of 'James' from a letter where he's signed his name more neatly than on this one. I'd say our letter writer is called James."

Sorrell smiles. "You're a genius, Daelene."

"Thanks." She blushes and buries her face in her work. "Hold on, I've got another one. I think it says 'Aunt Kitty' and it's at the top." She pauses. "Yup, your letter writer sent something to his Aunty Kitty before he wrote this one." She does another visual sweep. "No other impressions. He must have written those parts on the previous letter a little harder."

"Okay," Sorrell says, still standing close to Rose.

She looks up at him. "I'll get a sample of the ink and send it for analysis, but it'll be at least twenty-four hours before I can get that to you."

Daelene Rose will organize for a chemical analysis of the ink, and that will be matched against the FBI database to give us the type of pen that was used, and hopefully the brand. But twenty-four hours will be too late for Bowles.

"Great, thanks." Sorrell pauses. "And seriously, how are your cats?"

Rose gives him a light slap on the forearm. "Like you care."

"Well, I am more of a dog person." Sorrell straightens up.

"We'll have to agree to disagree on that point." She smiles. "I'll get this ink scraping and then we can walk the letter around to Harry if you like."

"Sounds good to me." Sorrell looks at me. "Harry Weaver is the forensic linguist."

We wait silently as Rose carefully takes scrapings of the letter and puts them in a test tube for ink analysis. After she's labeled the test tube with the case number, she puts the letter back in the evidence bag and signs and dates the Questioned Documents section of the form. She hands it to Sorrell. "You're all set," she says, stretching her arms upward. "I'll come with you for the walk."

"Thanks, Daelene." Sorrell looks at me. "Daelene's not coming for the walk. She's coming because she knows

Weaver will look at this—" he gently jostles the evidence bag "—faster for her than for me."

Perhaps Sorrell can work the ladies when he needs to, but not the men.

I follow the pair, feeling like a third wheel, but I'm not complaining when things are working out so well for us. Hell, I can be Ms. Invisible for a couple of hours if it gets us closer to Black's killer and, more importantly, closer to finding Bowles.

Daelene drops us off with Harry Weaver, urging him to look at the letter straightaway, before disappearing back to her own neck of the woods and promising Sorrell that she'll have a look at the printed letters from "A fan" as a priority.

With Weaver, I take out the high-quality prints of all four letters attributed to the same person, so he's got a bigger sample to look at. The more writing, the easier his job will be.

Leaving the handwritten letter in its evidence bag, he reads the letters once, then again, before passing them back to me. "The author of these letters spent quite some time in Wisconsin or the upper Midwest. He probably grew up there."

"Really?" I ask.

"Yes. In all the letters he or she has used the expression 'Believe you me.' That's very particular to that area."

Sorrell nods. "He's right."

Weaver looks at him strangely. "Of course I'm right."

It's certainly one of the disadvantages for me of being Australian. I wouldn't have a clue about regional slang.

"Thanks, Weaver." I hold my hand out and Weaver shakes it. "Look forward to working with you in the future," I say. I doubt many of my cases will require a forensic linguist, but you never know and it's plain good manners.

"Nice to meet you, Agent Anderson." He turns back to his work and, as though it's an afterthought, says, "Sorrell."

"Weaver." Sorrell gives a little nod at the acknowledgment, but that's it. I wouldn't go so far as to say that there's bad blood between the pair, but they're certainly not drinking buddies.

Back in the corridor, I stop. "Believe you me…I'm sure I've heard that expression recently."

Sorrell's face scrunches up in concentration. "I don't remember it." He pauses. "Any idea where you heard it?"

Now it's my turn to painstakingly try to trigger my memory, but I'm unsuccessful. "No. But let's ring our contacts and see if we can't find someone who spent any time in the Midwest."

"Assuming they'll tell us the truth."

"There is that. But it's worth a shot," I say. "We should try Peter Blake again too." He still hasn't returned our calls.

"Okay, prints first, then phone calls."

We make our way back to the shared lab space of Court and McAvey, but only McAvey's in the room.

"Where's Court?" I ask, after I've said hello.

"Court's in court." McAvey grins. "Never get tired of that."

"Yeah, well the rest of us do," Sorrell says good-naturedly, leaning on the nearest bench.

McAvey takes his gloves off and moves out from behind the bench. "Let me guess, you guys are here about those letters."

"Yeah," Sorrell says. "But like I said on the phone, another author's missing so we need to step things up."

"Her name's Katrina Bowles and she's an author from San Diego," I explain, hoping some more personal information will draw McAvey into this case and out of the other ones he's working on. Sometimes you need to play a little dirty. "She was reported missing this morning and it looks like she's our guy's latest victim. But we think she's still alive, for the moment at least."

"Shit." McAvey's suddenly serious. "Okay, tell me what you need."

We're both aware what a huge flood of evidence has come from Black's murder and today there's only McAvey working on it. But we need this information.

"I lodged some more letters last night," I say. "Most of them are with Daelene Rose, but we've got one that she's already processed." I hand him the evidence bag with the letter in it.

He turns the bag over in his hand. "This is your top, top priority?"

Sorrell and I look at each other and both nod.

Then Sorrell adds, "And the unaccounted print from the scene. Have you run it against the family's prints yet?"

"No, I was working on the letters first. But I'll do it right now."

I guess we've been sending him mixed messages—the crime scene, Black's original stash of letters, my batch from Holt's place yesterday…the poor guy doesn't know which way is up. And that's just our stuff, not all the other jobs in the queue.

McAvey jumps on a computer. "I haven't uploaded the family's prints into our database yet, but I can do that now." Getting fingerprints from surfaces is a multistage task: first you develop the print, usually with magnetic dust, then you digitize the print, then you upload it into the computer system to check against AFIS or any other prints you have relating to the case. But taking fingerprints directly from the source is much faster, using a digital scanning system called LiveScan. Sorrell would have used LiveScan to capture the Black family's prints, and then e-mailed the digital files to McAvey.

We watch while McAvey uploads the fingerprints and then sets his computer up to compare the unidentified print with the family database he's built. The computer takes less than ten seconds to perform the comparison.

"Looks like we've got a match."

"Damn," I say. We were hoping the fingerprint belonged to our killer, not someone in the family.

McAvey moves in closer to the screen, to verify the computer's match. "Yup. It belongs to Sandra Black."

Sorrell raises his eyebrows. "You really think we should dismiss it, Anderson? She's the jealous sister, who also happens to be an unpublished author."

I wince. While Sorrell's right from one perspective—I shouldn't automatically dismiss Sandra Black as a suspect—all I can think about is the way Black was posed and the mutilation. "I can't think of a case where a female killer sexually mutilated another woman." Female killers tend to murder for self-preservation or jealousy, not sexual pleasure. There have been some female serial killers—the Murderers' Club included a woman—but they're much more uncommon and they nearly exclusively target males. And to pose a female victim sexually and mutilate her breasts like Black's is a sexual act, albeit extremely perverse.

"It's hard to imagine *any* woman posing Black like that."

He sighs. "I know what you mean but she's a contender in so many ways. And she left a print there."

"She admitted she was there in March. The whole family's been there at some stage in the past year."

McAvey pipes in. "Fingerprints can last for ages. Depending on the surface, humidity…and a range of other factors."

I'm glad McAvey doesn't launch into a scientific lecture. I've read the forensic updates and the court rulings; I know they can't tell how long a print has been on a particular surface.

"Her fingerprint doesn't necessarily mean anything," I say with a sigh. "It's certainly not enough to make her anything more than a person of interest." I use the law-enforcement term.

"So, the letter?" McAvey snaps on a fresh pair of gloves and takes the letter out of the evidence bag. He holds it up, presumably looking for any partial prints that may have been made in the ink, but I've already looked for those and know there aren't any.

"We'll need to fumigate it," he says, looking up at us. "I'll do it now, but it'll take about half an hour for the fuming process."

Sorrell nods. "Thanks. We're sticking around here for the rest of the afternoon. We'll be in the meeting room on level two. Call us when you've got something."

"Sure."

"Thanks again, McAvey," I say, with genuine appreciation.

"That leaves us with DNA," Sorrell says to me once

we're in the corridor. "Then computers, then our calls about the Midwest." His height and long strides mean I have to almost trot to keep up.

"And don't forget Blake."

"How could I forget that?" Sorrell says before moving on to our next lab stop. "Sam Gold from DNA is in today and I play racquetball with him so we should be able to get him to cooperate."

Ah yes, it pays to be with someone who knows the lab techs.

"The bastard usually beats me too."

I consider Sorrell's height. "Good reach but your height slows you down?"

"Nah, Sam's just better than me."

On the fourth floor, Sorrell leads the way to Gold's lab. Gold looks up as soon as we enter. "Hi, Dave."

"Hey, Sam."

The two men shake hands.

"Still on for Monday night?" Gold asks.

"Always."

Gold nods and looks at me. "Hi."

Sorrell does the introductions. "Sam Gold, this is Special Agent Sophie Anderson. She's taken over Krump's role at the FBI."

"Ah, a profiler, huh?" He extends his hand to me.

"That's right." I take his hand and shake it.

Gold is a few inches taller than me, around five-eleven, with jet-black hair that's receding dramatically. He wears gold-rimmed glasses on his nose, probably for his long-distance vision, like Daelene Rose. A lot of scientists who start off with twenty-twenty vision become shortsighted after a few years of lab work because they are focusing on something so closely, day in and day out, and soon their eyes' lenses can't focus on things in the distance. A hazard of the job.

"I guess you're here to check on your DNA samples." He looks at Sorrell first, then me.

"You got it." Sorrell gives him a wink and goes for his leaning position on the nearest bench. I hadn't noticed Sorrell was a leaner until today, but it could just be that the lab benches are the right height for him.

"What's the number again?"

Sorrell rattles off the case file number assigned to all evidence from Black's murder.

Gold types the number into his computer. "Okay. The good news is we successfully got DNA from the panty hose, the tissue, the cotton-wool bud and the toilet bowl. Nothing from the vic's fingernails and nothing on the phone swab." He pauses. "Bad news is only one sample from the hose."

"Oh." Both Sorrell and I respond the same way. We were hoping the stockings would contain two discreet DNA samples even if they were comingled in the swab— one from Black and one from the killer. If only one DNA sample was found, it's much more likely to be Black's than the killer's, which also means the killer probably wore gloves. Just when things were looking up.

"Urine on the toilet is male," Gold continues, "and the DNA will finish processing in the next hour. I'll compare it to our samples on file first, then against CODIS if we don't have any luck."

CODIS, which stands for Combined DNA Index System, is the national DNA database. The samples on file that Gold refers to are from Werner, Holt, the cleaner and the paramedics who first responded to Werner's 911 call. It's common practice to take DNA swabs from all emergency-services personnel on site, in case they've inadvertently left a sample at the crime scene, which is easy to do. Someone sneezes and that's saliva, or they shed a hair. These small and involuntary actions can leave DNA. Given the urine's male, as a matter of procedure it'll be checked against Werner's sample, and the two paramedics, who were both male. Although if one of them actually used a toilet at a crime scene, we might have to shoot them.

"Thanks, Sam. We're in the meeting room on two," Sorrell says, pumping his friend's hand.

We stop off at Computer Forensics on our way back to the meeting room, but strike out there too. The computer guys haven't found anything strange on Black's computer—no viruses or keystroke recording programs or anything else to indicate a breach. They have started tracing the e-mails, but asked us to pick out suspect e-mails we'd like more information on first. Fair enough…it's no use them tracing every single e-mail back to its sender when it says something like, *Well done…loved your book.*

"So, let's start the ring-around." Sorrell flips open his phone.

We split up the case's main contacts before I move into the corridor, so we're not shouting over each other. On my list are Werner, the Black family and Emily Rickardian. Sorrell's got Randy Sade, Peter Blake and Loretta's agent and publisher.

Half an hour later I move back into the room to find Sorrell still talking.

"Uh-huh…thanks." He hangs up. "How'd you do?" he asks.

"No luck. George Black asked me about the case, of course, but said no one in his family grew up in the Midwest." In fact, I spent most of the time placating him, and assuring him that we are, indeed, doing everything possible. "Did you have any luck?"

"No go for Black's publisher and agent. I left a message for Sade and I still can't get ahold of Peter Blake." Sorrell pauses. "I think it's time to check the airlines. See if he flew down to San Diego yesterday."

"Yup." We need to escalate our investigations into Blake. Like Sade and Sandra Black, his connection is with Loretta Black, not Rickardian, but he's also MIA.

We spend the next thirty minutes checking with all the airlines to see if Blake was a passenger on any flights from L.A. to San Diego, but strike out.

"Maybe he drove?" I suggest.

Sorrell looks at the pile of documents in front of us. "Shall we swing by and see if his car's there? Should only take us about twenty minutes at this time of day."

"You're on."

Twenty

After checking the DMV—Department of Motor Vehicles—records for Blake's make and model of car, and registration details, Sorrell and I leave the pile of letters and e-mails. Twenty minutes later we're standing in the parking garage underneath Blake's building. It only takes us a few minutes to find his car.

"So where the hell is he?" For a second my stomach flips... Blake's a crime fiction author and he's missing. Could our killer have jumped genders and taken Blake too? But I talk myself out of it—the killer's too busy with Bowles to be simultaneously abducting a fourth victim.

We try the apartment buzzer again, but with no luck.

"Buzz him again," Sorrell suggests.

I lean on the buzzer for longer this time and a couple of minutes later the intercom system hisses to life.

"What?" says a croaky and annoyed-sounding Blake. At least he's alive and kicking.

I lean in to the speaker. "Mr. Blake, it's Special Agent Anderson and Detective Sorrell."

"Oh." He sounds surprised, but the door buzzes immediately and I push it before it locks again.

When Blake answers his door, he's in tracksuit pants and a T-shirt, with dark circles under his eyes contrasting against his pale skin. It certainly *looks* like he's been up all night writing. Or maybe up all night driving?

He gives us a tired nod and invites us in.

"How's the deadline looking?" I ask.

He puffs his cheeks out and blows the air out quickly. "Not good."

He crosses to his couch and sinks into it, motioning to the other chairs in the room. I take the armchair and Sorrell pulls over a chair from the dining-room table.

I sit down. "You been at it all night?"

"Yes. I slept for a couple of hours around four this morning."

"Anyone verify that?" Sorrell asks.

"No. Why?"

We ignore his question.

"You didn't speak to anyone? See anyone?" Sorrell takes out his notebook.

"No. I've unplugged from everything. The phone, the Internet." He runs a hand through his tousled brown hair. "You're lucky I even answered the door." He crosses his arms. "But you sounded persistent."

"We've been trying to reach you for some time, Mr. Blake," Sorrell explains.

"Is this about Loretta?" His face is crumpled with confusion.

"Yes." I lean in to one side of the armchair. I keep it simple. No need to tell him we've got another author missing if he doesn't already know—not yet.

"What was your relationship with Loretta?" Sorrell cuts to the chase.

"We saw each other at conventions, sometimes in the city. We were friends, I guess."

"When was the last time you saw her?" I ask.

"Um…" His eyes look up to the ceiling as he thinks. "Probably about a year and a half ago."

"Doesn't sound like she was a very good friend." Sorrell scribbles something in his notebook.

"I guess you could say we'd grown apart." He talks slowly, choosing his words carefully.

I sense Sorrell's going somewhere with the questioning, so I leave him to it.

He writes for a few seconds and then looks up at Blake. "Does that have anything to do with Left Coast Crime in 2004?"

Blake shifts uncomfortably. "I wondered if it was going to get out."

"What, exactly?" Sorrell again.

"Loretta and I were friends, good friends. But things got a little tense for us when our careers went in such different directions. She was suddenly a bestseller and I was struggling to get a new book deal with our publisher. Things were awkward between us on both sides. And then, one night, we tried to patch things up. We had a few drinks together, but wound up drinking way too much and…well, it sounds like you know the rest."

"So it's true?" I say. "You did have a physical relationship with Loretta?"

"Once, yes. And that made our already strained friendship impossible. Even when I saw her a year and a half ago it was at a party our publisher threw in L.A.

It was an unavoidable meeting, not a planned one." He sighs.

"If you and Loretta were friends, or used to be, why did you complain to your editor that she was receiving preferential treatment?"

"Well, it's the truth. And a little bit of pushing never hurt anyone. I was hoping maybe they'd promote my books a bit more."

"Did it work?" Sorrell asks.

He shakes his head. "Still waiting for my first bestseller." He sighs. "Maybe this is the one."

"Do you know Katrina Bowles?" I ask.

He shakes his head. "Should I?"

"She's an author, like you."

"Haven't heard of her."

After a long silence, I say, "She went missing in San Diego yesterday."

"Oh my God." His shock is either genuine or well acted. "That's terrible."

"Yes, it is."

It dawns on him again, just like it did outside the funeral home. "And you think I'm involved? That's why you're asking about last night?"

"We're investigating all avenues, Mr. Blake." Again, I downplay our interest in him as a suspect. "So, are you sure no one can verify your whereabouts last night?"

"No." He pauses. "Do I need a lawyer?"

"Let's take things one step at a time, Mr. Blake," Sorrell says.

"Where were you on April 21?" I ask about the night that Lorie Rickardian was killed.

"April 21? That's months ago. How the hell do I know?"

"You might want to find out, Mr. Blake," I suggest. "I presume you've got a diary?"

He takes a deep breath and stands up, nodding. "I'll get it."

He returns a few minutes later, diary in hand and open.

"I've got nothing written in for that date." His voice holds a hint of concern. The seriousness of the situation's hitting him. He flicks through the pages but shrugs. "I guess I was home."

Sorrell stands up. "We'll be in touch if we need anything else."

"Um…okay." Blake still seems confused and uncertain.

We're almost out the door when Sorrell turns back. "One more thing, Mr. Blake."

"Yes?"

"Do you have a copy of one of your books?"

I'm not sure where this is leading, but I trust Sorrell's going somewhere with it—and it's not just for his bedtime reading.

Blake nods and moves over to a nearby bookshelf, plucking a title from the middle shelf. "Here you go."

Sorrell takes the book and flips open the front cover before thanking Blake.

Once the elevator doors close, Sorrell turns to me. "If he is our killer—or even if the media finds out he's a suspect—I bet his books will become bestsellers." He waves the book in his hand.

"Yup. Imagine the publicity when we catch this guy… Blake or not."

"He doesn't have an alibi for Bowles. For last night."

I chew on my lip. "But the killer should still be in

San Diego, assuming he's following Bowles's plot. Torturing her."

"Unless he decided to get straight to the point with Bowles." Sorrell flips his phone open and shut for a few seconds. "I'm going to get a couple of plainclothes to watch Blake. See if he leads us anywhere."

"Good idea."

Sorrell makes the call and we sit out front in our car until the officers arrive in their unmarked car. The on-the-spot briefing is quick and to the point—"watch the guy."

Sorrell hands Blake's book over to the officers. "This is your target." He opens the book at the front cover, showing them Blake's glossy picture. Sorrell was thinking ahead.

We leave the officers to it while we go back to the lab and the tedious job of looking through Black's fan mail.

Although I feel that the suspect letters we've identified are much stronger leads, more worthy of our attention than the PDF of the last six months' worth of letters, it would be dangerous to let something potentially crucial slip through our fingers, especially when Bowles's life is at stake. And so, our reading pile includes all of Black's letters and e-mails for the past six months. I've read the first two letters on my pile when my cell rings. I recognize the number on display as Holt's and decide to take the call.

"Hi, Debbie."

"Hi, Sophie."

"What can I do for you?"

"Sorry, I know you're really busy." She sounds genuinely apologetic. "But I wanted to see if you've got news on Loretta's case."

"Nothing to report, I'm afraid."

"I see." She sighs. "I guess you're focusing on Katrina Bowles now."

"Don't worry, Debbie, we haven't forgotten about Loretta. I'm reading Loretta's fan mail as we speak."

"Good." She pauses. "You really think Loretta's killer has struck again? That he's killed Bowles?"

"It certainly looks like he's responsible for her disappearance." I'm not telling Holt anything that hasn't already appeared in the newspapers, but I'm hoping she'll feel better hearing it from me.

"Was the writing at her place?"

"I'm afraid I can't talk about case specifics, Debbie. You understand."

"Of course. I'm sorry. I'll let you get back to Loretta's fan mail."

"Thanks. And I will keep you in the loop as much as possible."

An hour later the meeting-room phone rings, relieving Sorrell and I from the boredom of reading yet another letter about how great Black is and how dark and compelling Benson is as a character. We both instinctively look at the digital display, which reads *Sam Gold*.

Sorrell scoops up the phone. "Sam. What have you got?" Sorrell pushes the speakerphone button just in time for me to catch Gold's response.

"Not good news. The toilet-bowl DNA belongs to Scott Werner, one in 1.2 million. The tissue was used by Debbie Holt, one in 1.4 million, and everything else matches the victim, Loretta Black."

"Damn," I say, frustrated.

"Told you it wasn't good news." Gold is apologetic.

"That's life in the big city," Sorrell says, but his face shows his disappointment. "Thanks for getting the results through for us."

"Yeah, thanks," I say.

"Anytime."

Sorrell hangs up and leans back in his chair. "We've still got the prints from the letters. And the beige fiber if we can find a match."

Before getting back into the hard slog of the letters and e-mails, Sorrell and I both grab a coffee. We've only just finished when the phone rings again. This time it's Daelene Rose.

"Okay, your first two exhibits were printed on an inkjet printer, with Staples printing paper. The printer matches the Canon PIXMA iP1600 inkjet printer. The last letter from 'A fan' was printed on a laser printer using a premium paper called Wausau Exact Premium Pastels, ivory color. The ink matches a Ricoh Aficio BP20, which is a laser printer."

Sorrell and I both jot down the details.

"And the one to Rickardian from 'A fan'?" I ask.

"Hold on." The sound of Rose thumbing through the evidence bags comes down the line. "Here it is," she says. "That's on the same laser printer, but Staples Heavyweight Printing Paper." She pauses. "I'll get on to the other letters as soon as I can, but I've got another urgent job I have to get back to first."

"Okay, thanks, Daelene. Want us to come up and walk the evidence to McAvey?"

"That's okay. I'll do that now."

"Look after those cats," says Sorrell before hanging up. Then, turning to me, he says, "So he changed from hand-written to inkjet to laser printer."

"We have to assume he got a printer sometime after the first letter." I shrug. "And then I guess he upgraded or maybe used his work's printer."

"Of course, work. Everyone prints personal stuff out at work. Corporate America loses lots of money from that."

"Exactly," I say. "You'd be hard-pressed to find any employee who hasn't used their company's printer at least once over any one-year period."

"True."

I sigh. "We're going to have to start thinking about how to track this fan if we don't get any prints. We're running out of time."

"I know. It's been ticking over." Sorrell taps his head.

I move over to the small whiteboard that's mounted in the meeting room. "Let's assume, for argument's sake, that our fan and the killer are one and the same person." Sorrell nods, and I write a list of what we know so far, combining the profile information with our forensics. Male, 35–50; First name = James; Caucasian; Grew up or spent time in Wisconsin or upper Midwest; Probably lives in San Francisco; Blue-collar worker—possibly in security; Recently separated or divorced or lost his job; High-school educated and possibly partially college-educated; May have met or known Rickardian; and drives an older-make sedan.

"Don't forget Aunt Kitty," Sorrell says.

"Who could forget Aunt Kitty?" I add it to the list and then point to the item before it. "We could do a DMV search in San Francisco for vehicles registered to someone with the first name James, looking at cars that are 1990–2000 models."

"Sounds good. And we could narrow it down with the age and race from the profile."

"That'd definitely give us a list of some description, but who knows how many names."

Sorrell tilts his head to one side. "San Francisco's not that big, you know. Not compared to L.A. at least. You're talking less than a million in total population."

Sorrell's right. With the parameters we've got, we may even come up with a manageable list. "You think it's risky to assume the letter writer lives in San Francisco, where he bought the paper from?"

Sorrell shrugs. "Maybe. But from what Daelene said, Salurtey sounds uncommon. And it's a lead we need to chase down."

"Yup. We should update everyone working on this with our forensics."

Sorrell looks at his watch. "Let's schedule a conference call for four o'clock. We should have something from McAvey by then too."

McAvey finally calls at 3:45 p.m. "Okay, I've got some preliminary results for you."

"Shoot." Sorrell has his pen poised over his notebook.

"I've found two sets of prints on that handwritten letter of yours."

"Yes?" Now things are getting interesting.

"One set matches the sample from Debbie Holt, but we've got one unidentified set. No matches from AFIS."

"That narrows it down some," Sorrell says.

"Anything else?" I ask McAvey.

"Daelene brought around another four letters that she said are priorities for you guys."

"That's right," I say, knowing he's talking about the other three letters from "A fan," plus the one to Rickardian.

"I've run those too. The one to Rickardian has got two

sets of prints. One matches the sample you gave me of the victim, but we've got another set too, and it's not the same print as the handwritten letter."

"It probably belongs to the victim's sister, Emily Rickardian," I say. "I'll organize a sample for you, McAvey." I jot the task down.

"Okay, thanks. Then we've got the three printed letters to Black. They've all got Holt's prints, one's got Black's prints, two have got the same prints as the handwritten letter and one has just got Holt's."

"Which one only has Holt's prints?" I ask.

"Um…" More shuffling of evidence bags. "The longest one. It starts with 'I read the latest George Benson novel with both fascination and repulsion.' You got a copy there?"

We do have copies, but I'm familiar enough with the letters now to know he's talking about the latest one, the one that arrived ten days before Black was killed. "It's the most recent one," I say for both Sorrell and McAvey. "At that stage he would have been planning her murder and probably took care to wear gloves when he handled the paper."

Sorrell writes it down. "Daelene's working on some other letters too, a couple of typed ones and two that use newspaper clippings. Can you jump those up when you get them?"

"I'll do my best, but I doubt it'll be today. You ain't the only ones chasing my tail."

"Don't forget about Katrina Bowles, McAvey." Sorrell's the one who says it, but he's voicing my sentiments too. Does McAvey's other case have a life at stake, now?

Sorrell and I sit in a pool of investigative depression.

Things always take so much longer than you want them to. When Sorrell's phone rings, we both jump.

"Sorrell," he says, somewhat desperately. "Hi, Mr. Sade. Thanks for the call back. I was just wondering where you grew up." Sorrell's jaw drops slightly and he raises his eyebrows at me. "Wyoming, hey?"

I visualize a map of the U.S.—that's our target area all right.

Twenty-One

I've got notes ready for the 4:00 p.m. meeting and we're just about to dial in when my cell phone rings. I look at the number with some annoyance but don't recognize it. Curiosity gets the better of me, as usual. I've still got a couple of minutes.

"I'll just get this," I say to Sorrell, backing out of the room. "Hello, Agent Anderson."

"Hi. I'm in L.A."

It takes me a few seconds to place the voice. "Justin?"

"Great, back to my first name."

"You are stubborn."

"It's one of my personality flaws…or strengths, depending on which way you look at it."

"Mmm…" I say, unsure which side to come down on— flaw or strength. "Listen, now's not a good time. I'm about to go into a four o'clock conference call and we've got a missing author."

"Of course, Katrina Bowles. I'm sorry, I didn't think. Next time I'm in L.A., though, I want to catch up."

He's put me on the spot. "Um…" The guy helped me catch NeverCaught, sent me flowers and has now flown down to L.A. Meeting up with him briefly in person might be the easiest way to politely stop Reid from chasing me. "Okay," I say. "It's a deal."

"Looking forward to it." His voice is lower for the last sentence and it makes me worry about what I've gotten myself into.

"See you later." I hang up, still conflicted. Justin Reid is too smooth, too suave for my liking.

Sorrell's face gets my attention and I realize it's four. Shit. But as I'm about to walk back into the meeting room the dizziness hits me. Damn, why now? Sometimes the visions only leave me a little giddy, but other times I can lose my balance altogether and feel nauseous. It seems to depend on the intensity and what I see—the longer or more macabre, the more physical effects I experience. What will this one be like? I have to make a split-second decision—let the vision come, even though Sorrell's right there, or repress it. But I don't have a choice, not with Bowles missing. I move to the door, effectively hiding from Sorrell, and hold on to the handle to steady myself.

I'm running through the woods, naked, and it's dark except for the light of a nearly full moon that's helping me fight my way through the foliage. My breathing is fast and labored and when I look down at myself I see blood. I'm covered in blood. My legs are shaky and the footsteps behind me are getting closer. God, no, please don't let him get me. Please!

I try to run faster, but my legs don't want to respond. I turn around, desperate, yet afraid to see how close he is to me. I scream when I see the silhouette only ten or so meters behind me and closing in fast. No! How did this happen? Why did I get in the car with him?

Now I can feel his breath, hard and fast on my body, and next thing I know an arm encircles my waist and pulls me to the ground. He's underneath me, holding me on top of him, using his legs and one arm to keep me trapped. I see a flick of something gleaming in the moonlight and I turn my head. It's a knife, long and shiny. I scream, but it's stifled when he clamps his free hand across my mouth and nose. I take short, sharp gasps, but I can't seem to get enough air. The knife comes closer to me but it doesn't touch me. Instead he rolls us over so I'm facedown and he's on top of me. Holding me down, he jams my legs open with his knees. I hear him unbuckling his belt and try to scream again, but all I get is a mouthful of dirt. For the first minute I cry as he rapes me, but then my tears stop. It's not the first time he's raped me over the past two days and it probably won't be the last. His breathing comes faster and he convulses on top of me. I let another shudder of tears out. I wish he'd just kill me and get it over with.

The door opens and I'm jerked out of the vision by Sorrell's face.

"Oh my God, are you okay?"

I blink several times, still trying to reassert myself in the real world, the here and now. My heart is pumping fast, like hers was, and my legs are shaky. I also feel beads of sweat across my upper lip and on my forehead, the physical reactions she experienced as she ran through the woods. But I notice I'm still standing, something I'm definitely happy about.

I straighten myself up. "Yeah." I force an evenness into my voice, despite the lingering terror. "Just a dizzy spell. I'm fine now."

"Really? You don't look so hot."

I get a flashback of the girl's naked body. Naked... they're always naked. It's part of the power dynamic between a victim and a perpetrator. Stripped of clothes, we all feel more vulnerable.

I make a move into the room and Sorrell backs up for me. I know he's being nice, but I hate the fact that he's fussing over me like I'm some delicate, helpless woman. But I guess the only other option is to tell him about the vision, and that sure as hell isn't happening.

"Seriously, Sorrell, I'm fine. I think I need to get some food into me and cut back on the coffee, is all." I force a smile before I glance at my watch. "Come on, let's get this teleconference happening."

"Are you sure?" Sorrell's concern makes me assume I still look a little pasty, like I've been running for my life.

"Definitely. We'll do the call and then I'll get something to eat."

Although he still looks concerned, he takes his seat and dials the number. We're the last to join and I apologize for the fact that we're a few minutes late.

Sorrell fills everyone in on today's forensic results and our ideas for a DMV search, while I sit there thinking about the girl from my vision. I try to concentrate on what Sorrell's saying, but I keep getting flashbacks. She's running. He's raping her. But worse than the flashbacks is the sickening sensation I can't shake. I feel violated, I feel frightened and I feel despair. They're all her emotions, but they're invading mine. I force myself back to the meeting.

"Good work," says Brady. "You're definitely getting closer."

"Thank goodness." I recognize the voice as that of Chief Saunders. "My phone's been ringing all day with press from everywhere. Even the U.K., Germany and Asia."

"Black's hot property," Sorrell says. "And the fact that she was killed by a serial killer when she wrote about serial killers in her fictional books…"

Silence for a moment.

"Not to mention we're now looking at another victim." It's Sullivan who adds in the latest abduction.

"Randy Sade, the journalist, his name's come up again too," Sorrell says. "Linguistics indicate our fan has a Midwest background, and we just discovered Sade does too."

"So is he back on the table?" Brady asks.

Sorrell and I exchange looks. We only had a chance to discuss this briefly before the meeting and, while Sade looks like the perfect suspect on the surface, he doesn't add up in so many ways. First and foremost, we can't link him to Rickardian or Bowles. His beef was with Black—she stole his idea and then stopped him from getting a book published.

"We keep coming back to him, but I'm not convinced he fits," I say, contributing for the first time.

"Alibis?" Brady asks.

"He would have had time to kill Black, but he was in L.A. this morning when Bowles was reported missing," Sorrell replies.

"But she could have been taken anytime between 12:00 p.m. and 5:00 a.m.," Sullivan reminds us.

"True," I say.

"What about Rickardian?" Brady asks.

"I checked with the airlines for flights to San Francisco for Rickardian's murder, but his name wasn't on any passenger list."

"Maybe he drove," Dusk says.

"Six-hour drive?"

I tap my pen on my notebook. "It's possible."

"What about the other author…Blake?" Brady asks.

"Home alone," Sorrell says.

"Keep on 'em," Brady replies before asking us when we plan to do the DMV search.

"It's next on our list," Sorrell says. "Anything from the L.A. hotline?"

Chief Saunders answers. "I spoke to the officer in charge. There are a few things he's got uniforms tracking down, but nothing looks very promising at this stage."

It's par for the course with a hotline. The officers are inundated with calls, mostly pranks or concerned citizens with irrelevant bits of information, but you can also get a case-breaking lead from the hotline, so everything has to be considered and examined carefully. However, managing the volume, particularly in a high-profile case like this, can be a nightmare. I remember when they discovered the bodies in Australia's Belangalo State Forest in what came to be known as the backpacker murders. The police set up a hotline and one of the calls was from a British man. He'd been traveling in Australia but had since returned home, and he phoned from the U.K., claiming he'd been tied up by someone he'd hitched a ride with, but had managed to escape. But with the hotline flooded with calls on a daily basis, it took nearly a year and a half before the information got to a senior detective who immediately recognized its relevance. After several more phone conversations, the British witness was flown back to Australia and he identified a suspect for the police. He then returned a few years later as the prosecution's star witness, and subsequently the suspect was convicted.

"What about the hotline in San Diego?" Brady asks.

"A few more reported sightings, but none of them are panning out," Levy says. "Mostly the usual attention seekers."

"How about the Pine Valley one?" I ask.

"The two uniforms I sent felt the woman genuinely *thought* she saw Bowles, but it's probably a case of mistaken identity because we haven't had any other reports and the witness said the woman was wearing sunglasses and a scarf, making it hard to see her face. I've asked the officers to stay put, just in case."

"Anything from you guys, O'Shaughnessy and Perez?" Sorrell asks.

Not surprisingly, it's O'Shaughnessy who responds for the pair. "Nothing this end. We heard back from Rickardian's publisher and compared her responses to the list you sent through for Black and Bowles, but the Thriller Writers' Association is still the only point in common."

"Okay." I sigh, wondering whether the association's worth pursuing despite Dusk's earlier comments that most crime-fiction authors will be members. "I also need to get prints from Emily Rickardian. Have you guys got them on file?"

"We took them at the time of the murder, but they've probably been discarded by now," O'Shaughnessy says. "I'll find out and e-mail them through to you one way or another."

"Great. We've found an unidentified print on the letter from 'A fan' but I'm betting it's Emily Rickardian's given she handled that letter." I shoot a questioning look at Sorrell, effectively asking him if there's anything else we need to cover. He shakes his head.

"We'll get on the DMV search," I say, "and e-mail you the list. Did you interview a James during the Rickardian case?"

Papers shuffle in the background before O'Shaughnessy comes back on the line. "No."

With everyone updated on the case, we say goodbye and hang up.

"DMV," I say to Sorrell as soon as the line is dead.

He shakes his head. "Let's get something to eat first."

Right. I'm supposed to be hungry.

Twenty minutes and one sandwich later, we're back in the lab, but this time borrowing a computer to look up the DMV records.

I bite my lip, thinking about the vehicle age I put in the profile. "Let's leave off the age of the vehicle for the moment," I say.

Sorrell looks puzzled. "You sure?"

"I don't want to miss our guy based on such a specific thing."

Sorrell nods. "We could always work off two lists. Best of both worlds."

We enter the other variables from the profile and the forensic results into the DMV search, typing in the first name of James, San Francisco as the city, male as the sex, Caucasian as the race and thirty-five to fifty for the age. Not surprisingly, we get over five hundred hits—five hundred and fifty-four, to be precise.

I wince. "Damn."

"List number one." Sorrell hits the print function and also copies and pastes the results into Word so we can forward them on to O'Shaughnessy, Perez and whoever else might be able to assist. I'm thinking IT input will definitely help us to narrow down the list.

"And on to list number two." Sorrell types in the year of manufacture as 1990–2000, as per my profile. This time the DMV records show twenty-six matches, a much more manageable list. He prints that list out and then goes back into the Word document, highlighting the relevant twenty-six names in the list of five hundred and fifty-four.

"I've got a guy in the Cyber Crime Division at Quantico who'll be able to help us refine that list." Special Agent Daniel Gerard could bring up everything we have on each person, using their IRS records, medical records, school records and so on, to exclude any potential suspects. "Actually, scrap that. It wouldn't be the best use of his expertise." Gerard's skills are well above those required to help us filter our list and I'd rather he was working on what takes up most of his time—online child pornography. I'm sure Sorrell or Brady will have someone closer to home we can use, especially given the L.A. Field Office has its own dedicated Cyber Crime Division.

"Let's use L.A. FBI," Sorrell says. "You've got a couple of good guys on your team there."

I think back to the org chart, which seems like weeks ago, but was only a few days back. "I'll talk to the head of the area and get someone assigned to us immediately."

Sorrell nods.

I call Melissa as my first point of contact, mostly because she's been so nice to me and is clearly on the ball.

She's about to transfer me to Ed Garcia, the head of the L.A. Cyber Crime Division, when she asks if I've heard from Justin Reid.

"Um…yes." I give her a truthful answer.

"And?"

"Nothing."

A pause, then: "Are you with Sorrell? You can't talk?"

"That's right."

"Damn!"

"Nothing to say anyway." Of course, I could tell her I've agreed to meet up with Justin, but I'd rather not share my social life with Melissa until I know her better. Besides, it may never eventuate and I'm really only meeting him to be polite. Nothing, not even Justin Reid, will change my mind about being single. I know what's best for me, end of story.

I get hold music for less than twenty seconds before the phone line buzzes to life, with Ed Garcia's deep, melodic voice.

"Anderson, I hear you need a resource."

"Yeah, I do. With Bowles missing we really need someone on this as a priority."

"Tell me what you've got."

I take Garcia through the details of our two DMV lists and the obvious areas someone could run a search on.

"Sounds simple enough. I'll get one of our junior support staff on it straightaway."

You really only need access to the right databases and a basic understanding of how they work, so Garcia's decision to hand it over to a junior team member makes sense. It's why I didn't bother contacting Agent Gerard at Quantico.

"Great. I'll send all the information through to you now. How long do you think it will take?"

"All going well, we should be able to narrow the list down for you by lunchtime tomorrow."

I bite my lip. That's too late for Bowles. "Any chance of getting it sooner? Of someone staying back?"

He gives me a good-humored snort. "Yeah, okay. I'll put Bob Green on it."

I take down the name. "Thanks, Garcia. I appreciate it."

I'm typing up the paperwork for Green and Garcia when I notice an e-mail from O'Shaughnessy, with an attachment, in my In-box. Sure enough it's Emily Rickardian's fingerprints. I forward the file on to McAvey before finishing off the paperwork and e-mailing it out. When I'm done, I join Sorrell in the meeting room once more, and we go back to Black's fan mail, hoping to find something.

We're about two thirds of the way through the PDF file by 6:00 p.m., and so far none of the letters have stood out or seem in any way related to Black's death and our serial killer. In some ways that's good news, because it lets us, and more importantly forensics, focus on the letters from our fan and the hate mail.

"Given the time, let's call Daelene and get an update." Sorrell picks up the phone. Daelene Rose answers after several rings.

"Hey, it's Sorrell." Sorrell puts the phone on speaker for my benefit. "Any news for us?"

"I'm sorry, Dave. I haven't got back to them yet. You around for much longer?"

"I'd say so. Call me on my cell in case we change venues."

"Okay."

"Sorry for cutting in to your nights again." Sorrell looks guilty.

I notice he said "again"—obviously Sorrell's used his charm on Daelene before, perhaps many times before.

"That's okay. Jason will be back soon and then things won't be so crazy."

"Speak to you later, Daelene." Sorrell hangs up. "McAvey." He taps in the fingerprint lab's extension, this time leaving the phone on speaker.

"Prints. McAvey." He sounds tired.

"It's Sorrell and Anderson. Any news?"

"The extra documents haven't come through from Daelene yet."

"I know, we just spoke to her. Anything else though?"

I butt in. "Did you get my e-mail with Emily Rickardian's print?"

"Sorry. I've been on another case most of the afternoon."

"Couldn't be as important as ours." Sorrell is half teasing and half serious. Someone's life lies in the balance right now, and when you're working a case like this, it's hard to think about other cases.

"Hold on, I'll run Emily Rickardian's print against the unidentified one on that letter."

Again, the process is fast, because we have a digital copy of the prints and the computer to run the search. Although, given McAvey's only comparing one print against another, he may even be doing the process manually.

"It's a match."

"Damn," I say, even though it is as I anticipated. "So we don't have the killer's print on that letter either."

Sorrell leans back in his chair. "Doesn't look like it."

"I'll wait around for as long as I can for the extra letters. Otherwise I'll be in first thing tomorrow morning—early."

"Thanks, McAvey. Call me as soon as you have something. It doesn't matter what time it is." Sorrell hangs up.

We're silent, but our eyes say it all. Sure, we've got leads on the go and even a few potential suspects on our radar in Blake and Sade, but time's running out and we're getting nowhere fast.

Dear Ms. Goodwin,

I really enjoyed your first six books, but when you switched from following prosecutor Dan James and started your new series with Detective Nathan Crane, you lost my respect and readership. You moved from carefully plotted, well-written and intelligent books to badly written clichés. Why?

The only thing I liked about your book was the killing method—drowning. I've always been fond of the less violent murdering methods and drowning is such a classic, right up there with poisoning. Old school, you know? And it has many advantages. For a start it's nice and clean…no blood, no mess. And I'm sure it's a more peaceful way to die. I was also glad to see you refraining from the explicit sexual homicides that seem to crowd our bookshelves. Whatever happened to the classic whodunit?

Do you think drowning would be a peaceful way to die? Would you prefer it yourself? Believe you me, most people would. I would. You shouldn't be frightened of death.

Yours sincerely,
A fan

Twenty-Two

My vision is hazy from reading letter after letter, and e-mail after e-mail, and my concentration is waning.

Sorrell groans. "Anything would be better than reading this crap." He arches his back.

"At least we're almost done. Should only take us another half hour."

Sorrell nods, but doesn't seem enthusiastic—it's 8:30 p.m. and we're both tired.

"Let's finish these and then head over to FBI and see how Bob Green's doing. We need that list." I try to stay positive.

"A suspect list. That sure will be nice."

"Yup. And then it will be off to San Francisco to see 'James.'"

"Yeah, I wouldn't leave it to O'Shaughnessy and Perez." Sorrell stands up, continuing his stretch.

I follow suit; my back is sore from hunching over a desk for so long too. "Brady said they're working another homicide now. So I guess their attention is split." But even on full attention I'd question their commitment. I'm the opposite—if I know I missed something I throw myself at the case one hundred and ten percent, to try to make up for the mistake. That's what I'm doing now—I can't bear the thought that Bowles could be paying for my oversight. I push away the thought of her fingers being cut off one by one.

"Let's just hope that our letter writer lives in San Francisco and wasn't just visiting when he bought that paper."

I nod and sit back down, moving back to the letters and e-mails—the sooner we finish reading them, the sooner we can move on. But it's the same story—nothing unusual or incriminating, nothing worth getting forensics to focus on. It's frustrating when you spend a lot of time on one lead only to discover it's a dead end, but that's the nature of police business. You don't know something's irrelevant until you've found it and examined it from every angle. At least we can cross one thing off our list and head to the FBI field office, ready to hound Bob Green.

It's 10:00 p.m. by the time we're making our way through the deserted open-plan offices to the tech section. There's one guy still on duty, and I presume I'm looking at Bob Green. I walk up to the man and am about to say, "Green?" when Sorrell beats me to it.

"Hey, Green."

Green looks up and smiles at Sorrell. "Hey. What's up?"

"Green, have you met your new profiler?"

"Not in person, no. Today's my first day back from vacation." He stands up and puts his hand out. "Bob Green."

"Hi," I say, shaking his hand. "I'm Sophie Anderson. Sorry for ruining your first day back."

He shrugs. "I think that's why Garcia gave it to me... I'm fresh." He smiles. "Welcome aboard, anyway." He sits down again. "I'm just finishing up your request now. I've got you down to fifty-four names, including eight from your highlighted batch."

"That's fantastic news." It's certainly the best news I've heard all day, but that wouldn't be hard. "Hopefully your computer's got the killer's name on it." I motion to Green's computer screen.

"Better yet, only a few guys grew up in your target area. I've put those names first. Give me about fifteen minutes to print it all out, with the license photos and everything else I've got on the fifty-four guys. Okay?"

"Sure. We'll be in meeting room number..." I try to think of the most spacious room "...number three."

While we wait for the file, I mark up the main points from the profile on the whiteboard, so we can refer back and forth to it.

Age: 35–50
Race: Caucasian
Organized offender
Blue collar—maybe security guard
Recently separated or lost his job
Children or close to children
Car: Older sedan
No criminal record
Grew up or spent time in Wisconsin or upper Midwest area

Green's timing is perfect and he arrives with a folder in hand just as I write up the regional detail.

"There you go." He passes me the file. "If you don't need me anymore, I'm going to head home."

I'm already flicking through the pages when I respond, "Sure. Thanks."

Green says goodbye and makes a hasty exit. It's well and truly past home time.

I open the file on the table and the first face and name stares up at us. "I think our guy's in the older end of the age range from the profile. The fact that he handwrote his first letter to Black makes me think he's more old school. And he did, and perhaps still does, write to his Aunt Kitty."

"Okay, well let's sort them by age. Thirty-five to forty, forty-one to forty-five and then forty-six to fifty."

"Sounds good." I flick through the pages, making three separate piles across the desk. Then we start with the pile of forty-six to fifty-year-olds. I'm hoping maybe I'll get something psychically if I'm looking at the photo of "A fan."

We spend the next couple of hours reviewing every person on our shortlist in detail, spending more time on the four Jameses who currently live in San Francisco but spent at least part of their school years in Wisconsin or the upper Midwest. During the process I get a few obscure flashes of people at work or with their families, but nothing that tells me the person is our killer. Maybe things would go better if I was by myself and able to go through my relaxation techniques, but that won't be an option until whatever time it is when I scurry home for a few hours of sleep.

"Maybe we *should* send O'Shaughnessy and Perez out to see them, especially these four." Sorrell taps the pages of the four men in front of us. "At least they're on the ground now."

"You think O'Shaughnessy or Perez will answer their phone at this time?" A glance at my watch tells me it's just gone midnight. Only twelve hours left for Bowles if the killer follows the plot exactly.

We're silent, but the peace is interrupted by Sorrell's phone ringing.

He looks at the caller ID. "Looks like the lab," he says, before hitting the answer button.

"Hi, Daelene. Hold on while I put you on loudspeaker." Sorrell presses a button on his phone and lays it on the table.

"Hi, Daelene," I say.

"Hi, Sophie."

"I've finished the extra letters. I've got paper and ink on them, but it's nothing particularly unusual, nothing we could use to help us *find* our guy."

I want to sigh loudly and heavily, or stamp my foot, but I control myself. Besides, Daelene's stayed back extremely late for us. Once more, forensics on the letters will be about confirming our suspect is the doer, rather than pointing us in his direction.

"And what about the one with the cutout letters?" I think back to the sexual anger in the note—the writer thinks of all women as whores who should be punished.

"I've matched some of the letters used to the *San Francisco Examiner,* but there's a second source in there that I can't identify." She pauses. "Sorry, not very helpful, huh? I've taken them down to prints."

"Thanks, Daelene," Sorrell says. "Was McAvey still there?"

"I'm afraid not." She pauses. "But he's more of an early riser than a late-nighter."

Once Sorrell hangs up, we go back to staring at the three piles of suspects.

"Let's call them all—" Sorrell points to the nearest file "—and ask if they've got an Aunt Kitty."

I raise my eyebrows. "Simple, yet effective. I like it."

Sorrell smiles. "And if we just mention the Aunt Kitty, there's no way our guy will think we're part of the murder investigation, or that we're onto him."

"Hang on…" My sluggish mind processes things. "If the fan's our killer, he shouldn't be home, not if he's holding Bowles in San Diego somewhere."

Sorrell's silent at first. Then he says, "True. But we can at least eliminate some people and get the list real tight."

"Sounds like a plan."

Despite the lateness, we start the calls. So there'll be fifty-four Jameses in San Francisco who'll be pissed off at us. A small price to pay for Katrina Bowles's life.

Twenty-Three

I'm running through the woods, and he's behind me. I scream as loud as I can, but it's a feeble, sickly gurgle in my throat. My voice is weak from hardly drinking anything for days and weak from the breathlessness of running. But even if I could scream at the top of my lungs, no one would hear me. It's just me and the wild animals out here...and he's the wildest of them all.

I dart left and right, avoiding the bigger trees, but letting the smaller ones clip my body and face. I'm covered in scratches, but scratches are nothing. I know what he'll do to me when he catches me, he does it every time, but I still run. The day I stop running, I know he'll kill me. And while part of me wants that, part of me wants to hang on. They must be looking for me. Looking for him. Surely someone knows this bastard is loose and on the hunt.

I wake up to my 6:00 a.m. alarm, groggy from lack of sleep. I always find it hard to go to bed at all when I'm working a time-critical case, no matter how late it is and how tired I am. But I know I can't function without at least a couple of hours' sleep. I force myself into an upright position and suddenly remember my dream…the woods again. Who the hell is she and how is she related to this case? I'm also frustrated by the knowledge that this could have been something that happened years ago, or something that will happen in the future. Maybe this girl is already dead, or maybe I'll get a chance to save her.

I replay the dream over and over again while I'm in the shower, trying to see something new, notice something new. I'm still standing under the pulsing, warm water when my phone rings in the other room. I turn off the taps and grab a towel before running into the bedroom and hunting around for my cell. I pick up just in time.

"Didn't see this one coming." I recognize Sorrell's voice.

"What?"

"McAvey just phoned me with a positive ID on some of that hate mail Daelene processed last night."

"Yes?"

"Three of the letters were covered in Sandra Black's prints."

"Really?" I shake my head, leaving droplets of water on my shoulders.

"No wonder she was reluctant to give us a fingerprint sample. And no wonder the letter writer knew about Loretta's spending spree."

"So that was one of the letters?"

"Yes. That, plus the 2004 one where she agrees with the *Chicago Tribune*'s negative review, and one of the hate mails you'd picked out from earlier this year."

We're silent for a few seconds.

"It's pretty hardcore," I say. "She signed one of the letters off with 'Watch your back, bitch.'"

"I know." Sorrell pauses. "Still think she couldn't pose her sister like that?" Sorrell asks. "And the mutilation could be about hatred, not sexual degradation."

I raise my eyebrows. "It certainly makes the print at Black's house more suspicious now. And she is a struggling author." I sigh. "But in answer to your question, I still don't think a woman would pose the body like that, or concentrate mutilation on such a female part of the body. The breasts so obviously represent womanhood."

"But couldn't that just be about the book? And that's where Sandra Black's hatred stems from—her sister's fame as a writer."

I'm silent, considering this. The books and replication of the fictional works are complicating our crime scene, complicating my normal profiling methods, that's for sure. What belongs to our killer and is about him—or her—and what's simply about mimicking the fiction? I think back to my visions and dreams from Black's and Rickardian's murders and there's nothing in them that can rule out a female perpetrator. Black's crime scene screams male. Rickardian's...

"But Rickardian's nightdress was pulled up, and that wasn't in her book. That is a sexual act, one that the killer felt compelled to do before *he* left the scene."

Now it's Sorrell's turn to be silent as we bounce ideas off one another. In the end he agrees but says, "Let's go see what Sandra Black's got to say for herself."

"Definitely."

"We've got something else promising." Sorrell's voice is excited.

"Yes?"

"Another AFIS match. It's from that threatening letter made out of cutout letters."

"Really?"

"The guy's name is John Santana and his priors include sexual assault."

Sorrell's happy with the link to sexual assault, but I'm not so sure. While I'm not surprised that someone who wrote a letter showing such disrespect and violence toward women is guilty of sexual assault, I doubt Black's work made him act. Like I said to Dusk, crime fiction doesn't incite sexual assault or homicide. But it's possible Santana was already a rapist, and now he's picked a new type of woman to target—authors.

"Where does he live?" I ask.

"Oregon…Eugene. Know anyone up there?"

"We've got an office in Portland. How far's that from Eugene?"

"Couple hours' drive." Sorrell pauses. "I'll contact the local cops and maybe speak to his parole officer."

"Okay. I'll call our Portland Field Office and see if they've got anything on the guy. I'll also find out if we've got agents in Eugene."

"Meet you at Sandra Black's home in…forty-five minutes?"

"See you then."

As soon as we hang up, I use my laptop to jump online and into the FBI's network to find the after-hours contact details for the Portland office. I choose the head of the Violent Crimes Investigative Department as my contact and also discover we have agents in Eugene, so I take down the cell number of the agent in charge up there.

I try the Portland contact first. "Special Agent Crone."

I can tell I've woken him, but his voice is still alert. I introduce myself and apologize for the early call.

"Quite all right, Agent Anderson. What can I do for you?"

"Do you know a John Santana from Eugene? His priors include sexual assault."

"Sure, I know Santana. Career criminal, that one."

"You looking at him for anything at the moment?"

"Don't think so. But I'll give a ring around in Eugene and double-check if you like."

"That'd be great." It also saves me a call.

"What's your interest in him?"

"He sent Loretta Black a nasty bit of fan mail."

"Really? And you think he's tied in to her murder? And that other author's?"

"Not sure yet. But we're running prints on all the fan mail and seeing where it leads us."

"Uh-huh. Well, Santana's on parole and shouldn't be leaving Oregon. Give me some dates and I'll see if I can verify that Santana was in Oregon."

I give Crone the dates of Black's and Rickardian's murders. "I've got a colleague with the Beverly Hills PD who's going to contact the local Eugene forces and Santana's parole officer."

"Okay. I'll make sure we don't double up. You should hear back from me soon."

Sandra Black lives in a small two-story town house in Hermosa Beach, a coastal suburb about thirty kilometers south, and slightly west, of downtown L.A. Thanks to big sis, Sandra Black's doing damn well for a struggling, unpublished author.

I see Sorrell leaning against his car about half a block away from Black's town house. Once I find a parking space, I double back on foot.

"How'd you go?" I ask.

"Managed to get ahold of one of the cops who worked a couple of rape cases against Santana. I don't like the sound of this Santana one little bit."

"FBI Portland knew him too. Career criminal."

"That and more. His last rape victim nearly died. She was found in a laneway, bleeding profusely from her abdomen. He'd stabbed her while he was having sex with her and then left her for dead. They got a conviction, but only fifteen years. He's been out of jail and on parole for the last seven months, and they're keeping a close eye on him."

"How close? Have they been able to clear him for our murders and the abduction of Bowles?"

"They're getting back to me on dates."

"Same with FBI."

"Sandra Black?" Sorrell stands upright.

"Let's do it."

We walk the half block to Sandra Black's home and ring the doorbell of the intercom system.

"Hello?" Her voice is muffled and croaky and we've obviously woken her up.

"Ms. Black, it's Detective Sorrell and Agent Anderson. We want to talk to you about your sister's murder."

A pause, before static comes through the intercom for a second followed by, "Okay, I'll be down in a minute."

Sorrell and I lean against opposite sides of the railing that leads up the four steps to Sandra Black's stoop. Windows on either side of the front door are decorated with flower boxes.

"This'll be interesting." Sorrell looks up, perhaps imagining which room is Sandra's bedroom.

"Yes, it will be." I sigh. "I'm wrecked."

"Me too."

"You've spoken to her more than I have." I motion with my head to the front door. "You can lead the interview."

Sorrell nods, just as the door opens. Sandra Black wears a pair of running shorts and a fitted T-shirt. She's bra-less and barefoot.

"Detective Sorrell." She looks at me. "Agent Anderson. What can I do for you?"

Sorrell gives her a pleasant smile. "Hi, Sandra. Sorry to wake you up."

"Not at all. Anything I can do to help the investigation." She puts her hands behind her back awkwardly, but not fast enough for me to miss the shaking.

"Come in," she says, standing back and holding the door open for us. "It's terrible about Katrina Bowles. Have you found her yet?" Now she clasps her hands together in front of her body.

I bite my lip at the reminder. "No, not yet."

"But we have got something new on Loretta," Sorrell says. "Let's sit down."

Sandra's eyes dart from Sorrell to me. "Of course." She leads us down the hallway and we take our first right, into her living room. Two maroon two-seater couches face one another, with a dark wood coffee table between them. Sandra sits on one of the two-seaters and Sorrell and I take the other. The room is decorated with dark wooden furniture, almost Japanese in style, complemented by maroon and cream furnishings, and it reminds me of Holt's decor. Maybe they shared design ideas. On a counter in the corner is a maroon vase with white lilies, which are either real or extremely good fakes.

"So, what is it?" She leans forward.

Sorrell maintains eye contact. "We know about the letters you sent Loretta. The hate mail."

She's silent at first, but gradually her face falls, until tears stream down her cheeks. At first she takes swipes at the tears as they fall, and then she puts both hands up to her face.

Sorrell and I watch her reaction silently.

It's a minute or so before she looks up. "Please don't tell Dad. He'd never understand."

"You've got more to worry about than your father, Sandra."

"What do you mean?" She pauses, and the penny drops. "You can't think…you can't think that I had anything to do with Loretta's murder."

The shock and outrage in her voice sound real, but I know Sorrell won't leave it there.

"You had motive. Money and jealousy."

"Yes, but…but I could never kill Loretta. My own flesh and blood." She clutches at her chest with both hands.

"But you could write nasty and threatening letters to her?"

I keep quiet, observing the exchange.

"That's different." Sandra pushes herself backward and brings her legs up, cross-legged, on the couch. "Loretta had it all, and Dad…he never stopped talking about her. He didn't care about what I did. You know, he's never read one of my books, but he's read every one of Loretta's several times over. And she really wasn't even that good!" She shakes her head. "It drove me crazy, living with that. So…so I wrote Loretta a nasty letter about two years ago.

It made me feel better." She shrugs. "And then I wrote a couple more letters when Loretta or Dad said or did something obnoxious." She pauses. "It was cathartic for me."

"Was killing her cathartic?" Sorrell hits her with it hard.

"This is madness!" She stands up. "I didn't hurt my sister!"

Sorrell takes out his notebook and flips through the pages. "You don't deserve to be published, you don't deserve to live."

Sandra wrings her hands together. "I was angry. I didn't *mean* it."

Sorrell's silent and stares at Sandra for some time before speaking again. "When did you last see your sister?"

"I told you, at the launch."

Sandra is distraught, too distraught to be asking us more pertinent questions, like, "What about Rickardian and Bowles? Why would I kill them?"

"You sure about that?"

"Yes."

For the first time I have a question for Sandra. "Why did you even go, if you hated her so much?"

"First off, I didn't hate her. I was just frustrated that she'd done so well and I still can't find a publisher for any of my books." She shakes her head. "And I *had* to go to the stupid launches. I'd never hear the end of it if I didn't turn up to the L.A. launch, not when I live here."

Sorrell waits a beat, leaving time for me to follow up, but I don't feel the need to. "When was the last time you were at Loretta's house?" he asks. "Honestly. We found your fingerprint there." Sorrell's bluffing, choosing not to mention that the fingerprint could have been there since March.

She pauses, still breathing fast from crying and fear.

"Two weeks ago to give her my latest manuscript. I asked her to read it and pass it on to her agent."

"What did she say?"

Sandra grits her teeth. "That she'd pass it on if she felt it was good enough." She snorts. "And that it would take her a few weeks to get to it with her other commitments."

Ouch. That had to have hurt. On the one hand I see Black's point—you don't want to recommend something crappy to your professional associates—but it's still a tough game to play with your sister.

"And no one knew about this meeting with her?"

Sandra shrugs. "I didn't tell anyone. I was embarrassed that my sister could treat me like that."

"But she did help you out in other ways." Sorrell sweeps his hand out around him, indicating the house.

She hangs her head. "Yes. Loretta bought this house for me five years ago."

Sorrell and I exchange a look.

"I know, I stink," she says, sinking back onto the couch. "My sister puts me up rent free and I send her bitchy notes." She looks up. "God, *please* don't tell Dad."

Sorrell puts his notebook away. "Like I said, Sandra, you've got more things to worry about than your father."

"But I didn't touch Loretta! I swear to God!"

Sandra's still crying tears of shame as we leave.

"My gut tells me she's a dead end," Sorrell says as soon as we're down the stairs. "But I'm going to get some of my guys to tail her."

"Okay."

Lucky for us the case is high profile. Otherwise we'd never have enough cops at our disposal to tail Blake and Sandra Black around the clock.

We're walking to our cars when my phone rings.

"Anderson, it's Crone." He speaks quickly. "We may have something for you."

"Yes?"

"I sent two of our Eugene agents to check on Santana's current whereabouts. When no one answered at his home, they canvassed the street and have had two independent reports of a woman screaming late last night. They're about to go in."

Could it have been Bowles? Would he transport her? It's certainly a big deviation from the book and the only way he'd be able to do it is by car, and that's a long drive. "How long would it take to drive from San Diego to Eugene?"

"Katrina Bowles?"

"Yeah."

"Over twelve hours." If Bowles was taken at the earlier end of our timeline, it's possible.

"I'm ordering my agents in. Do you want to stay on the line?"

"Yes, sir."

I instantly get hold music and while I'm waiting I fill Sorrell in on the details.

"Holy smoke. So we could have Bowles?"

I scrunch my face up. I want to hope, I do, but why would our killer transport the victim back to Eugene? And why deviate from the book's plot so much? "I don't know, Sorrell."

We wait next to Sorrell's car until finally, after fifteen minutes, the hold music cuts off and Crone's voice comes on the line.

"Anderson?"

"Yup, I'm here."

"We've got Santana and he did have a woman with him, but it's not Katrina Bowles. The woman says she knows Santana and claims they were having an argument, that's all."

What could this woman be thinking, choosing to spend time in Santana's company? I'm glad it's nothing more sinister, but it still leaves Katrina Bowles in the hands of another sexual predator.

"Thanks, Agent Crone."

I hang up.

"Well?" Sorrell says.

"Apparently it was a domestic dispute between Santana and a woman who was with him of her own free will. Not Bowles."

Sorrell nods. "We've still got a bit of time to find her."

I sigh. "Yeah, but not much." I start walking to my car. "See you back at the field office?"

"Yeah."

In the car, I can't help but think about another sexual predator, and another victim—the girl in the woods. Maybe Dusk can help me. I punch in his number. "Hey, Dusk. It's Anderson."

"Hey. Any news on Bowles?"

"No." I don't bother telling him about Santana.

Dusk's silent for a little while, also aware that the clock is ticking.

I move on to the purpose of my call. "Dusk, have you ever read a crime book about a woman running through the woods and being chased by a man?"

"Um…no, I don't think so. Why?"

"Long story." I hope this will be enough to dismiss

Dusk's question, and just to make sure I say, "I've gotta go, Dusk. And if the woods rings a bell, let me know."

"Will do."

I run through the dream again, but nothing's specific enough to help me. The woods could be anywhere, the girl could be anyone, the man chasing her could be anyone. Again, there were no faces, no cars, no houses, nothing. I think back to the vision I had about the girl last year, when I was working the D.C. Slasher case, and try to picture her. She had short blond hair, with a slight wave in it, and I thought she looked petite. It's possible I'd recognize her as a missing person, or an author photo…possible. And maybe VICAP would have some matches for me.

Back at the FBI field office, it's time to start ringing our Jameses again. We got through to thirty-five of the fifty-four last night, with no hits on an Aunt Kitty, so today it's back to the others. Time's running out for Bowles, but until there's a body, I won't give up hope.

Sorrell's set up to call from meeting room three and I call from my desk—it would be too difficult to both make the calls from the same room, especially if one of our suspects overheard us asking someone else exactly the same questions.

But before I start on my half of the remaining nineteen names, I open up VICAP and plug in the variables from my recurring nightmare. I search under woods for the body-dump locations or the attack locations and cross that with both rape and murder victims, but because I don't know the cause of death I'm overloaded with matches. Were the women stabbed, strangled, shot or something else? Has there even been more than one victim? My gut tells me yes—the person chasing me in the dreams and visions seemed to know what he was doing, seemed to have a routine down.

The few dead female vics that have been found in woods don't match my girl, so maybe this guy's victims have been buried in the woods but not found. And in terms of rape victims who are alive, nothing matches either—no one's reported being held captive in the woods. And victims like my girl would be covered in scratches from all the branches and shrubs.

The final thing I decide to do before getting back to my list of suspects is to check through the e-mailed updates from both the L.A. and San Diego call centers, but nothing's panned out so far. No more sightings in Pine Valley, or anywhere else. The lead was probably too different to Bowles's book and therefore the plot the killer will be following, but it was worth looking into. I go back over the information about Bowles—the apartment, her girlfriend, her book. I wonder how Anne Cooper's faring, given her hysterical state at the press conference, but mostly I think about the letter, or rather the absence of one. Why would our fan communicate with the other victims, but not Bowles? Was she a spur-of-the-moment target, rather than planned, as his other victims were? If so, maybe he didn't have time to write a letter. But our killer is an organized offender, characterized by meticulous planning. He doesn't kill on impulse. And the correspondence seems important to him, an essential part of his pattern of contacting his soon-to-be victims. Unless…

"Shit!" I say out aloud before almost running to the meeting room. Sorrell looks up as soon as I burst in.

"I can't believe it!"

Sorrell keeps staring at me, puzzled.

"The witness from Pine Valley said that the woman she saw was wearing sunglasses and a scarf…maybe she was trying to disguise herself." I emphasize the last few words. I continue. "They set this up…for the publicity. Bowles hasn't been abducted, she's hiding out in Pine Valley."

Sorrell doesn't look convinced so I keep going.

"Did you see Cooper at the press conference? She was a mess. The Cooper we met was tired, yes, but she was nervous, not distraught. At first I thought she was simply worried, but she wasn't. She was nervous because she was lying to us." I shake my head, thinking back to all the questions about how many people were on the case and if we were still investigating the other leads. Her questions were fueled by guilt.

Sorrell crosses his arms, allowing himself to believe it. "Bowles got her publicity, that's for sure. I bet her books are selling now."

We immediately call Levy and Sullivan. Like Sorrell, at first they can't believe it, but then they see the thread of logic. Cooper's tears at the press conference looked genuine, maybe genuine enough to upset Bowles in her hideaway, so much so that she broke cover to reassure her.

As soon as we hang up from Levy and Sullivan, I call Cooper on speakerphone. Levy and Sullivan will go and see her in person, but I can't just leave it without confirming it on the phone and giving her a piece of my mind. And maybe Sorrell will join in. He certainly looks tired enough, and annoyed enough.

The phone's answered after two rings.

"Yes?" Her voice still sounds ragged, but I guess it's an act.

"It's Special Agent Anderson, Anne."

"Yes? What is it, Agent Anderson?" She manages to continue the act, as if she thinks we've got news for her about Bowles.

"Give it a rest, Anne. We know this is all a publicity stunt."

Her silence is all the confirmation I need.

Sorrell takes his swing. "We flew out from L.A., leaving an active investigation, to try and apprehend the killer before he killed your girlfriend. Do you have any idea how much trouble you're in?" Sorrell's angry but not aggressive. He's also brought up a damn good point—we could charge both Cooper and Bowles with obstruction of justice, at the very least.

"I…I…I didn't know at first. Then after the press conference Trina called me. She said she couldn't stand seeing me like that."

The behavioral differences between the woman at the press conference and the one we spoke to in San Diego back up her claims.

She continues, "Trina knew I wouldn't approve. That I wouldn't be able to go to the police and report her missing if I knew where she really was. But then when she saw me at the press conference, she called and told me everything. Told me to keep it up just for a few days." Cooper's voice is breaking. "Trina's a great writer, but her first two books didn't do well and if her third one doesn't go better, she may not get another book deal."

"Anne, don't even try to explain it. You can save that for court."

"Court?" Suddenly her voice is more alert.

"Obstruction of justice. See you then." I hang up, still angry. But despite the anger, I am relieved. We don't have another victim and I was right about the escalation. That's two out of two.

Half an hour later, Brady and Saunders run another press conference, this time a brief one to inform the press and public that Bowles has been found alive and well. For the moment, he calls it a "misunderstanding" between Bowles and her girlfriend, but we've still got legal avenues open to us if we want to pursue it later.

Back at my desk, I check my messages. One from Reid. I call him back and his secretary puts me through.

"I guess you're free for dinner now."

I manage a shocked half laugh, half sigh. "How do you find these things out so quickly?"

"I have my ways."

I bite my lip. I still don't think going out with Justin Reid's a good idea, but I did say I would. "How about a quick drink?" I suggest, thinking this would be less intense than dinner.

"You don't eat?"

I smile. "I eat. But I think a drink is a better idea."

"Guess a woman has to be careful these days." His tone is teasing. "Just because I'm the owner of SysTech doesn't mean I'm a good guy, right?"

"Stop giving me a hard time." I also make sure my voice is light. Truth is, I wouldn't mind sitting back and having a couple of drinks tonight, now that Bowles is safe and there's no need to work the case 24/7. But I don't admit that to Reid. Instead I say, "I was up most of last night working on the Bowles thing…before we found out she was okay. I doubt I'll make it past eight o'clock tonight, so I think drinks is a better idea."

"Whatever you say." Justin doesn't sound convinced.

"Let's make it six, but you can pick the venue."

"Done. I'll meet you at the Caroon Bar. It's in Beverly Hills."

"Okay, I'll find it."

Sorrell and I spend the rest of the day going through our suspect list for San Francisco. By 5:30 p.m. we've managed to eliminate everyone except for four people, including one who has documented time in Wisconsin and one in Minnesota. We've also booked flights for Saturday morning to check out the four men.

"Sure you don't want to leave it till Monday?" Sorrell asks, but I get the impression he's keen to move as fast as possible.

"I know we don't have the urgency of Bowles, but I still want to put this bastard behind bars as quickly as possible. Besides, the killer might not be our fan, might not be James, and we need to find out one way or another."

I still feel that the letters are linked to the deaths—both authors receiving letters from "A fan" is simply too coincidental. But there's another thought that's been preying on my mind…and it bothers me. I first thought of it at Black's funeral, when I was questioning if Sorrell's instincts on Werner as the killer were better than mine.

"What's up?" Sorrell is staring at me.

I shrug. "Nothing."

"Come on, Anderson. Don't hold out on me now."

I pause. "It's just…well, the investigation took a sudden turn when we found out about Rickardian, right?"

"Sure."

"Well, what if that was the plan all along? What if our killer's been planning Black's death for months, maybe longer, and decided that killing another author first was the best way to ensure the investigation changed from personal to serial killer?"

Sorrell scrunches up his face. "It'd certainly change things." He pauses. "Sandra Black, Randy Sade, Peter Blake and Scott Werner would all be in the picture, big-time."

"Yup." I drum my fingers on the table. "And both Blake and Sade aren't alibied for the night Black died. Nor for Rickardian. We should check out Sandra's alibi too." I bite my lip. "Just in case."

"And you know how much I like Werner for it."

"If he hired a hitman?"

"Exactly. But that'll be darn hard to trace if he did it right." Sorrell shakes his head. "I don't think he's stupid enough to go into a rough part of town and solicit thugs." He pauses. "So what do you wanna do?"

"Let's see how things pan out with our four guys in San Fran tomorrow. Blake, Werner, Black and Sade aren't going anywhere. Not if they think they've committed the perfect murder."

Twenty-Four

When I arrive at the Caroon Bar at nearly 6:15 p.m., I feel decidedly underdressed. Sure, I'm in a suit like most of the other patrons, but mine's obviously not a designer label and I'm not flashing any bling like the other women. For an instant I'm anxious, embarrassed to be turning up to meet a man like Reid in a place like this when I'm dressed so conservatively. I even hesitate at the door, although I wouldn't seriously think about doing a runner and standing the guy up. But then I come to my senses—it's not a date, and even if it was, the venue choice is obviously meant to impress me, and I refuse to be impressed by glitz.

I enter the bar, not strutting, but at least striding.

A well-dressed man approaches me. "Do you have a booking, ma'am?"

I need a booking for a bar? "I'm meeting someone."

"Yes?"

"Justin Reid."

The manager's face instantly changes from door bitch

to lapdog. "Ah, Ms. Anderson. Wonderful to have you with us. Please follow me." He walks me upstairs to a window table. Reid's on his cell phone, but as soon as he sees me he tells the person on the other end he has to go and stands up. Nice to see he's got manners.

"Sophie." He smiles. "I was just wondering if you were going to stand me up."

The manager pulls out my chair and I sit, noticing the bottle of Dom Pérignon on ice.

"Sorry, I got held up at work." Even though the FBI offices aren't far from the bar, the traffic on a Friday night was unbearable. Plus I spent a little bit of time reapplying makeup after Sorrell left for the day.

"Champagne?" The manager motions to the bottle.

Reid looks at me. "If you don't like champagne we can order something else."

"Champagne's fine," I say, purposefully keeping my voice neutral. I love a glass of champagne, but I'm not going to admit that to Reid.

Reid leans back and looks at me, letting the manager pour the champagne and set it back in the ice. Reid seems comfortable in the silence, waiting until the manager leaves before raising his glass. "Cheers."

We gently clink glasses. "Cheers," I say, noticing an expensive-looking platinum-and-diamond ring on his little finger. Even Reid's got bling on. But despite the diamonds, it's tasteful and small.

He takes a small sip, daintier than I would have expected. "Hard day at the office?"

"A little." I lean back and glance out the window at the magnificent skyline view. "You?"

"Not really. I don't do that much in the company these

days, to be honest." He takes another sip. "It's all meetings, and in most cases the decision's already been made. I'm just the final threshold they have to cross." He chuckles. "Do you play chess, Sophie?"

I'm a little thrown by the apparent topic change. "I know how to play, but it's not a game I really enjoy."

"I see. I was going to make the analogy between myself and the king in chess. I may be important, but I don't do much on a day-to-day level. I don't really hold the power anymore."

"So who does?"

"My managing director. He's the queen, if you like. He can go anywhere he wants, do anything he pleases."

I'm sure Reid's more active and important than he's letting on, but I don't stroke his ego. There's no doubt in my mind that he's got more than enough volunteers for that job.

"So does it keep you busy?" I ask.

"That and the charity work I do."

I know Reid is involved in a youth outreach program for young African-American offenders in San Francisco—that's how he met Heath Jordan all those years ago, the man we discovered was AmericanPsycho and the president of the Murderers' Club.

"What charities are you involved in?"

He lists several, including World Vision, Amnesty International, the AIDS Fund and the Make-A-Wish Foundation. The list is impressive.

"Wow," is all I manage in response. Then: "That's good of you to, you know, put back in instead of using your wealth for material possessions and wining and dining."

I look at the bottle of Dom Pérignon on the table and Justin follows my gaze. "I'm sorry, I didn't mean…"

He smiles. "I thought you might feel like that. So I got the nonvintage instead of the vintage."

I laugh. Truth is, I do appreciate good wine and food. "If I could afford it, I'd be tempted by expensive wine," I admit. "Definitely more likely to indulge in that than clothes and shoes."

"I don't think many women would side with you on that one."

He might be right, so I let him get away with the sweeping generalization. I take another sip of the Dom Pérignon, enjoying its complex flavors. "So, is your business finished in L.A.?"

"Yes. I nodded and signed."

Again, I get the feeling he's downplaying his role or maybe just omitting details, like the signing was for a multimillion-dollar contract of some sort, but I go with the image of him nodding and signing. "I'm sure you did it very well."

Justin smiles. "I'm well practiced."

The manager comes back with a plate of hors d'oeuvres and places them in the center of the table.

Justin leans forward. "It's not *dinner,* just something small to enjoy with the champagne." He smiles.

The deal was drinks but I'm not going to complain. Even though I had a late lunch, I'm feeling the beginnings of hunger pangs. I take a blini that's been topped with smoked salmon and crème fraiche.

"So, how are you enjoying L.A.? It's a big move, East Coast to West Coast." Justin chooses a piece of sushi.

"It is a big move. But not as big as moving from Australia to the U.S."

"No, of course not." He pauses. "I'm sure your family and friends are very proud of you."

Proud isn't the word I'd use for my parents…well, maybe they are proud, but that's overshadowed by their concern. They lost one child, and the thought of losing another must be unbearable.

"Yes, they are proud." I don't know if it's a lie or not, but Justin hardly needs to know the internal workings of my family. "What about your parents? They must be thrilled with your achievements."

He makes a slight shrugging gesture. "My mother died when I was very young, and Dad passed away a year ago."

"Oh, I'm so sorry." First the inadvertent dig at his choice of expensive champagne and now this. "I've really got foot-and-mouth tonight."

"Not at all." He smiles. "My dad was proud of me. I started the company ten years ago, and created the first version of NetSecure a year into that. So Dad got to see most of the product's success."

I nod. "It's nice that at least one of them was around."

I can't help but feel a little sorry for Justin Reid now, despite his success. Having studied psychology before moving into criminal psychology, I know how damaging the loss of a parent can be for a child. It's something you deal with but can never truly recover from. Just like my brother's death.

"Do you like the champagne?" he asks.

"It's delicious."

"Have you had it before?"

"No, I haven't." I don't know why, but I feel embarrassed to admit this.

"Well, I'm glad to be the one to introduce you to it. I'm looking forward to sharing more bottles with you."

I put my champagne glass down. I need to nip this in the bud. "Look, Justin, you seem like a nice guy, but I really don't think a repeat of this is a good idea."

Justin sighs. "Because of Heath?"

"Yes. But that's not the only reason."

"I'd like to hear your other reasons then, Sophie." Underneath his smooth tone I sense a hint of pain.

"I'll be honest with you, Justin. I'm just not interested in seeing anyone at the moment."

"But you are single?"

"Yes, and I want to stay that way, at least for the moment."

"Bad breakup?"

In most cases it would be a safe bet on Justin's part, but not this time, not with me. Yes, I did break up with someone in the past six months, but that's not the only reason I've ditched the dating game. With everything that's happened and that's happening in my life, I don't need more complication. And with visions of terrified women being chased and raped, I'm not exactly dying to jump into a relationship with a man.

"Not exactly." I decide to go for a slightly watered-down version of the truth. "I *was* seeing someone over here and, yes, things didn't go as planned, but it's got more to do with my work than him."

"You're ambitious, focused and you don't want a man distracting you?"

"My work's important to me, yes, and it needs a lot of time and focus."

"It must be hard to put it out of your mind at the end of the day. Seeing what you see."

"Yes."

"Is it…is it gruesome? Horrible?" He wrinkles his nose at the thought.

"A lot of it, yes. But I love the idea of helping people, of bringing the bad guys to justice." I smile. "Does that sound trite?"

"Not at all." He pauses. "But it must be hard, seeing victims, mostly women and children, every day."

I take another sip of champagne, not willing to let him see that he's hit the nail on the head. "Yes, it is." I manage to say it without emotion.

He nods. "So this will be our one and only date?" Again, there's a hint of hurt in his voice.

"Yes, I'm afraid so."

We spend the next hour and a half talking mostly about the differences between Australia and the U.S. and talking about travel. Not surprisingly, Justin has traveled extensively, and I've always had a bit of a travel bug myself. We've been to many of the same cities in Europe, although I imagine our accommodations were somewhat different, especially given most of my European travel was as a backpacker. Still, we're able to talk about our most-loved places and both agree that Paris is our favorite European city.

I know that Justin was probably hoping drinks would extend into dinner, but I make sure I cut the evening short, despite the fact that I'm enjoying his company.

"Thank you for a lovely evening, Justin, but it's time for me to go."

"You must be hungry, though?"

"No. The hors d'oeuvres have filled me up enough."

He smiles. "Then perhaps I shouldn't have ordered them. An oversight on my part." He pauses. "Are you going to Tucson for Heath's pretrial conference on Monday?" he asks.

I hesitate. I have to be very careful what I say to Justin. Despite his apparent acceptance of Heath's crimes, there's still probably a part of him that doesn't believe it, that feels loyal to Heath. He even appeared as a character witness at the preliminary hearing—but that was a few months ago. A lot can change in that time. "No witnesses are required at a pretrial." I dodge the question.

"No. So I guess I won't be seeing you Monday."

"You're still standing by him?" I try to keep the incredulity out of my voice.

"I am." He pauses. "I know I said a couple of months ago that I thought maybe he *could* have done those horrible things, but there's still a part of me that can't reconcile that with the man I know. Jordan and I have been friends for ten years now. I rely on him, and he relies on me. And there aren't many people I can say that about."

"So you think he's innocent?"

"No offense, but it wouldn't be the first time it's happened, would it? Innocent people go to prison. It's a fact of life."

"But—"

Reid holds up a hand. "Sorry, I shouldn't have brought it up. At this stage, I'm going to give him the benefit of the doubt and if I'm wrong, so be it."

I want to lay out all the evidence for Reid, to make him see sense, but instead I say, "You'll take a hammering for it in the press."

He shrugs. "I can cope."

"And your shareholders?"

"If SysTech shares take a dive over this, they'll soon recover. The media has a short attention span."

"Maybe you're right." I stand up and sling my handbag over my shoulder. Justin stands too.

"Good night." I hold my hand out, but instead of shaking hands, Justin leans in and gives me a gentle but decidedly seductive kiss on the cheek. A shiver travels through my body, but it's not a pleasurable one.

"You okay?" he asks, a hint of smugness in his face. He thinks his kiss has had the desired effect—but it felt cold, not warm, like someone walking on my grave.

"I'm fine, thank you. Good night." I take a few steps away before turning back. "Justin, how did you know I'd transferred to the L.A. office?"

He shrugs. "I have my ways."

"No, seriously."

"I've got some friends in the Bureau." He rocks on his feet. "I have to confess I was checking up on you, and one of them mentioned you were about to start in the L.A. office."

"Who?"

"Now that would be telling." Although he says it jokingly, I can tell that I'm not going to get any more information out of him. I'd still like to know who was talking about me, but instead of questioning him further, I wave goodbye and head home—to my empty apartment and empty bed. But empty's fine by me at the moment, especially after Reid's kiss.

I'm home by 9:00 p.m. and channel-surf for about half an hour, before opting for a much-needed early night. I should read Rickardian's book, but I'm in no mood to read about death and murder, so instead I opt for my usual fantasy novel. I'm just about to drop off when I see her again.

He holds my head with both hands and with a quick and hard movement, I hear my neck snap. I just have time to think, Thank God it's over, *before darkness engulfs me.*

Twenty-Five

Sorrell and I land in San Francisco at nine the next morning. We spent part of the flight mapping out our stops to avoid backtracking—first Redwood City, then Mountain View, then across the bay to Union City before moving all the way up to Oakland.

We knock on the apartment door of James Crater, a forty-five-year-old recently divorced accountant. He matches the profile in some ways—such as his age, 1995 Mustang and recent divorce—but not in other ways, such as his education level, occupation and regional background. Unlike the other three people on our list, we did manage to contact him, but Sorrell felt he was a little edgy and worth following up.

We both wait expectantly, aware that in these situations anything can happen—from no answer to a potentially violent confrontation. Seems that everyone owns a gun these days. Both Sorrell and I have our holsters unclipped, ready for that possibility.

The door's opened by a tall redhead, whose face is covered in mild acne scars and loads of freckles. "Yeah?"

"I'm Detective Sorrell." Sorrell flashes his badge. "We spoke on the phone yesterday."

"Yes, of course. What can I do for you?"

"Mind if we come in?" I ask, before also showing my ID and introducing myself.

Crater backs away and lets us in, but Sorrell's right—the guy's nervous about something.

A beat of silence.

"Look, if this is about my ex-wife…"

He trails off, but both Sorrell and I keep quiet. Sometimes silence alone is enough to get people talking. It can even be better than asking questions. This time it has the desired effect, and after a moment Crater keeps talking.

"I swear, it's bullshit. I didn't touch her."

Sorrell and I exchange a look, disappointed that his nervousness is nothing to do with our case. We both relax a little—probably won't need our guns this visit.

Sorrell lowers himself onto the couch. "It's not about your ex-wife, Mr. Crater."

Crater sits down, still uncertain, but I remain standing. The apartment is a hodgepodge of furnishings and very obviously the product of splitting everything down the middle: one older cream couch and a new but cheaper-looking red couch; a glass coffee table that may or may not have been part of the settlement; and an empty glass cabinet—guess the ex got the actual glasses.

"What's it about then?"

"You said on the phone you don't have an Aunt Kitty?"

"That's right." He's still hesitant, not quite sure where this is going.

We've already discovered the source of his nervousness on the phone yesterday, but now that we're in his living room we may as well ask a few more questions.

"Do you read much, James?" I ask.

"Not really. Sports magazines and newspapers mostly."

I nod. "What about crime fiction?"

"No. Not my thing."

A glance around the room seems to confirm this. There are several sports magazines lying on the coffee table, but no bookshelves and no books in sight.

"You still haven't told me what this is all about. If it's not about my ex…"

"We're investigating a murder, Mr. Crater." Sorrell crosses his legs.

Crater's jaw drops open. "Murder?" He looks at us both. "Who's dead?" Now his voice is fearful—he's worried someone he knows has been killed.

"We're investigating the Loretta Black and Lorie Rickardian murders," Sorrell explains.

"Oh." Crater visibly relaxes, but then his eyebrows come together in confusion. "And I can help you how?"

"We're looking for someone who wrote Loretta Black and Lorie Rickardian fan mail. We think they may be able to help us with our investigation."

Crater shakes his head. "Sorry, not me. What makes you think I wrote to them?"

Sorrell stands up. "Don't worry about that, Mr. Crater. We obviously got the wrong person. Thank you for your time." Sorrell and I both make our way to the door.

"Sorry," Sorrell says to me once we're outside. "I did try to push him on the phone to see what was making him nervous, but he wasn't forthcoming."

"An in-person visit is much more confronting than a phone call."

"Yeah."

Our next stop is a family home in Mountain View. This is the listed address for James Rowe, a thirty-five-year-old bouncer we haven't been able to contact. The house is a single-story white brick home, with orange-brown trimmings—gutters, window frames and door frames. A double garage is to the left of the front door. It's Saturday morning and the street is busy, with kids riding bikes, men washing cars or mowing the lawns and women out gardening or watching their children. But all's quiet at Rowe's house.

"How does a bouncer afford this?" I say, looking around at the other houses on the street. I don't know San Francisco, but I imagine this area wouldn't exactly be cheap.

Sorrell shrugs. "Maybe he's got a sugar mommy."

We ring the doorbell and wait, again alert and ready for anything. We hang around for a few minutes before ringing again. No answer. We move on to the next-door neighbors. We try the house to the right first, simply because there's a man out front polishing his brand-new SUV.

"Hi there," Sorrell says.

The man looks up. "You looking for James?" He motions with his head back to James Rowe's house, making it obvious that he noticed us on his neighbor's stoop.

"Yeah. Know if he's about?"

"He works Saturdays. His mom will be in, but she's going a little deaf. Probably didn't hear the doorbell."

"You know where James works?" I ask.

"Yeah." He pauses, making the transition from helpful to suspicious. Nice to know he's protecting his neighbor.

Sorrell gets his badge out. "I'm Detective Sorrell, and this is Agent Anderson."

I fish out my ID and hold the folder open.

The man gives both IDs a cursory glance, happy enough that we are who we say we are. "He in some kind of trouble?"

"What makes you say that?" I leave the question open.

The man shrugs—our silence doesn't work this time.

"Has he been in trouble before?" I prompt.

"No. But he works at Garden City in San Jose, so I thought maybe something was going on there."

"Garden City?" I say.

"The casino."

I nod my understanding. His security job could lead to problems—Rowe oversteps the mark and beats up a customer, or an evicted gambler decides to take it out on the security guard.

"Will he be at work all day?" Sorrell asks.

"Uh-huh. But if you knock real hard Mrs. Rowe might just hear you. She's more likely to hear the knock than the buzzer."

Makes sense—when people lose their hearing it's usually the higher frequencies that go first, and the doorbell was quite high-pitched.

"Thanks for your time." Sorrell turns on his heel and I give the neighbor a nod before following suit.

Once we're out of earshot I say, "Let's knock. See what she says about her son."

We walk across the front lawn and back to the door, but before we have a chance to knock, the door opens. A woman in her seventies with tightly curled white hair and a summer dress stands in the doorway.

"What are you doing on my property?" she asks.

Sorrell and I both identify ourselves, making sure we speak loudly.

"That's no excuse for trampling over my flowers." Her hands go to her hips. "Young people these days…you've just got no respect."

We stepped *over* the garden beds, not on them, but I don't bother explaining this to Mrs. Rowe.

Sorrell apologizes, falling into line like a schoolboy—or more likely pretending to fall into line. He seems to judge people well and to know exactly what tactic to take with them to get the best results.

Mrs. Rowe begrudgingly accepts the apology. "Least you know you've done wrong."

We both bite our tongues.

"So, why are you trampling over my lawn anyway?"

"You own this house, ma'am?" I ask, trying to make my tone as polite as possible while still loud.

"Certainly. Frankie, my late husband, and I bought it forty years ago."

Explains why a bouncer can afford such a nice home. He lives at home with his well-off mother.

"Do you mind if we come in, Mrs. Rowe? We think your son might be able to help us with a very important case." Sorrell's voice is a perfect combination of respect and charm. Plus he's pandering to her parental pride, indicating her son could be helpful in a "very important case."

"James isn't here."

"That's okay." Sorrell smiles. "Maybe you can help us."

"Certainly, Detective, if I can. Please come in."

She offers us a cup of coffee, which we accept, before seating us in the living room. Sorrell and I look around while Mrs. Rowe makes the coffee. The house is homey, but it looks like it was last updated sometime in the seventies, judging by the wallpaper, light fittings and carpet. The furniture is also in need of a major facelift or, better yet, replacing. The fact that James Rowe lives with his mother in such an outdated environment immediately makes me draw conclusions about him. Firstly, he's a mommy's boy and probably an only child. That, coupled with his mother's obviously dominant personality, tells me that he's ruled by his mother. Yet he's a security guard, so I'm thinking he looks sterner or more threatening than he is, so he's probably a big guy. Gentle giant? Not if he's our killer. I think back to the DMV search and his photo. It was only a headshot, so hard to tell size. I move in for a closer look at the photos on the mantelpiece and sure enough, James was towering over both his parents from what looks like about fourteen years of age. The photo progression shows him filling out sideways to match his height, but he's only slightly overweight, with most of his width being broad shoulders.

Mrs. Rowe returns to the living room with a tray. The crockery pattern is very sixties, perhaps even one of the Rowes' original wedding presents. Guess they don't make stuff like they used to.

She puts the tray down and offers us cream and sugar before handing us each our coffees. The cantankerous woman is almost totally gone, replaced by a helpful citizen doing her civic duty, or perhaps trying to make sure her precious son helps law enforcement.

"Now, what can we do for you?" she asks, once her own coffee is poured.

"We're actually investigating Loretta Black's death," Sorrell says loudly.

"No need to shout, young man, I can hear you well

enough." She taps her hearing aid, which is pointing directly at Sorrell.

"Sorry, ma'am."

She nods. "Loretta Black. That is a big case. I've seen it on the news every day for a week now."

"Yes, she was found last Saturday," I say.

Again Mrs. Rowe nods. "And you think my James can help."

I give Sorrell a look, so he'll let me speak. "Yes, Mrs. Rowe. We believe Ms. Black was recently at Garden City, where your son works. He may have seen something, something important."

"Really?"

"Yes." I pause. "Did he mention anything about Loretta Black?"

"No. And he usually does tell me if anyone famous comes to the casino." She takes a sip of her coffee. "Mind you, I doubt he'd recognize her. He's not much of a reader, our James."

"So he's not a fan of Loretta Black?" I ask for confirmation.

She shakes her head. "No. Like I said, not a big reader. God blessed my James with many talents, but brains—" she taps her head "—wasn't one of them." She sighs. "Frankie was so disappointed too. He was a lawyer, you know."

Sorrell and I both give her a few nods that we hope will cover all bases—from acknowledgment to condolences.

We ask her a few more questions about Black, and also bring up Lorie Rickardian, but it's obvious we're barking up the wrong tree. And James Rowe isn't going to hide a love of books, or crime fiction, from his white-haired mother. After we finish our coffees we politely excuse ourselves and thank Mrs. Rowe for her time.

"Let's hope the day gets more productive," I say as we clamber back into our rental.

Next is our Union City stop, James Baker. Baker, our Minnesota man, lives in a small, single-fronted weatherboard, that's a bit more weathered than board on the outside. The front garden, however, is immaculate, with neat flower beds in full bloom and a perfectly manicured knee-high hedge leading from the front gate to the front door. We open the red wire gate. The house is set back about thirty meters from the fence, with two steps up to a narrow veranda. Potted plants in ceramic pots line either side of the door. I listen for any noises inside before ringing the doorbell. My right hand rests on my holster to give me a few milliseconds of advantage if I need it. After two washouts I'm not quite as wired, but I'm still alert.

When a minute passes with no answer, I ring the doorbell again. Another minute passes and I shrug my shoulders. Guess he's not home. Not surprising given we haven't been able to reach him on the telephone.

I peer into the front window.

"Hey, what are you doing there?"

Sorrell and I both turn around to the source of the suspicious voice—a woman in her late fifties. She wears her gray hair short and layered. Her pink lipstick matches her pink T-shirt, which sits on top of loose white shorts that show off her slim legs.

"We're looking for James Baker," I say.

Her eyes narrow slightly.

"My name's Special Agent Anderson. I'm with the FBI."

She still looks a little suspicious. "He's on vacation. Won't be back until tomorrow." She takes a packet of cigarettes out of her back pocket and lights up.

I look back at the mailbox. I'm certain I would have noticed a buildup of mail. Sure enough, it's clear. "What about his mail?" I ask.

"I've been collecting it for him and watering his garden and plants." She motions toward the veranda with her cigarette hand before taking another drag. "He's in Florida."

Sorrell takes a few steps toward her. "How long has he been away for?"

"Five days."

That still leaves him open for Black's murder seven days ago. He kills her and then hops on a plane. I move closer to the neighbor. "Do you know if he reads much?"

She snorts, and streams of smoke fly out of her nostrils. "I'll say. If he's not reading, he's gardening."

Sorrell's phone rings loudly. He answers it, but immediately tells the caller that he'll phone them back.

"Baker retired?" I ask the neighbor.

She eyes us suspiciously again. "You got some ID on you?"

I show her my ID and explain that Sorrell's Beverly Hills PD before he shows her his badge.

"He works part-time as a security guard at the Legion of Honor Museum."

I nod. Not only does that match his last tax return with the IRS, it matches the profile.

"What's he like?" Sorrell asks, taking out his notebook.

She takes a long drag of her cigarette. "You think I'd collect his mail and water his plants if he wasn't a nice man?"

Sorrell shrugs. "Maybe you're just being a good neighbor."

She smiles. "I'm not the neighborly type. But James… he's good to me. We've been neighbors for ten years and during that time my husband, Gary, passed away." Her tone softens. "James is always helping me out around the house. He's a good man. A gentleman. And there aren't too many of them left." She gives Sorrell a slightly accusatory look, seemingly hinting that Sorrell's no gentleman.

He doesn't take the bait. "So, what sort of books does he read?"

"Anything and everything, I think. But I know he likes thrillers." She pauses. "James isn't in any trouble, is he?"

The fact that it's taken her this long to ask that question shows her high opinion of James. It was way down her list of possible reasons why law enforcement could be visiting Baker, not her first assumption.

"We're just asking some routine questions," Sorrell says diplomatically.

"For an investigation?"

"Yes," he replies.

"Do you know if James has an Aunt Kitty?" I ask.

"Yes, he does."

Now we're really getting somewhere. Not only does James Baker fit the profile, he's got an Aunt Kitty, just like our mysterious fan.

"Does this have something to do with her? He'll be devastated if anything's happened to his Aunt Kitty."

"We can't discuss that at this point." Sorrell's dodging of the question makes it look as if our presence is related to the aunt.

She takes another hard drag on her cigarette. "I hope nothing's happened to that little old lady."

"Does James have children?" I ask, thinking about our fan's anger at the authors for creating bad role models.

"Nope. He's a bachelor. But he's like a father to his two nieces."

Man, it doesn't get much better than this.

"When does James get back?" Sorrell asks.

"Sunday morning, I think. But I'm not sure exactly when."

I nod. "Okay, thanks. We'll come back later." But we won't be waiting here for him. We should be able to find his name on a booking from Florida to San Francisco, and I'd rather be his welcoming committee at the airport.

If we felt that there was a chance evidence could be destroyed or someone's life was in danger, we could legally enter James Baker's home and search it. But there's nothing to indicate the situation's that urgent, and if we do go in without a warrant, anything we find might not be admissible in court. So we'll have to wait.

Walking back to the car, Sorrell tells me that his phone call was Sandra Black.

"What did she have to say?"

"I didn't really give her much of a chance. Said I'd call her back."

In the car, Sorrell dials Sandra Black on speakerphone.

"I just had a call from some Detective Edwards," she says.

"Yes, he's helping us out on your sister's case," Sorrell explains.

"But I told you yesterday, I didn't have anything to do with Loretta's murder."

Sorrell gives me a look. Sandra Black is being downright naive, thinking we'd take her word for it without following up.

"We still need to know where you were the night of your sister's murder." Sorrell's voice is patient.

"But I don't see what business that is of yours, or this Detective Edwards."

"We're investigating a murder," I say. "And your finger-prints were found at the scene and on some extremely incriminating mail."

Silence.

"We can ask around, Sandra. Maybe give your dad and brother a call, ask if they know where you were."

"No!" She whimpers into the phone. Then: "Okay, okay. I was out with friends for dinner, and then we went to a bar. I guess I got back home about two."

"And your friends can verify that?"

Sandra Black gives us a few names before we hang up.

"Two…it doesn't give her much time, but it's within the realm of possibility." Sorrell pulls out onto the I-880.

"Depends how long the killer spent with Black before he…or she…killed her."

Sorrell says. "Last stop coming up. Oakland."

The chance of James Arrow from Oakland also having an Aunt Kitty are smaller than a Las Vegas jackpot, but we can't drop the lead, especially since he did spend part of his adolescence in Wisconsin.

But James Arrow turns out to be a bust—the only thing we were interrupting was a hangover, not plans to kill crime-fiction authors.

"Looks like James Baker is our man," I say in the elevator ride down from James Arrow's apartment.

"Uh-huh. Let's find out as much as we can about him before he flies in tomorrow morning."

There goes what little of my weekend is left. But Sorrell's right. Now that we've got confirmation that the guy's got an Aunty Kitty and reads crime, we need to ramp up our investigation.

"He must be our letter writer," I say. "Let's hope he's our killer too."

From Oakland we head over the Bay Bridge to downtown San Francisco. The sky is clear and the views from the bridge are stunning. It certainly makes me want to sightsee rather than canvass associates of James Baker. But we're here to work, to catch a killer.

"So, Baker's neighbors and work colleagues," I say.

"Yup." Sorrell pauses. "That'll keep us busy for the rest of the day."

"At least we've got a good suspect." It would have been terrible to strike out with all four guys on our list.

"Match us a couple of fibers and we're done." Sorrell's referring to both the beige fiber found in Loretta Black's hair and the navy carpet fiber found at Lorie Rickardian's house. Hopefully we'll discover that James Baker has a navy carpet and a beige sweater.

Twenty-Six

Baker's flight is due to land at 11:15 a.m., but Sorrell and I make sure we're at the gate, waiting, from 10:30 a.m. Ground staff confirmed James Baker did board the plane in Florida, so now we just have to wait. I've got his picture in my hand and I glance at it every few seconds, even though I'd easily know him by sight now.

Baker's flight is delayed by a few minutes but finally, at 11:25 a.m., the passengers start streaming out. My eyes flick to each passenger in turn, moving on to the next person only when I'm one hundred percent sure I haven't got James Baker in my sights. For some people that means I don't even have to study their faces—women, children and men who are obviously under forty can be dismissed instantly. But for each male that looks like he's in our target age range, I carefully examine each facial feature and his face as a whole. Toward the middle of the pack I see Baker.

Baker looks all of his forty-nine years—perhaps Florida is a regular vacation for him and he spends too much time in the sun. His hair is dark brown with lots of gray at the temples, and his face is broad with large features and leathery, tanned skin. He's about six feet and looks like he keeps in shape. I also notice he's quite dressed up for a man back from a vacation in the sun—he wears brown trousers and a cream long-sleeved shirt.

I nudge Sorrell.

"Yup, I see him." Sorrell moves forward first, and I take an extralong step to catch up with him. We both take out our IDs.

"Mr. James Baker?" I ask, even though I know it's him. He nods. "Yes."

I note his reaction. He doesn't seem nervous or worried. But it's amazing how people will protest their innocence, even when faced with the murder weapon in their house.

"I'm Agent Anderson with the FBI and this is Detective Sorrell. We'd like to have a few words with you."

Sorrell takes Baker by the arm and leads him away from the curious onlookers. I guess this show's better than whatever they ran on the flight. Sorrell ushers Baker into the corner of the gate lounge, the most private place in a very public area.

"Is everything okay?" Baker puts down his leather carry-on bag.

I study his face. "Have you written letters to Loretta Black and Lorie Rickardian?"

He looks a little thrown, but says, "I wrote letters to Loretta Black."

"And you signed them 'A fan'?" This time it's Sorrell who asks.

"That's right, yes." He looks us up and down. "I wrote three letters to Ms. Black."

Looks like Baker's having problems with his arithmetic. "You mean four to Loretta Black and one to Lorie Rickardian?" I say.

He shakes his head. "No." He looks at us both, from Sorrell to me, then back again. "What's all this about anyway?"

Sorrell still holds Baker's arm, as if he's worried the man's going to make a run for it. "I presume you heard about Loretta Black's murder."

"Of course, it's been all over the news. And they've linked it to Lorie Rickardian's murder too."

Sorrell nods. "Exactly. *We* have." Sorrell puts enough emphasis on the word "we" that it should be obvious to Baker that Sorrell and I are involved in the investigation.

The penny drops. "You can't think…you can't think that *I* had anything to do with those poor women's deaths?"

"You were obsessed with them." Sorrell's voice hardens.

Time to move venues.

"Mr. Baker, if you're innocent, I'm sure you won't mind coming down to FBI headquarters and answering our questions somewhere more private." I hold up both arms, gesturing at the busy airport backdrop.

He looks hesitant at first, but then puffs his chest up. "Certainly. I've got nothing to hide and anything I can do to help…"

We wait with him for his luggage and then load him and his possessions into our rental car. I sit in back with Baker, just in case he suddenly changes tactics and decides on a drastic move. Looks can be deceiving, and, if he's like most serial killers, Baker's public face will be very different to his private murderous fantasies and actions. One thing serial killers often have in common is that their

neighbors will vouch for what a nice guy he was…"quiet."
But a human being who's capable of murder, particularly
serial murders, is capable of pretty much anything.

We walk through the almost-deserted field office, taking
Baker straight into one of the interview rooms and offering
him a drink. He opts for coffee and we leave him and his
caffeine in the room to stew together. Sorrell and I watch him
from the observation room, formulating our plan of attack.

"I think you should lead the questioning," I say.
"Baker's old school, traditional, and he'll respond better
to a male authority figure."

"Sure." Sorrell's flicking through the files. "I'm
thinking we start with the letters. If he admits to those on
record, we can get a search warrant for his place, even if
he doesn't confess to the crime itself."

"It'd be nice to get inside his house and confirm the
printer and paper." Before we can get a judge to sign a
search warrant, we need to prove probable cause. A concrete admission on tape that Baker wrote the letters should
be enough. Once we have that, we'll go looking for a beige
sweater and navy carpet to place him at both murders.
"And see if he'll give you his fingerprints, so we can
compare them to the fan mail."

Sorrell nods. "I'm going in." He makes his way out of
the observation room.

I haven't seen Sorrell in action in the interview room
and I don't know what his style will be. Most cops nowa-
days know they have to pretend they understand, even
agree with the perp's actions. But some still like to play
hardball, and that won't work with Baker. He needs
someone who can understand his cause, and Sorrell
seemed about to go for the aggressive angle at the airport.

"Take it easy on him," I say. "Indulge his need for vengeance."

Sorrell turns and gives me the tiniest of smiles. "I can do that."

Baker looks up when Sorrell enters the room.

Sorrell forces a bigger smile. "So, Mr. Baker. Like I said at the airport, I'm Detective Sorrell from L.A. and we're investigating the murders of Loretta Black and Lorie Rickardian."

Baker nods.

"So, you first wrote to Loretta Black in 2004. Is that correct?"

"Yes."

"And is this the letter you wrote?" Sorrell puts a photocopy of the handwritten letter on the table.

Baker immediately claims ownership of the letter, but still picks it up and looks at it.

"We'd like to verify that with your fingerprints."

Baker shifts uncomfortably in his chair. "I don't know about that. I don't have to give them to you, right? No one should *have* to give their fingerprints…unless they're charged," he adds as an afterthought.

"No, you don't." Sorrell wisely changes the topic. I can see Baker will take us down the road of privacy and police powers. "So at this point you enjoyed her books?"

"Yes. That's correct."

I can't work out if Baker's deliberately keeping his answers brief or if it's just because so far Sorrell's only asked him questions that require a short answer.

"And this is the second letter you wrote, in 2005." Sorrell puts the photocopy of the second letter on the table.

"Yes."

"And why did you change from handwriting to a computer printout?"

Baker crosses his arms. "I finally succumbed to the digital age and bought myself a computer and printer."

That marries with our own thoughts on the change, particularly given his age. If he didn't use a computer much, or at all, at his work, then his exposure could be limited. They're few and far between these days, but there are still some people who prefer the old-fashioned ways.

Sorrell continues with the letters. "Next was this one, which you sent in 2006. This is when you became unhappy with the level of violence in Black's books."

"Well, it's true isn't it, Detective? I'm sure you don't thank modern-day TV and crime-fiction books for your increased workload. People kill too easily, wouldn't you say? And for no good reason."

Sorrell smiles. "I couldn't agree with you more. And you're right, I see it in this job every day. Our murder rate just keeps going up and up." Sorrell pauses, giving Baker the chance to take up the baton.

He obliges. "Exactly." Baker slams open hands onto the table. "And it drives me crazy. You know it's no longer safe to walk around at night. No one truly feels safe in our cities these days. And I'm sure L.A. is much worse than here."

Sorrell leans back in his chair, like he's in deep contemplation. "True. True."

"And authors like Black are contributing to the problem."

Sorrell gives one nod. "She committed horrible crimes against our society, didn't she?" I recognize the phrasing Sorrell chooses from Baker's fourth letter.

Baker's eyes narrow. "Um…yeah, I guess you could put it that way. Correct, Detective."

Sorrell takes out the fourth letter. "Well, that's exactly the way *you* put it, Mr. Baker."

Baker picks the letter up and reads it. "I didn't write this."

"Come on, Baker. We know you wrote these letters."

"I wrote three letters. I didn't write this one." He taps the letter with his index finger, while still holding it with his other hand. "This letter's vulgar. With the part about the woman's spread legs. I certainly wouldn't write that."

"Come on, Baker, I understand where you're coming from. I really do. Loretta Black's work damaged our society and you set that wrong right."

"No." He shakes his head emphatically. "I didn't."

Sorrell stands up. "We're going to find evidence that links you to the murders, James. Why not make it easier on yourself?"

"What? This has gone far enough. I want a lawyer."

"Interview suspended at 12:15 p.m.," Sorrell says for the videotape. He makes his way to the door. "Give me a minute."

A few seconds later Sorrell's standing in front of me. "What do you think?"

"I think we've got enough for a search warrant, and for a court order on his fingerprints, but not enough to charge him. Let's cut him loose with surveillance and go search his house."

Sorrell nods. "Do you want to organize the warrant while I organize a lawyer to stall and keep him here? We don't want him going home and destroying evidence."

"Will do." I move straightaway to phone Dusk. He'll

know a judge for the warrant and will hopefully be able to get some agents to keep an eye on Baker once we release him—even though it is a Sunday afternoon.

An hour later we're driving Baker home—he thought it was out of the kindness of our hearts, but meeting us at his house is a forensics team, and I've got a faxed copy of the signed search warrant in my pocket. Sometimes the wheels of justice turn slowly, but when you're at the tail end of a high-profile investigation with a strong suspect in your sights, the wheels can spin mighty fast. We also got a court order for his prints, and once we scanned them in, I sent them to McAvey. Baker has admitted to writing three of the four letters to Black, so I'm sure his prints will be a match. And the fourth letter is the one we assume he wore gloves for.

A large SUV is out the front of Baker's house. It's black and screams FBI.

"What's going on?" Baker asks.

I fish the search warrant out of my pocket and hand it to him. "We're searching your house for evidence."

"But you can't do that. I didn't have anything to do with the murders!"

"They all say that, Mr. Baker." I take the search warrant back from him.

"I gave you my stupid fingerprints."

"Because you had to."

He doesn't have a comeback. Instead, he's good enough to open his front door for us—well, he is when we point out that the warrant gives us the right to break in and ruin his door or window.

"You can watch, Mr. Baker, but you need to keep out of the way of the forensics team," Sorrell says. "Otherwise we can charge you with obstruction of justice."

Baker's house is a three-bedroom, but one room's been converted into a study. We instruct the evidence-collection team to take the printer, computer and paper back to the San Francisco lab for testing, while we look around the rest of the house.

The house is carpeted throughout in cream, not navy, but Baker does have a few beige-colored clothes. I instruct forensics to bag these items. The search warrant also includes his car, which we discover in the locked garage. Again, it matches the profile—a 1994 Ford Lincoln Town Car—but I'm disappointed to find it has black carpeting, not navy.

Because the victims weren't brought back here, we don't fingerprint the house, but we do complete a thorough search for anything else that may link Baker to the authors. It takes Sorrell, me and the forensics team four hours to process the house, but the only obvious link we find to Black and Rickardian are their books on Baker's book-shelf. I jot down all the other authors that appear on his shelves—a tedious task, but one that's important because I need to know who else he wrote to, who else he might have been targeting. I'm satisfied we've found our letter writer, but have we found our killer?

Twenty-Seven

Monday morning I'm sitting in the San Francisco Field Office when my phone rings. It's Darren.

"Hi," I say. "Good weekend?"

"The weekend was fine, but everything went to hell this morning." Darren sounds stressed.

"What's up?"

"Heath Jordan."

"What's happened?" Lots of things flash through my mind—he's escaped, he's been killed in prison, he's committed suicide, he's somehow plea-bargained his way out of the death penalty—and while I'm not in favor of the death penalty, that would be a major political debacle given the heinous nature of the crime.

"Can you fly down?"

"What!" It must be bad. "What's happened, Darren?"

"Heath Jordan's attorney, Harry Strongson, has just claimed that Jordan isn't AmericanPsycho, and that Brooke Woods can corroborate it."

"But she never saw AmericanPsycho."

"Strongson says she never saw AmericanPsycho, but she *did* see Heath. According to Strongson, she saw Heath Jordan on the video stream, but while AmericanPsycho was online." He pauses. "The claim is that the face was blurred, like it was being obscured by some software program, but that the build is unmistakable."

"His build is distinctive, but not unique." Heath Jordan's as tall as Sorrell's six-six, maybe taller, and he's nearly double the width. He looks like a professional American football player or a heavyweight boxer.

"I guess it's possible he purposefully hired someone who resembled his build to try to clear himself later on."

I shake my head. "Why has this just come out now? And what about the computer evidence?" We found log-in data for AmericanPsycho on both Jordan's home computer and his work computer. Both computers were used to log on to www.murderers-club.com and communicate online with the other three serial killers. But I also remember Gerard mentioning anomalies on the computer.

Darren sighs. "I don't know. But I'm hoping to get some answers real soon. We're about to go and see Brooke and then we're meeting with Strongson."

"I'm afraid I can't fly down, Darren. I can't leave this case at the moment. But can you hook me into the meeting via phone? I want to hear what they've got to say for themselves. But first I've got to call Agent Gerard."

"Will do."

"Hey, Darren?"

"Yup."

"We've still got Brooke's original statement on video, and her testimony from the preliminary hearing. That's gotta count for something."

"Let's hope so. If we can't confirm that Jordan's AmericanPsycho, we won't have him for murder."

"We've got the conspiracy charges," I say. "He was part of this scheme, one way or another, and people died. We can still get him for murder." I bite my lip… God I hope I'm right.

"I hope so." Darren pauses. "How's your current case going? Any news on forensics?" It's good of Darren to ask, but I know he's just being polite. It's hard to think about any other cases with the prospect of Jordan getting off.

"Not yet. Sorrell's at the San Francisco lab at the moment." I say goodbye and ring Agent Daniel Gerard as soon as I've hung up.

"Hello?" His voice is a little terse.

"Gerard, it's Anderson."

"Anderson…hi. Look, I'll have to call you back. We've got a bit of a problem here."

"This is urgent, Gerard."

"Can't be as urgent as this."

Now I'm curious. "What's up?"

He hesitates. "We've got a computer breach." I can hear guilt in his voice. Gerard's not responsible for the FBI's security, but with his background as a hacker, I'm sure he's consulted on the subject.

"Okay," I say, immediately understanding the seriousness of the situation. Only an extremely accomplished hacker would be able to get into the FBI system and there's a lot of incredibly sensitive information on our computers. "Call me back as soon as you can. Looks like Heath Jordan may not be AmericanPsycho."

"What?" He's distracted, but he still cares about the case.

I sigh. "We've got a visual ID from Brooke. She says he was on the video stream while Psycho was online."

"Yeah, and we can believe everything she says." Gerard met Brooke Woods during the case and knows exactly the type of predator she is.

"True. I don't know much yet, but I'll fill you in as soon as I do. Sorry to distract you."

He sighs. "My fault for picking up the phone."

I fill Dusk in on the latest developments while I wait for Darren's call. It's forty-five minutes before it comes.

"Okay, we're at the prison and I'm walking to an interview room now."

It's a couple of minutes later that the sound of footsteps and chairs being moved subsides.

"Hi, Brooke. You remember us—I'm Detective Carter and this is District Attorney Cole."

"Of course."

"And we've got Agent Anderson on the phone too," Darren continues. "We've just come from Heath Jordan's pretrial conference and his lawyer said you could testify that Jordan is *not* AmericanPsycho." Darren keeps his voice even and free from any emotion.

"That's right."

"So you're changing your story?"

"No. I was asked before if I recognized a photo of Heath Jordan and I answered truthfully, that he looked like the guy on the video stream."

"But you knew at the preliminary hearing three months ago that we were prosecuting Jordan based on the belief that he's AmericanPsycho." This time it's Sam Cole's voice. "You never mentioned that he was online and in the video picture simultaneously."

"You didn't ask."

Brooke's been jerking us around. "I thought you wanted revenge on the president for setting you up," I say.

"I did, Agent Anderson. But when you guys fucked it up, I decided you deserved to be at the very bottom of the pit you'd dug for yourselves."

I resist the temptation to yell at her down the phone. At least she's off the streets…and out of the bars and clubs where she used to pick up her male victims.

"So you will testify that Heath Jordan is not American-Psycho?" I ask, keeping my voice even.

"Can't be in two places at once, right?" Her voice is syrupy sweet.

"You just blew your deal, Ms. Woods," Cole says. "Guess you better make peace with yourself."

She laughs. "Nice try, but the deal is tight. I know it and you know it. I've fulfilled my part of the bargain. I'll still testify about the Murderers' Club, about what we all said online, who was killed, everything. And *that* is the deal I signed."

"Why now? Why tell us now?" I ask. It would have been more dramatic to wait until the trial—to force a mistrial even. That would have jerked us around more and caused the maximum damage to our case and to our public profile.

"I had a visitor yesterday."

Darren tries to get more details out of Brooke, but she's not talking.

Back in the corridor, Darren says, "We're on our way to find out who Brooke's mystery visitor was yesterday."

The prison keeps a record, so Brooke's decision not to divulge that information is about power, nothing else. She knows it's only a matter of minutes before we get the information, but she likes the idea of prolonging our time in the dark.

"I'll call you back." Darren hangs up and I wait, going over the old case. I thought we had them all…I thought Never-Caught, Andrew Picking, was the last of the murderous group.

Within five minutes my cell's ringing.

"Shoot," I say straight off.

"Harry Strongson, Heath Jordan's attorney, was her visitor. We're on our way to see him now." Again, Darren arranges to call me back once he and Cole are with Strongson.

So if it was Strongson, then either Heath Jordan finally broke his steely silence, or something else happened that made Strongson follow up on Woods. But how did he know that Jordan's identity as AmericanPsycho was in doubt if it wasn't Jordan himself who told him?

This time I have to wait thirty minutes for the call.

"We're with Harry Strongson now, Sophie."

"Hi, Agent Anderson."

"Hi. Is your client with you, Mr. Strongson?"

"No. He's been taken back to prison."

"What the hell's going on, Harry?" Cole says. "We know you were up with Brooke Woods yesterday."

"That's correct, yes."

"Jesus Christ, Strongson. Enough with the games."

Darren and I keep quiet for the moment—this is lawyer talk.

"New evidence," Strongson replies.

"Come on, what new evidence? You know you're obliged to share that with us."

"Certainly. And I'm going to do that now. But Heath only told me about it yesterday and I had to corroborate it."

"Why is he suddenly talking?" I ask.

"Who knows, Agent Anderson. But he did make the declaration soon after I gave him an envelope."

"Envelope?" Darren asks.

"It was delivered by courier to my office. That's why I visited Jordan in prison yesterday. And then he instructed me to talk to Brooke, said that she could clear him."

"Do you know who the note was from? What it said?"

"No. And even if I did, I wouldn't tell you."

I roll my eyes.

"If it's part of your new evidence, we've got a right to it. You know that, Strongson," Cole says.

"I won't be presenting the letter as evidence, Sam. You're lucky I even told you about it."

To compel Jordan to show us that letter—if he hasn't destroyed it already—we'd need a court order.

"How do you live with yourself, defending people like him?" Cole asks, taking the moral high ground as only a D.A. can.

"I'm paid to do a job."

Maybe it's Reid we should be taking the moral high ground with. He's the one who's bankrolling Jordan's defense with San Francisco's best and most expensive criminal lawyer. He promised Jordan representation as soon as he was arrested. I think back to the chilling kiss and am instantly hit by a wave of dizziness so strong that I'm relieved to be sitting down.

I unlock the shack and drag the body behind me. I look down at the four bullet holes in Danny Jensen's chest and the semidried blood on his shirt. I smile, happy that he's dead. I open the door and pull Danny closer to the edge of the pit. I kneel down and use both gloved hands to roll him into the pit. His body hits the mummified corpses of the others.

It's dark, but I run a flashlight over the pit, checking on my handiwork. I smile. I'm unstoppable and soon they'll all be dead. I take off my gloves, revealing my only jewelry—one diamond-and-platinum ring.

Oh my God, I've seen that ring before. My stomach starts to convulse, my mind flashing back once more to Justin Reid's kiss. I manage to control the desire to vomit, but only just. I know who the real AmericanPsycho is. It was never Heath Jordan, he was Reid's fall guy. The henchman turned scapegoat. We've been played, and I was part of Reid's game all along. The help with NeverCaught, the roses, the "date." Bile begins to rise up my throat once more.

"Darren," I say, my voice barely above a whisper.

"What? What's wrong?" Darren's instantly concerned, reading my shock well, even over the phone.

"They've been buying time. Buying time for the real AmericanPsycho."

"You know who it is?"

"Yeah, I do." Again, flashes of the flowers, the champagne, the kiss make me feel ill. "I think it's Justin Reid."

"Don't be ridiculous, Agent Anderson." Strongson is outraged—not surprising given he knows Reid. Not surprising given everyone thinks Reid is the epitome of good, wholesome business.

"Sophie, are you sure about this?" Darren asks.

"I'm pretty sure, Darren." I put enough emphasis into my words that even long-distance, Darren must guess that a vision was involved. "I'm in San Francisco now." I pause. "Time to pay Mr. Reid a visit." I stand up as I'm talking, ready to take off.

"This is outrageous!" It's Strongson's voice, and I'm sure most people would agree with him. An upstanding citizen like Reid hiding his true, murderous face?

"Mr. Strongson, do not interfere in this. Call Reid to warn him and I will find something to charge you with."

Silence. Strongson knows that at the very least I'd be able to slap an obstruction charge on him.

I soften my voice. "I'll let you know how it goes, Darren."

"Watch your back, Sophie," Darren manages before I hang up. I've got to get moving. If the note for Heath Jordan was from Justin, he's probably already on the run. I just hope we're not too late.

I pick up reinforcements—Dusk and two other FBI agents—and hotfoot it over to Palo Alto and Reid's SysTech office. On the way over I call Gerard.

"Gerard, I think I know where your breach came from."

"Really?"

I try not to be offended by the surprise in his voice.

"Reid. Justin Reid."

"We have been looking at Trojan horses," he says, slowly piecing together what I'm telling him. "Reid could have planted a Trojan horse with a back door to our system in that code we downloaded from his server a few months ago." He pauses. "Oh my God…you think he's American-Psycho, don't you?" His voice is incredulous, showing his surprise that the Reid he knows could be a psychopathic killer. But he also knows that it adds up.

"Yeah, I do. We're going to pay him a visit now." I bite my lip, knowing in my heart that we're too late. Jordan was willing to take the fall for Justin, and if he's suddenly changed his story now, it's probably because he's been given the all-clear. The note must have been from Justin Reid.

We pull up outside SysTech. It seems like only a few days ago that we were rushing into the building to take down Jordan, and now…

We bypass security instantly and catch the elevator to the top floor. Our guns are drawn and we all wear bullet-proof vests. I lead the way to Reid's office, moving quickly past his secretary, Carolyn. She tries to intercept us, but I put my hand up in a stop signal to silence her. I swing Reid's office door open. He's standing in the far corner of his office, admiring the view.

"On your knees, Reid! Now!"

"But—" He starts to turn around.

"FBI, on your knees or we'll fire." I don't really believe that he'd turn around with a gun in his hand, but there's no point taking a chance.

He kneels down. "Don't shoot."

"Hands behind your head."

He puts his hands behind his head. "Okay, I'm down. Now listen to me, I'm not Justin Reid."

"What?" I keep my gun pointed at him, but move closer. Once I'm within physical range, I pull his arm so his body turns slightly. "Who the hell are you?"

"My name's Albert Ramirez. I've got a twelve o'clock appointment with Mr. Reid."

Carolyn races in behind us. "What are you doing?"

"Looking for Mr. Reid," I reply. "Where is he?"

"That's just it…I don't know." Carolyn's forehead wrinkles with worry.

"When did you last see him?"

"Friday. I tried to call him on his cell, but no luck. I'm worried about him."

Worried? If only she knew.

Twenty-Eight

My attention is well and truly divided. The realization that Reid is AmericanPsycho and the true mastermind behind the scheme four months ago fills me with a rage so fierce I can barely function.

Over the past twenty-four hours our efforts to locate Reid have been useless, despite his high-profile and recognizable face. We've checked all the airports and the Canadian and Mexican borders, but as far as we can tell Justin Reid hasn't left the country. Then again, Reid can afford the best fake ID money can buy. My bet is he flew out of the U.S. the day he had the letter delivered to Jordan, or even the day before, if he was playing it safe. We've got agents going over camera footage from the airports in San Francisco, but that will take days.

With a court order, we accessed Reid's banking details, only to find that all of his investments were cashed in the past few months and his U.S. accounts drained. He's transferred the bulk of his money somewhere... God only knows where. Key SysTech staff have been interviewed, and have revealed that Reid rushed through a few deals, including the one he made in L.A. last Friday—the night he met me for a drink. I keep flashing back to him sitting across the table from me sipping Dom Pérignon, all the while smug in the knowledge that *he* was the killer I'd been looking for. And obviously his chess analogy was a joke on me too—he figured we were playing a game of chess and he was maneuvering all his pieces just where he wanted them.

I call Agent Daniel Gerard, who has been working around the clock since the discovery of Reid's true identity.

"Hi, Gerard. It's Anderson."

"Hi." I can hear the fatigue in his voice.

"Anything?"

"We've confirmed that our breach was a Trojan horse, and that it was embedded in the program we downloaded from Reid's secure server to locate NeverCaught." He pauses. "But I'm still unraveling the web to tie that directly to Reid and not SysTech in general."

"SysTech could mean any employee."

"Yes. And given how well he covered his tracks last time, during our investigation of the Murderers' Club, I know I'm dealing with a pro…a genius."

"You've got the brains to match Reid."

He sighs. "Thanks. But it doesn't feel like it at the moment."

"Do you know what he accessed in the FBI network?"

"Yeah, and you're not going to like one of the items, Anderson."

"Go on," I say hesitantly.

"Your calendar."

"That's how he knew I'd been transferred. Friend in the FBI my ass."

"Sorry?"

I fill Gerard in on the fact that Reid had known about my transfer…and sent me welcoming flowers.

"Not the kind of admirer a girl wants." His tone is grim.

"No." I move us back to the case. "What else did Reid access?"

"All the files on the Murderers' Club."

"Not surprising."

"No. As you know, I'd been working on the evidence on and off. I guess Reid realized I'd eventually uncover the real identity of AmericanPsycho."

"Would you have?"

"Truthfully, it's hard to say for sure. But yeah, I think so."

Reid's a calculating man, cool under pressure. And I know he thinks like a psychopath—his first thought would have been to kill Gerard…fix the problem. So my guess is he decided that would bring too much heat. I don't bother voicing my conclusions to Gerard. No point informing him of his potential brush with death.

"So where to from here?"

"I've still got to find something to definitively tie Reid to the Murderers' Club, and to murder," he says.

My vision linked Reid to the Murderers' Club—I saw him lower one of the victims' bodies into the pit near the bunker. But that won't hold up in a court of law, that's for sure. And Reid must have killed before. Then it hits me…the visions I've been having about the girl in the woods…they've nearly all been after I've had contact with Reid. Two after phone calls, one after the date. He's the killer in the woods!

"Gerard, can you find out what properties Reid owns? See if there are any out of the city."

"Sure. Hold on a sec."

I hear furious typing in the background. Within a few minutes, Gerard says, "It's well-hidden, behind companies within companies, but he's got a place in Groveland, California."

"Shit. I gotta go, Gerard. Thanks."

Three hours later we're making our way up the dirt driveway of Reid's country retreat in Groveland. From a satellite view, we discovered a large house sitting on two acres of cleared land amongst a thirty-acre property. That's plenty of room for Reid to stage his hunting game with its human prey. But how many victims has he claimed? Not to mention, where the hell is he now?

We're accompanied by a large FBI team, staffed from the San Francisco Field Office. Dusk and I ride together, and both Darren and Agent Daniel Gerard are anxiously waiting by the phone for news. I don't envy them—I couldn't sit this one out—but neither of them could get here fast enough.

We didn't get any heat readings from the bird, but I'm still hopeful that the girl from my dreams is alive. Or that at least one victim is still being held captive. I'd like to save one girl from Reid's deranged sense of fun. I can only imagine how these women must have felt, being picked up by *the* Justin Reid. Many of them probably recognized him and were thrilled to be getting attention from such a powerful and charming man.

The driveway is rough, and our vehicles bounce around. As far as the others are concerned we're simply checking out one of Reid's properties, now that we know he's a killer. And even though nobody's looking forward to what we might find, I'm the only one who has an insight into exactly what that will be. Reid was smooth, practiced. The Murderers' Club was not his first taste of killing, and neither was the girl from my dreams. He had his killing routine down pat, no doubt after years of practice and refinement.

A light blue weatherboard house comes into view through a cluster of oak trees. The driveway seems to become a little smoother, as though this section has been graded recently, and suddenly we emerge into the clearing. With the house in sight, I instinctively check my gun, ammunition and vest.

"You ready?" Dusk asks, breaking the silence.

"Sure." I keep my eyes focused on the house, thinking of the girl from my vision. Who is she? Is she in that house somewhere? Or did Reid have enough time to put his affairs in order—in every sense?

I radio the base, checking for the latest satellite images. "Any heat signatures?" I ask.

"No." A pause. "All's quiet and has been for the past twenty minutes." It's been twenty minutes since I checked in with them last. I'd wanted to check in every minute, but I'm cautious not to show my obsession with Reid. Lots of people in the L.A. office know Reid sent me flowers, and by now that knowledge may not be confined to the one office.

I take a few deep but silent breaths in preparation. I visualize drawing my gun and firing on Reid—at the moment, that's a pretty nice thought. But I push the desire away… I'm law enforcement, not judge, jury and executioner.

The car pulls to a halt and Dusk and I pile out on the far side of the house, using the car as a shield, just in case. The other four cars pull up, and the agents take their positions. Once the cars are angled across the driveway and blocking the front of the building, I move us forward. Dusk and I make the first move, directly to the front door via the large veranda that extends around the house. I look through one of the glass panes and can instantly see that the house is empty. And I mean empty. No furniture, nothing. I guess that's what happens when you've got months between committing a crime and the prospect of being brought to justice. Especially if you've been in the FBI's computer system and can pinpoint at exactly what time your crimes will be discovered.

I motion to the other units to take their positions. I try the door…it's open. The arrogant bastard didn't even bother to lock up after he'd cleared off. My already boiling blood takes a further hike. Man, I want this guy.

My gun's drawn as I push the door open. I wait for a few seconds, not willing to put the possibility of booby traps past Reid—nothing about him would surprise me now. I think back to the bomb blasts in the Mojave Desert, which must have been triggered by Reid in the comfort of his office.

The seconds drag by like hours, but nothing happens. I move forward, and am relieved when we don't all go "boom." I move into the house with Dusk and four other agents hot on my heels. The front door opens onto a small area and a staircase, with a dining room to the left and a living room to the right. I motion two of the other agents upstairs, two to the living room, and Dusk and I take the dining room. The house will be easy to secure without furniture. We're moving toward a swinging door, probably to the kitchen, when a bout of dizziness hits me. I pause for a second.

A woman sits at a dining-room table. Her arms are free but she's tied to the chair around her waist. Opposite her is Reid, smiling.

She wears an evening dress, torn, and her face and arms are covered in scratches.

I come out of it quickly. It was a different woman to my other vision, which makes it at least two victims. While this doesn't surprise me, somehow I still feel an overwhelming sense of grief. And fear—could I have ended up as one of those women? Was that his plan for me before he realized his identity would soon be uncovered?

We move into the kitchen, which is empty except for a single red rose in a glass vase on a kitchen bench. The rose looks like it's only been fully open for a day, maybe two. Dusk looks at my face, which I keep expressionless, despite my fear and anger. The rose could only be meant for me.

The kitchen's a dead end, so we move back into the hallway via the dining room. Under the stairs is a door, which we open. Another staircase leads down to the basement. I fish the torch from my pocket and hold my gun in my right hand, the torch in my left. We move down the stairs slowly. Part of me is ready for anything…anyone…and part of me believes that Reid had too much time to sort things out, too much time to leave anyone alive. At the bottom of the stairs I see a cord for a pull-down light switch, but the bare bulb reveals another empty room. Just like the rest of the house, the basement is a bust.

We meet the rest of the indoor team near the front door, and move out the back to rendezvous with the agents sweeping the back of the property. We're moving back through the kitchen and toward the back door when my earpiece crackles.

"Agent Anderson?"

"Yes."

"I think we've got something out back."

I join the four agents sweeping the back of the house, who are all standing over one area just on the border of the cleared land. As I get closer, I see a large flower bed covering an area nearly the size of the house. There are lots of bursts of different colors from flowers in full bloom, contrasted by rich, dark earth—some recently upturned. The flower bed has all the makings of makeshift graves— disturbed earth and plants that are thriving on the natural fertilizer of decomposing human flesh. I was too late for these women and I sat across from their killer drinking champagne. I don't have to imagine their terror—I felt it firsthand through my visions, and I feel it now.

With a wave of nausea comes the dizziness.

I'm running through the woods, and he's behind me...again. I don't know how many times we'll do this dance, how many times he'll make me run for my life, only to catch me, rape me and then take me back to my dungeon. But maybe this time I'll outrun him. Maybe this time I'll see someone, someone to help me.

I keep moving, the branches of trees swiping at my face and body, opening up new cuts—some over the old, some on fresh skin.

I can hear his breath, hard and fast behind me. But it's the sound of someone catching up to me, not of someone laboring. He's too fit for that. If only I was fitter. If only I could run faster, or for longer.

A hand grabs my arm and jerks me to the ground. We go through it all again. Him on top of me, me crying. When it's over, I stumble to my feet and start crying. It's different to the tears I've cried before…different this time. This time, I don't think I'll ever stop. He comes toward me and cups my jaw in his hands. He leans in, gives me a tender kiss that sends shivers of dread down my spine. He pulls back from the kiss, smiles and flicks my neck around.

A large snap spreads through me, ringing in my ears. It's over.

A few hours later, a technician with a ground-penetrating radar system methodically scans the flower bed, but the light fades before he can finish. His rough count at dusk—twelve bodies. It will take us days, maybe weeks, to carefully excavate the area, then piece the skeletons back together for identification. Some of the bodies will be matched on dental records, and some will be matched against missing persons using facial reconstruction. And some may always remain nameless.

Justin Reid must have been killing women for years—leading his double life for years. Probably since well before he met Heath Jordan. In fact, now it seems probable Heath Jordan was recruited by Reid for his darker skills as well as his potential as a computer programmer. They were a match made in heaven. And now Reid's in the wind, probably left the country, and Jordan's trying to weasel his way out of murder charges. Ultimately it will be up to a jury to decide if Jordan knew what he was part of. If they decide he did, he will be convicted of conspiracy to murder and conspiracy to kidnap—and he'll face the death penalty. But if they believe Heath Jordan's story, his jail time will be limited…he may even get off scot-free.

I'm going to stick around in Groveland for as long as I can to oversee the investigation of Reid's country property. But I can't forget about Black—and I haven't. On the way back to my hotel, I phone Sorrell while Dusk drives.

"Anything new?" I ask.

"The computer guys are done with James Baker's computer."

"That was fast."

"Yeah, I know. Guess the San Francisco lab's not as busy as the L.A. one."

"Stands to reason," I say, thinking about the population differences and L.A.'s high crime rate.

"They found a total of twenty-eight letters to seven different authors on the computer and final tests on his printer confirmed a match for the second and third letters to Black."

"And the first and the last letters?"

"The first has been positively matched to his handwriting sample, and that print is definitely his."

I pause. "And the fourth letter to Black?"

"That's the sticking point. It's not on his computer system and, as you know, the printer doesn't match."

We turned Baker's house and car upside down yesterday but there was only one printer, and the printer at his work doesn't match the fourth letter either. This, coupled with his denial of writing the fourth letter and the letter to Rickardian, concerns me. Could he be telling the truth? And if he is telling the truth, who wrote the fourth letter from "A fan" and the one to Rickardian? As is often the case in a murder investigation, we've got more questions than answers.

"And the paper?" I ask.

"The computer paper found at Baker's house was different to that used for the printed letters."

We come to a T-intersection and Dusk takes a right. "Doesn't necessarily mean anything. Lots of people swap papers, buying one that's on special or at the cash register as they're shopping."

"We did find some Salurtey. Baker admits he still uses it occasionally for handwritten correspondence."

"Again, it ties him to the letters, but not the murders."

"Exactly." Sorrell moves on. "Trace is due to start on our fibers today."

Sorrell's referring to the samples we took from Baker's clothing. "Still nothing on the navy fiber?"

"No. We can't find any navy carpet we can associate with Baker. I checked his workplace again myself today."

I sigh.

"How's it going there?" he asks.

"Oh, terrific." I shake my head. "We just found twelve bodies, buried out the back of Reid's place here in Groveland."

"Holy smoke."

"Uh-huh."

"Guess I'm having a better day than you, then."

"Wouldn't be hard. Any other news?"

"We've still got Baker under surveillance, but nothing else to report."

I say goodbye and help Dusk out with directions. We're pulling up in front of the guesthouse when my cell phone rings.

"Agent Anderson."

"Anderson, it's Brady." My boss does not sound happy. Maybe I'm spending too much time out of the office.

"Yes, sir?"

"We've got another one."

"Sir?"

He gives me a big sigh. "Another dead author."

"What? Where?"

"A body was found underneath the Santa Monica Pier. Looks like it may have been dumped out at sea and then washed up. We're waiting on a positive visual ID from the family, but the woman was carrying ID of Jane Goodwin, a local crime writer turned scriptwriter."

"Shit!" I automatically think about Baker. "What's the time of death?"

"Prelim tests indicate roughly twenty-four hours."

"That would leave Baker in the clear. He's been under round-the-clock surveillance."

"Uh-huh."

That's why Brady's so unhappy. He knows our prime suspect can't have been responsible for Goodwin's murder—and that means probably not Black's or Rickardian's either.

We *are* back to square one. "You looked up Goodwin's most recent book, sir?"

"Yeah." Again Brady's voice is discouraged. "Her fictitious victim was drowned by an unfaithful husband during a boating outing."

I'm speechless, literally. It was probably all the press around Bowles that made our guy escalate. He knew he wasn't responsible for her disappearance and it made him angry enough to kill his next target. He wanted the attention firmly on him and his punishment of the authors and not on some staged disappearance. Most serial killers have an ego when it comes to what they do, and a kind of sick pride. To think that someone was copying his MO, his signature, must have pushed him over the edge. I shake my head. How could Bowles and Cooper have been so stupid?

"You still there, Anderson?"

"Yeah, I'm here." Now my voice is despondent. "Have you told Sorrell?"

"Nope. I'll leave that to you. And you may as well call the whole surveillance team in. No use tailing Baker now."

"Yes, sir." I say goodbye to Brady after vaguely discussing plans to fly back to L.A. "Sorry, Dusk. Doesn't look like I'll be checking in with you."

He looks at me questioningly.

"There's been another murder, another author."

"Oh my God, who?"

"Jane Goodwin. You know her?"

"Oh yeah. She's one of my favorites. And her last book finished with a real cliffhanger."

He seems disappointed that he'll never know the ending.

Dusk suddenly realizes what he's said. "Sorry…I…I didn't mean it to come out like that."

"That's okay. I guess a lot of her fans will be upset about not knowing what happens to her characters. Let's hope we can find out what happened to her."

Twenty-Nine

I make my way back to San Francisco, driving straight to the airport to meet up with Sorrell. We organized to meet at the gate for our L.A. flight, and on the way I visit the airport bookstore and pick up a copy of Goodwin's latest book, *Revenge*. The title makes me wonder if the dead woman somehow gets revenge on her cheating husband, or if he was getting revenge by killing her. Guess I'll have to read the damn thing to find out.

In this case, it also looks like the story will be told backward, because it opens with the husband on trial for murder. Flicking through the pages, I soon realize the story is told through courtroom proceedings, coupled with flashbacks from the husband's and dead woman's perspectives. It makes my job harder, because I don't know which version is the truth—that's probably something that Goodwin reveals only toward the end, or perhaps that's the cliffhanger Dusk mentioned. I find the most relevant part from the victim's perspective.

* * *

Alex takes the bottle out of the wine cooler and I hold my glass forward. The champagne's bubbles threaten to spill over the edge but Alex has timed it just right.

"Happy tenth wedding anniversary, darling."

We clink glasses.

"It's been a wonderful ten years." I don't mention the not-so-wonderful parts—me waiting for him to get home from work. But I guess that's just one of the drawbacks of being married to a successful man. And there's no denying that Alex does make me happy.

I gaze at the ocean, and enjoy the rhythmic sound of the waves hitting the side of the boat. "And what a beautiful anniversary present." Both the boat and the champagne were a surprise.

"Anything for you, darling. Come on. Let's go for a swim." Alex takes off his shirt and hat, leaving only his shorts, which double as a bathing suit.

"Now?" I look over the edge. It's deep—scary deep.

"It'll be fun, Katey." He comes in close for a hug.

"I don't know. I'll watch."

His arms encircle me. "Where's that adventurous woman I married?" He pauses. "You're not going to get boring on me, are you?"

My gut clenches, and those old worries that I could be boring Alex resurface.

"Okay, I'll do it." I start to take off my sundress, but Alex gathers me in his arms and lifts me up, jumping overboard at the same time. I'm unprepared and water goes up my nose before I swim to the surface.

"What are you doing?"

Alex is laughing and my anger dissipates. I suppose I do look funny.

I splash some water in his face and he reciprocates before diving under. This is a game we haven't played for years, and one that I always hated. I look around for him, waiting for him to come up underneath me and grab me. It's unsettling, but I know Alex is just having one of his "I'm a big kid" moments.

Almost a minute passes and I start to panic. What's happened to him? Are there sharks in the bay? Just as I start to swim back toward the boat, I feel hands around my ankles. He pulls down hard and a gush of water flies into my nose as I go under. We move upwards together and both take an almighty gasp as we break the water's surface. Alex is out of breath from being under for so long, and even after I take the breath in I can't stop coughing and spluttering. Alex's face changes...he looks scared and sad. But it only lasts for a minute before his hand is on my head, pushing me under. At first I think it's another one of his games. I fight, because it's my natural instinct, but I'm not fighting for my life.

Soon, though, I'm panicking. I can't breathe. I start pulling on Alex's hands and arms, trying to make him understand that I'm in trouble, that he needs to stop. And then I remember his face...oh my God. It couldn't be. My tugs on his arms turn to des-

perate scratching. I even have the sense to look for
his body and try to kick him in the groin. I make contact, but the water weakens my force, acting like a
natural layer of protection for Alex. He pulls his legs
up, covering his groin, but I haven't hit him hard
enough for him to even loosen his grip on my head
and hair. I pour all my energy into one final assault,
pushing myself upwards toward air and life, but Alex
is too strong.

Putting the book on my lap, I look up to see Sorrell
hovering over me.

"You made good time from Groveland."

"Yeah, I did."

He looks at the book on my lap. "Well?"

"The way it's recounted from the victim's point of view
in the book could easily be what went down with Goodwin. The woman in the book was taken out to sea, thrown
overboard and then someone held her under the water
until she drowned."

"Motive?" Sorrell asks.

I shrug. "From what I can gather from my skim-reading,
the wife thought of the husband as successful but he had
gambling debts, a mistress to pay for and a life-insurance
policy on the wife."

"I love the classics. The husband did it. They're so
much easier than random killings or serial killers."

I close the book. "You still think Werner could have
killed his wife? And Rickardian and now Goodwin too?"

Sorrell shrugs. "I'd get Rickardian…you know, throw
us off his scent…but Goodwin? What would be the point?"

I nod. "It's the same with all of our remaining suspects

though. Werner, Sade, Blake and Sandra Black all had a problem with Black. As far as we can tell, they had no links to Rickardian."

"Maybe Goodwin will tell us more."

Sorrell and I go straight from the airport to the coroner's office on North Mission Road, slightly west of downtown L.A. The Goodwin case has been assigned to Lloyd Grove, the same forensic pathologist who performed Black's autopsy, and he agreed to wait so we could witness the postmortem examination.

When we arrive, the body has been stripped, x-rayed, weighed and measured. These first steps, we all agreed, could easily be conducted in our absence. In addition, blood has already been drawn and will be forwarded to the lab with everything else once the autopsy is complete.

Jane Goodwin lies faceup and naked on the table. Her short blond hair is now dry, but matted together, probably from the salty seawater.

"Okay," Grove says. "We took extensive photos of her clothes, of course, and didn't find anything unusual. My assistant has organized for the clothes to be dried and packaged for processing."

I nod, but it's doubtful, to say the least, that any evidence would have survived in the water. Dumping a body in water, any type of water, has some advantages in terms of forensics but more disadvantages. On the plus side it can preserve older bodies for longer, delaying the decomposition process, but this can also be a negative because it can make it harder to establish time of death. Other disadvantages include the destruction of evidence by the water itself or by fish or other creatures that may feed on the body. Water means even skin scrapings under the nails will loosen and dissolve away, potentially destroying the perp's DNA. And that can make finding a killer very tough indeed. In our case, Grove estimated Goodwin had only been submerged for roughly twenty-four to thirty-six hours, which gives us some hope—at least it's not weeks.

Grove begins the autopsy with a visual examination, which includes studying the body, front and back, and combing the hair for any trace elements, foreign hairs and other evidence. Next Grove conducts the standard rape examination, and examines other openings in her body such as her ears and mouth. He finds nothing. It's the same story with the fingernail scrapings. Next are the fingerprint and footprint cards for the autopsy record. These would often be used for identification, but in this case, Goodwin's husband has positively ID'd her.

The last thing Grove does before opening her up is to switch off the lights and examine the body under a UV light source. In the case of Goodwin, Grove finds a few small lingering bruises and some new ones, but the water has washed anything else away. He notates the position and size of each bruise. It's likely the recent ones occurred while her attacker was overpowering her, trying to drown Goodwin, but it's hard to be sure. Most people have a bruise or two at any given time.

Grove reaches for his scalpel and makes the standard Y-incision, cutting down Goodwin's chest.

I let out a small sigh, and Sorrell gives me a look.

"Sorry." I shrug my shoulders. "I always hate that first part."

He nods. "Me too."

"Me too," Grove jokes as he finishes the Y-cut at

Goodwin's abdomen. He peels back the skin to reveal organs, and starts the internal examination. He's able to confirm drowning as the cause of death, based on high levels of water in the lungs. He takes samples of the water in Goodwin's lungs, which will be matched against a sample I presume he took underneath the pier. If she drowned in that water, it should match, but if she was drowned with tap water and then the body was dumped, the water analysis will tell us that too. Grove proceeds with the autopsy, weighing and inspecting the organs, but it doesn't tell us much. Goodwin was a normal, healthy forty-year-old woman before she drowned.

Sorrell and I stand on the front steps of the coroner's office.

"Where to now?" he says.

I laugh. "I was about to ask you the same question." I sit down on the step and Sorrell follows suit. "We need to go back to finding the link, but now we've got another variable to add—Goodwin."

Sorrell looks up at the setting sun. "Do you think we have to worry about another victim?"

I shake my head. "I don't think escalation would have been a factor for our guy if Bowles hadn't staged her disappearance and made everyone think the killer had struck again. He wanted to get our attention again, and the media's, by killing his next victim. I'm going to redraft the profile…now that the killer and letter writer aren't one and the same person." I knew it was a risk to use the letters as one of my profiling inputs, but it was a risk worth taking at the time.

Sorrell sighs. "I hate to think what's being run on the news now."

I rest my chin in my hands. "Brady said they're talking about another press conference. Probably first thing tomorrow morning."

"Good idea. Especially in this town." Sorrell stands up and offers me his hand. I take it.

"Home?" he asks.

"Yeah. I'm beat." I am tired, but I also need to see if I can induce a premonition or have one of my dreams. I still don't like relying on this gift of mine, and I don't completely trust it, but history has taught me that everything I see means *something,* it's just a matter of finding out what that something is. And while I can't give evidence in court about a vision, I can push the investigation in a certain direction if I think it's warranted. And Lord knows we need a direction.

"What about the letters?" I ask Sorrell. "Are McAvey and Court still processing them?"

"Uh-huh. And I'm siphoning through any AFIS matches to Edwards to check out. But so far, the few fans that were in the AFIS database have been clear. Alibied, too old, in prison…" He trails off.

"Okay. I'll talk to Goodwin's family and friends tomorrow. And fill out the list for her too. Maybe she'll help us discover the link." In some cases the point of intersection for the victims, and the killer, becomes clearer the more victims you have—it's more data to put into the pool.

I lie on the bed, with photos of Rickardian, Black and Goodwin surrounding me. Every few seconds I pick up a new photo and study it. It's hard to focus on this case and not on Justin Reid, but I force myself. After about fifteen minutes I stop looking at the photos and move on to my relaxation techniques. I figure it's like setting up a clean canvas, ready for an image to be painted on. Once my mind is blank and my body relaxed, the dizziness comes.

Black stands next to her casket and looks at me with pleading eyes...Black's tied to a chair and someone paces in front of her...Black's gasping for breath, a stocking pulled tightly around her neck...Black's on the tiled floor, and the killer's leaning over her, drawing the lipstick mark...A computer screen fills with the words from the last letter from A fan...Bowles's disappearance is on the news, with Anne Cooper crying...The cover of Goodwin's book, Revenge*...Goodwin's under water, taking her last breath...Goodwin's floating facedown under the Santa Monica Pier...Goodwin's on the slab, a Y-cut running down her body.*

The onslaught of images stops as suddenly as it started, lurching me back into reality. And with the images come a quick succession of varied emotions. I'm left with a lingering sense of confusion and fear from both Black and Goodwin. But part of the vision was from the killer's perspective, and anger overshadowed any other emotions the killer may have been feeling.

I grab a pen and paper, eager to write everything down as soon as I can. The whole thing was so fast, with each image literally flashing into my consciousness for less than a second.

Propping myself up farther on my two pillows, I rerun it again, trying to decipher the elements. There must be something I'm missing, something I've forgotten. I sigh, frustrated. And why wasn't Rickardian present in some way? Time to have another go, this time with Rickardian. I pick out all the crime-scene photos from Rickardian's case and concentrate solely on them. When thoughts of Black or Goodwin come to mind, I push them away. Rickardian, I want more on Rickardian. Nothing comes, but I don't give up. I just keep lying there, periodically looking at photos of Rickardian. I'm aware of time passing—more than two hours—but I try not to dwell on it. I've never spent so much time forcing a vision.

Rickardian's book cover…Rickardian sitting in her bay window, reading, while I watch her…Rickardian's house is dark…I'm walking up the stairs to Rickardian's bedroom…I'm scared…I stop on one step and think about going back, but I keep moving…Rickardian's asleep in bed…I clamp my hand down over her face and drag her out of bed—she's older and weaker…I slam the crowbar into her head, one, two, three, four times.

The killer's mind is stronger this time, like a dream that's hard to come out of, that keeps pulling me back into sleep. I can feel the hesitation—he nearly didn't kill Rickardian, there was an instant when he thought seriously about backing out. I feel giddy, slightly nauseous…and incredibly tired. Inducing two visions in a row has taken its toll. I manage to sweep the photos off my bed and slip underneath the covers. But I don't cleanse my face, I don't brush my teeth, I don't change out of my clothes…all I can think about is sleep.

I'm sailing, relaxed and happy on the ocean…I'm drinking wine and eating. Then my plate's empty except for a few olive pips. I'm in the water, cold and frightened, my clothes clinging to my body. A hand pushes me under and I fight for a breath, fight my way up.

I wake up to the alarm screeching in my ear and sit bolt upright. My mind is racing, thinking of my dream. I was on a yacht—not surprising, given Jane Goodwin was drowned. I saw the murder from her perspective; someone's hand was holding me under the water. I was fighting, Jane Goodwin was fighting, just like her character in *Revenge*. But eventually her lungs were filled with water, not air. It's logical that Goodwin was taken out on some sort of a boat, and a yacht would marry with her book's plot. So did the killer hire a yacht, or does he own one? A deceptively minor comment of Sorrell's comes racing back to me. Loretta Black's will. There was a yacht in her will. And she left it to her husband, Scott Werner.

Thirty

I get ready in record time, and arrive at Santa Monica Pier at 7:15 a.m. My motivation is twofold: check out the crime scene and hopefully find Black's yacht. At this time of the morning it's mostly joggers and roller-bladers keeping me company on the pier. Guess it's still a little early for the tourists—they are on vacation, after all. The famous pier is elaborate—more like a theme park than a traditional pier—with a carousel, Ferris wheel and other amusement-park rides at one end and restaurants running along its length. Street stalls also dot the pier, although many are closed at this time of the day.

I've got about twenty minutes before Sorrell's due to arrive, so with my copy of Goodwin's *Revenge* in hand, I cross the boardwalk and head for the beach. Goodwin's body was found yesterday afternoon, as the tide came in. And it was a few hours later that the ID was phoned through to the FBI. I take off my slip-on shoes and let the cool sand slide between my toes. Another few hours and the sand will be red-hot. The beach itself is busy for this time of morning, with some people taking their early-morning dip and others opting for a walk. I wade in ankle-deep water underneath the pier and study the author photo in Goodwin's book, hoping it might bring on a vision. I'm staring at the photo when I feel a compulsion to look up.

Goodwin's standing in the water near one of the old, wooden posts, shaking. Her hair is wet and a white dress clings to her body. She looks at me uncertainly.

Goodwin disappears like a fast-departing train, shrinking into nothingness as I'm startled out of the vision by a passing runner.

I'm about to try again when my cell rings. It's Sorrell.

"Hi, Sorrell."

"Hi. I'm here."

"Okay, I'm on the beach, under the pier."

"I haven't parked because I've been thinking about what you said, and if we're looking for a yacht, we need to go to Marina del Rey. That's where all the yacht clubs are. I'm at the pier's entrance."

"Okay. Stay there and I'll be up soon."

I break into a light jog, making my way back onto the pier and toward the main street, the Pacific Coast Highway. I spot Sorrell at the pier's entrance, illegally parked. Not that he has to worry about getting a ticket. I brush as much sand off my feet as I can and slip my shoes back on before hopping into the passenger side.

"Sorry about the sand," I say.

"No problem." He does a U-turn and turns right onto the highway, heading us south and toward Marina del Rey.

We could have called Scott Werner, or even George

Black, to find out where Loretta's yacht is moored, but we decided to keep our cards close to our chests. No use scaring our killer into running—it's bad enough that Reid's in the wind. Just thinking of Reid makes me clench my fists. I'll give it another couple of hours before I hassle Dusk for an update on Reid's Groveland property and the bodies.

There are several yacht clubs at Marina del Rey, and after striking out on the first two, we finally get a hit at the Corinthian Yacht Club.

The guy on duty is young, about twenty, and wears shorts and a pec-hugging T-shirt. "Yeah, the Blacks' boat is moored here."

"Really? Do you know if it was taken out the day before yesterday?" I ask.

"I wasn't on duty, but I'll check." He punches a few keys on his computer. "Yup, here it is."

"Do you know who took it out?" I move closer.

"Sure."

Sorrell leans in too. "Scott Werner?"

"No. It was Debbie Holt."

"Holt?" Sorrell and I say in unison.

I try to process this discovery, and my shock and denial soon turn to acceptance and anger. The chances of Holt being on the bay at roughly the same time as Goodwin's murder are a million to one. It can't be a coincidence, it just can't. And if she is guilty, part of her plan was to pull me into the investigation so she could stay close to the case, hoping I'd feed her info.

"Was she with anyone?" For a strong case against her, and for a search warrant, we'll probably need a positive visual ID of Holt and Goodwin together. Otherwise, it's all too circumstantial.

He looks at his computer screen. "It does say she had a visitor, but I'm not sure who that was."

I glance around the room, looking for a camera. "Do you take video footage in here?"

"No. But maybe the guy who was working saw someone else."

"Can you call him…now?" Sorrell leans even farther into the counter.

"Um…"

"It's important enough to disturb him," Sorrell reassures him.

While he's on the phone, I cast my mind back to Holt's apartment. I was sitting in her office, so I try to visualize the printer. I turn to Sorrell. "She's got a Ricoh printer."

"The printer used for the fourth letter to Black and the letter to Rickardian."

"Yup. And she had access to the first letters, she knew his writing style, knew to sign the letters off from 'A fan.'"

"I've got Jim O'Connell on the phone for you now."

We both look up at the yacht-club attendant.

"He says Debbie Holt was with another woman."

I hold my hand out to the phone, and the guy hands it to me. "Hello, Mr. O'Connell, is it?"

"Yes."

"I'm Special Agent Sophie Anderson with the FBI. We need to see you urgently. Did you get a good look at Ms. Holt's companion?"

"Pretty good. I'd probably recognize her again. Is that what you mean?"

"Yes, that's exactly what I mean," I reply. "Where are you now? Can we come and see you?"

"Sure. I'm in View Park."

I take down the address and soon Sorrell and I are clambering back into his car and hightailing it over to View Park. When we show O'Connell the photo of Goodwin from her book, he's certain she's the person he saw with Holt at the marina, but he does add that Goodwin didn't come into the main area, but waited outside. She was also wearing a wide-brimmed hat and glasses to protect herself from the sun. Sorrell looks at me with a small, satisfied smile on his face. We've got enough for a warrant.

Thirty-One

"Misdirection," I say to Sorrell when we're back in the car. "It's the premise of magic tricks."

"What?"

"Black was the target all along. Rickardian and Goodwin were smoke screens, directing our attention firmly toward a serial killer and away from those closest to Black. It was a damn good scheme too."

Sorrell nods. "Let's get the warrant and see if we've got matching fibers…and maybe we'll turn something else up at her place."

Three phone calls later, Sorrell and I are waiting outside a judge's chambers with Jim O'Connell's written statement.

Sorrell shakes his head. "Told you it was the money."

I smile. "Yeah, you did." I hesitate. "But you think she killed three people just to get her cut of the will?"

"Five percent is a lot of money. Probably more than she would have seen as Black's assistant in a lifetime."

I shake my head. "But Werner said Holt didn't even know she was in the will." I pause. "I think there might be more to it than that. The crime scenes were personal, particularly Black's."

Sorrell shrugs. "I guess we're about to find out."

"I'll give Holt her dues, she set this up well, creating crime scenes and the letters to drive us a certain way, to lead to a certain profile."

"Maybe she should have been a novelist."

"She is. Black told me Holt was working on something at the Academy."

Forty-five minutes later we pull up, warrant in hand. In addition to our crime-scene techs, we've brought along two uniforms, just in case. But Holt's not a high flight risk so we haven't bothered with anything more dramatic, like SWAT. She's got no idea we're onto her…the perfect crime, right?

We ring the buzzer and Holt lets us in, no questions asked.

"Hi, Debbie." I manage a fake smile.

"Hi, Sophie. Any news?" Her voice is thick with concern—yeah, right.

"No, nothing I'm afraid," I lie. "How's your book coming?"

"My book." She hesitates, obviously surprised by the question. "Good. Really good in fact."

"What did you say it was about, Debbie?"

She shrugs. "You know…murder. I'm keeping it under wraps."

"Serial killer?" Sorrell weighs in on the conversation.

"Yes. I guess it won't do any harm telling you that." She smiles. "You have to be careful in this business."

"I believe Randy Sade would agree with you," Sorrell says.

"Guess he probably would." Holt looks at us both. "So, what can I do for you?"

I decide it's time to lay our cards on the table.

"Have you heard of an author called Jane Goodwin?" I ask.

"Of course. Like I told you, Loretta always made me keep on top of the competition."

"Have you read her most recent book, *Revenge?*"

"Yeah. I read it about six months ago, when it first came out." Holt's still cool, giving no sign that we're hitting a nerve. "Did you want a drink? A coffee or a cold drink?"

"No thanks." I can't relax into the act that much. Sorrell also declines the offer.

Holt motions to the couches and we all sit down.

I continue. "The main character was drowned."

"Yes, I remember. Killed by her husband."

I nod. "Have you been on Loretta's yacht recently, Debbie?"

"I went for a sail a couple of days ago, as a matter of fact. Clear my head after everything that's happened."

"Do you often go out on their boat?"

"Maybe once a month. More in summer." She leans on the arm of her sofa. "I love sailing. I've sailed all my life. Loretta always said I could use the yacht whenever I wanted to, and Scott's been kind enough to leave that invitation open."

"That is kind of him," Sorrell says.

Silence.

"Jane Goodwin's dead, Debbie." I pretend I'm delivering news, not making an accusation.

"What? That's terrible." She stands up. "Is it the same killer? As Loretta and Lorie Rickardian? It must be."

"Yes, we believe it's the same killer." I stay seated, and now I'm the one as cool as a cucumber.

Silence again, which Holt soon fills. "I can't believe it."

"Really?" I pause. "That's strange, Debbie, because a witness at the Corinthian Yacht Club saw you and Jane Goodwin together."

She shakes her head. "I was by myself. Your witness must be mistaken."

"I don't think so, Debbie."

"I really don't know what you're talking about, Sophie." She raises her voice in indignation. "What are you implying?"

Now I stand, pacing, but slowly. "What am I implying?" I pause for effect. "That you killed Lorie Rickardian, Loretta Black and then Jane Goodwin."

"Why, that's absurd." Her voice is outraged, but we've got too much evidence against her for me to be convinced of her innocence. Even my vision of Black at the funeral makes sense now. Black held up her hand, motioning for me to stop. I thought she was telling me not to come any closer, but maybe that wasn't it at all. Stop…halt…Holt.

"When did you decide to do it? Was it after the first letter from 'A fan'? The second? The third? We know it wasn't after the fourth, because you wrote that. Just like you wrote the letter to Lorie Rickardian and signed it from 'A fan.'"

Debbie's silent, so I keep going. "Your carpet is gray. So where's the navy carpet? Your car?"

"I really don't know what you're talking about, Agent Anderson." I notice she uses my official title for the first time since the Academy. Is she trying to distance herself from me, or show respect?

I pull the search warrant out of my pocket. "We've got a warrant for this apartment. Everything in it."

"You can't go through my stuff." The cool facade is fading ever so slightly.

"Debbie, you know very well that, with one of these, we can."

"You're out of your mind. Why would I kill Loretta?"

"Money," Sorrell says. "Plain and simple."

Holt shakes her head. "Typical cop. It's not always about money, Detective Sorrell."

"So what is it about?"

She takes a breath in, like maybe she's going to confess, but then changes her mind.

Sorrell calls in the techs who were waiting downstairs and they get started. I oversee the process in Holt's bedroom, firstly going through her cupboards. We find two beige sweaters—either one of them could match the fiber we found in Black's hair.

Back in her study I notice the Ricoh printer is an Aficio BP20, just like that used for the fourth letter to Black and the one to Lorie Rickardian. I also find her manuscript.

Holt shouts when I pick it up. "No, that's private!"

"Ah, your book." I start to flick through the pages but Holt makes a dive for me.

"Get away from that!"

The uniform watching her grabs Holt by the shoulders, but that makes her fight more wildly.

"Cuff her," I say. "Assaulting a police officer."

The uniform pulls out his cuffs and reads Holt her rights.

"Even if you have evidence that puts me at the scene, it doesn't mean anything," she says, regaining her cool. "I was Loretta's assistant, I was around her all the time. I had contact with her, there'll be traces of me everywhere inside that house." Holt's referring to the Locard Principle on which forensics is based: that every contact leaves a trace. The perpetrator will leave trace evidence of himself, or herself, at the crime scene and will inadvertently take away trace evidence from the crime scene or the victim on his, or her, person. And Holt's right—she was in that house all the time, around Black all the time. Of course there'll be traces of her presence at the Black house and vice versa. We'll need more evidence to nail Holt for this crime. She's committed a near-perfect murder, or rather murders, but there's no such thing as *the* perfect murder, not in my book at least. We'll get something…we better get something.

Thirty-Two

Holt sits in the interview room, coffee in hand, a picture of serenity. So far she's waived her right to a lawyer, but that could change at any time. She's confident, all right. I walk in and take a seat across from her, case files and her manuscript in hand.

"Tell me about your killer," I say to Holt and open her manuscript, which I've spent the last half hour skimming through.

She peers at the pieces of paper on the table and realizes that I'm talking about her fictitious killer, Corey Chambers. I've opened the manuscript at the point where he's introduced, and we both stare at the page.

He sat hunched over his desk, pressing harder and harder with each word. They thought they were so clever, filling his world with violence, but soon they'd get a taste of it firsthand. Soon he'd be filling their worlds with violence. Soon it'd be their turn and they'd pay.

"What about him?" A slight smirk plays across Holt's lips.

"Anything you like." I pause but she doesn't fill in the blanks. I know from what I've read that Holt's killer is scarily close to my profile. He is the twisted fan, convinced that crime fiction promotes violence and driven by the delusional belief that he must cleanse society of the writers.

"When did you start writing this, Debbie?"

"About a year ago."

"You've done a lot of research?"

She shrugs. "Most of it I'd already done for Loretta." She pauses. "But I did have to research profiling more extensively. To really get inside his head."

I skip ahead, looking for the first murder scene.

He took the same route to the park that he'd taken many times. Before it had only been for research, reconnaissance, but this was no practice run.

It had taken him a long time to choose his first. His first victim was so important. In the end, he'd opted for the writer with the most descriptive and violent scenes. Sasha Lane. She was the one who deserved to die the most, although it had been a tight race.

He left his car on the west side of the park at 6:00 p.m. and jogged from there. She always arrived between 6:15 p.m. and 6:30 p.m., and only ran on weekdays. Like him, she was a creature of habit.

"So the visit to the Academy was for you, not Black?"

"I did enjoy that particular research, yes. But as you

know, Loretta was thinking about featuring a profiler in her next book."

I look down at the manuscript again. The first murder is described in detail, over pages and pages. Even though I don't read crime fiction, I can't imagine this is normal for the genre.

I read the first act of violence out aloud to Holt. "'He smiled, before pulling her down to the concrete and smashing her head against the bitumen. He enjoyed the crack of bone and the faint squelch as her skull knocked against her brain. He watched a trickle of blood erupt from her skull and was surprised to find himself aroused by the dark, sticky substance.'" I look up at Holt, but her face remains impassive. "And that's tame, isn't it, Debbie?"

"Like I said, I did a lot of research to make sure I really got inside the killer's mind."

"Do you think you were successful?" I ask.

"You tell me, you're the profiler."

I cross my arms and stare at Holt. "I thought better of you, Debbie, than to kill for money. I really did." Holt didn't kill for money; I know that. I haven't read her book word for word, but the skim reading I have done tells me this wasn't about the money. This is about a woman who became so absorbed in the mind of a killer that she became one herself.

"For money?" Holt takes the bait. "I don't care about money. You're as bad as Detective Sorrell."

"Why else would you kill three people? If not for the money?"

"I haven't killed anyone."

"Come on, Debbie. You're good, I admit that, but you're smart enough to know when the game's up. We've got a match on your sweater, you know."

She shrugs. "So? Like I said, I spent a lot of time with Loretta…at her house."

"We've placed you at the Corinthian Yacht Club the day before yesterday with Jane Goodwin."

Holt shrugs again. "Your witness is mistaken. You know false IDs happen all the time, Agent Anderson. I've come across it in my research for Loretta."

Holt's right. Faulty eyewitness identifications are one of the leading causes of wrongful convictions—a fact that her defense attorney will no doubt bring up at trial.

"Come on, Debbie. We've got the fiber, we've confirmed that you weren't in L.A. on April 21 when Lorie Rickardian was murdered. We're checking out car rentals in San Francisco now, and soon we'll have you at all three crime scenes, on the days of the murders. And this book—" I wave the heavy pages around "—is more than we need. Your fictitious killer matches my profile in just about every way. You based it on 'A fan,' right?"

She's silent.

I run through my profile.

"I profiled our killer as thirty-five to fifty, and your killer, Corey Chambers, is forty-eight. He's an organized offender, obviously, and used his victims' fictional plots as his template for killing. He works as a security guard and his wife left him soon after their son was convicted of rape. He snapped, blaming crime authors for his son's imprisonment and his marital breakup. He drives an older, American model sedan, has a high IQ but is only high-school educated. He has no criminal record and his signature is to leave the words "Your turn" at the body-dump sites."

I got the profile right, it's just that I was profiling a

person who didn't really exist, a killer created by Holt using her sick imagination and a few real fan letters as fuel.

Holt sits silently, but I see a hint of something in her face. I study the slight smirk closely. She *wants* to confess, she *wants* us to know how smart she was to create the killer, to fool us. A little more pushing and she'll break. But I have to insult her, not flatter her. "You won't get the money, you know. Your share of Black's estate will be frozen."

She's still silent, but the smirk has vanished and now I can just make out the slightest bit of tension on her forehead.

"Why did you want that kind of money anyway, Debbie? What, you want to buy designer clothes and a fancy house? Is that what's important to you?"

She pushes her chair out from the table. "It's not about the money. You people just don't get it!"

Now we're getting somewhere. "It's about your jealousy. You were jealous of Loretta." Again, I'm feeding her something I know to be untrue.

She shakes her head. "P-lease. The woman was nothing without me. I practically wrote *Ladykiller* and she got all the money and the fame. Why do you think she put me in the will?"

"That's what Scott Werner said. That you were invaluable to Loretta."

She nods. "I've got a pretty good imagination myself, you know."

I clear my throat. "Maybe, but Loretta was the published, successful author. She was the really imaginative one." I pause, watching Holt unravel a little bit more. "Your book doesn't strike me as particularly inspired."

"What are you talking about? It's genius. Pure genius."

I shrug. "I've read the murder scene. The way you sexualize your killer's actions reminds me more of pornography."

"So I've successfully captured the killer's point of view." She smiles, triumphant.

"Sexual homicide is about many things, and yes, sexual gratification for the killer is one of them. But you're glorifying the act, Debbie. It's not just graphic…it's…" But I can't think of the right word. I could say it was the ramblings of an insane person, but I don't want to give Holt any ammunition for the insanity plea. Disturbingly, the sections I've read make me wonder if Holt found the murders sexually arousing herself.

I shake my head, trying to accept Holt's twisted mindset.

"I'm breaking new ground. Taking the genre to new heights." Holt stands up and starts pacing. "I'm smart, you know, Sophie. Real smart."

I shrug again and remain silent.

"You think some hack could plan this?"

"Plan what?"

She smiles. "Like you said, my killer and your profile are one and the same person." Holt smiles again. "Smart, huh?"

"To set up the crime scenes like that?" I stand up next to her. "Yeah, I guess that was smart." I pander to her ego again. "When did you decide to do it?"

Holt's still smiling, still pleased with herself. "Six months ago, when I opened the third letter from 'A fan.' It sparked my imagination and I thought, what if this guy got so pissed with Loretta's swearing and violence that he killed her? I'd already studied profiling a bit, and felt that I had a real sense of who this guy, the letter writer, was."

I nod. "Go on." Holt based the killer loosely on what she knew about James Baker from his three letters.

"I thought it would make a great concept for a book—a crazed fan going after crime authors."

"And that's why your manuscript is so incriminating."

"It wouldn't have been. I could have released it in a year's time and said 'inspired by real-life events.' No one would have known. No one would have guessed." Her eyes still gleam as she stops for a quick breath. "And then I created 'A fan' properly. I treated him just like I would any other character. I gave him a name, motivation, age, back story…everything. I knew the clearer a picture I had of him, the better I could make the crime scene look and the easier it would be to fake letters from him. When I was ready, I sent a letter to Rickardian and signed it from 'A fan.'"

"So my profile was based on someone you created." I voice the obvious, the conclusion I'd already come to.

"Yes! Genius." She smiles, caught up in her own ego.

"What made you pick Lorie Rickardian?" I ask.

Holt jolts, my question bringing her back to earth. "I'd read her book recently. The method of killing seemed—" she pauses "—achievable."

I try to keep the coldness I feel toward Holt out of my blue eyes. She's managed to develop the same detachment many serial killers feel for their victims. She's talking about choosing Rickardian, killing Rickardian, as though she were choosing a shampoo brand at the supermarket.

"So Lorie Rickardian died because she had the least disturbing killing method for you to replicate?"

She nods, like it's the most obvious thing in the world.

"And the footprint in the dirt near the back door? Did you plant that?"

She smiles. "Why of course. I bought a pair of size ten work boots, slipped one on, made the impression then turned my foot to one side to smudge it." She pauses. "Of course, I knew I couldn't just push the boot down into the earth by hand, that it would need my full weight in it."

Holt's right. Forensics can usually give us a weight range based on the sort of soil and how deep the impression is. If the tread digs in really deep, they know the person wearing the shoe is heavy or was perhaps carrying another person.

"You still got that work boot?" I ask.

She looks at me as though I'm stupid. "Of course not. I dumped them in a charity box the next day."

When she's silent for several seconds, I prompt her. "And then what?"

"Then we waited. We knew most serial killers tend to start with six to twelve months between their kills, sometimes even more, but we couldn't wait that long. We couldn't afford to lose our nerve. So we waited until *Ladykiller* was released, and picked a date."

A knock at the door interrupts us. "Excuse me, Debbie." I fake a smile—as I said, sometimes during questioning we need to give an Oscar-winning performance.

I open the door and step outside.

"'We'?" Sorrell says. "It's bloody Werner."

I sigh. "I don't think so, Sorrell."

"She just said 'we' half a dozen times. She's got a conspirator."

I voice the sickening realization I've come to. "She's not

talking about a real person, Sorrell. She's talking about her and the killer from her book, Corey Chambers."

Sorrell screws his face up. "But…"

"I don't think she knows anymore where her book ends and real life begins."

"That's insane." He rubs his forehead. "Fuck it!"

I'm stunned by his outburst, but I know where he's coming from. The insanity plea's looking mighty good for Holt and she doesn't deserve a cushy ride. But it also explains why a woman was able to kill like a man, and leave a classic male-perpetrator crime scene after her. When Holt was killing Rickardian, Black and Goodwin, she was in character. She was Corey Chambers, the crazed fan.

I go back inside with the intent of steering the interview back to reality, back to the facts…if I can.

"Did Loretta know it was you? While she was tied up?" From my vision at the start of this case I'm pretty sure the answer is yes. Black didn't look frightened, didn't look like she thought her life was about to be taken from her…because she didn't think Holt was capable of it.

"She knew. She thought it was a joke at first. She didn't think she was in danger. But she was wrong."

"What did you do with the rope afterward?"

"It's long gone, Sophie. Long gone."

I pause before deciding it's no use asking her where it's gone to. She's smart enough to make sure it's not somewhere we could find it. "What about Goodwin, then? Why her?"

"There was never meant to be a third victim. *I'd* decided against it. But then Bowles disappeared and the press linked it to us. But I mean, Katrina Bowles? She wasn't worthy of our attention, wasn't worthy of our kind of genius. How could you even think it was related to Black and Rickardian?" Holt pauses, waiting for my response.

"You're right, of course. And I should have guessed once I read her book."

Holt nods. "Trash, right?" This time the question is rhetorical. "It was insulting, and another victim was the only surefire way of getting the media's attention back on our cause. *He* picked Goodwin. We'd met her briefly at Loretta's launch. She lived in L.A., her victim drowned at sea and we had access to a yacht. He was right, it was meant to be. I wrote the letter while Bowles was still missing."

"So Goodwin received a letter from 'A fan'?"

"Of course."

We hadn't followed up and asked Goodwin's husband if she'd received a letter from "A fan" because by then Baker was in the clear.

Holt smiles and I sense Goodwin's murder wasn't purely about practicality—she'd had a taste of killing and she enjoyed it. Although perhaps it was the Corey Chambers in her that was feeling the pleasure.

We're both silent for a minute or so. Holt looks around the tiny interview room and, for the first time, she looks sad. "It was supposed to be the perfect crime." Reality is hitting her hard.

"You, of all people, should know there's no such thing as a perfect murder, Debbie," I say.

"On the contrary, there is. As *you* should know."

I don't think there is such a thing as a perfect murder, but I can't deny that people get away with murder every year. And Holt was better placed than most to pull it off. She'd researched profiling, police procedures, forensics, everything. She created a fictitious killer, and then cast herself in the leading role. It was a smart plan…very smart.

"Why did you drag me into this?" Again, I know the answer to the question. They say good lawyers never ask a question they don't know the answer to, and sometimes that strategy can work for us too. Especially when you're getting a confession on video.

"I wanted to be as close to the investigation as possible. When you said at the Academy that you were about to move to L.A., I thought all my Christmases had come at once. I felt confident that with you on the case, I'd be able to make more of an impact on the investigation. And for a while, it worked."

"You threw us a few bones?"

"Sade and 'A fan.'" She nods. "Then Peter Blake. It wasn't too hard pushing you in certain directions."

"We were following standard investigative techniques, and you used your knowledge of homicide investigation to feed us leads you knew we'd run down."

Her only response is a smile.

"We're going through your lipsticks now, Debbie. Will we find a match to the writing at Loretta's and Rickardian's homes?"

She laughs. "No. And you won't find stockings that match the one on Loretta either."

Holt seems to be telling the truth, but we'll still check all her lipsticks and the stockings. No point throwing evidence away if it's there. "You couldn't write your message on Goodwin. That must have pissed you off. Chambers couldn't mark her."

She shrugs. "We wrote it on her, but I knew it'd wash off by the time she was found." She sighs. "What does it matter? She got the message, didn't she?"

Thirty-Three

Holt's trial will start in a few months. There is evidence that places her at all three crime scenes, but we didn't find the boots, matching lipstick, the rope or panty hose. What we do have is so much better: her not-so-fictitious book and her confession, recorded on video. The case is airtight for three counts of murder.

Heath Jordan is a different story. He's now claiming he didn't know what was going on—that he was an ignorant participant in the Murderers' Club rather than a willing conspirator. He's gone from saying absolutely nothing for four months, to suddenly becoming very communicative, pleading his innocence. He kept his mouth shut for Justin Reid, but I can't see Jordan as innocent. He knew what he was involved in all right. But will a jury agree with me?

I think about Justin Reid and feel a swelling of outrage and frustration. He got away. It took four days and a team of agents going over footage from every single surveillance camera at the two main San Francisco airports, plus agents on the ground checking flight records for charter flights, but eventually we found him. Traveling with a false passport under the name Nathan Rhodes, he caught a United Airlines flight to Paris the day before the letter was delivered to Jordan. I should have guessed he'd head for Paris—it is his favorite city, after all. But that's where the trail went cold. The contact details on Reid's entry card led nowhere. We've alerted Interpol, but Reid's got the funds and contacts to buy himself another new identity, and new documentation to go with it. It's just a matter of time until he strikes in Europe. He may have changed hunting grounds, but he's still a hunter.

The phone on my desk starts ringing, bringing me out of my daze.

It's Melissa.

"Hi, Melissa."

"Hi. Um…Sophie…I don't know how to say this."

"Yes?"

She takes a deep breath. "There are a dozen red roses here for you."

"What?"

I bolt to her desk. My breathing is shallow and fast as I pull the card from the center of the bouquet. I tear open the envelope, hands shaking slightly.

Written on the card in big letters are the words *Checkmate.* Beneath them, in smaller writing, it says: *Until we meet again, JR.*

MCN2624RR

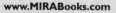

REQUEST YOUR
FREE BOOKS!

2 FREE NOVELS
FROM THE ROMANCE/SUSPENSE
COLLECTION PLUS 2 FREE GIFTS!

YES! Please send me 2 FREE novels from the Romance/Suspense Collection and my 2 FREE gifts (gifts are worth about $10). After receiving them, if I don't wish to receive any more books, I can return the shipping statement marked "cancel." If I don't cancel, I will receive 4 brand-new novels every month and be billed just $5.74 per book in the U.S. or $6.24 per book in Canada. That's a savings of at least 28% off the cover price. It's quite a bargain! Shipping and handling is just 50¢ per book.* I understand that accepting the 2 free books and gifts places me under no obligation to buy anything. I can always return a shipment and cancel at any time. Even if I never buy another book from the Reader Service, the two free books and gifts are mine to keep forever.

185 MDN EYNQ 385 MDN EYN2

Name _____ (PLEASE PRINT) _____

Address _____ Apt. # _____

City _____ State/Prov. _____ Zip/Postal Code _____

Signature (if under 18, a parent or guardian must sign)

Mail to **The Reader Service:**
IN U.S.A.: P.O. Box 1867, Buffalo, NY 14240-1867
IN CANADA: P.O. Box 609, Fort Erie, Ontario L2A 5X3

Not valid to current subscribers of the Romance Collection,
the Suspense Collection or the Romance/Suspense Collection.

Want to try two free books from another line?
Call 1-800-873-8635 or visit www.morefreebooks.com.

* Terms and prices subject to change without notice. Prices do not include applicable taxes. Sales tax applicable in N.Y. Canadian residents will be charged applicable provincial taxes and GST. Offer not valid in Quebec. This offer is limited to one order per household. All orders subject to approval. Credit or debit balances in a customer's account(s) may be offset by any other outstanding balance owed by or to the customer. Please allow 4 to 6 weeks for delivery. Offer available while quantities last.

Your Privacy: Harlequin is committed to protecting your privacy. Our Privacy Policy is available online at www.eHarlequin.com or upon request from the Reader Service. From time to time we make our lists of customers available to reputable third parties who may have a product or service of interest to you. If you would prefer we not share your name and address, please check here. ☐

BOB09

P.D. MARTIN

32604 THE MURDERERS' CLUB   ___ $6.99 U.S. ___ $6.99 CAN.

(limited quantities available)

TOTAL AMOUNT $ _____
POSTAGE & HANDLING $ _____
($1.00 for 1 book, 50¢ for each additional)
APPLICABLE TAXES* $ _____
TOTAL PAYABLE $ _____

(check or money order—please do not send cash)

To order, complete this form and send it, along with a check or money order for the total above, payable to MIRA Books, to: **In the U.S.:** 3010 Walden Avenue, P.O. Box 9077, Buffalo, NY 14269-9077; **In Canada:** P.O. Box 636, Fort Erie, Ontario, L2A 5X3.

Name: _____
Address: _____ City: _____
State/Prov.: _____ Zip/Postal Code: _____
Account Number (if applicable): _____

075 CSAS

*New York residents remit applicable sales taxes.
*Canadian residents remit applicable GST and provincial taxes.

MIRA®

www.MIRABooks.com